CRY ME A RIVER

A NOVEL OF SUSPENSE

PATRICIA HAGAN

VANDAMERE PRESS

Published by
Vandamere Press
P.O. Box 5243
Arlington, VA 22205

Copyright 2001
Patricia Hagan

ISBN 0-918339-55-3

Manufactured in the United States of America. All rights reserved, which includes the right to reproduce this book or any portion thereof in any form whatsoever, except as provided by U.S. Copyright Law. For information contact Vandamere Press

Acknowledgments

I wish to dedicate this novel as an expression of appreciation to the following:

For their assistance in answering my many medical queries: Drs. Robert Barker, Bruce Minkin, Evelyn Lyles, and James W. Ralph.

For insight on the inner workings of a sheriff's department: Lt. Wayne Ayers, Buncombe County Sheriff's Department, Asheville, North Carolina.

For funerary research: Ray Lindsey, licensed mortician and RN, Fayetteville, North Carolina and Dr. William T. Bass, forensic pathologist and former professor, University of Tennessee.

For sharing his memories of an Alabama cotton mill in the 60s, my uncle, O. B. Wright, Pell City, Alabama, and to his daughter and my cousin, Julia Skelton, Pell City, Alabama, for general research.

To those who believed in this novel and loved it as much as I do: My publisher, Art Brown of Vandamere Press and my treasured friends: Dan and Elizabeth Cowley, Bob Robison, Barb and Jim Ralph, and Gary Staley.

And, most importantly, the Class of '57, Sylacauga High School, Sylacauga, Alabama for fond memories and vivid imagination to last a lifetime.

PART I

CHAPTER 1

Halloween Eve, 1969

It was nearly three in the morning before Sheriff Luke Ballard dared hope the Halloween pranksters were through for another year. He and his deputies, Matt Rumsey and Kirby Washam, had been patrolling all night, but vandals had still managed to strew trash on lawns and send rolls of toilet paper spiraling onto tree limbs. Some of the unpopular high school teachers would wake up to flat tires.

The "biggie" had been the cruel trick played on poor Betsy Borden, and Luke was itching to get his hands on the "sickos" responsible. Betsy had been off her rocker ever since her husband and three kids were killed a few years back when lightning hit their tar paper shack and set it on fire while she was at prayer meeting. Folks figured Eddie Borden was passed out drunk, and the kids were too little to save themselves. Betsy's kin had offered her a home, but she refused to sleep indoors because she was scared of another fire, so she bedded down with the chickens in the roost house.

Then tonight, just after midnight, one of Betsy's neighbors called the sheriff's office to say he'd heard her screaming bloody murder. When Luke got there, he'd found her curled up in a ball in the chicken droppings under the roost, babbling that Eddie's ghost had come back to haunt her for not being home that night to save him and the kids.

The ghost turned out to be a pulley stretched between two trees drawing a white sheet back and forth. Luke had coaxed Betsy out of the roost house and showed her it was just a Halloween prank. She hadn't said a word, just stood there looking like a whipped hound dog, then turned and crawled back inside.

Luke knew firsthand just how mean some folks could be in Hampton, Alabama. It was why he had left, but the hunger for revenge had brought him back, and when he showed a few people paybacks were hell, he'd go again, never to return.

Like a lot of southern towns, Hampton's business section squared around the courthouse. Luke saw the supermarket windows had been soaped, and he just could make out the signs advertising 59 cents a pound for ground beef and a quarter for a dozen eggs.

He hit the brakes and came to a dead stop in front of the movie theater. *Easy Rider* had been playing nearly a month, and the glass case next to the ticket booth had been broken and the poster of Peter Fonda was gone.

Shaking his head and thinking how he and his deputies were going to be blamed for not being on their toes to stop all the meanness, Luke drove on down to the end of Elm Street and the railroad tracks that served as an unofficial border between town and the mill village.

In the distance he could see the lights from the mill itself. Operating around the clock, it was the financial heartbeat of Buford County. Everybody was tied to it either by employment or dependency on the payroll to stay in business.

He made it a point to avoid the village as much as possible. It stirred too many bad memories. He hated the area around the tracks even more. Kearney's Corner was a cluster of rundown wooden shacks built behind a greasy cafe and cheap gas station. It hadn't always been so trashy. As the story went, right after the Civil War, it was where the trains stopped at the water tank. Jebediah Kearney built a little stand and bought vegetables and fruit from desperate farmers and sold them to the rail passengers at a big profit.

Business boomed when carpetbagger Cleve Hampton built the cotton mill to take advantage of workers willing to work for peanuts to keep their families from starving. Kearney's Corner was passed on to his descendants, and eventually the motor court was built, but the town grew in the opposite direction. The depot was moved, trains no longer stopped there, and the superhighway to Birmingham came in at the other end of the county. By then, Jebediah's great-grandson was the owner. To keep the business going, he got into gambling, prostitution, and selling moonshine. But all that was before Luke got elected sheriff. Things were different now.

He turned into the parking lot, red dust from the dry clay settling on the hood and fenders of the white Torino. At once, a screen door opened and banged shut, and Junior Kearney came toward him waving his arms. "What the hell are you doin' here, Luke? You'll drive away my customers. Nobody wants to turn in when they see the sheriff's car, and there ain't no reason for you to spy on me anyhow, 'cause I ain't doing nothing wrong."

"And the only reason you aren't doing anything wrong is because I *do* keep an eye on you." In the glow of a mercury yard light, he could see Junior's face and how he'd aged since he'd got his comeuppance. Still, Luke had gone light on him because even though he'd treated his mother like shit all those years, he had given her shelter when she was homeless, unwed, and *pregnant with him.*

Junior's face crumpled. "Please. Just get out of here before you run off what business I've got left. I swear I ain't doing nothing wrong. I don't have no whores working for me. The guys have to bring their own. And I ain't selling moonshine, neither."

"And we made a deal, remember?" Junior leaned in the open window, looking as desperate as a drowning man gulping for air. "I did what you wanted, and I'll never live it down. You made me look like a fool in front of God and everybody. Isn't that enough? What more do you want? How come you got to keep hounding me?"

Any other time Luke would have hung around just to aggravate him, but he was tired and ready to call it a night. "Just keep walking a chalk line, Junior, because if you make one little slip, you can bet your ass you'll do hard time."

As he drove away, he glanced in the rearview mirror and saw Junior raise his middle finger. He didn't care. He was just living for the day when he could see the whole damn town reflected in his mirror.

The radio crackled. He heard Matt calling in to Ned Tucker, the dispatcher back in the basement office at the courthouse. Ned answered, sounding tired. Luke knew as soon as everybody signed off for the night, he would lean back in his chair and sleep the rest of his shift.

"Tell the sheriff I'm going ten-seven," Matt said.

Luke pressed the button on his mike. "Where's Kirby?"

Ned answered. "He went off a half hour ago. Didn't you hear him?"

"Must have been when I was chasing off the brats soaping the windows at the library."

Matt asked how long he was going to stay on duty, and Luke

explained he was about to call it a night. "Alma has to work today and wants me to take Tammy shopping in Birmingham, so I need to get to bed pretty soon."

He released the button. He was going to bed, all right, but not his own. Once he signed off with Ned, he planned to head out to the country where the sweetest girl in the world was waiting. At least he *hoped* she was still waiting, just like he hoped it was still safe to sneak in her house.

The evening before, when he and Emma Jean Veazey had run into each other accidentally on purpose at Creech's filling station, she'd said her husband, Rudy, was complaining that his stomach hurt. She was afraid he might call into work sick. If he did, they wouldn't have a chance to be together for a couple of weeks because his shift was changing to days. And with her working at the laundromat, she wouldn't be able to get away.

Luke needed to see her bad, too, and not just for the lovemaking. He had made up his mind they couldn't keep sneaking around. Rudy was a hot-headed redneck who would fight at the drop of his fertilizer cap. Luke wasn't worried about tangling with him. He just shuddered to think of what Rudy would do to Emma Jean if he found out. Besides, he knew he loved her and wanted to be with her for always.

He had done a lot of thinking and come up with a plan he was sure would work. He had confided in an old army buddy in Birmingham who was manager of a big supermarket. The friend promised Emma Jean a job and even said she could stay with him and his wife where she'd be safe. Once Luke got her there, he would tell Rudy to his face how it was.

He'd have to tell Alma real quick, too, because the story would spread like butter on hot grits. Not that she would give a damn except for her pride. They only got married because she was pregnant, not because they loved each other. But he knew she didn't want a divorce, because she had things just like she wanted them: complete control over their daughter Tammy and her job as a floor supervisor at the mill, which paid more than his job as sheriff. Plus the respectability of marriage, which was real important to women raised like her. *A sorry man is better than no man at all*, they liked to say.

As for his own future, he didn't plan to hang around Alabama for long. He figured he could always find a job just about anywhere in law enforcement. He also had his disability pay from the army, and with his job and Emma Jean's working, he could pay child support and they would still live well.

Life was going to be good again. He just felt it in his bones. President Nixon was said to be bringing 75,000 troops home from Vietnam by the end of the year. Maybe soon, the hellish war would be over and everybody could get back to peaceful times.

But before he made too many plans he needed to make sure Emma Jean felt the same way he did. He was pretty sure she did, although she'd never come right out and said so. Tonight he was going to find out for a fact.

Finally signing off, Luke headed in the direction of Sid Dootree's farm where Rudy rented a tenant shack. It wasn't much, but Emma Jean had fixed it up nice with what she had to work with. Luke liked the location. It was on a side road that dead-ended in a swamp, so there was never much traffic, especially this time of night.

He was almost to the turnoff when the radio crackled.

"Base to sheriff. Come in."

For a few seconds Luke was tempted not to respond, but Ned knew he hadn't had time to get home yet. It might look funny. He snatched up the mike. "Yeah, I'm here. What is it?"

There was a brief, hesitant silence, then, "Just got a call about somebody messing around at the cemetery."

"Who was it—Cecil Curry? Hell, he's always hearing noises over there. He ought to move. He's too big a sissy to live near a graveyard."

Another pause. "It wasn't Cecil."

Luke glanced impatiently at the clock on the dash. It was almost 4 a.m. It would start getting light around 6:30 a.m. If Rudy had gone to work—and he wouldn't know till he saw whether his pickup was in the driveway—he and Emma Jean would have less than three hours together. He didn't have time to check out the cemetery. "So who was it, Ned?"

"They wouldn't say . . . just said they saw lights in there and hung up."

"So what do you expect on Halloween? Remember that old legend about the talking grave? Some kids are fooling around, that's all, and I'm too tired to care."

"The talking grave is at the Hampton monument. That's not where they saw the lights."

Irritated, Luke snapped, "Damn it, will you just tell me word for word what they did say and get it over with? I've been in this car almost twelve hours now."

Another maddening moment of silence, then, "They said the lights were near where your momma is buried. I thought you'd want to check it out. Maybe I should call Matt for backup. He's probably not got to bed yet."

Luke had already spun the car around so fast it jumped the curb and knocked down Lula Porter's mailbox. "Listen and listen good, Ned. I don't need backup, and you just forget that call ever came in. You hear me?"

Ned heard Luke click off. He understood, all right. Luke liked to do things his way, and he didn't always go by the book. And Ned wasn't at all surprised about how it was going to be this time. Everybody knew how Luke felt about his momma, and, Lordy, he felt sorry for whoever was up there messing around her grave.

Luke took a short cut to the cemetery and came in the back way. If the vandals didn't know they had been spotted, he might be able to catch them. And if he did, by the time he finished with them, they wouldn't go near a cemetery again till they were in their own coffins.

Mess with his momma's grave, would they? Lord, he was going to make them pay. And he had a good idea who they were, too—the Scroggins boys. They had it in for him, and Rossie, the oldest, had even hinted at something like this. Easing the patrol car behind a utility shed, Luke carefully, quietly got out. He was in the oldest section where some of the graves dated back to the 1800s.

Bare tree branches rattled together like bones, and spidery beams of moonlight cast an eerie glow over the crumbling, mold-crusted tombstones. The new section was on the hill above. His stomach twisted with anger to see lights flashing around right where his mother was buried.

Most of the moonlight was spilling into the main path, which had no trees to block his view. Wanting to keep to the shadows, he had to cross graves, which meant moving slower than he wanted. It was dangerous going. Earlier burials had been in wooden coffins, not in vaults. When they had rotted, the graves had sunk. He didn't want to risk stepping in one of the holes and breaking an ankle. The funeral home was supposed to keep the graves up, but evidently Hardy Moon was getting lazy. Luke made a mental note to say something to Hardy's wife, Lucy. She'd straighten him out.

Luke set his jaw to think about Hardy. If he was behind this instead of the Scroggins boys, Luke was going to wreak revenge all over again. And this time it would be much worse.

As he got closer, he saw there were two lights, which probably meant only two people were involved. He calculated it had been about 15 minutes since he'd got the call, and they were still there. But what the hell were they doing? He was getting madder with each careful, plodding step.

He moved around the Hampton family monument. It was the tallest and biggest in the cemetery, and the one he had been referring to with Ned as the *talking grave*. For as long as he could remember, it had been the focus for a silly prank the kids liked to play on newcomers to town. He had done it a few times himself when he was a teenager. A new kid was told the legend of somebody going to the grave at midnight and quietly asking, "What do you want for supper?" After turning around three times, the bodies buried within the iron picket enclosure would answer. If the new kid refused to try it, he was forevermore branded a chicken—something boys wanted to avoid at all costs.

The trick, of course, was to intimidate somebody into doing it. After he'd asked the question and spun around without anything happening, he was informed, amidst taunting laughter because he was so stupid and gullible, that the corpses had, indeed, answered. They didn't want anything for supper, so they said . . . nothing.

As it turned out, it was, ironically, a Hampton who put an end to the tradition. It happened the first year Luke was elected sheriff. Old lady Clara Hampton had died, and Hardy had her grave dug the evening before her funeral was scheduled. The kids who played the joke on two unsuspecting newcomers didn't know about it. The newcomers fell in the grave, and the kids thought that made it all the funnier and took off, leaving them to climb out by themselves.

What they had not known, however, was that the hole was way deeper than six feet in order to accommodate an expensive vault. Neatly dug by a backhoe, the walls were straight up with nowhere to get a handhold in the red clay. As it turned out, that didn't matter anyway because one of the boys died of a broken neck the instant he landed. The other boy broke his leg and went mad from pain and having to lay next to his dead buddy all night.

It wasn't till late in the morning that the funeral procession arrived. It was summer, and the dead boy was already starting to smell. The other kid's hair had turned stone white. His name was Robbie Kershaw. Luke would never forget helping to lift him out of the grave. He was babbling and drooling, and his eyes were rolling around his head like he'd stuck his finger in a light socket. The last Luke heard, he was still in the state insane asylum down in Tuscaloosa.

Luke unbuckled the strap over his gun handle. If he wasn't able to take them by surprise, they might come at him swinging shovels or some other weapons.

In the glow of the lights, he could see the canopy over Jake Petrie's waiting grave. His funeral was set for ten the next morning. Luke was real grateful to the person who called in because he would have hated mighty bad not to have found out about any vandalism before then. Now he'd have a chance to make repairs and be spared the humiliation of everyone knowing about it.

His view was temporarily blocked when he had to go around the last obstacle, huge box hedges planted around the Odom family plot. Chester Odom owned the local nursery and, even though none of the graves were occupied, he had already landscaped them. He said he did it to make sure he would have a nice resting place, but everyone knew the old coot used it to advertise his business. Why else would he have a little sign stuck in the ground proclaiming, *"Odom's Nursery—Let us make your loved one's resting place a garden of Eden"*? Hardy kept taking down the signs, but Chester put them right back up.

Luke stepped around the end of the hedge, blinked against the lights . . . and cursed to realize he'd been had. Two flashlights had been tied to low-hanging branches from a tree over the grave. It was undisturbed, and the bouquet of artificial pink and white roses he'd put there over a month ago was still in place at the foot of the marker carved with the inscription:

ORLENA PEARL BALLARD
1923–1964
DEVOTED MOTHER
ASLEEP IN JESUS

Hands shaking with rage, Luke took out his pocket knife and reached up to cut the ropes. While he was really pissed off to think somebody had dared rile him this way, he was relieved it wasn't worse and told himself he still had time to make it to Emma Jean's. The evening wasn't totally ruined.

. . . *until the shots rang out.*

He was a perfect target, framed by the glow of the flashlights, there on the windy hillock in the black of night. The first bullet smashed into his shoulder, and he dropped to his knees with a gasp. The second ripped through his thigh, and he pitched forward to dig his fingers into the gummy red clay to try and propel himself forward in a frantic attempt to escape the ring of light that rendered him a helpless mark. The third shot struck him in the head.

Across the road in one of the mill shacks, Cecil Curry had awakened at the sound of gunfire. He rushed down the hall and grabbed the big flashlight he kept beside the front door. He didn't like living so close to a graveyard, but the house was the only one the mill had available to rent when he'd gone to work there six months ago. His wife, Nancy, teased him about being scared of the dead, even though he tried to make her see he felt it was just his duty to check out anything unusual.

"What's wrong?" she called sleepily as she padded down the hall after him. Through the open door she could see him standing at the edge of the front porch, sweeping the cemetery with the big light. It gave her the willies. "Listen, it's just some kids fooling around 'cause it's Halloween. Come on back to bed."

"I heard gunshots," he said grimly. "And it's not Halloween no more. It's after four o'clock. I'm gonna call the law and report it."

Nancy frowned. He had called the sheriff's office twice before and both times the noises he'd heard turned out to be tomcats fighting. Folks were going to start laughing at him behind his back, and she didn't want that. "It was probably a truck backfiring on the Birmingham highway. Come on back to bed."

Cecil thought about the way Sheriff Ballard and his deputies had looked at each other and snickered the last time he'd called them out. "You're probably right. Just a backfire."

He let her lead him back inside. They were almost to the bedroom door when they heard the sound of a car roaring out the cemetery gates, squealing tires.

"Whoever come out of there was up to no good," Cecil said, looking over his shoulder toward the front of the house.

Nancy gave his arm a tug. "It's none of our business. Now let's get some sleep. First thing Monday, I'm calling the mill office and see when they'll have another house so we can move. You're going to drive us crazy if we stay here."

Luke also heard the car as he struggled to drag himself by his arms, eyes filling with blood streaming from the wound in his head. It was a long way down the hill to where he'd left the car. Through the dizzy haze overwhelming him, he knew he had to try and reach the car and use the radio to call for help. Clenching his teeth, struggling to breathe, he mustered all his strength for a mighty thrust forward, then felt himself hurtling into the gaping black hole that was Jake Petrie's grave.

As he lost consciousness, Luke knew the terror Robbie Kershaw must have known when his mind exploded.

CHAPTER 2

Emma Jean wrapped the ham sandwich she had made for Luke in wax paper and put it in the icebox. She noticed the compartment at the top needed defrosting. It made Rudy awful mad to see it caked with ice, but she was not worrying about chores, his losing his temper, or any of the fretful things that filled most of the waking hours of her life. She was thinking about the one person in the world who made her happy and worrying why it was after four o'clock, and he hadn't shown up.

He hadn't even called with his signal—one ring and hang up

meant he was tied up with sheriffing business and couldn't come; two meant he was on his way. They didn't dare chance talking, not on a six-party line. Myrtle Letchworth, the old busybody down the road, would wake from a sound sleep at any hour if she heard somebody's line ringing just to see what she could hear. Then she could gossip about it the next day at the beauty shop she ran in the trailer behind her house.

It just wasn't like Luke not to give either signal since he knew she'd stay up waiting till he did. He had told her earlier at the gas station that he was going to try to get to her house early because he knew it was going to be a while till they could see each other again with Rudy changing his shift. And then he had added, smiling mysteriously, that he wanted to talk about something important. So Emma Jean was feeling real anxious, but there was nothing she could do about it, no one she could call. Certainly not the sheriff's office. Somebody besides Luke might answer, and what could she say?

With a sigh, she took the dish rag from the sink and began to wipe the top of the yellow and white chrome table. The kitchen was small, like the rest of the house. There was hardly enough room for the table and the four chairs with their cracked vinyl seats. The sink was old and chipped and had all kinds of nasty looking stains that put blisters on her hands when she tried to scrub them out. Rudy said his ma said Emma Jean was a sloppy housekeeper. When she had dared to point out the stains had been there when they rented the old tenant house, he had slapped her. She tried not to talk back to him. He couldn't stand that in a woman. He said his pa never put up with it from his ma, and he wasn't going to take it off her either.

Next she made sure there were pieces of old fried bacon in the mousetraps under the cabinets. The mice came in from the fields, and bacon lured them better than cheese. Rudy said it was cheaper, too, because his pa gave them bacon when he killed hogs, but cheese cost money.

She went into the sitting room with its worn sofa and chairs that Miss Bertha—that's what she called Rudy's ma—had given them. She didn't care for Miss Bertha because she was always criticizing her to Rudy. That made Rudy meaner than ever, but Emma Jean still tried to do everything she could to get along with Miss Bertha.

She glanced around the room with loathing. The tacky plastic flowers stuck in Coke bottles that Miss Bertha had given them were nothing but dust collectors. She didn't like all the pictures of Jesus on the wall either, not because she didn't believe in Him, because she did. She just wasn't a fanatic about religion like Miss Bertha and the other members of their kooky church, Thunder Swamp Pentecostal Holiness. Situated way back in the woods about four miles out of town, folks there got a bit crazy sometimes with their hollering and carrying on. It scared her half to death the first time she saw somebody doing what was called talking in tongue. It was an old man. All of a sudden he had jumped up out of his seat and started dancing around and waving his arms and yelling things like, "Praise Jesus," and "Glory, glory." Then he had started making sounds like "ollee-lollee-wallee-ewww-yahhh," and the next thing Emma Jean knew he was down on the floor, thrashing around, with his eyes rolled back up in his head and his tongue flicking in and out of his mouth like a lizard. She had tried to leave, but Miss Bertha wouldn't let her out of the pew, and since Miss Bertha weighed about 300 pounds, folks didn't get by her if she didn't want them to.

Emma Jean had come home that day and told Rudy about it and swore she would never go back. He said folks would talk about her if she didn't go to church every Sunday. When she'd asked how come he didn't go, he hit her a time or two and said if she didn't learn to watch her mouth, he'd kick her out on her butt. Secretly she thought that would be a blessing except she didn't have any money and no place to go. She also knew he didn't mean it and would kill her if she ever tried to leave.

The linoleum floor was cold, and she was barefooted, so she walked into the bedroom with its cheap shag carpet that she had bought at Woolworth's Five and Dime for $19.95 with some of the money she had earned picking tomatos for Sid Dootree during the summer. She never got a chance to spend what she made working at the laundromat because her boss gave her pay direct to Rudy, who hadn't raised hell about her using some of the tomato-picking money because the bedroom floors were raw wood, and he was always getting a splinter in his foot.

Actually, she despised the bedroom most of all with its old rusted iron poster bed. It took up almost the whole room.

Clothes had to be stacked in orange crates in the corners or hung on nails in the wall, but Rudy said all they needed was the bed anyway.

She sat down and ran her hand across the pillow where Luke would put his head if he showed up. Thanks to him she had a few good memories from the old sagging mattress. Luke hadn't wanted to lay on the bed, saying it was bad enough to have sex with another man's wife without doing it right in his bed. She had begged him though, shyly explaining how she wanted to be able to think about something nice happening there. Then she would be able to just close her eyes and think about him when Rudy was having his way with her. Luke had understood and never said another word about it, but she could tell he liked it better when they did it in the back seat of the patrol car or in a motel.

Lord, she loved him so much and brushed tears from her eyes to think about it. Still she couldn't believe she'd been blessed to have him love her in return—which she believed with all her heart he did.

He was handsome but not like a movie star. He was raw-boned and good-looking from his expressive brows to the square lines of his jaw. He had smoky brown eyes and his hair was a straw blond color, neatly trimmed in a crew cut.

He was tough through and through with a hard, muscular build and big, broad shoulders. He made her feel that, as long as she was with him, nothing in the world could ever hurt her. And he also had a gentle side, holding her after they made love like she was so precious she might break.

Over and over she wished she could have met Luke instead of Rudy, but Luke had been in the Army, not the Air Force, and he had never been stationed at Patrick Air Force Base on the east coast of Florida. There was no way they could have met at the Sputnik Lounge at Cocoa Beach where she worked as a cocktail waitress. She went there from Tennessee, running away at sixteen, because, after dodging her stepfather's groping hands for years, he had finally crawled in her bed one night and forced her to put her mouth on his thing. When she told her mother, she was accused of lying and got a beating with a belt. Emma Jean realized then things would only get worse and hit the road.

Broke and desperate, she swiped a purse from an older girl on the bus so she could use her driver's license to get the job at the lounge. All she had to do was keep her thumb over the name while the bookkeeper copied down her birth date.

The tips were good. She shared the rent on a trailer with two other girls, and life would have been just fine if the customers had kept their hands to themselves. Eddie, her boss, said that if she wanted to keep her job, she'd better grow up and see that's how it was. Things were getting pretty miserable when Rudy came along. Eddie was giving her a hard time, saying he knew she was using a false ID, that she was nowhere near twenty-one, and if she wasn't nice to him, he would turn her in. She was trying to keep him at bay till she could find another job, but then one night, a drunk customer ran his hand up her miniskirt and squeezed her crotch. It made her so mad she smacked him over the head with the tray of cocktails she was carrying. The customer jumped up and grabbed her and started hitting her. That's when Eddie came in yelling she was fired, and right in the middle of it all, Rudy suddenly appeared to come to her rescue and whisk her away.

Over burgers at an all-night cafe, he told her he'd had an eye on her for the last few nights he'd been coming to the lounge. He said she reminded him of Sandra Dee with her blond hair and blue eyes, but he had held off trying to make a date with her till he could figure out what kind of girl she was. He didn't want somebody cheap, and he won her heart when he confided that his mother had always told him not to date a girl unless she was the kind he might want to marry one day. Emma Jean thought that was sweet. She thought *he* was sweet, and cute too, even though something about his eyes scared her sometimes.

His discharge was coming up, so there hadn't been time for much of a courtship, but Emma Jean didn't mind. He said he loved her and wanted her to be his wife and take her home with him to a little Alabama town called Hampton. They got married only two weeks after they met, and Emma Jean still shuddered to think of their wedding night when all the trouble began.

They had left Florida in Rudy's beat-up Ford pickup truck right after the early morning ceremony at the courthouse in Titusville. Less than an hour up the road Rudy said he couldn't wait any longer to really make her his wife. In the time they had known each other, they hadn't gone beyond tongue-kissing and heavy petting because he said he wanted things to be right. Emma Jean had only felt a teeny bit guilty to let him think she was a virgin, thinking of that time with Johnny Grice back in the ninth grade, a mistake she had tried to put out of her mind.

When they stopped at a seedy-looking motel, the man at the desk grinned nastily at Rudy for wanting a room in the middle of the day. He made Rudy so mad he yanked the marriage certificate from his pocket and yelled at the man that they were man and wife and, if he didn't wipe that silly smirk off his face, he'd do it for him.

Emma Jean was so embarrassed. Once they were out of the office, she said that she wished they'd waited till night. Rudy told her to shut up, that she was his wife, and he'd say when they went to bed.

The room was awful. It smelled like smoke and pee. The sagging bed with its stained spread and a cigarette-burned dresser were the only pieces of furniture. The floor was covered in cracked linoleum, and roaches had scurried to hide when the door was opened. Frayed curtains were nailed to the dingy windows. There was a toilet without a lid in an alcove next to a cheap metal shower stall. Then there was no time to look around because Rudy had already taken off his pants and started tearing at the shirtwaist dress she was wearing. She tried to fend him off by telling him it was her best dress and he was going to ruin it. He said he didn't care, ripped the front, and then yanked off her bra. Emma Jean lost her temper then and tried to push him away, which only made him mad. Then he threw her down and shoved himself into her.

By then she was crying so hard she couldn't stop. He had turned into a monster, but the worst was yet to come. All of a sudden he was hitting her, yelling how he could tell she wasn't a virgin, and calling her a whore. He accused her of lying to him, and she tried to tell him she hadn't lied. He hadn't asked her if she was a virgin. Besides, it only happened one time with one boy when she was just a kid.

He had his way with her and then hit her till she was dizzy. He told her if she thought she was going to run around on him, she was crazy because he'd kill her if he ever caught her. Afterwards, he went out and bought a bottle of whiskey, then got so drunk he passed out. Emma Jean cried most of the night, wondering what kind of hell she had got herself in and how she could escape.

The next morning he told her he hated having to hurt her but said it was her fault for having fooled him. He went on to say that, while he never would have married her if he had known she was soiled, she was his wife now and as long as she learned her place he'd take care of her. He warned her again that he'd kill her if he ever caught her running around. Then he stopped at the first store they came to and bought her a new dress.

So began her miserable existence as Rudy's wife, but all the while she dreamed of finding a way to get away from him. She tried taking corresponding courses to get her high school diploma, but he found out when he happened to get the mail before she did one day. He whipped her with a belt until she admitted she stole the money from his wallet to pay for the course. He warned her that he'd better not find any more of her "book shit" as he called it.

Defeated, she went to the post office to mail a letter to the company telling them not to send anything else. There was no one there that day except the clerk, Ruth Pederson. Ruth was a nosy sort, and by the time she got through grilling Emma Jean about her black eye, the whole story just spilled out. Ruth told her not to worry, that she would keep her lessons and all mail from the school right there at the post office for Emma Jean to pick up. If she could keep her things hidden at home, Rudy wouldn't know. So far he hadn't found out, but she hadn't been concentrating on her studies much since Luke came into her life. She no longer worried about the future, just about the here and now and being with him whenever possible.

Wearily, she turned off the garish bulb hanging from the frayed cord in the ceiling and got in bed. She supposed she should take off the lavender baby doll pajama set she had bought especially for this night and put on one of her old nightgowns. Otherwise, Rudy would want to know where she got the set. Worse, he would wonder how she paid for it now that tomato season was over. He never gave her any money of her own. It was Luke who insisted on giving her a few dollars now and then, and she had saved that money till she had enough to buy the pajamas.

Suddenly she heard a soft creaking sound as the kitchen door opened. She bolted upright, joy spinning through her body, to realize Luke had made it after all. If he was running late, he hadn't taken time for the phone signal, but that was all right. He knew she'd be waiting.

Playfully, she scrambled from the bed and hurried to the living room to grab one of the dusty roses from a Coke bottle and stick it between her teeth. Then she raced back to the bed to strike a seductive pose by leaning back with her legs spread wide and bosom thrust forward.

She could hear him making his way in the darkness, and when he reached the bedroom door, she called out huskily, "Oh, Luke, baby, you don't know how I've been praying you'd make it."

The overhead bulb flashed on, flooding the room with a sickly yellow light. The rose dropped from Emma Jean's mouth. It was Rudy.

"I was right."

Her blood curdled with terror.

"You *have* been screwing that son of a bitch."

Slowly, his eyes slitted in that menacing glare she had learned to fear, Rudy started toward the bed. It was then that she saw the gleam of the butcher knife in his hand.

The coffee was hot, but Alma Ballard was hotter.

She sat at the kitchen table, dressed for work in green slacks, white blouse, and an orange jacket emblazoned with *HAMPTON MILLS* on the back and *SUPERVISOR* on the front. White cotton socks cuffed her dingy sneakers, and her straight brown hair was pulled back in a ponytail held by a rubber band.

A glance at the clock brought a fresh rush of anger. It was after six-thirty. She was due at work at seven, but no way was she leaving till she found out where Luke was, damn him. If something bad had happened, he should have called unless, and she gritted her teeth to think about it, he had fallen asleep somewhere with his girlfriend. She dug down in her pocket and brought out a crumpled pack of Camels. Lighting up, she inhaled deeply, then blew the smoke from her nose as she absently picked at a piece of tobacco caught between her teeth.

Luke thought he was so clever, but she had heard the rumors about him and Emma Jean Veazey, and she was worried about it. Sure, she had suspected from time to time that he'd been with women in the past, but they were just fly-by-night floozies. If he was seriously involved with Emma Jean, it might be something to worry about. She even thought about talking to Rudy Veazy so he could put a stop to it, then decided against it. Rudy might kill him, and Alma didn't want him dead, not that she gave a damn about Luke any more than he gave a rat's ass about her. She just didn't want Tammy to have to live with the shame of having the man she thought of as her daddy murdered for screwing another man's wife.

Alma drew on the Camel so deeply that the smoke stung her lungs. Maybe she should feel guilty about making Luke think Tammy was his, but she didn't. After all, Tammy could have been if Jimmy Tate hadn't gotten her pregnant first. In all fairness, when she started going all the way with Luke, she hadn't known she was already pregnant. She and Jimmy had broken up over Sylvie Grice, and she wanted to make him jealous, so she went out with Luke, who was trying to make Sara Daughtry jealous.

As it turned out, Jimmy didn't care because he and Sylvie made up, ran off to Mississippi, and got married. So when Alma realized she was going to have a baby, she pointed the finger at Luke, figuring he was better husband material than Jimmy, anyway. Besides, her daddy didn't even have to make him marry her because Miss Orlena, Luke's mother, saw to it that Luke would do the right thing. After all, who in all of Hampton should know better than Miss Orlena how important it was for a boy to accept his responsibility? She surely had her cross to bear, raising Luke in shame with the whole town knowing he was a bastard.

So they were married, and Alma moved in to live with Luke and his mother at Junior Kearney's motor court. Only Luke didn't stay long. He had only agreed to the marriage if his mother would sign for him to join the Army, which was what he did, dropping out of school to go marching off.

He had not been around when Tammy was born, and Alma wondered if he would have even come back at all, if not for his mother. He sure never pretended to care anything about *her*. He never wanted to have sex with her, which was fine. Alma had never enjoyed sex anyway. It was only good for making babies. Look at her own mother, for goodness sakes. Ten children. Each of her sisters had several babies before they were twenty, making them old before their time. She had sworn it wouldn't happen to her. So she had left Tammy with Miss Orlena and gone to work at the mill, eventually climbing up the ladder to become a floor supervisor and earn a nice salary.

She stubbed out the cigarette. Things weren't really so bad even if she and Luke couldn't stand each other. Thanks to his getting a VA loan, they were able to buy a house. Alma enjoyed being a respected member of the community, even though Luke wouldn't step foot inside her church—Gospel Light United. He said they were fanatics because the women couldn't wear lipstick, and dancing and watching television were considered sins.

Smoking was also forbidden, she thought guiltily as she lit another cigarette. But as long as nobody knew about it, she was going to keep it up—especially when her nerves were bad, like now. Where was Luke anyhow, damn it?

She didn't want her tidy life messed up, which meant it was time to put a stop to things between him and Emma Jean before they went too far. Emma Jean might be trying to talk him into running off with her, and he might be crazy enough to do it. After all, he had been acting funny lately, and when anybody mentioned his running for sheriff again next year, he wouldn't talk about it.

She had to find out where he was, damn it, and if he was off somewhere with Emma Jean, there was going to be hell to pay.

She reached for the phone.

Wilma Farrell was busy filing her nails. No one was around the courthouse because the sheriff and the deputies had worked most of the night. She didn't expect them until lunch time, and she was looking forward to a quiet morning.

The phone rang, and she answered, hoping it was nothing important.

"Is he there?"

Wilma recognized the voice. "I haven't seen him this morning, Alma. I figured he'd sleep late." She started clearing her manicure supplies from the top of her desk. So much for an easy morning. Luke was probably on his way in.

"Well, he isn't sleeping late *here*," Alma fired back curtly, at the same time wishing she hadn't. She didn't want to make Wilma wonder why she was upset. Softening her tone, she added, "I just thought maybe there was more vandalism than usual last night, and he was still working."

"You mean he hasn't come home?"

"If he had, do you think I'd be calling?" *So much for not sounding upset.*

"Well, I don't know of anything that would have kept him this late."

"Well, look at the log, damn it."

Wilma's brows rose sharply. Everyone knew Alma Ballard called herself a Christian, so she must be really aggravated to curse. She quickly scanned the log. "Nope. Nothing here—but wait . . ." She saw that something on the very last line had been erased but couldn't tell what it was. "No. Nothing."

"Then what time did he sign off?"

Wilma saw the time noted for Matt and Kirby but nothing for Luke. "I guess he forgot to call in."

"He wouldn't do that. He's the sheriff, you idiot. Where's Ned?"

Wilma knew Alma was very angry now, but there was something else, a sense of urgency in her voice that was downright scary. "He left when I got here about thirty minutes ago. Said he was going fishing. Do you want me to call the deputies and see if they know anything?"

"Don't bother. I'll take care of it myself."

Alma slammed the receiver down, fuming to think Luke could only be at Emma Jean's. She had seen the schedule and knew Rudy was working nights. Luke was probably so hot to get over there he forgot to sign off for the first time. After quickly phoning the mill to say she'd be late, she snatched up her purse and car keys.

If Luke had, indeed, fallen asleep in the little tramp's bed, she was going to yank his butt right out of it, then beat the hell out of Emma Jean. Enough was enough.

Wilma immediately called Matt. He was her nephew, and they were close. They had been talking about Luke's carrying on with Emma Jean Veazey and how it might be getting serious.

Matt was still asleep, but she told Ruthie, his wife, that it was an emergency, and he finally came on the line. He listened, then said, "I can't say anything over the phone, Aunt Wilma, but you know what I'm thinking."

She knew all right. He was agreeing with her that Luke was going to be in big trouble if he was snoozing in Rudy Veazey's bed. "Well, what do you think we should do?"

"I'd better drive out there and look around."

She felt relief, but not much and urged, "You'd better hurry, because I think that's where Alma is headed, and from the way she sounded on the phone, Lord help them both if she gets there first."

Chapter 3

Cleve Hampton, III, or "Buddy," as he was known to intimates, fought the impulse to send the golf putter crashing against the wall.

Murline Pruitt watched nervously. She well knew his temper and dreaded how he'd react to hearing Alma Ballard had called in saying she'd be late.

He set the putter aside. "Did she say *how* late?"

"No, just that there was some kind of family emergency."

"Damn it. First Rudy Veazey leaves sick and now this. How the hell am I supposed to keep that section of the plant running overtime when both the foreman and floor supervisor are out? Nobody likes working Saturdays, but that's too bad. What's wrong with Veazey, anyway?"

"I was told when he clocked out around four he claimed he had a stomachache."

"Call his house. Tell him about Alma not showing up and, if he wants to keep his job, to get his butt back down here."

"I tried, but I kept getting a busy signal, so I called the operator, and she checked and said the phone was off the hook."

She jumped as Buddy kicked the side of his desk. "Then he's fired. Check the personnel files for who's next in seniority and promote them to his job."

After Murline rushed from the room, Buddy opened the bottom drawer of his desk and took out the flask of vodka he kept there for the times when life seemed unbearable. Thanks to Luke Ballard, it was almost empty.

Buddy had a ten o'clock tee-off at the country club but couldn't leave till a replacement was found for Rudy. He just wished he could fire Alma, too, but didn't dare. Not now. Hell, he wished he had never promoted her in the first place, but she was a good worker, and he'd felt sorry for her raising her kid alone. Like everyone else, he never thought Luke would come back to Hampton to stay; only, he'd been wrong. Now here he was, the richest man in Buford County, having his strings pulled by a redneck sheriff and the only way he would ever have any peace was for the son of a bitch to die.

His private line rang, and he answered, cringing to hear Burch Cleghorn's voice.

"Hey, it's me. Listen, I called your house, but the maid said you were at the office. Since it's such a nice day I figured you'd be heading to the golf course later, and I want to invite myself along if it's okay."

Buddy gritted his teeth. "I'm playing with Thad Greer."

A few seconds of silence was followed by Burch whining, "But he wouldn't care if I came along if you said it was okay."

"He might feel uncomfortable."

"That's ridiculous. I mean, it's time people start forgetting."

Buddy snickered. "You're a fool to think they ever will."

Burch's voice cracked. "Yeah, Luke made sure of that, didn't he? He fixed me, all right. But I'm not the only one. I still think he had something to do with Hardy's deeding the funeral home back over to Lucy and letting her boss him around ever since. He'll get to you, too, if he can."

Buddy was silent for a moment, not trusting himself to speak, lest he give away his own fury. The truth was, Luke *had* gotten to him. The one mercy was that no one else knew—not yet, anyway. Finally, he said, "I'm not as stupid as you are, Burch."

"Okay. Okay. But it's not fair. Sara Daughtry is nothing but a slut, and she came out smelling like a rose, while I . . ."

"Nobody knows it was her you were with, and Luke threatened to kill you and make it look like an accident if you said she was, didn't he?"

"Yeah, and I could kill both of 'em with my bare hands."

Buddy shook his head in disgust. Burch was getting on his nerves. "Look, I know you're going through a rough time, but I've got problems of my own here."

Burch welcomed someone else's troubles to get his mind off his own. "What's going on?"

"We're running overtime. Alma Ballard is the supervisor, but there's a family emergency, and she's going to be late if she shows at all. Rudy Veazey is the foreman on that side, and he went home sick."

Burch gave a nasty chuckle. "Maybe Alma's emergency is that Luke wants to pork her for a change, instead of Rudy's old lady. Maybe she wants to get it while she can."

Buddy matched his coarse humor. "And maybe Rudy stayed out for the same reason—to pork *his* old lady while Luke isn't around."

"I doubt Rudy knows Luke is screwing her. If he did, he'd kill both of them."

"Then maybe we should see to it he finds out," Buddy laughed. "That would make a few folks happy, wouldn't it?"

Burch seized on Buddy's sudden switch to a good mood. "Sure would, old chum, but how about the golf game? I'll come on over to your office and . . ."

"Another time. I've got to go." Buddy hung up and thought maybe he shouldn't have been so brusque, but the fact was, if not for him and Hardy Moon, Burch wouldn't have any social life at all. Buddy knew his marriage was wrecked, but his wife had stuck by him because she couldn't afford to leave. After all, how could she support herself at her age when the only thing she had ever done in life was play bridge and have three kids? And Burch couldn't afford to keep her up separately. His practice had gone to hell after the scandal, and while he still had a few out-of-town clients, his days of high living were over. Burch's life had been ruined forevermore, and worse, if Luke had his way, he'd do the same damn thing to Buddy's.

─────

Burch was still in bed and thought maybe he would just stay there all day. He had no reason to get up. Nobody wanted anything to do with him, which was why he hated weekends. Monday through Friday he had his work, such as it was, plus he didn't have to be around Irene, who let him know every chance she got that she hated his guts.

Luke Ballard. The name boiled like bile in his gut. God, he wished him dead.

"Burch?" Irene appeared in the doorway. It was not yet eight o'clock but she was dressed in a blue polished cotton dress, her hair still perfectly coiffed from the beauty parlor the day before. She wore stockings, medium high heels, a touch of rouge and lipstick. Every day for the twenty-four years they had been married she got up early to make herself as attractive as possible. Only now she did so out of habit, not to please him.

Burch did not respond, pretending to be asleep, hoping she would go away. She yanked the covers off his head. "I don't want you hanging around the house today."

He rolled over to meet her contemptuous glare. "Why not? I happen to live here, you know."

"Much to my sorrow and humiliation," she fired back. "Now my church circle is meeting here this morning to make plans for the Christmas bazaar, and I don't want them to see you because it will remind them of what you did."

He snorted. "As if out-of-sight, out-of-mind means anything to those old biddies. They'll still gossip."

"Shame on you. They're fine Christian women. If they weren't, they wouldn't have anything to do with me. God knows, everybody wonders why I stay with you, anyway."

"Well, *we* know, don't we, dear? Because you can't do anything except play bridge and pour tea, and, therefore, cannot support yourself."

Her eyes narrowed. "I want you out of here."

"I'll stay in my room and won't come out." They slept separately in opposite ends of the large house.

"I'm giving you one hour, Burch."

"I'm not going anywhere, and you and your pious friends can go to hell."

"How dare you talk to me that way? I've been a good wife and raised three fine children. And look how you've treated me. Look what you did to me, to our marriage, and . . ."

He leaped out of bed, ran into the bathroom, and slammed and locked the door after him. He'd heard it all before and was sick of it. Turning on the shower full force to drown out her screaming, he let the water run while he opened the medicine chest and took out the bottle of aspirin. He gulped down several to try and stave off the headache that was sure to come. By the time he was dressed, she had given up and left.

He snatched up the phone and dialed the funeral home. Hardy answered, and Burch said, desperately, "Let's go play golf or do something. I've got to get out of here. Irene is in one of her moods . . ."

"No can do. I've got the Petrie funeral at eleven this morning."

"What about after?"

"I have a body to prepare." Hardy never said embalm. He had been taught in mortuary school that the word bothered some people.

Burch bantered, "Is it Luke Ballard, by any chance?"

Hardy chuckled. "Don't we all wish? Maybe one of these days. But at least I've got another creep to put away that I can't stand—Jubal Cochran. His next-door neighbor found him on the bathroom floor when she checked to see why he didn't answer the phone or come to the door."

"What happened?"

"I'm putting heart attack on the coroner's report."

Jubal had owned the hardware store. Burch had known Jubal all his life but felt no remorse over his death. Jubal was one of the holier-than-thous who had wanted to crucify him after Luke and Sara set him up. Jubal had also told all over town that there was hanky-panky going on at the funeral home, but when Burch reminded Hardy of that, Hardy cut him off.

"I don't care anymore, and I've got to get busy. Call Buddy and see if he'll play with you." Sometimes Hardy felt sorry for Burch because he and Buddy were the only men in town who would have anything to do with him. This was not, however, one of those times. He had too much to do. He was also anxious to get started on Jubal because he enjoyed embalming people he didn't like.

Burch said, "I did, but he's got a mess on his hands." He recounted the situation at the mill.

Hardy snickered. "Well, that's real interesting, seeing how the rumor is that Luke is screwing Rudy's old lady."

"Yeah, me and Buddy were talking about that. Maybe they

all got together for a foursome of a different kind—Luke, Alma, Rudy, and Emma Jean."

They laughed together, but Burch, reluctant to end the moment of camaraderie, was too loud and exaggerated and Hardy finally interrupted. "Call me later, and maybe you can come by for a beer."

"How about if I come over now? Maybe I can help with something."

Hardy knew all Burch would do was sit in his private office and sip whiskey from the pint he carried in his pocket. "No, thanks. Besides, Buddy might call you once he gets things under control at the mill."

Burch sighed. "You know something? I've got a feeling Luke is responsible somehow. Damn him, Hardy, he just louses up everybody's life, doesn't he?"

"That he does," Hardy said quietly, soberly. "That he does."

He hung up the phone and walked to the embalming table.

Jubal's eyes stared blankly as Hardy smiled down at him. Gleefully, he whispered, "You didn't know when you went to bed last night you'd be here with me this morning, did you, you son of a bitch?"

And, with a fiendish laugh, he slapped Jubal's cold, unyielding face.

For long moments, Burch sat staring at the phone.

Jubal had started a lot of speculation about wrongdoings at the funeral home, but no one was sure exactly what they were because no charges were ever filed. Hardy refused to talk about it, and all of a sudden, Jubal shut up about it.

Still, at the mention of Luke's name, Hardy got a look on his face that was downright scary. Burch shuddered to think how much Hardy would probably enjoy it if he ever got Luke on that embalming table.

Ozzie Poole parked his rusty old pickup next to the supply shed, got out, and stretched lazily in the crisp autumn air. He was wearing his good overalls, clean and pressed, something he always did when there was a burying. He tried to look nice in case the family came back before the grave was filled in. Mr. Moon tried to get them to stay away till everything was covered and the flowers laid on top, but sometimes they hung around. Ozzie didn't want folks to think he had no respect for the dead.

Hank Wheeler pulled his '54 Chevy in right beside him. Ozzie scowled to see Hank had on the same clothes he had worn the day before. They were grimy and dirty, and his brogans were caked with red clay. Hank never cared how he looked, and that really griped Ozzie.

"Well, I hear we got our work cut out for us today," Hank said by way of greeting. "Heard Jubal Cochran kicked the bucket last night, so I reckon we'll be digging another grave."

"Not for a day or so. Mr. Moon don't like graves open longer than necessary."

Hank's brows lifted. "Then why in thunderation did we work our butts off diggin' old Lem's last night? Gave me the creeps, it did, bein' Halloween and all. He didn't even tell us to start till late afternoon. It was almost dark when we got done."

Ozzie shrugged. "Because the funeral is this morning, dummy. We wouldn't have had time to do it now."

Hank grunted. "I'd have been glad to come to work early instead of being around this place when the shadows start fallin'."

Ozzie unlocked the shed, went inside, got a roll of artificial grass, and slung it over his shoulder. He motioned for Hank to do the same, but Hank shook his head and walked around back, saying he had to pee.

"Too much coffee this morning. I was trying to wake up."

"Well, make it quick. We've got to get this grass rolled out."

All of a sudden Hank called, "Hey, Ozzie. Come here and look at this."

"I don't want to watch you take a piss, for crying out loud. What's wrong with you?"

"How come the sheriff hid his car back here?"

At that, Ozzie walked around the shed, and, sure enough, there sat the white Ford Torino with SHERIFF, BUFORD COUNTY, printed on the doors and across the trunk. "Well, darn if he didn't," he said in wonder.

They both eased closer, then jumped at the sound of the radio crackling, followed by Wilma Farrell's plea, "Sheriff, come in. Where are you? Come in, please. This is an emergency."

Hank and Ozzie looked at each other, and Hank said, "Maybe we should tell her he ain't here, but his car is."

Ozzie chewed the inside of his jaw. "I dunno. That's messing with law business, and we could get in trouble."

"But she says it's an emergency."

"Yeah, but it ain't up to us to get involved."

"I say we answer it."

"I say we go look for the sheriff and tell him Wilma's trying to get up with him and let him handle it. If his car's here, he's got to be around someplace."

Hank decided that sounded like a safe thing to do and fell in step behind Ozzie as they began walking up the hill.

Matt Rumsey's uniform was rumpled and smelly with sweat but it didn't matter. After his Aunt Wilma called, he'd grabbed his clothes off the chair where he'd left them the night before, dressed, and rushed out. He hadn't even taken time to answer Ruthie's questions about where he was going. Besides, if he had, he knew she'd be on the phone before he backed out of the driveway, anxious to spread the news that Alma Ballard was on her way to finally whip Emma Jean Veazey's butt. There was no need to sound the alarm, at least not until he found out for sure what was going on. Maybe Luke wasn't there and had fallen asleep somewhere in his car.

Yeah, right, he wryly thought.

He had sensed Luke's restlessness the night before and knew it probably had to do with his planning to meet Emma Jean, which meant Rudy had to be working third shift. Now Matt wished he'd had the nerve to talk to him about it earlier to try and make him see how he was playing with fire. Bad enough if Alma found out, but if Rudy ever caught him, it would be like Godzilla Meets King Kong. Matt had arrested Rudy a few times for beating up on people at the grill when he got drunk and turned mean. He was big and stocky and strong as an ox. Luke was trained to fight special forces style, and Rudy would come at him like a madman. All hell would break loose, and they could kill each other if somebody wasn't around to break it up fast.

He was also worried about Luke's having a gun because he might shoot Rudy and be done with it. He hated the son of a bitch, but if he was in bed with Emma Jean when Rudy got there, he would have taken off his holster. Rudy might see where he left it, go for it, and . . .

Matt mashed his foot harder on the accelerator. Rounding a curve, he saw Alma's car up ahead and quickly pulled up alongside her to yell out the window for her to pull over.

Clutching the steering wheel tightly, she took her eyes off the road long enough to roll down her window, dart an angry glance in his direction, and yell back, "Just stay out of this, Matt. It's between me and Luke and that hussy."

"Pull over, damn it." He swerved toward her ever so slightly but was careful not to rub metal, afraid she might panic and lose control.

"Go to hell."

He stomped on the gas and shot by her, intending to warn Luke but stiffened at the sight of Rudy's pickup on the shoulder of the road in front of his house.

Turning in the driveway in a cloud of dust, he roared into the backyard and skidded to a stop. Luke's car was nowhere in sight and all was quiet, except for the cackling chickens that had panicked and scattered at his approach.

Something wasn't right. He could feel it in his bones. Things were *too* quiet. Why hadn't Rudy come charging out of the house demanding to know why he had come tearing into his yard like the devil was on his heels? Relieved not to find Luke there, and wanting to avoid a run-in with Rudy, Matt quickly whipped the car around, then cursed to realize Alma had driven in right behind him.

He pulled up beside her. "Look, he isn't here. It's all a mistake. Now let's go before Rudy starts asking questions and things get stirred up for no reason."

Alma laughed shrilly. "No reason? Then what are you doing here? You thought he'd be here, too, didn't you? That's why you came—to warn him."

"We can talk at the cafe. I'll buy you a cup of coffee. Come on, Alma." He didn't know what he was going to say to her. All he was thinking about right then was making tracks fast.

"You *did* think he'd be here," she repeated, tears welling in her eyes. "You know about them, don't you? Just like everybody else in town. Well, I'm sick of everyone laughing behind my back. And it's time Rudy found out. He'll put a stop to it, and . . ."

She fell silent, eyes going wide, and Matt turned to follow her gaze just as her scream of horror broke the stillness. Emma

Jean was standing on the back porch looking like a zombie, staring straight ahead but not seeing anything. She was naked and she was also holding a knife.

Matt bolted out of the car, yelling over his shoulder for Alma to stay put. As he sprinted across the yard, he saw that Emma Jean was covered in blood. Instinctively, he drew his pistol. "Drop the knife, Emma Jean. Now."

She blinked a few times, opened her hand to let it fall to the ground, and then sank to the steps. He kicked the knife out of her reach. Then, as a precaution until he found out what was going on, he swiftly handcuffed one of her wrists to the porch railing. She did not resist. He asked what had happened, but she didn't respond.

Slowly opening the screen door, he stepped inside the kitchen. He could smell the familiar metallic odor of blood, and his gaze dropped to the floor to see bloody footprints coming from what appeared to be the bedroom. Moving in that direction, he called, "Rudy, are you in there? It's Matt Rumsey."

With a chill of foreboding, he sensed there would be no answer. Sucking in a deep breath, he stepped through the door and froze. Before becoming a deputy sheriff, Matt had put in some time with the volunteer rescue squad and had seen his share of blood and gore . . . but nothing like the carnage before him now.

Rudy was cradled in a bed of blood, the floor a carpet of what looked like a thick, red pudding. His mouth gaped open in a silent scream, and his eyes were wide with the sightless glare of death.

There was nothing anybody could do for Rudy, and Matt needed to radio for an ambulance for Emma Jean. Until she came out of shock, there would be no answer about what happened. Meanwhile, Hardy Moon, who was also the county coroner, needed to come do his thing and clean up the mess.

Matt started to turn away, but hesitated, did a quick double take, then spun around to lean over Rudy's body to make sure his eyes weren't playing tricks on him. They weren't. Emma Jean had taken a bite out of Rudy's dick.

Holstering his gun, Matt backed out of the room, wondering just what Rudy had done to make her go nuts. He had seen it in her eyes. She was lost in that netherworld where the mad go to escape what they can't face.

But what about Luke? Where did he fit into all of this? If he had been here, and Rudy had surprised the two of them, Matt knew there was no way he would have run off to leave Emma Jean to face the music alone. He would have stayed and had it out, no matter the consequences. It wasn't Luke's way to run.

Emma Jean was right where he had left her, but now she had company. Curiosity had gotten the best of Alma. Standing over Emma Jean, she demanded, "What's going on? How come she's all bloody, and why won't she talk to me?"

"She's in shock."

"But what about the blood?" Alma persisted. "And where is Rudy?"

"Dead. And don't go in there unless you want to have nightmares the rest of your life." He caught her elbow and steered her toward his car. "I've got to radio for help."

Alma tried to pull away from him. "I want to go home."

"You don't have any business driving the shape you're in."

"I don't want anyone to find me here. They'll know I was looking for Luke. Besides, I don't want any part of this. Now let me go."

"Not till I talk to Luke and find out what he wants me to do with you." He wrestled her into the back seat of the car and slammed the door, locking her inside.

She beat on the window. "You can't do this to me, damn you. I've got to get home."

He grabbed the microphone. "Car nine to base." He did not wait for Wilma to acknowledge. "I've got a ten-thirty-three at the Veazey place. Get an ambulance and the coroner out here quick."

Wilma came back at once. "Is Alma with you, Matt?"

"I'm afraid so. Look, it's bad out here. Real bad. Rudy is dead, and it looks like Emma Jean did it. She's in shock. I've got to talk to Luke. Have you found him yet?"

"Matt, I . . ." her voice broke.

He tensed. "What is it?"

She choked the words out. "The call just came in a few minutes ago. I was going to call you, but I had to get the ambulance on the way first. Luke's been shot. Ozzie and Hank found him at the cemetery in Jake Petrie's open grave. They said it looked like he'd been there all night."

Alma screamed, "She did it. I know she did. He must've met her there to tell her he wouldn't leave me for her, and she got mad and shot him, then came home and killed Rudy, and . . ."

Matt growled at her to shut up, that she didn't know what the hell she was talking about. Then, worriedly, he asked Wilma, "How bad is he?"

"They say he's breathing, but he's lost a lot of blood. You all go on to the hospital and meet the ambulance there."

Matt reminded, "I can't leave a crime scene when I'm the only officer here. Find Kirby and get hold of Hardy and tell him to get his butt out here to pick up the body."

In the back seat, Alma collapsed in alternating fits of crying and cursing out the window at Emma Jean, who was oblivious to everything around her.

Matt released the mike button. There was nothing else to say, and he was feeling too sick to his stomach over the whole mess to talk anymore.

Chapter 4

The injection machine made a gentle whirring sound in the otherwise silent room as it pumped embalming fluid into Jubal's body. The procedure was almost over, and Hardy had enjoyed every moment. Usually he closed the eyes right away, but he had wanted to imagine Jubal could actually see what was happening to him.

He noticed oozing from the mouth and nose, which wasn't unusual when death came from heart failure. It was caused by fluid in the lungs, and Hardy wiped at it with a dirty rag.

He had stripped off Jubal's pajamas and tossed them to the floor. Ordinarily, out of respect, he would cover the genital area with a towel. But not Jubal. "I always knew you'd have a little pecker," he said, tweaking the limp organ between thumb and forefinger. "And your balls look like prunes."

The phone rang again, and Hardy irritably wondered who had been calling every few minutes for the past hour but still he did not answer. If it was business, whoever it was had no choice but to call back since his was the only funeral home in town. It was probably one of Lucy's gabby friends, but she had gone to Birmingham for the day.

He reached for a tube of airplane glue as he said to Jubal, "I'm charging for eye caps, but that's not what you're getting. You're not worth it." Dripping the glue over the dry eyeballs, he pulled the lids shut, satisfied there was no tell-tale oozing of the sticky solution around the lashes. The family would never know they had paid an extra ten dollars for nothing. Thinking about it made him remember Luke's warning, but Hardy had to take a chance this time. It was the principle involved—the principle and the fact he hated Jubal and wanted to screw his estate as much as possible. Besides, Luke would never find out about it.

There was a sudden pounding on the back door. "I'm busy," he yelled irritably. "Come back later." He figured he had another half hour to work on Jubal before time for Jake Petrie's funeral.

"Mr. Moon, it's me—Ozzie. And it's real important."

"Why aren't you at the cemetery getting ready for the Petrie funeral?"

"I was out there, and that's when I found Sheriff Ballard in Jake's grave, and . . ."

Hardy nearly tripped in his haste to open the door and yank Ozzie inside. After listening, heart pounding, to his story, Hardy sent him back to the cemetery, then called Buddy, who had already heard.

"Get over here," Buddy said brusquely.

"How'd you find out?"

"Nancy Curry phoned in to spread the news. She lives near the cemetery and heard the commotion."

"What about Burch? Have you talked to him?"

"He's on his way. Now hurry up."

Hardy hung up and pinched Jubal's arm. It felt firm like it was supposed to, as though rigor mortis had returned caused by the saturation of the muscle with the embalming solution. Aspiration of the thoracic area was next, but that would have to wait. Carelessly, he tossed a dirty sheet over Jubal's body and hurried on his way, ignoring the phone, which was ringing again. He paused only long enough to leave a note pinned to the door saying where he had gone and that he would be back shortly.

Buddy looked from Burch to Hardy, then bammed a fist on his desk. "All right, which one of you is responsible?"

Hardy shook his head. "Not me."

"Me, either," said Burch.

"Okay," Buddy allowed, "Nobody wants to own up to it, but I just hope the person paid to do it keeps their mouth shut."

Burch dared suggest, "And what about you? We've talked about this, you know—how it looks like maybe Luke's got a vendetta going. First it was Junior Kearney, and we know Luke probably had something to do with that. Then he went after Hardy" . . . he darted a glance at Hardy . . . "and don't try to deny something happened to make you let Lucy take over. He had to be behind it.

"And," he added chokily, face crimson with a sudden rush of anger, "I told you it was him that set me up. So you were next on his list." He pointed a shaking finger at Buddy.

"Yeah, that's right," Hardy chimed in with a firm nod. "Only maybe you're too ashamed to admit it."

Resisting the impulse to squirm in his chair, Buddy managed an amused chuckle. "That's crazy. The whole thing is crazy."

"Is it?" Burch leaned across the desk, eyes wide with fear. "Think about it."

"That's ridiculous," Buddy said. "He's just an asshole, that's all, and I only want to make sure you two cover your tracks if you were involved in any way with what happened."

"Does anybody know how bad he's hurt?" Burch asked.

Hardy related Ozzie's story about how the rescue squad said his pulse was weak and things didn't look good.

"Well, maybe he won't make it," Buddy said hopefully. "I'm going to call his office and see what I can find out."

Burch was quick to protest, "Maybe we shouldn't act concerned. It might look suspicious."

"Don't be an idiot," Buddy scoffed. "I'm the richest and most prominent man in the whole damn county. It's only natural I'd inquire when the sheriff's been shot."

He reached for the phone just as the intercom buzzer sounded, followed by Murline saying, "Wilma from the sheriff's office is on the phone, Mr. Hampton. She says it's important."

"This may be it," Buddy said, excited. "It's only natural I'd be notified if he's dead." He punched a button to take the call. "Cleve Hampton here, Wilma. What can I do for you?"

He listened, brow creasing, eyes falling on Hardy as he confirmed, "Yes, he's here. Just a minute. But let me ask you—is it true what I've heard about Sheriff Ballard?" He grimaced with disappointment to hear Luke was still alive but managed to sound properly concerned. "I am so sorry to hear this, and I want you to keep me informed and let me know if there's anything I can do."

Covering the mouthpiece with his hand, he quickly whispered to Burch, "They've been trying to reach you. They finally went to the funeral home and saw the note you left on the door. Now be calm and act natural."

Hardy took the phone. "Yeah, Wilma, what's going on?" His eyes went wide. "Well, I'll be damned. Sure. Sure. I'll get over there right now. I just need to call the preacher and tell him he'll have to do the Petrie funeral alone."

He hung up with a grin. "I've got a body to pick up, all right—Rudy Veazey. Looks like his old lady killed him."

He started for the door but turned to ask Buddy, "What did Wilma say about Luke?"

"That he's in critical condition, and they're moving him to Birmingham."

Burch, for the moment, wasn't thinking about Luke. "They're saying Emma Jean did it?"

"Yeah. But I don't know any of the details."

Burch leaped to his feet. "I'll go with you. She's going to need a lawyer." Even if she couldn't afford one, he knew he would represent her anyway. He had nothing to lose except time and sure as hell had plenty of that lately, thanks to Luke. God, he hoped the bastard died before they could get him to Birmingham.

Buddy stared after them.

So far, Luke had only put his plans to ruin him in motion, but it hadn't actually happened. And if he didn't make it, then it never would.

"Die," Buddy whispered, tears stinging his eyes. "Please, you bastard, die."

News spreads fast in a small town, and Hampton was no exception. By the time Matt and Alma arrived at the hospital, the waiting room was crowded with people anxious to hear details of what had happened to their sheriff. So far, no one else knew about Rudy Veazey's murder. Wilma had called Kirby and got him to take over for Matt so he could get Alma to the hospital. Everyone assumed he had gone to her house to pick her up.

Matt watched as members of Alma's church flocked around her. The minister, Daniel Conley—everyone called him "Preacher Dan" —was praying out loud, beseeching God to forgive Luke's sins and not send him to roast in hell. Since he wasn't bothering to ask that Luke survive, it appeared to be a foregone conclusion—to Preacher Dan anyway—that Luke was a goner.

Matt swallowed against the lump in his throat. He had known Luke his whole life, and while most people thought Luke was cold-hearted and didn't give a damn about anybody or anything, Matt knew differently. Sure, Luke had been a hellraiser back in high school, but he'd been treated like dirt for being born a bastard. It was only natural he'd fight back. Maybe he did have a chip on his shoulder since he'd come back from the war, and maybe he had made a few people eat shit. So what? Matt figured they must have had it coming.

All in all, Luke was a good man and had done a fine job of cleaning up the town since he got elected sheriff and if he did die, Matt would never rest until he found out who was responsible and saw to it that they paid. Maybe he wouldn't even bother going by the law. Maybe he would just take the murdering skunk out on some back road, put a bullet in his head, then tie a sack of rocks around his ankles, and toss him in the Coosa River to feed the catfish.

The doors to the ambulance bay swung open and Sue Watson, Alma's neighbor, rushed in with Tammy. Tammy, face white as a sheet, spotted Alma and ran to throw herself in her arms. Some of the folks down on their knees started to get up to make room for her, but a scathing look from Preacher Dan kept them where they were as he continued to intone, "Cleanse his soul, Lord, and spare him from the fires of hell. Don't let his Christian loved ones suffer to know he'll spend eternity in Satan's furnace."

Alma was worn out with Preacher Dan and turned her attention to Tammy. "We don't know anything, yet, honey."

Tammy was feeling guilty to think how she'd dreaded going to Birmingham with her daddy that morning. They had never been close, and she really hadn't thought much about him until she realized she didn't want him to die. "Miss Sue said somebody shot him. Do they know who it was?"

Matt thought how he could name half a dozen people who could have pulled the trigger. Maybe more. He wished he had gone to the crime scene but wanted to be at the hospital to get first-hand information about Luke. At least he had thought to radio back to Wilma and have her get hold of Wendell Wheat, a part-time deputy, to help Kirby out at the Veazey place. Emma Jean was acting downright spooky, and the ambulance hadn't left yet to go get her. It was still parked outside. Matt knew that the doctors did not know yet if it would be needed to transfer Luke to Birmingham.

God, he wished he knew what had happened. He just couldn't picture Emma Jean going loco and killing Rudy. He remembered the time he and Luke had gone out there when Rudy had beat her. She hadn't said a word, just cowered in a corner with her hands over her face, refusing to sign a warrant. So it was hard to imagine her slashing him to death, much less getting mad enough to take a bite out of his dick.

He was thinking about calling Wilma to see if she'd heard anymore from Kirby when all of a sudden a ripple of gasps went through the room like a shower of pebbles thrown in water. Kirby and Wendell were walking in with Emma Jean. A blanket was wrapped around her, and they was having to hold her up.

Alma shot a look at Matt. She had followed his orders to keep quiet about Rudy, but now she worried what people were going to think with Emma Jean being brought in looking like she did.

Then it happened. Myrtle Letchworth, thinking that maybe Emma Jean had shown up out of concern for Luke shrieked, "You shameless hussy. How dare you embarrass Luke's family this way? Have you no shame?"

Preacher Dan was quick to admonish, "Judge not lest ye be judged, sister. You can tell she's sick. Look at her." He was staring at Emma Jean's bloody feet and legs. "She's hurt."

Myrtle screamed, "No, she ain't. She ain't hurt a'tall. Maybe that's Luke's blood. Maybe she's the one who shot him."

Preacher Dan had heard the gossip about Luke and Emma Jean's adulterous affair and quickly realized things were about to get out of hand. He tried to restrain Myrtle, who was trying to get closer to Emma Jean, but she was beyond control.

"She's the one. She did it because he wouldn't leave Alma for her. Whore of Babylon. We ought to stone her."

Alma was suddenly goaded by the realization that Myrtle's theory matched her own. Emma Jean, she figured, had gone crazy after she realized what she'd done and rushed home, only to find Rudy waiting. Naturally, when he discovered she wasn't there in the middle of the night, he figured she was off somewhere with Luke. They got into a fight, and Emma Jean had killed him.

Alma pushed Tammy from her arms and started through the crowd toward Emma Jean. "You murdering bitch. You shot my husband and then killed yours."

Matt quickly moved to grab her as Emma Jean, still supported by Kirby and Wendell, raised her head long enough to look at Alma blankly, then lowered it again, still in shock.

"What did you say?" someone shouted. "Did you say she killed Rudy? Rudy's dead?"

Alma screamed back, "She stabbed him. I saw her with the bloody knife in her hand, only Matt told me not to say anything. We just came from there, and I know what I'm talking about. She shot Luke because he wouldn't leave me for a whore like her."

Kirby yelled, "Matt, get her out of here now."

Matt gave her a shake. "Alma, shut up."

Wrenching from Matt's hold, Alma managed to rake her nails down Emma Jean's face, then grabbed her by her neck and started choking her. Emma Jean, in her stupor, made no effort to defend herself. Alma was quickly pulled away, but, by then, bedlam had erupted as everyone in the waiting room began to surge forward, yelling and screaming all at once.

Matt jerked Alma's arms behind her back at the same time Tammy came running to kick him in his shins and tell him to get his hands off her mother. Preacher Dan tried to help and got clobbered in the eye with Myrtle Letchworth's handbag and turned away in a yelp of pain.

Matt shouted to Kirby, "Get Emma Jean out of here."

Preacher Dan, one hand covering his rapidly swelling eye, urged, "Take her on back in the emergency room. I think Myrtle has gone to tell the Veazey family about Rudy, and there's no telling what will happen when they get here." Then he turned to Alma, who was struggling against Matt, who had grabbed hold of her again. "You need to calm down, sister. Your child needs you."

Alma reached out for Tammy, and Matt let her go as he saw Dr. Ben Campbell coming out from the back. Dr. Campbell glanced about with a frown, obviously annoyed by all the commotion. "Is Mrs. Ballard here?" Alma stumbled forward, and he motioned her to go with him. Matt was right behind them, and so was Kirby, still holding Emma Jean.

Once the doors to the waiting room were closed, Dr. Campbell demanded, exasperated, "What are all of you doing back here? I only asked for Mrs. Ballard." Then he noticed the blood on Emma Jean. "What happened to her?"

"We aren't sure," Matt said. "And it's not her blood. She isn't hurt. Not physically anyway." He quickly explained how she was apparently in shock and also under arrest for the murder of her husband. Either Matt or Kirby would have to stay with her. "And we needed to get her out of sight," he was quick to add, "or else we were going to have a riot on our hands when the Veazey family gets here."

Dr. Campbell motioned to a nurse. "Get this woman to a room. I'll be in to check her over as soon as I can." He put his hand on Alma's shoulder. "Come with me."

Matt trailed after them, leaving Kirby with Emma Jean.

Once inside an empty cubicle, Dr. Campbell gently told Alma, "Luke is in critical condition. We're moving him to Birmingham." He described his wounds, how he had been shot three times, probably with a .22 rifle. "The bullets that hit his shoulder and thigh didn't do much damage. They went through clean without shattering bone. It's the one still in his head I'm worried about. It struck the top of his head at an acute angle of, I'd say, between twenty to thirty degrees, probably as he was falling from his other wounds. Had he been standing erect, he'd have been killed instantly."

Matt snatched at the hope, "Will the doctors in Birmingham be able to get it out?"

"I can't answer that. I only know we don't have a surgeon to do it here." He thought about what the x-rays had shown, how the bullet had gone through the left side of the cerebrum, hit the inside of the skull, then slid down into the temporal lobe. So far, there was no sign of a subdural or extradural hemorrhage and no sinus laceration. The bullet might also eventually shift around and damage pulmonary arteries. If not removed, Luke would die. But it was also possible that surgery might also dislodge the bullet and cause instant death. Lord, he was glad it was all being taken out of his hands.

"Is he awake?" Matt asked. "I'd like to find out if he can tell me anything about who did it."

"He's in a coma." Dr. Campbell turned to Alma. "We'll be loading him in the ambulance in a few minutes. You'll need to get someone to drive you to Birmingham because it's best you don't ride with him."

Alma, who had remained composed throughout the conversation, quietly said, "I'm sure I can find somebody." She walked out.

When they were alone, Matt looked Dr. Campbell straight in the eye. "Okay. Give it to me straight. What are his chances?"

Grim-faced, Dr. Campbell replied, "Frankly, Matt, I'll be surprised if he makes it to Birmingham."

Chapter 5

August 1965

Luke stared out the window of the bus at the rolling Alabama hills. He always hated coming home and hadn't been there in quite a while. He and Alma had never gotten along and never would. Tammy was spoiled rotten and acted like she couldn't stand him. He couldn't wait to get away, despite his mother's wanting him to stay. She was the only reason he came back anyway. She was after him not to reenlist when his time was up in a few more months, but his life was the army.

Alma didn't care, but his mother argued Tammy needed a father. His defense was that it was Alma's choice not to move to

California to be with him. Not that he wanted her. He liked his life just fine like it was.

A sniper's bullet to his left thigh had bought him a ticket back to the states, and now he was a drill sergeant, whipping new recruits into shape. He was stationed at Camp Pendleton, assigned to the Marines, and loved California. He lived off base in a shack on the beach with a little Mexican gal hotter than a chili pepper who knew a zillion ways to take him around the world.

He was happy, Alma seemed content with the way things were, and his mother had stayed so drunk the past few years she didn't know whether she was coming or going most of the time anyway. But now she was *going*, according to what the doctor told Alma. At forty-two, her liver was giving out, her heart was acting up, and there just wasn't anything anybody could do. She had lived a hard life, and that, plus the whiskey, had taken its toll. He knew it was time for him and Alma to have a serious talk because, once his mother died, it made sense they should get a divorce since he didn't plan on ever coming back.

He smelled the odor of rotten eggs—sulphur from the paper mill. That meant he was getting real close to Hampton. Seeing familiar landmarks triggered memories like reading lines in a diary. Sadly, few were pleasant.

The bus lumbered past the football stadium where, in his senior year as quarterback, he was leading the team to a second 2-A division championship when the coach called him into his office one day to tell him there had been a change concerning homecoming weekend. As captain, Luke was supposed to escort Julie Faircloth, who was the team's candidate for queen, onto the field for the pre-game ceremony. But Coach Martin said Tim Speight would take her instead.

Luke wanted an explanation, and Coach Martin said he hated to be blunt, but the fact was that Julie's father was the mayor. He wanted someone from a prominent family to escort his daughter since there would be pictures in the paper, the school annual, and so forth. Luke understood then because he had put up with snubs all his life. Mayor Faircloth did not want his daughter escorted and photographed with Orlena Ballard's bastard son.

Luke had said it didn't matter to him, then took out the rage boiling inside by playing his guts out at the homecoming game.

He hogged the ball, even running when the play called for him to pass. He got tackled a lot and fumbled a few times. Some of his teammates got annoyed and accused him of show-boating, but the final score shut them up. The Hampton High Bulldogs won 49-0, and Luke had scored every touchdown.

Vengeance had been sweet. So many pictures of Luke were plastered on the front page of the *Hampton Herald* that coverage of the homecoming ceremonies was reduced to one paragraph announcing Julie had been crowned queen with no room for a photo.

The bus rolled by the Bulldog Cafe, and Luke imagined he could still see the blood on the sidewalk from that summer night in '56. He had taken Judy Turnage to the movies and had enough money left over from his week's pay as a bag boy at the A&P to buy her a burger and a Coke. But when they got to the cafe, Rudy Veazey was there, mad as hell to see Judy out with Luke, because he had been dating her.

Just then Rudy spotted Luke's mother riding by with Junior Kearney in his pickup truck and yelled to ask Luke how come his last name wasn't *Kearney* since everybody in town figured Junior was his daddy. Luke was furious but ignored Rudy's insults and steered Judy on inside. Then, just before the door closed after them, Rudy laughed to his buddies that maybe Luke should be called Luke *Heinz* instead, like in *Heinz-57*, since his whore-momma probably screwed fifty-seven guys the night she got knocked up.

Luke had whirled about so fast his hand missed the doorknob and went through the glass instead. A lot of the blood spilled on the sidewalk that night was probably his, but most of it had to have been Rudy's by the time Luke finished with him. They were both arrested for fighting but let off with a stern lecture. They had hated each other's guts ever since.

Luke didn't look for trouble, but he didn't run from a fight either. Yeah, he had worn his hair long back then. A "DA" it was called. Duck's ass slicked back and plastered with Vitalis. But he was no punk. And his mother was no whore.

Sure, she had been Junior's woman for a long time. What other choice did she have when her folks kicked her out, pregnant, with no place to go? But when Junior tossed her aside after she lost her looks because of heavy drinking and hard work, he had let her keep on working at the motor court. She cleaned cabins, and she also worked as a waitress in the cafe. She didn't mess with other men, no matter what folks said.

Passing the park, Luke was reminded of another slight, the Easter he was nine years old when his mother dyed a basket of eggs and took him there for the annual egg hunt. The ladies in charge had turned as many colors as the eggs scattered in the grass when they saw Orlena and her bastard kid in tow. It had been Ramona Hampton—Mrs. Cleve Hampton, herself—who had curtly told Orlena that they had way too many children, and, goodness, she was so sorry.

Luke remembered how his mother had blinked back humiliated tears as she squeezed his hand and whispered to him that it didn't matter and turned to lead him away. But Luke had hung back just long enough to snatch an egg out of the basket and sail it through the air to smash on the back of Mrs. Hampton's head. Then he and his mother had took off running, laughing all the while. Later she scolded him and said he shouldn't have done it, but he knew she was secretly glad.

He saw the First Baptist Church with its tall white steeple and manicured lawn and recalled another of his mother's futile attempts to have him accepted. She had offered to teach vacation Bible school one summer and, again, was rudely rejected, this time by Irene Cleghorn, who cruelly told Orlena she was unqualified. So his mother had sent him anyway, but Mrs. Cleghorn had turned him away, claiming there was no room for him.

To keep from hurting his mother, Luke had left home every morning like he was going to Bible school, then hidden till after it was over. She had never questioned why he didn't bring home handicrafts like the other kids, and he had wondered if he managed to fool her after all.

The bus pulled in behind Creech's gas station, which served as the depot. Luke waited till everybody else got off, then took his duffle bag from the overhead rack and made his way out. The heat slapped him in the face like an invisible hand. Only hell could be hotter than Alabama in August. His uniform felt like he was wearing a thick wool blanket, but it, along with the coveted green beret denoting Special Forces, and the ribbon for the Silver Star he'd been awarded for heroics in Vietnam, were the only things he'd ever had to hold his head up about in his life, and he wore both proudly.

Taking out his handkerchief, he wiped at his brow and neck as he glanced about. He wasn't surprised no one was there to meet him. His mother was in the hospital, and Alma would be working.

"Luke. Luke Ballard. Is that really you?"

He turned toward the gas pump and saw a girl waving at him from the window of a black Ford pickup. "I don't believe it."

She jumped out of the truck and started toward him. He grinned when he recognized Sara Daughtry. Only she was Sara Daughtry Speight now, and every bit as pixie cute as she had been when he fancied himself in love with her back in 1956. Her cinnamon-colored hair was pulled back in a ponytail, and cutoff jeans revealed her shapely, tanned legs. A sleeveless blouse, the tails tied in a knot beneath her bosom, accented her still narrow waist and flat stomach even though she'd had two kids. She threw herself at him, and he wrapped his arms around her and hugged her tight. Sara was, and always would be, special.

Aware that the guys working at the station, as well as a few customers, were watching, he let her go. "You look just like you did when you'd run to meet me on the field after a game, Sara. I swear, you haven't changed a bit."

"Oh, really?" she laughed and gave her waist a pinch. "If I tried to get into my old cheerleading outfit I'd bust the zipper. That was eight years and twice that many pounds ago."

"Well, I'm way ahead of you."

"You're still gorgeous."

"Hey, enough of this or I'll grab you like I did back then and take you parking in the cotton field and try to get that zipper undone myself."

She gave him a playful punch under his chin. "You've got more important things to do than flirt with me. I know you've come home because of your mom. I heard she was in the hospital. Come on, and I'll take you to the mill to get your car from Alma."

He hoisted his duffle bag over his shoulder. "Thanks. I don't think I'd enjoy walking in this heat."

"I'm glad to do it. It's not much out of the way, and Dewey won't care when I tell him why I took so long getting back."

Luke did not fail to notice how her voice softened when she spoke her uncle's name. Dewey Culver was much more than just Sara's uncle by virtue of his marriage to her father's sister. He was the man she had loved since she was only fourteen years old—and also the reason she had held back from loving *him*. She had told him so by letter years after he had to marry Alma. He was in Vietnam by then, and she had explained that she just felt driven to confide everything to him. He had written her back that he understood—even though he didn't—and warned her she was playing with fire but wished her well.

His letter had opened the door for Sara to unload all her problems and she had written often after that. She told him the reason why she had married Tim Speight right after graduation. She and Dewey agreed she could not spend her life living for stolen moments, and, most importantly, she wanted children and a home of her own. Tim seemed to be the kind of guy parents hoped their daughters would marry. He had a good job in the steel mill in Birmingham and the future looked bright. The only thing was, once they were married, Sara had discovered how he really was: tight with money, domineering, and verbally abusive. She took solace in the son and daughter born within the first three years they were married, and, eventually, in Dewey's arms. It didn't matter he was old enough to be her daddy. They loved each other and lived for the precious times they could steal away to be together.

The letters had fallen off since Luke had come back from Vietnam, and he hadn't heard from her in a while. "So how are things between you two?" he asked.

"Fine, but we don't see each other much this time of year," she said. "He's got quite a truck garden, you know, so it keeps the whole family busy, and believe me, if Dewey wasn't family, Tim would never let me work for him. He thinks all I should do is stay home, keep house, and bake cookies."

"The ones you sent me in Nam were pretty good. They didn't last long, either. The other guys would steal them out of my pack."

"If you'd written more, I'd have baked more. That's what you get for being so lazy."

"It wasn't altogether being lazy, Sara," he soberly reminded. "I was always afraid Tim would find out." He had sent his letters to Sara's cousin, and Sara would pick them up at her house, but he worried just the same.

"And I was always afraid you'd get killed with mine in your pack and they'd be sent home to Alma. Then there would have been *two* new graves in the cemetery—yours *and* mine."

He tossed his bag in the back of the truck, then went inside the station and bought a frosty cold bottle of Coca-Cola and a bag of salted peanuts. Climbing in the cab beside Sara, he poured the peanuts into the Coke, then took a long swallow and sighed. He had forgotten how good the two tasted mixed together because, for some strange reason, he only thought to do it when he was in Alabama. Anywhere else just didn't seem natural.

He asked about her kids. She said they were great. The boy, Tim Junior, had just turned six, and the girl, Bonnie, would be four in a few months.

"I saw Tammy last week," she told him. "The church camp she's attending came by Dewey's farm on a day trip. He showed them around and gave them free watermelons. She's really growing, Luke. What is she now? Eight?"

"I think so. Alma reminded me a few months ago we'd been married eight years, and Tammy came along about five months later." His tone was bitter as he added, "I sure as hell messed up when I had to get married. I never loved Alma, and you know it."

"But sometimes people learn to love each other."

"Not this time."

She gave his arm a pat. "You'll meet somebody some day, Luke. Wait and see. Till then, just try and hold things together for Tammy's sake. That's the only reason I'm staying with Tim now. When my kids are grown, I'm leaving him and to hell with what folks think."

She eased into a parking space in front of Woolworth's Five and Dime. "I've got to run inside and get some Band-Aids. One of the workers has a blister. Want to come with me? I won't be but a minute, but it's hot out here and air-conditioned in there."

He reached for the door handle. "Sure. Anything to beat this heat."

He froze at the sight of a sheriff's deputy dragging a little colored girl out the front door. She looked to be eight or nine years old, and she was crying and begging him to let her go.

"What the hell?"

Sara grabbed his arm. "Whatever it is, stay out of it, Luke."

He shot her an incredulous look. "But she's just a little kid and look how he's treating her. There's no need for that, and—hey—I've seen that kid before. A picture of her, anyway. She's Ocie Rhoden's girl."

"Who's Ocie Rhoden?"

"You remember him. He was the drum major at East Hampton High." East Hampton was the colored high school, and the white kids loved to go to their football games on Monday nights. They enjoyed the spirited music and antics of the band, especially high-stepping, high-strutting Ocie.

"Oh, yeah," Sara responded thoughtfully, "but how do you know that's his daughter?"

Luke felt his guts tighten at the way the pot-bellied deputy was shoving her around as he screamed into her face that she was going to jail. "He was in basic training with me at Fort Benning. We stayed in touch and ran into each other in Nam. He showed me her picture. He's still over there, risking his life so fat-assed gestapos can bully his kid."

His last words were drowned by the slamming of the door. He was out of the truck and sprinting across the sidewalk just in time to grab the deputy's arm.

"Hey, whaddaya think you're doing?" the deputy roared.

Luke gave him a rough shove. "I'm saving you from getting your face punched in, tough guy, because that's what's going to happen if you don't get your hands off her."

With a curse, the deputy went for his gun, but Luke was quicker. Pinning the deputy's arm behind his back, he spun him around and pressed his face against the wall. "You don't want to point a gun at me unless you plan to use it, and if you do plan to use it, you better be fast. Now how come you're picking on Ocie's kid?"

The little girl rallied from her terror to cry in wonder, "You know my daddy, mister?"

"I sure do, honey."

The deputy growled, "You're interfering with the law, buddy. She was stealing."

The child, buoyed by Luke's intervention, spoke up to defend herself. "That ain't so. I was just lookin' at a doll and holdin' it and walkin' around pretendin' it was mine, but I was gonna put it back. I don't steal."

The deputy, despite Luke's hold and his face mashed so hard against the brick wall, snickered, "Niggers are natural-born thieves, you lyin' little pickaninny."

Luke mashed his face harder into the wall to shut him up as he asked the little girl, "Where's the doll?"

A clerk who had been standing in the doorway watching called out, "I have it." She held up the doll. "She dropped it when he grabbed her."

"Was she trying to hide it?"

The clerk hesitated. She did not want to dispute the deputy's word.

"Well, was she?" Luke repeated loudly, impatiently.

She shook her head. "I don't guess so."

He released the deputy. "You stupid jerk. Don't you know you can't arrest somebody for shoplifting until they leave the store with the goods? As long as she was inside, she wasn't guilty of a damn thing."

"Well, you're the one in deep shit now."

"No, you are, for dragging her out and accusing her of shoplifting."

"If I had waited till she left, she'd have took off, and I never would've caught her, fast as pickaninnies can run."

Luke narrowed his eyes and thought for a minute. Then it dawned on him, and he chuckled, "Faster than you, that's for sure, *Howie*." He had recognized him—Howell, Howie for short—Camden. He had been a fat slob in high school and still was.

And Howie recognized him as well. "You might've won a medal, Ballard, but that don't mean nothing around here. The sheriff is gonna be plenty mad when he hears what you did, and—"

"And you tell him I'm real worried about it, okay?" Dismissing him, he asked the clerk, "How much is the doll?"

She looked at the square white tag stapled to the doll's gingham dress. "Two-ninety-nine."

He pulled out his wallet, handed her three one dollar bills, then took the doll and gave it to the little girl. "Now it's yours. Your name's Patti Sue, isn't it? I remember your daddy telling me."

"Yessir, it sho is, and I thank you, sir. Thank you so much." She hugged the doll tightly, glanced at the deputy fearfully, then turned and ran to disappear around the corner of the building.

A small crowd had gathered, and Sara hurried on inside to buy the Bandaids. When she returned, Luke was back in the truck, and Howie was gone, but a few men stood just down the sidewalk, talking and looking in Luke's direction.

"I wish you hadn't done that," she said nervously, turning the ignition key with a shaky hand.

"You can't mean that. You actually wanted me to stand by and let that bully mistreat her? You heard her—she didn't steal anything."

"You don't understand. Sheriff Grady isn't going to like your interfering, and he can be real mean, especially when it comes to coloreds."

"Then he's got no business being sheriff."

"I agree. He's up for reelection next year, but nobody wants to run against him because they're scared of him."

"That's bullshit."

"Easy for you to say. You don't live here."

"I'd say it if I did."

"But you don't," she repeated, then warned, "but your family does, so mind your own business, Luke, or Sheriff Grady could make it rough on them to get back at you."

Taking a swallow of peanut-laced Coke, he said, "That would be his last mistake."

Ben Cotter, retired postmaster, Jubal Cochran, manager of the auto parts business next to Woolworth's, and Clyde Bush, owner of the Bulldog Cafe, stared after them as Sara drove away.

"He sure as gun's iron stood up to Howie," Ben said.

Clyde agreed. "Yep. And I always liked that boy. He was a good boy, too, which is surprising when you think of how some folks treated him because he's a bastard. I remember the time he broke the glass in the front door of the cafe when he got in a fight with that punk, Rudy Veazey. Whipped his butt, he did. And you know what else?"

Ben and Jake shook their heads.

"Gave me a dollar a week out of his salary at the A&P until he paid for fixing it."

Jake mused aloud, "Well, it's a shame he don't live here. He'd be a good one to run for sheriff against Grady."

"Maybe we can talk him into it," Ben suggested.

Clyde snorted. "It'd take more'n talk, I'm afraid. Lot's more. 'Cause somethin' tells me unless something big happens to change his mind, when Orlena Ballard kicks the bucket, we've seen the last of Luke in this town."

Sara stopped at the front gate of the mill. Inside the fence, workers were sitting at picnic tables, taking their morning break for coffee and cigarettes. "I see Alma, and she isn't going to like your being with me, Luke. Hurry and get out and maybe she won't notice."

He did not move as he looked at the woman who was his wife and wondered what it would be like to be married to someone he could look forward to coming home to . . . like Sara.

Sara glanced at her watch. "I have to get back to the fields, anyway. Now you be sure and tell your momma I'm thinking about her, you hear?"

"I will, and thanks for keeping in touch with her." He paused to gaze at her thoughtfully, then said, "She always hated that we didn't wind up together."

"I know." Sara swallowed hard. "If not for Dewey, maybe we would've. But you're still my friend and always will be, Luke. I want you to know that."

Suddenly he found himself asking the question that had burned in his gut ever since she first told him how it was with her and Dewey. "What makes him so special, Sara?"

She stared through the window, beyond the mill and toward the Cheaha mountain range in the distance as she tried to frame her answer. "It's hard to explain if you've never been there, Luke . . . if you've never felt that way about anybody. It's a kind of warm, hand-holding kind of love that makes me feel like as long as I'm with him nothing or nobody can hurt me. And it doesn't matter if the sun is blazing down, or rain soaking me to the bone, or so cold my toe nails pop off.

"He's in my heart, Luke," she said wistfully. "Every hour of every day. No matter how rough things get, I know he's with me. I think it's the way we're supposed to feel about Jesus. I don't mean to sound sacrilegious. That's just how it is. And I know if folks found out, they'd think it was just for sex, but that's not so. That's just a part of it. The important thing is our *heart* love, not our *body* love."

She was suddenly embarrassed to have become so carried away, especially over something so personal. "You asked me, and I told you, and I sincerely hope one day you'll understand what I'm talking about."

Luke doubted that would ever happen. "Just be careful and don't get caught. If Tim ever found out, he'd divorce you and take the kids. And Dewey's marriage would be wrecked, too, if your daddy didn't kill him first."

"We never take any chances, and look how many years we've been together. Besides, you've got enough to worry about without me. So scoot. Alma's seen us, and her eyes are shooting daggers."

Norma Breedlove turned to see what was making Alma look mad enough to bite a nail in two. "Hey, isn't that your old man getting out of Dewey Culver's truck with Sara Speight drivin'? What's he doing with her?"

Without a word, Alma got up and started walking across the parking lot. She was not about to make any comment that would give Norma more fodder for gossip. Luke got out of the truck, and Sara wasted no time driving away.

Alma couldn't help thinking that he was a fine-looking man, even if he did already have some lines around his eyes, and his nose was crooked from when he broke it playing football. He was tall and well-built, and she knew lots of women thought she'd made a real good catch when she married him. Of course, they didn't know the truth, that he didn't love her and never had. But he was hers, by golly, as long as he went on believing Tammy was his daughter.

Alma thought of the promise she had made herself, how she was going to make things better because she didn't want to lose him, which is what might happen once Miss Orlena died. Luke would never come back and probably want a divorce, and if that happened, Alma knew at her age she'd probably never find another husband. So she was going to seduce him, and she smiled to think about it. When his leave was over, he'd be so crazy about her he'd want to get out of the army and settle down and be a real family man. Before, it hadn't mattered, because she knew as long as his mother was alive, things would stay the same. Only now, she was worried, and the first thing she was going to do was not to say anything snotty about him riding with Sara.

Luke took a step backwards, stunned, as she threw her arms around his neck and hugged him.

"Lordy, I'm glad you're home, but why didn't you let me know when you were coming? I'd have taken off work and met the bus."

She was still clinging to him, and Luke wondered what the hell was going on. She never hugged him, never touched him, and he had expected her to blow up about Sara, anyway.

He unwound her arms and mumbled he hadn't known exactly when he'd arrive. "I just need to get the car so I can go to the hospital. I'll be back to pick you up when you get off work."

He watched as she dug into the pocket of her pedal pushers for the keys. She wasn't a bad looking woman, he thought, if she'd wear a little makeup and fix herself up. Back in high school she had been a knockout, in a trashy kind of way, and she still had a nice shape.

She handed him the keys. "I went by the hospital on my way to work this morning, but she was asleep. I hate to say it, Luke, but I don't think she's going to live much longer. She's real bad off."

He felt the guilt that washed over him every time he thought about how he should have come home more often. It was worse now, knowing his mother was going down for the count. But hell, there was no life for him here and never had been, and not for her, either. But whenever he would point that out to her, she'd argue it was the only home she'd ever known and she wasn't running. So she stayed . . . and she drank . . . and it was killing her.

And Luke supposed he was going to always feel guilty about not being there to try and make things easier for her, but what could he have done except be miserable with her, which wouldn't have done either of them any good?

He scanned the parking lot and spotted the green Bel Air and turned to go. Alma caught his arm. "Tammy is really looking forward to your being here, too, Luke. I'll fix your favorite supper, fried chicken and turnip greens, and then we'll all go to the hospital together. But later, we need to have ourselves a talk."

"Yeah, sure," he said uncertainly. She was acting real strange. Maybe she had met somebody else and was being nice because she was going to ask him for a divorce. Well, that would suit him just fine. "See you later."

He found his mother asleep, bedded down in a ward with three other women. Two of them were crazy with old age, babbling and moaning. The third looked like she was already dead but nobody knew it yet. He turned on his heel and went straight to the nurses' station and told her, in no uncertain terms, that he wanted his mother moved to a private room as soon as possible.

The nurse, face as stiff as her starched white cap, explained a private room cost twenty dollars a day but ward beds were only eight. He told her it didn't matter, just to move her. Then he returned to the ward and pulled the curtain around the bed and sat down.

Staring at his mother, he thought of so many things he had always wanted to ask but never mustered the nerve—like just who was his daddy? And why hadn't she married him? Was it because he already had a wife? And did he live in Hampton? And how come he hadn't at least helped out with money so she wouldn't have had to take crap off Junior Kearney after her folks kicked her out? Junior wasn't his daddy. She had told him that much, at least.

What, exactly, burned inside her like a gnawing canker that she'd had to try and seek solace in a bottle all these years? She could have given him up at birth for adoption and gone away to start a new life, but she told him that thought never entered her mind. He was her baby, her son . . . the only good thing that had ever happened to her in her whole life, and she wasn't about to give him up, no matter what folks thought. So many questions, and the time for answers was running out.

Her hair, which had turned gray way before its time, hung loose and limp. As he pushed a few strands back from her face, her lashes softly fluttered at his touch, but she did not awaken.

"Oh, Lordy, Momma," he whispered raggedly, "just what were the demons in your life?"

Only when he finally left did Orlena open her eyes.

Maybe, she thought, wishing desperately that she had a drink, *the time had finally come to tell him about the demons.*

CHAPTER 6

Every time Luke went home, the cabin seemed to get smaller. The kitchen and sitting area were all in one room. There was only one bedroom, and the bath had been added on later and took up half of what used to be the back porch. Alma and his mother shared the bedroom, and Tammy slept on the sofa. When he was there, Tammy moved in with his mother, and he and Alma took the couch—not that it mattered. He couldn't remember the last time they'd had sex.

He was sitting on the front porch with Tammy while Alma fixed supper. He tried to make small talk but didn't know what to say.

A car pulled into the parking lot, and Luke watched as a man got out and headed straight for a cabin. The door flew open before he got there, and a woman with hair the color of egg yolks and wearing only a slip eagerly waved him inside.

"That's Miss Roxie's place," Tammy said. "And that man is one of her cousins. Momma says Miss Roxie has lots of cousins that come to visit. She's real nice. She gives me candy sometimes."

He knew then that was how Alma explained the whores Junior had started keeping, and he made up his mind to get his family out of there no matter how much his mother argued about it. Junior's place had always been a dump, and now the sheriff was apparently too busy harassing negroes to care about anything illegal going on there.

His attention was drawn to a black Ford as it pulled up to the back door of the cafe. A man dressed in black peg-legged pants and a bright pink shirt got out. He walked to the trunk, started to open it, then saw Luke watching and changed his mind and went on inside.

Tammy said importantly, "That's Mister Virgil. He brings bottled water to Mr. Kearney. I've seen him unload cases of it in big Mason jars. He must have a good well or something, huh?"

Luke gave an absent nod, burning to think how Junior had not only turned the motor court into a whore house but was also selling moonshine in what was, in theory, a dry county. A few minutes later the man came out, got in the car, and, with an annoyed glance at Luke, took off with a screech of tires, red dust flying.

Junior followed and headed straight for Luke. "Well, well," he sneered. "The soldier boy came home 'cause his momma is sick. Ain't that sweet?"

Luke stood, pulling Tammy with him. He gave her a gentle push and told her to go inside, then turned on Junior. "Skip the bullshit, Junior. I see what's going on here with your whores and moonshine, and I don't like it."

Junior spat a wad of tobacco juice to land near Luke's feet. "So why don't you take 'em and git?"

"That's exactly what I plan to do."

"Good." Junior nodded as though it were all settled. "So how's Orlena doin'?"

"What do you care?"

"What do I care?" Junior hooted. "Ain't you forgettin' something, boy? If not for me, you'd probably been born in a back alley somewheres. I gave your momma a roof over her head, remember?"

"She worked for it in more ways than one," Luke reminded him with hooded eyes.

Junior frowned. Luke was a big fellow, and he'd heard how he'd had a lot of special training in the army to make him real mean. Instinctively, he retreated a few steps. "You just let me know when you plan to move, and the sooner the better. I can use this cabin for one of my girls."

"Luke," Alma called uncertainly from where she stood just inside the rusting screen door, "Supper's ready."

He left Junior standing there and went inside. As soon as he got to the table, he curtly declared, "Tomorrow we're going to find someplace else for you all to live. You aren't staying here any longer, and that's final. If Momma makes it out of the hospital, I'll set her straight how it's going to be. You should have written me what's been going on here. *Cousins. Bottled water.* Jesus, Alma." He stabbed a drumstick with his fork and put it on his plate.

Tammy watched with wide eyes, and Alma cleared her throat, sending a message to Luke to cool it. They ate in silence, except for Luke's saying how good everything was. Alma had been cooking ever since she got home and had outdone herself, which puzzled him, because she had never gone to this trouble before.

"It started up in the last year." Alma had waited to say anything till they were on their way to the hospital after dropping Tammy off at a girlfriend's house to spend the night. "First it was the women. Just a few at first. Then every single cabin was taken by them, except for ours. Junior is sorry as they come, Luke, and I've sure never had no use for him, but he has taken care of your momma. He hasn't asked her to move."

"I wish he had."

"So do I, because things keep getting worse. There's the gambling, and sometimes there's big fights that spill into the parking lot. We don't go outside after dark, and I try to make sure Tammy sleeps at one of her friend's on the weekends when it gets real bad."

"Have you ever called the sheriff?"

"Oh, yes. One night when there was a big fight and a man got cut up. Deputies came and broke it up, but they didn't arrest anybody, and things kept right on. So I don't bother, anymore, especially when I've seen the deputies going in the cabins where the women are. And I'll let you figure out why," she added with a roll of her eyes.

"And you didn't write me about any of it."

"Orlena wouldn't let me. She said you'd come home and raise hell, and there was no need. You know how stubborn she can be. That old motor court is the only home she's ever had, and she wasn't about to move anywhere else. She said there was nowhere else in this county where she'd be welcome, anyhow."

"So she felt welcome around whores and drunks and gamblers." He slammed his palms against the steering wheel. "Well, I promise you one thing: she's spent her last night there."

At the hospital, Luke was glad to run into the doctor as he was making his rounds but not pleased over what he had to tell him.

"Orlena has cirrhosis of the liver caused by her drinking," Dr. Campbell explained. "Ordinarily, the damage can be reversed with abstinence if it's caught in time, but apparently your mother had symptoms she ignored. Now she has fever, jaundice, and she's in a lot of pain. There's also some sepsis—that's when bacteria invades the body—and I'm also seeing signs of heart failure."

Luke felt like he'd swallowed a brick and had to force his words around it. "Is there any hope she can pull out of this? I swear, I'll do whatever it takes to make her quit drinking. I'll sign for her to go to Brice's if you think it'll help."

Dr. Campbell shook his head. "I'm sorry, Luke, but I'm afraid it's too late. The damage is done."

Alma had already gone in his mother's room, and Luke followed, glad to see she was awake. Earlier, there had only been one IV bottle dripping a clear liquid into her veins, but now there was a second, flowing red. Dr. Campbell had explained a blood transfusion might make her feel better since she was so anemic.

Orlena managed a feeble smile as Luke took her hand, her voice thin as an eggshell when she spoke. "Oh, son, it's so good to see you . . . even if I did have to get sick to bring you home."

"You just get well, and I promise it won't be so long between visits anymore."

"I think I'd like it better if you just get out of the army before you get killed and come on back home where you belong. I love you, son, and I've missed you."

He had to speak around the brick again, only this time it had settled deeper in his chest. He found himself wishing men had the social freedom to cry like women to relieve the pressure, like Alma was doing, only she had turned away so Orlena wouldn't see.

It was hard, but he managed to keep his voice from cracking. "I love you, too, Momma. I always have. I just wish I could have made things easier for you."

"I wouldn't trade a minute of the time I've had with you, but I'd change how you was brought into the world if I could help it.

I'd see to it folks didn't look down on you for being born like you was." A tear slipped from the corner of her eye.

He brushed it away. "None of that, you hear? If that's what it took for me to have you for a mother, it was worth it."

Alma, feeling like she was intruding on a private moment, said, "I'll wait for you downstairs, Luke. Goodnight, Orlena." She kissed Orlena's cheek and hurried out.

Once they were alone, Orlena looked him straight in the eyes and said, "I want you to know I was never a whore, Luke. You have to believe that."

"God, Momma, I know that."

"I know folks said I was."

"Well, they didn't know what they were talking about. You were young. You made a mistake. You probably thought you were in love, and . . ."

"I never told you I loved nobody," she cut him off. "I never told you anything. And you knew better than to ask questions after that time you came home from school when you were in the third grade crying and wanting to know what a bastard was. I told you, and then you went back and beat up the kid that called you one. That's why I never told you how it happened, how you came to be. I was scared you'd kill somebody, but maybe I should have. Maybe I should've let you take the revenge I couldn't, and then I wouldn't have had to drink so much to keep from thinking about it and wouldn't be here in the shape I'm in, and . . ."

She began to cough, hard, husky, and then the wheezing began as she lost her breath, and her head lolled back as a terrified look came over her face.

Luke mashed the call button and within seconds a nurse swished into the room. She took one look at Orlena and ran for the oxygen tank that stood in a corner and quickly rolled it to the bed. Barking instructions to Luke, they had the plastic tent spread in no time, covering Orlena from head to waist. The nurse went to get medication, though Orlena seemed to be resting comfortably as she breathed in the oxygen.

"She'll sleep now," the nurse said as she injected Orlena with a sedative. "You might as well go. We'll call if there's any change."

But Luke made no move to leave right away, for his mind

was whirling to wonder what his mother had been about to say. Never before, even in her darkest moments of despair and disappointment, had he heard her speak of retribution against his father. And now he burned to know why.

～～～

It was dark when Luke and Alma got home, and everything seemed quiet.

"It's because you're here," Alma said. "Junior is scared you'll make trouble."

Luke went straight to the refrigerator. "No beer?" He scanned the shelves.

"Afraid not."

"I'll go get some. Maybe I'll stop by the Comet and see if any of the guys are around." The Comet was a drive-in cafe on the Birmingham highway, where he could usually find some of his old high school buddies, like Matt Rumsey. Matt hated his job at the mill, didn't get along with his wife, so he hung out at the Comet.

At the front door, Alma positioned herself in front of him. "Don't go."

He lifted a brow. "You scared to stay by yourself?"

"It's not that." She took a deep breath, then slipped her arms around his neck and pressed against him. "I want you to take me to bed."

For an instant, Luke thought he hadn't heard right, but then she squeezed his crotch. "*Now*, Luke. Let's go to bed *now*."

Hell, he was only human, and she got results the way she was rubbing him. He felt himself getting hard. She felt it, too, and began trying to pump him up and down through his trousers.

He unzipped his fly. "It's easier this way."

His swollen penis leaped into her hand, and she drew back for an instant, startled. She hadn't felt a man's thing since Jimmy Tate. The few times she and Luke had had sex, she hadn't touched him, hadn't wanted to, didn't want to now, and wouldn't if not for wanting to hang on to her marriage. She pulled him into the bedroom by his erection, and he laughed and did not protest.

He took off his clothes. She took off hers. They laid down side by side, and he thought of Coquina, his Mexican girlfriend waiting back in California. She always put on a show for him when she undressed, playing music on the radio while she stripped like a pro. Maybe she was. He didn't know and hadn't asked, but it made him crazy to watch her.

"Still got your diaphragm?" he asked, not wanting to take any chances.

She nodded and went to put it in while he waited and wondered what was going on, but it didn't take much to figure out she was worried about what would happen to their marriage if his mother died. Alma's way of thinking was just like all women of her upbringing: any man was better than no man at all. She didn't want to face being a divorcee with a kid to raise all by herself in a jerkwater town like Hampton, Alabama.

It was over quick, with Alma as lifeless as a store mannequin. Afterwards, he got up to take a shower, but she padded after him, the sheet wrapped around her.

"Luke, we need to talk. I've been thinking about us and how we could really have a good life together if we tried. I mean, we have got a daughter, and . . ."

The sound of the water running drowned her out, but she was waiting to start in again as soon as he finished.

"I'm going to make us some hot cocoa, and we can have a nice talk about where we're going to move. I was thinking we could maybe buy a house out in the country. Tammy would like that, and your momma would, too. She's always said she wished she had a garden."

He pulled on his pants and yanked on a shirt. "She isn't going to live that long, and you know it."

"But there's still the three of us, Luke."

"You know I hate this place."

"But it's your home."

"No, it isn't. And when my mother dies, I am never coming back."

"But what about us?"

He was almost to the door but whirled around to challenge, "Yeah, what about us, Alma? Do you want to move to California? 'Cause that's where I plan to live. I'll take you and Tammy with me if you want to go, because it's my duty. But you and I both know this marriage stinks and always has."

Her eyes narrowed. "But I don't want to move, and your place is here with me and Tammy."

He could tell she was getting mad, and he didn't want to fight. "We'll talk later."

She ran behind him. "No, we're going to settle things right now. Your taking me to bed proves you still want me, Luke."

"It proves I'm a man, and you made me horny."

"You can't divorce me," she screamed from the open front door. "I won't let you, damn you. Now you get your ass back in here. You aren't running off to hang out all night drinking with your white trash buddies."

He turned to look at her incredulously. "Alma, have you lost your mind? Everybody can hear you, yelling like a fish wife. Get back in the house." In the glow of the yellow bug light hanging from a frayed cord, she did look mad, eyes wild and bulging.

She took tiny running steps towards the edge of the porch to continue her tirade. "After what I just did for you, you owe me, damn you. Now get in here."

"What you just did for me?" He echoed with a shake of his head. Maybe she really was crazy. They had had sex for the first time in years, and now she thought he owed her. "Go ahead and yell for the whole damn county to hear. I don't care." He hurried toward the car.

She ran down the steps, struggling to keep the sheet wrapped around her. "Did you hear what I said? You aren't going out drinking. Your momma's in the hospital. It isn't proper."

According to Alma, nothing he ever did was proper. She let him know that every time he came home, so to avoid trouble, he'd learned through the years to just keep his mouth shut and count the days till he could leave again.

He had the car door open and was almost inside when she threw herself at him and began to pummel his chest with her fists. "You bastard. I hate you."

Bastard.

God, he hated the word that was so easily flung by people in anger. Maybe it wasn't meant to be taken literally, just an ugly name. But in his case, it was so.

He *was* a bastard, and it really pissed him off when anybody called him one, and if he hadn't been raised to believe every southern male was supposed to act like Ashley Wilkes, he'd have busted Alma in the mouth then and there. Instead, he yanked away her sheet.

Horrified to be standing there naked where someone might see, she turned and ran up on the porch. Just before Luke drove away, he heard her shout, "I never loved you, Luke Ballard. Never. And I wouldn't have married you if I didn't have to. Go to hell, you *bastard, bastard, bastard . . .*"

He drove like a bat out of hell, not slowing till he swerved into the Comet's parking lot, gravel flying as he skidded to a stop next to Matt Rumsey.

Wanda Potts, one of the curb girls, was hanging on the side of Matt's car. "Lord almighty, who's that crazy fool? He almost hit me."

Matt scrambled out to greet Luke. "Good to see you, man. When did you get in? Why didn't you call me? Hey, I'm sorry about your momma. I heard she wasn't doing good. Can I do anything? Let me buy you a beer. Wanna go inside?"

"Out here is fine. Get in. Good to see you, too."

Wanda took their orders, then Matt introduced her to Luke. Between loud pops of her chewing gum, she acknowledged, "I've heard of you. You're the big war hero. And you were captain of the football team back in '56. I remember 'cause I was a cheerleader for Alex City, and when we played y'all, all the girls were talking about how cute you were. Still are." She winked and walked away, hips swinging in skin-tight jeans.

"You banging her?" Luke asked, watching every wiggle.

Matt laughed, "Yeah, but it don't matter if you'd like to tap it. She's got enough for two."

"She had on a wedding ring."

"Makes it safe, 'cause she's tied down, too. I never mess with a single chick. They make noises about me getting a divorce and marrying them, and I say no way, *Ho-zay*. If I ever get unhitched, I'll stay that way. Now tell me about your momma. How's she doing?"

"I guess she's holding her own right now." Not wanting to talk about it, he abruptly changed the subject. "I want to hear about the sheriff."

Matt grinned. "Figured you would. It's all over town about your run-in with Howie this morning, or, as he's better known—*Barney Fife*."

"Why? Barney never picks on little colored girls."

"True, and Andy Taylor is no Bo Grady, either. But lots of

things have changed since Bo got elected, Luke, and none of them for the good. Bo hates coloreds, and ever since that civil rights march in Selma last spring, he's vowed the ones in Buford County will stay in their place or wish they had."

"And have they?"

"Yep, 'cause Bo and his deputies knock heads to make sure they do. But there's other stuff going on, too, like at Junior's place. You've probably already seen that, though, like how he's selling moonshine. Beer and wine ain't enough. He's got to deal in the hard stuff. And he's got prostitutes working. Then there's the gambling. Hell, it's even rumored he's got cockfights going on in the woods out back sometimes."

Wanda brought their beers and an order of fries, which she said was a welcome home present to Luke from her. She flirted a few minutes, then got the message she wasn't wanted and left.

"Well, he'll probably be voted out next election," Luke said. "Let's hope so, anyway."

"Don't bet on it. Nobody's got the balls to run against him."

"Including you?"

Matt hooted. "Hey, man, all I've done since high school is work at the mill. I don't have the experience needed to be a sheriff."

"And what kind did Grady have?"

"He's a Korean vet, and he bragged about being in the military police before the army stuck him in some special unit overseas. Besides, folks were ready for a change. Seemed like old Jesse Peagrover had been in office since World War II and he was ready to retire. So he didn't put up a fight. Bo slipped right in, and he's here to stay unless somebody is willing to go up against him.

"How about you?" Matt said suddenly, brightly. "Hell, you're a war hero."

"I've got a job, remember?"

"Yeah, but your time's up soon. What then?"

"I reenlist, and when Mom dies, I tell Hampton, Alabama, to kiss my ass and never come back."

"You really hate this place, don't you?"

"Can you think of a reason I shouldn't?"

"Yeah. You've got a wife and kid here."

Luke shook his head. "I'm not like you, Matt. I can't stay in a dead marriage for a kid's sake, especially not in a town that treated my mother like dirt because some asshole knocked her up and then ran out on her."

"Well, if you were sheriff, maybe you could use your badge to get even and kick some butt."

"A tempting thought to be sure, but I think I'd rather ride off into the sunset and not look back."

A car pulled in on the other side and Kirby Washam, another close buddy from high school days, joined them.

The evening slipped away, and then the neon lights bordering the roof of the drive-in began to blink. Wanda came to ask if they wanted one final round.

"How come you're closing early?" Matt looked at his watch. "Wow, it's almost midnight. Where did the time go?"

"You drank it away, like you always do." She blew a bubble and let it pop. "So? You want a last round or not? I've got other customers you know."

Matt reached across Luke to squeeze her arm. "But only one that wants to take you home. How about you and me having a last round together?"

She threw back her head and laughed. "You gotta be kiddin'. Last time I rode off with you *was* the last round for me and you, buddy, 'cause you ain't worth shit when you're drunk."

Luke pounded the steering wheel as he and Kirby broke into gales of laughter as Matt yelled curses at Wanda's retreating, swinging rear.

"Okay, okay," Luke said finally. "Maybe we'd better call it a night. We've all had enough."

"Yeah, I guess so." Kirby opened the back door and started to get out, then hesitated. "Hey, isn't that Sara Speight pulling in? What the hell's she doing here this time of night?"

Luke got out to meet her, and the instant he saw her face knew something was wrong.

"It's your mom," she said in a rush. "Lynn Waller, the nurse on night shift on your mom's floor is my cousin, and she called me to ask if I had any idea where you were. Alma told her she didn't know."

He slammed his hands down on top of the car so hard it shook. "The hell she didn't."

Sara suspected Alma had lied. She knew Luke would never go off and not leave word where he was with his mother so sick but didn't say so. "I told Lynn I thought I knew because you usually meet up with the guys here."

"I'll get over there right away. Thanks for finding me. Alma's just showing her butt. I'm sorry to have put you out like this."

"You know I didn't mind. Would you like for me to go to the hospital with you?"

He shook his head.

If his mother was ready to tell him about the demons, he damn sure didn't want anybody else listening.

Lynn gave it to him straight. His mother was slipping away. The signs were all there: a rise in body temperature, falling blood pressure, and irregular pulse. Lynn had called Dr. Campbell, and he said all they could do was try and make Orlena as comfortable as possible because it was almost over.

Orlena's eyes were closed, and she lay very still. Luke asked if she were in a coma. Lynn said no, just sedated, then left and said if he needed her to press the button.

The oxygen tent had been removed. Luke drew a chair close to the bed, then sat down and leaned over to press his cheek against his mother's hand. He hoped she knew he loved her, even though he might not have shown it like he should have. Everybody, he supposed, felt guilty when somebody they loved died. His guilt came from leaving home. But he hadn't been able to help her when he was there, remembering all the times he'd come home from school to find her passed out drunk. So he had no reason to believe that if he had stayed around things would have been any different.

He thought how pretty she used to be before her skin became puffy and mottled by spider webs of broken veins. And he couldn't remember a time when her bloodshot eyes didn't remind him of an Alabama roadmap.

He almost didn't hear her as she whispered his name, soft as a baby's sigh. He straightened but held tight to her hand. "Yes, Momma. I'm here."

With a feeble hand, he motioned to the bedside table and water pitcher. He poured a glass, held it to her parched lips as she drank, then she said she wanted to be propped up so she could talk better. "I've got to tell you how it was, Luke, and there's not much time."

It was like an icicle plunged into his heart. After all the years of wanting the truth, now he wasn't so sure. Maybe she should take it to the grave with her. "Tomorrow," he said. "You'll feel better tomorrow, and you can tell me then."

With a sad little smile, she slowly shook her head. "There are no tomorrows for me, and I've got to tell you about the yesterdays so I can go in peace. I promised myself I never would, but lately I've come to realize it's not right that you don't make them pay for what they did to both of us."

She began to cough, and he moved quickly to lift her head higher up on the pillows to help her breathe. All the while, one word was burning in his gut like acid: *them*. She had said *them*. Did that mean there had been more than one? Suddenly he found himself wishing she would go on and die then and there without telling him because something boiling inside of him warned that once he knew the truth his life would never be the same.

When the coughing subsided, Orlena continued. "But I don't want you to kill them, Luke. Promise you won't do that. They have to live and suffer like I have. Make them know what it's like to be shamed and have folks look down on them. But don't do anything to get yourself in trouble, and never, ever, let them or anybody else suspect you know."

Luke felt sick to wonder if she had slept with so many back then that she didn't know who his daddy was. He prayed not. Let her have made just one mistake that left her pregnant and not, God forbid, the town whore back in 1939.

Her eyes closed as she drifted away, and he let her hand go and sat back in the chair. Staring at the IV bag with its tube snaking to the needle in the back of her hand, he wondered if it were the sedative making her talk crazy. But, he suddenly decided, if that weren't the case, then the best thing for him to do was leave while she slept. Tomorrow she'd be glad he left before she said things she might later regret.

He started to get up, the chair squeaked, and Orlena's eyes opened. They locked gazes—hers, wild and determined; his, desperate with pleading for her silence.

"I was raped, Luke, and there were three of them."

Knees buckling, he sank back to the chair, hands curling into fists to press against his temples.

"And when you hear my story, you'll understand why I never told you before . . . and how none of what happened was my fault."

Her voice broke as she begged, "I want you to make them cry like I did all these years, Luke. I want you to make them *cry me a river* . . ."

Then, with a sigh, wrenched from the depths of her tortured soul, Orlena reached out for his hand with cold fingers. Clutching in desperation, she took him with her to the night that wrenched away all hope and changed her life forever.

She led him back to 1939 . . .

Orlena was exhausted. It was nearly eleven o'clock, and she wasn't anywhere near finished with her mopping. She was also freezing. The coal furnace wasn't able to heat the big, drafty mill like it should, and every time she had to wring out the mop in cold water, she was chilled to the bone.

She was working on the floors outside the offices. From the other end, beyond the big steel doors, she could hear the almost deafening noise from the machines as third shift toiled away. Her family all worked second shift.

Her father had been there nearly twenty years, and her mother had joined him a few months after Orlena was born, and she was sixteen now. Orlena's four brothers had quit school to hire on, but she was determined to graduate. Her father said that was a waste of time, especially for a woman. She needed to get married, have babies, and eventually go to work at the mill like everybody else. Meanwhile, he made her work at whatever she could to bring in some money.

The night cleaning job paid ten cents an hour. She was allowed to keep fifty cents out of every pay envelope. She had the mill owner's son, Buddy Hampton, to thank for her job. He had always been nice to her. She had a secret crush on him, too, but knew it was hopeless. Boys like Buddy didn't date village girls, and, besides, he had a girl: Ramona Booker, the Methodist preacher's daughter. She was the one who rode with him in the fancy car his daddy bought him for an early graduation present, a bright red Mercedes-Benz sedan.

It was understood that when Buddy graduated from Auburn Polytechnic Institute he would marry Ramona. Orlena did not like her. She was a snob and also a hypocrite, not acting at all like the Christian she pretended to be, what with her daddy being a preacher and all. She was all the time belittling the mill kids and hurting their feelings.

Orlena wrung out the mop and began swiping at the floor again, thinking how there was no harm in dreaming about Buddy. He was so cute with his blond hair and twinkling blue eyes. He was also captain of the football team and said to be one of the best quarterbacks Hampton High had ever had.

But Buddy could be mischievous, and she smiled to think about some of the pranks he'd pulled and got away with because of who he was. The teachers didn't dare punish him. After all, they, like everybody else in town, probably had a relative who worked at the mill and could lose their job at the snap of his fingers.

Finally, the eleven o'clock whistle blew, and Orlena wished she could catch a ride home but couldn't leave till she was finished. She was way behind, too, because somebody had spilled Coca-Cola all over the floor, and it was hard to clean up.

The door to the weaving room opened, and Willard Poultrie poked his head out. "Better come on if you're riding with me, Orlena."

Willard had a flatbed truck, and he gave everybody who could pile on it a ride home. "I wish I could, Willard, but I've got to get this mess up." It would be a long walk for her, too, and freezing cold out.

"Buddy Hampton and those smart-alecky pals of his did that. I saw 'em in here while you were mopping the other end. They were spraying each other with cola. Sorry, but I'll have to leave without you."

"It's all right," she said, suddenly not minding the mess if it was Buddy's. "Goodnight, Mr. Poultrie."

It was almost midnight before she was able to leave. There was no moon, the night so black she had to trust her instincts to take her in the right direction. Once she crossed the railroad tracks, there was a wooded area to pass by, then she would be in the village with its row after row of identical shotgun shanties. Bare limbs of trees overhead clattered together like wooden swords as the wind howled. She could hear a dog barking way off somewhere. A cat bolted from the brush beside her, and she choked on a scream and told herself she was being silly. She had walked home lots of times at night and nothing ever happened.

Lights appeared from behind, and she moved to the shoulder of the road. If it stopped, she would bolt into the woods and hide till she knew who it was. Sure enough, it began to slow and she lunged into the bushes.

"Hey, Orlena. Don't be scared. It's me—Buddy."

She turned back. "Buddy? What are you doing here?" She saw that he had quickly gotten out of the car and was standing in front of the lights. He was wearing his football sweater with a shirt and tie and knickers, and, like always, her heart skipped a beat at the sight of him.

"I'd hoped to catch you before you left the mill so I could give you a ride home."

"You did?" She couldn't believe her own ears.

"Yeah, I got to thinking about that mess me and those crazy pals of mine made and how your cleaning it up would probably make you late and miss your ride. I'm real sorry, Orlena. Get in, and I'll take you the rest of the way. It's the least I can do."

She did not hesitate, knowing it was probably the only chance in her life she would have to ride in such a fine car, but that wasn't what mattered. Being with Buddy, if only for a short while, was a memory that would last a lifetime.

He opened the door for her. "Pull that lap robe around you."

He hurried around to his side and got in, then melted her with a wide grin. "You look so cute sitting there. I've always thought you were the prettiest girl in school."

She could not speak nor breathe in what had to be the most wonderful moment of her life.

He took a flask from beneath his seat. "Here. It'll warm you right up."

Wanting to please him, she drank and was instantly seized by great, choking gasps as the whiskey hit her stomach like liquid fire.

He laughed and slapped her on the back, then took a big swallow himself. Wiping his mouth with the back of his hand, he said, "Hey, how'd you like to go for a little ride?" Without waiting for answer, he took off with tires spinning.

Once they were on the highway and speeding along, he said,

"There's just nothing like driving at night when nobody's around. I can go as fast as I want."

Despite how happy she was to be with him, Orlena was scared. They seemed to be hurtling through the night. Suddenly she blurted, "Does Ramona mind when you drive so fast?"

"Are you kidding? She can't stay out this late. Her parents hate this car anyway. Her mother told my old man it was a sin for him to spend so much on a car when he could give the money to the Lord. And you know what he said? That she had no call to lecture him because, if it weren't for him, there wouldn't be a church, and her husband wouldn't have a job preaching there, so she'd best keep her nose out of his business."

He took another drink. "But your folks don't even know you're out, sweetheart. That's what's nice about being with you. And we can do anything we want." He squeezed her thigh.

Orlena jumped.

With a chuckle, he began to run his fingers up and down, kneading the flesh through her thin wool skirt. "Don't be scared. I've always wanted to touch you, 'cause you've got meat on your bones. Not like Ramona. She's nothing but skin and bones." He made a face.

Orlena giggled and relaxed a little. If he wanted to touch her, it was okay. That meant he liked her.

She leaned her head back and dreamily said, "I don't think I've ever had such a good time."

"Well, honey pie, it's only going to get better."

She fell against him as he swerved off the highway without warning and onto a dirt road.

She righted herself. "Where are we going?"

"Ever been to Hampton Pond?"

She shook her head. She knew about it though. Everybody did. It was where Buddy and his friends went to swim in the summer. His family owned it, and every year on the 4th of July, there was a big picnic, and girls were invited with their families, of course. But Orlena had never been included. Village folks never were.

"Well, you're going now. There's a little cabin with a fireplace, and I'll get us a fire going in no time so we can warm up before heading back to town. I think Dad's got a bottle stashed away there, too." Turning the flask up, he downed what was left, then tossed it aside.

The car was bumping along, and Orlena found herself being constantly jounced against him, and while that was nice, she was getting nervous. "I don't know, Buddy. Maybe we shouldn't. I mean, if anybody ever found out, my reputation would be ruined, and my pa would kill me."

"How's anybody going to find out? You think I'd tell? Hell, no. It'll be okay. Honest." He pulled her close. "To tell you the truth, I've had my eye on you for quite a while, honey pie, and I've been hoping we'd get a chance to get to know each other better. You're a cute dish."

Orlena felt the blood rush to her cheeks. "Th . . thank you," she stammered. "It . . . it's nice of you to say that."

"Nice?" He squeezed her. "Honey pie, you're what's nice, and me and you are gonna have lots of fun together, okay?"

She felt silly just bobbing her head up and down as she whispered, "Okay," but couldn't think of anything else to say.

"Yep, we're gonna have us some good times, all right. You can stay out nearly all night, since your folks are bound to be sound asleep by the time you get off work. They won't know how late you get in, and if they do, hell, tell 'em you had to work overtime. If they check, I'll see that you're covered. And if you're real nice, I might even fix it so the hours you're out with me will show up on your time card. How's that? You'll be getting paid to have fun with me."

He squeezed her again, and this time his hand dropped to her breast, which unnerved her almost as much as what he had just said. Dear Lord, she couldn't stay out all night. She was a good girl, and sooner or later someone would find out, and then she'd be ruined forevermore. Besides, his saying she'd get paid to be with him somehow didn't sound nice.

She eased away from him. "I couldn't do that, Buddy, and I really think I should be getting home."

"Oh, don't be a baby."

She knew he was annoyed, but she persisted, "Please, Buddy. If my pa wakes up and finds me not home, I'm going to be in all kinds of trouble."

"That won't happen, now relax. You're starting to get on my nerves with your whining. We're gonna have us some fun."

He gave the steering wheel a sharp yank to the right, and a log cabin seemed to appear like magic, big and ghostly in the lights.

"Buddy, I want to go home." Fear was a spider, creeping up her taut spine.

"Not till I have another drink."

"I'll just wait here," she said thinly.

He grabbed her arm. "Come on. It's too cold out here."

She yielded, not wanting to make him any madder than he already was. He might just go off and leave her, and then how would she get home?

He found the key hidden over the door and let them in.

Striking a match, he glanced around and found an old oil lantern. Once it was lit, Orlena could see the tiny room and its sparse furnishings: a sofa, a long wooden table with benches down both sides, and an iron-postered bed. One corner of the room was set up as a kitchen, with cabinets and countertops and a sink with a water pump beside it.

"Pop thinks he's so smart," Buddy said as he stooped by the fireplace and pulled at a loose board. "He always makes everybody leave before he hides his hooch, but I've been knowing where he kept it since I was in knickers." He took out a bottle, drank, then offered it to her.

She shook her head firmly. "No. No more. I don't like it."

She was starting to really get scared at the way he was looking at her like he could see right through her clothes. "Okay, Buddy, you've had your drink. Let's go."

"Not till we warm you up, sugar." He set the bottle aside. "You've been wanting this, and don't pretend you haven't. I hate a tease."

He tried to kiss her, and she pushed him away. "Stop it, Buddy, please. I'm not that kind of girl."

"Not that kind of girl," he mimicked, screwing up his face as he shoved her away from him so hard she stumbled and fell back on the bed. He threw himself on top of her. "Don't be stupid. I can make life real easy for you and your family. You can use extra money, and I've got plenty. All you gotta do is be nice . . ."

"No, Buddy. Let me go." She pounded on his back, shaking her head from side to side. "If you don't, I swear I'll tell. . . ."

He slapped her, and as she whimpered with pain, shouted, "You little fool. You say one word, and your whole family gets fired. And nobody would believe you, anyway, because I'll say you threw yourself at me, wanting favors, and when I turned you down, you took revenge. Now don't be stupid, Orlena."

She continued to fend him off, and he finally lost his temper and hit her till she was dazed. Then he found a rope and lashed her arms to the bedposts.

"I don't want to have to rip your clothes," he said calmly as he proceeded to undress her. "You probably don't have many."

He was pulling at her bloomers when she rallied and kicked him. With a painful grunt, he fell back, but only for an instant. He doubled up his fist and pressed it against her chin. "No more, understand? Or you'll have a broken nose to explain."

Terrified, she could only lay there as he had his way with her. It hurt terribly, and when he saw the blood afterwards, said, "So you've never done it before. Who would've thought?" He shrugged. "Oh, well, it doesn't matter. Somebody had to be first."

Orlena was crying, and he yelled at her to shut up. Between sobs, she begged him to let her go, but he told her he wasn't through with her yet. She saw how he kept going to the door and looking out, and she wondered, through the pain racking her body, what he was waiting for. Then headlights flashed, and fresh terror ripped to the core of her soul as Buddy shouted, "Hey, it's about damn time you got here. I need to be home before light."

Orlena stared in wide-eyed horror as Hardy Moon and Burch Cleghorn walked in. They were Buddy's best friends.

"Oh, please, God, no." She strained at the ropes as they came toward the bed, both of them grinning.

Burch said, "You really did it, Buddy. You really got her here."

"But what's with the ropes?" Hardy pointed and looked to Buddy for explanation. "You said she'd be easy. You said you'd give her a few bucks, and she'd do us all."

Buddy explained, "She turned out to be a tease, but don't worry about it. It's all an act. She makes like she don't like it, but she does."

"Is that so, Orlena?" Burch fumbled with the buttons on his

fly. "You playing games with us? Well, that's all right with me. Just so I get what I want."

He lowered himself on top of her, as Hardy told him to hurry up so he could have his turn.

And Orlena closed her eyes and prayed to die.

CHAPTER 7

Luke kept a grip on Tammy's arm to keep her from stumbling as they walked toward the funeral home. Hardy Moon, whom Luke could now easily kill with his bare hands, had really let things go to pot since he married Lucy Taylor and took over the business. The yard was mostly weeds, the picket fence was rotting, and the two-story Victorian house made him think about the one in *Psycho*. After what his mother had told him on her death bed, Luke was tempted to start acting like Norman Bates.

"Thanks to Hardy, this place is a disgrace," Alma grumbled. "Too bad it's the only funeral home in town."

Luke could agree with that but for a reason Alma would never guess. His first impulse had been to have his mother taken to a funeral home in Birmingham, but that would have raised questions he didn't want to answer. In order to limit Hardy's contact with her, Luke refused to have her embalmed.

As they neared the front porch, Alma whined, "It's not right you won't talk to me, Luke. I told you I was sorry about what happened, but I was mad at you, and besides, I didn't think it was that serious, that your mother was really fixing to . . ."

Alma fell silent as he nodded toward Tammy. It wasn't the time to talk about it, and he didn't want to anyway. It was over. And so was his marriage. He was leaving as soon as he moved them from Junior's place. He planned to stay in touch with Tammy, help with her support, and if she ever wanted to visit, he'd send her a ticket. But he was through with Hampton, by God, even though his gut burned with hunger for revenge.

Since his mother had poured out her soul, he had thought of nothing else, except trying to come up with a way to make Buddy Hampton, Burch Cleghorn, and Hardy Moon pay . . .

and pay big. So far he hadn't figured out a way to do it short of cold-blooded murder.

Alma was worried about how Luke was acting. Now, more than ever, she wanted to hold her marriage together, but he was freezing her out. He hadn't even talked to her about the funeral arrangements, and she considered it a slap in the face that he'd asked Sara Speight to see to everything.

She had also been surprised when Hardy called to indignantly inform her that Luke had refused to let his mother be embalmed and asked her to get him to change his mind. Alma had then called Sara to ask why that decision had been made, and Sara had explained that it was Luke's doing, and it was perfectly legal because embalming was not required if the body wasn't to be transported across the state line.

"Well, people will talk when they hear she wasn't," Alma had argued, then tartly added, "And you ought to stay out of it, anyway."

Sara had responded in a patronizing tone that had made her all the madder. "I'm just doing what Luke asked me to do, Alma, and trying to make things as easy as possible for him. I'm worried about him. He's taking this real hard."

Furious, Alma had fired back, "Well, you'd best remember he's *my* husband, Sara, and let me do the worrying about him."

Sara had calmly retorted, "If you're upset about his asking me to help, perhaps you should talk to him about it."

Alma had slammed the phone down. *Talk to Luke?* That was a laugh. He'd been like a zombie since Orlena had died. Lynn Waller said that when she went into the room before the end of her shift Saturday morning, Orlena had been dead for some time and starting to get stiff, and Luke was just sitting there like he was in a trance.

She decided to try again to reach him. "Don't you think it was nice of Preacher Dan to say he'd do the funeral, Luke? After all, Orlena didn't have a church, but I've been going to Preacher Dan's, and he said he'd be glad to. His church is the Gospel Light United out on the Talladega Highway. He came and got it started up here last winter, and it's really growing. Folks come from all over."

Luke had no use for churches, and neither had his mother, not after the way they'd both been treated. But, she deserved a Christian burial, no matter what folks thought of her. And the way he saw it, the whole damn town owed her an apology for how they had treated her all these years. It didn't matter they didn't know the truth and never would. If they were such good Christians, they shouldn't have sat in judgement and condemned her to find the only peace she knew in a bottle of whiskey. They had killed her, the town and the devils that had raped her.

The door opened and Hardy stepped out on the porch, a practiced look of condolence on his pudgy face. "My sympathies, Luke."

Luke pushed by him. The air inside was thick with cloying odors: stale cigarette smoke, flowers from past funerals, old ladies' heavy colognes. Wine-colored velvet drapes, thick with dust, sealed out any hint of sunlight, and the overhead chandelier with its small-watt bulbs cast an eery light over the faded, sickly wallpaper with its pattern of purple roses.

The house had been built before the turn of the century. The floors were warped with age, and it was like walking uphill to pass through the parlor, cluttered with worn sofas and folding chairs. They were almost to the viewing room. Luke could see a corner of the gray metal coffin and stopped where he was and said to Alma, "You and Tammy go ahead."

Hardy exchanged a puzzled glance with Alma, who shrugged. Then she took Tammy's hand, leading the way as she said, "Now remember, sweetie, it's like Grandma is just sleeping. She's gone to be with the angels, and one day, if you're very, very good, you'll see her again, and . . ."

Luke shut out the sound. He didn't want to think about angels and the afterlife. It was the here and now that had him tied up in knots.

"Don't you want to see her, Luke?" Hardy asked solicitously. "She looks real nice, even if she is starting to turn a little dark because you didn't want her embalmed. It's a good thing you set the funeral for today, by the way. I couldn't have guaranteed we could open the coffin by tomorrow. But you go on in, and . . ."

"I will when I'm ready."

"Well, of course," Hardy said uneasily, "and you just take all the time you want, Luke. We've got a while yet. It's a shame you weren't up to being here last night. Some folks came to pay their respects, and I know they would've liked to see you."

Did Buddy Hampton come, Luke felt like screaming? Did he come to pay *his* respects to the woman he had raped? And what about the honorable attorney and church deacon, Burch Cleghorn?

Luke knew he had to stop thinking like that or he was going to lose control and kill Hardy here and now. Then he'd wind up going to jail while Burch and Buddy went their merry way. He wanted all three of them to suffer, by damn.

He saw Tammy was crying as Alma brought her out of the viewing room, leading her to sit in the parlor. Hardy wandered away, and Luke continued to just stand there, reluctant to see his mother in her coffin. He heard others arriving. People from Alma's church, he supposed. He had not expected much of a turnout for the funeral. His mother had been a loner and had no close friends that he knew about. Matt and Kirby and their wives would probably be there, and Sara, of course.

Out of the corner of his eye he spotted Norma Breedlove heading straight toward him, all set to gush sympathy. To escape, he stepped quickly into the viewing room and closed the door after him. Wooden legs carried him to the coffin. Sara had told him she had chosen what was called a "full couch" model, which had one long lid, because it didn't cost as much as the other kind that was divided top and bottom, and all of his mother could be seen, not just from the waist up.

He could not bring himself to focus on her face just yet. Instead he fastened his gaze on her hands, which were clasped just below her bosom. There were no rings on her fingers. She had never owned any jewelry. Other things were more important, she always said, but he knew it was only because there had never been any extra money. They had barely survived when he was growing up. His clothes had come from Salvation Army barrels. So had hers, but she said she didn't need much. After all, it made no difference what she wore to clean cabins at Junior's Motor Court or wash dishes at his cafe.

Finally, he forced himself to look at her. Somebody had put makeup on, rouge, powder, lipstick. Even her eyebrows had been darkened with a pencil. She almost looked as pretty as she used to before the whiskey took its toll.

He didn't have a lot of good memories growing up, and the ones he did have were mostly thanks to her. Even though she'd had a rough time supporting the two of them, he had never once heard her complain. What she did say was that he was the biggest blessing she had ever been given. Now, knowing what he did, he marveled that she could have felt that way because, if things had been different, some nice guy would probably have come along and married her, and she'd have lived a good and happy life instead of winding up with a lifetime of pain and misery.

Luke was unmindful of how his hands, gripping the coffin, had begun to shake. He was fast becoming lost in the throes of the vision of how it had been for her that cruel, fateful night when he had been created by the wild sperm from any one of three devils.

"I'll get them for you," he whispered, his grip on the edge of the coffin growing tighter, his hands shaking harder.

Out in the parlor, Norma asked Alma, "How is he doing?"

"Not too good. I think he's sort of in shock."

"Well, he wasn't in shock when he asked Sara Speight to make all the arrangements, was he? I tell you, Alma, you ought to raise hell with him about that. You know how folks talk, and everybody is wondering why he did it. It was your place, not hers."

Alma gave a dismal nod. "I know. I tried to tell her that, but she doesn't care. I've always hated her," she whispered out of the corner of her mouth.

"Well, if I were you, I'd keep an eye on them two. They were sweethearts back in high school, remember?"

Alma didn't say anything. She didn't like being reminded.

Norma sighed. "So when's he going back to California?"

"He hasn't said." She was not about to confide how Luke was giving her the silent treatment.

"Well, it might be best if he went to get him away from her."

"He said he wanted to move me and Tammy away from Junior Kearney's. He'll do that before he leaves."

Norma patted her hand. "Well, you do like I told you and keep an eye on things. She's after him, for sure, and, speak of the devil . . ."

Alma saw Sara walk in and was annoyed that she was wearing a black skirt and blouse like she was in mourning. She wasn't family, for God's sake, but she was sure trying to act like it. Alma had rushed out the day before and bought a black cotton dress to wear, but *she* had the right. Sara didn't.

Sara glanced around, spotted Alma, and hurried over. She gave Tammy a quick hug, then asked in the soft, patronizing voice Alma despised, "Is Luke in there with her?" Without waiting for answer, "How's he doing?"

Eyes glittering with anger, Alma snapped, "Don't you worry about how he's doing, Sara. I'll see he does all right."

Norma snickered, and Sara, red-faced, walked away.

Afterwards, they left her on the outskirts of the village by the railroad track, which divided it from the rest of the town. She stumbled along in the depths of night, bruised and bleeding, barely making it home to her bed before anyone woke up.

As Buddy shoved her out of the car, he warned her again that if she ever told anyone, he'd see to it that her family lost their jobs, their home in the village, everything. Who would believe the word of a mill girl over a Hampton, anyway, he had taunted.

So she never said a word, not even when she realized she was pregnant. Her father had beat her senseless as he tried to make her name the boy responsible. Finally, he kicked her out, her family abandoning her for all time.

The pictures of his mother's attack became more vivid in Luke's mind. Suddenly it was as though he had actually been there, all those years ago, to witness the heinous violation of his mother.

Sara knocked, and when there was no answer, she hesitantly opened the door. "Luke? Is it okay if I come in?"

She gasped to see how he was holding onto the coffin, which was teetering precariously to and fro. It was sitting on a folding table, the legs of which looked none too sturdy.

She hurried to grab his wrists and try to pull his hands away, but he held tight. "Luke, let go. Please. You're going to make it turn over. Now come with me. It's time for the funeral. Please, Luke . . ." She began to cry.

He held fast, his face as frozen as his mother's.

Sara turned and ran back into the parlor and beckoned to

Kirby, who was standing nearby. He saw her expression and came at once. Speaking so others could not hear, she told him in a rush, "It's Luke. I'm afraid something awful is going to happen if you don't get him away from that coffin."

But before he could act, something awful *did* happen. The table legs buckled and collapsed, and the coffin tipped over. Luke came alive at the last second and tried to right it, but he was not quick enough. Kirby tried to help but stumbled into Luke, causing both of them to fall to one side as Orlena tumbled out of the coffin and hit the floor with a dull thud.

And then she began to roll . . .

Like a log, over and over she went, limbs still stiff from rigor mortis, which had not yet dissipated in the thirty-four hours or so since her death. She hurtled down the slanting floor toward the parlor, which had become a scene of bedlam as the hysterical mourners scrambled to get out of her way.

Norma Breedlove fainted as Orlena's eyes popped open, the cheap glue Hardy had used unable to keep them shut as she rolled. Her mouth, also glued instead of the gums having been wired together, gaped open in a silent scream of protest over such indignity. She continued across the now empty parlor, finally coming to a stop when she hit a row of metal folding chairs, knocking them over with a loud clatter.

For a few moments, nobody made a move or sound as they watched warily from the hall. Finally, wordlessly, Kirby and Luke simultaneously started toward her.

Hardy ran to right the table, and, with Preacher Dan's help, lifted the coffin and put it back in place, then stood back as Kirby and Luke positioned Orlena inside. Luke, carefully and reverently, tucked in the satin border of the lining, then closed the lid with a finality so fierce it seemed to echo not only throughout the funeral home . . . but all of Hampton, as well.

It had finally stopped raining. Luke was soaked, but he didn't mind. He was at his mother's grave to say good-bye before taking the noon bus to begin his journey back to California. The funeral was two days ago, and he had managed to get Alma and Tammy settled into an apartment. Alma said folks would talk about his leaving so quick. He told her, not for the first time, he didn't give a damn. That made her mad, and she told him to get the hell out. So he had done just that, walking all the way to the cemetery, but he hadn't minded.

It was going to be a long bus ride all the way to California, but he didn't care about that either. He needed the time to think about whether he wanted to reenlist. The army offered a pretty good bonus, but some really big money was being dangled under his nose like a gold carrot. The CIA agent he had met with secretly had made him a real tempting offer. All he had to do was work as a mercenary, a soldier of fortune, hiring himself out as a paid killer and helping to smuggle illegal arms to guerillas in places like Laos. It was dangerous, but he was well-trained, and, besides, he didn't have much to live for, and sometimes wondered if he ever had. He felt real guilty about not fulfilling the promise he'd made to his mother to take revenge. The truth was he still couldn't think of anything short of murder.

"I'm sorry, momma," he whispered.

He threw his duffle bag over his shoulder and turned from the grave and was surprised to see Matt and Kirby walking up the hill with Clyde Bush, Ben Cotter, and Jubal Cochran following. Matt waved, and when he got closer, called, "Hey, Luke. I'm glad we found you. We went by the apartment, but Alma said you headed off in this direction, so we figured you'd be here."

Luke frowned. "Something tells me you didn't come to give me a ride into town."

Matt didn't mince words. "Lily Rhoden got beat up real bad last night, and a cross was burned in front of her house."

With an angry oath, Luke slung his duffle bag to the ground.

Matt continued. "She was out of town Friday when all that bull happened at the five and dime with her kid, so when she got home yesterday and heard about it, she went tearing off to the sheriff's department to raise hell. She said Howie had no business treating her kid like that. The sheriff told her she was lucky the thievin' little pickaninny didn't get locked up and next time he'd personally see to it she was."

Kirby jumped in to add, "That's when Lily got really pissed. She said she had some friends in the NAACP. She said they would be real interested in hearing how black kids are treated in Buford County and maybe the sheriff might just have a civil rights march on his hands before long."

Matt related how the Ku Klux Klan, in white robes and hoods, had descended on the Rhoden shack around midnight, carrying torches and the cross, which they set afire. When Lily had run out the front door swinging a broom, things got worse. A few of the Klansmen knocked her around, and she wound up battered and bruised, both arms broken and her nose smashed.

Luke was having trouble hearing over the roaring in his ears, but it got through to him that Patti Sue had also been dragged into it. The gutless cowards had taken the doll he had bought for her and made her watch while they tied it to the cross and burned it. When she wouldn't stop screaming, one of them had slapped her and busted her mouth open. It would probably have got worse but somebody had the courage to declare enough was enough, and they finally left.

Ben spoke for the first time. "I marched right over to the courthouse as soon as I heard about it, Luke, and asked the sheriff what he planned to do about having Klan trouble here. He said they weren't locals, and as far as he was concerned, there *is* no trouble."

Clyde joined in. "Yeah, right. He also said none of it would've happened, anyway, if you hadn't butted in when Howie was trying to arrest the kid for shoplifting. He said if anybody's to blame, it's you, and he's damn glad you don't live here because you're nothing but a troublemaker."

"We're hoping you'll show him how much trouble you *can* make," Jubal said. "We want you to run for sheriff. You'll win hands down. Folks are fed up. Don't worry about what it will cost. We're already collecting money. I started off your campaign fund with a hundred dollars," he added proudly.

"And I kicked in the same," Clyde said.

Ben assured he was good for a like amount.

"Well, I'm afraid I don't have that kind of money," Matt said, "but I'll give what I can. So will Kirby. And we'll get out and rustle up from other folks, too."

"Just say you'll do it, Luke," Kirby pleaded. "We're with you all the way."

Luke was silent as he turned back to the grave, eyes narrowed, lips a thin, tight line.

Matt put a hand on his shoulder, "Listen, me and Kirby know how much you hate this place and how bad you want to leave and never come back, but you can still do that once you get things cleaned up around here."

"That's right," Kirby chimed in, "But another thing you better think about is your own kid, because a lot of what happened last night was to get back at you, the way they burned the doll and all. So who's to say the sheriff won't do something to hurt Tammy?"

Luke kept staring at his mother's grave. He wished there had been more flowers. Matt and Kirby and their wives had chipped in to buy a nice wreath. Alma's church had sent a small spray. Junior bought a cheap potted plant. If not for the casket piece of pink and white carnations that Sara had ordered and paid for, the raw mound of red clay would be exposed.

"Luke, we need you," Ben persisted. "Buford County needs you. You're our only hope, the only man qualified who can kick Bo Grady's fat ass right out of office."

Jubal pointed out, "You'd have the power to clean things up the way they oughta be, Luke."

Power.

Luke seized on the word.

He would have the *power* to fulfill his mother's wish. He did not have to think about it any longer. "All right. I'll do it."

As he spoke, Luke felt the imaginary ghostly hand that had been squeezing his ankle to urge him on, let go and return to the grave.

At last, his mother had begun to rest in peace.

PART II

Chapter 8

September, 1968

The Bulldog was the only cafe in town. Situated across the street from the main door to the courthouse, the Hampton High School colors were reflected in the red and white awnings hanging over the plate glass windows. Inside, a marble-topped counter ran the length of one wall, with shelves of dishes and glasses behind the soda fountain where Clyde mixed what was considered the best cherry Coke in the state of Alabama.

Along the counter, covered plates displayed Ardis Bush's homemade bakery specials of the day: pies, cakes, cookies, and muffins. On the other side of the room were the booths, red vinyl-covered benches and wood tables scarred from generations of high school kids' carvings when Clyde wasn't looking. The truth was, he didn't mind the graffiti and wouldn't have refinished the tables for anything in the world. He knew it made the cafe a treasure trove for high school memories.

Square chrome-topped tables and wooden chairs filled the middle of the room with a small floor space left in front of the jukebox for dancing. Outdated calendars and posters listing the Hampton High Bulldogs' football and basketball schedules adorned the walls. Hanging right next to the cash register was Clyde's most treasured possession, a framed photograph of him with his arm around Lana Turner. She had popped into the cafe one day years ago when the car carrying her from Atlanta to Birmingham had broken down. Clyde had sent a copy of the picture to her in care of her studio in Hollywood, and she had obligingly autographed it to: *"My favorite Alabamian who makes the best cherry Coke I ever tasted, love and kisses, Lana Turner,"* and sent it back. Clyde swore he wanted it buried with him in his coffin, but Ardis told him no way.

Across the street, Luke eased his patrol car into the space marked *Sheriff*. He didn't think he had ever needed a cup of Clyde's strong coffee more in his whole life. It was Saturday night, still early, and he was already exhausted. He had just left a wreck where three people had been killed, and, since it was the first night of the county fair, he still had to check things out there.

As always, when he got to the door, his eyes went to the spot where his hand had gone through the glass the night he'd had the fight with Rudy Veazey. Rudy had left him alone after that, except to give him dirty looks from a distance. Eventually Rudy had quit school and bummed around before joining the Air Force to keep from being drafted into the army and the infantry, which would have shipped him to Nam and straight into combat. He was back in town, working at the mill, and Luke was glad he seldom saw him.

Luke sat down in the back booth, which had been his favorite spot since his dating days with Sara. He smiled at *"Luke + Sara"* scratched into the wood along with the date, *"9/12/56,"* and thought again how she would always have a special place in his heart.

The cafe was empty, unusual at any time, but especially on a Saturday night. Sally Pope, who had been a waitress there as long as he could remember, promptly brought a mug of steaming coffee. She had grease and catsup stains on the front of her uniform, and strands of hair stuck out from under a net. When she smiled, he could see lipstick smeared on her teeth, and he got a whiff of onion breath.

"Was the wreck as bad as they say?" she asked, eyes shining with morbid curiosity. "Did they really have to take the bodies out in pieces like we heard?"

"Not quite." He began stirring the coffee to cool it. Clyde made damn good coffee, and it would be a sin to waste the flavor with sugar or cream. Besides, the stronger the caffeine fix this night, the better.

"Did the ones who got killed die right quick?"

"Looks that way."

She slid into the bench across from him. "And were they really so messed up their coffins won't be open?"

"I don't know. That's up to Hardy Moon and what kind of job he can do." The wreck had happened when Ronnie Turnage, drunk judging from the liquor bottles strewn around, missed a sharp curve near Sycamore on the Talladega highway and plowed straight into a tree. His wife, Inez, had fallen out when the door flew open on her side. She had missed the full impact, but her legs were broken pretty bad. Wiley and Lorraine Hendon in the back seat had also been killed.

"Know what else I heard? That Ronnie probably missed that curve because him and Inez were fighting. Somebody who was at the dance in Talladega said Ronnie and them were there, too, and Ronnie was pissed off over how she'd been carrying on with Bobby Ray Walston. It was Ricky Bowden who told me. He and Annie stopped by a while ago. He said Inez was a sight, and the more she flirted with Bobby Ray, the drunker Ronnie got."

Luke wasn't surprised. He knew just about everything that went on in town, and it was common knowledge Inez fooled around. He'd had her himself, but it was only that one time, right after he was elected sheriff in a record-setting landslide when he was sort of full of himself with his badge and patrol car and all, and doing some wild and crazy things. But no more.

Sally continued, "Well, I'd just like to ask Inez what it feels like to know she made her old man kill himself and take two others with him. I don't see how she can look folks in the eye, the little strumpet."

"And I don't see how you expect me to stay in business if you don't get to work." Clyde gently pulled her to her feet. "Now how about getting the sheriff a big slice of Ardis's pecan pie?" He sat down and winked at Luke, "I know it's your favorite."

"Well, I've sure eaten enough of it in the past two years."

Clyde sighed with satisfaction, "And, you know, Luke, they've been *good* years, too. You cleaned this place up just like everybody knew you would."

Luke recalled how the first thing he had done was to come down hard on Junior Kearney and put a stop to the goings-on at the motor court. He'd had enough on him to put him away but that would have been too easy. Luke wanted reprisal in a special way, and if he was patient, he figured sooner or later the right opportunity would come along.

The same was true with his other targets. He would know exactly when to drop the hammer. Besides, he hadn't wanted to zero in on them at once. It might look too obvious. So he was biding his time and keeping his eyes and ears open all the while.

He had also made Klan activities come to a screeching halt. The ones responsible for injuring Ocie's wife were never identified, but things had been quiet since. Ocie had been discharged from the army and gone to work at the mill, and all seemed peaceful.

"That wreck was a bad one, huh?" Clyde probed.

"Afraid so. It took nearly two hours to pry Wiley and Lorraine out. Hardy was finally getting ready to load them in the hearse when I left."

The door opened and a crowd of teenagers swarmed in to settle at the front of the cafe. Clyde glanced over his shoulder. "The movie must have let out. Guess I'd better get busy frying burgers. I'll be back in a while to talk some more."

"I've got to run along. I need to get over to the fairgrounds and check things out."

Clyde grinned. "Lots of luck, sheriff. I hear the cooch show is a real sizzler this year. Packin' 'em in like crazy. Tootie Byrd was in here a while ago and said he saw the first show. When word spread what a certain little gal was doing with a Coke bottle, the line to buy tickets was a mile long."

Luke shook his head in disgust. It happened every year, and just as soon as the wives and church folk got wind that the hoochy-coochy show was back, his phone would be ringing off the hook. He usually let the strippers get away with it for the first few nights, depending on how raunchy they got, and then he'd run them out of town.

"Did Tootie happen to know the girl's name?"

"No. He says she's new. He doesn't remember ever seeing her before. She's got this routine where she comes out all wrapped up in animal fur before she strips buck naked."

Luke stood. "Save the pie for me, and I'll try to get back before you close."

Luke went to the toilet, and when he came out saw that Hardy Moon was sitting on a stool up front, the center of attention as the teenagers fired questions about the wreck victims. "Go see for yourself if you want to," he said with an airy wave. "They're right outside."

The teens made a dash for the door.

Hardy glanced up at Luke. "I guess you've seen enough for one night, right, Sheriff?"

As he did every time they met, Luke wanted to slam his fist into his face. "How in the hell can you let them look at those bodies?"

Hardy stiffened. "All those people at the scene saw them. What's wrong with a few more?"

"The families of the victims won't appreciate it, and you can be sure they'll hear about it."

Hardy scowled. "You know, sometimes I think you're an all right guy, but there are times you can be a real prick, like now. If I'm not breaking a law, get off my back."

Afraid of what he might do if he didn't get away from him fast, Luke walked out of the cafe and pushed his way through the crowd gathered around the hearse. One of the kids had crawled in the back and unfastened the gurney straps from around Wiley Hendon's body and pulled back the sheet to display his face, which was a mass of blood with big gaping holes where his nose and eyes used to be. A girl looking on was puking in the gutter. Another was leaning against a telephone pole crying. Luke hoped they had nightmares the rest of their life. He yanked the boy out and slammed the doors. "The show's over."

All the while he was thinking what a fine day it would be when he finally found a way to bring the hammer down on Hardy Moon.

―⁂―

The fair was set up just off the Birmingham highway on the land used for softball fields during the spring and summer. It wasn't much of a fair by big city standards, but the locals always looked forward to it. The local 4-H club had livestock and small animal exhibits, and there were judgings for best pickles, preserves, and baked goods. But, by far, the reason people came out was for the midway with its ferris wheel, bumper cars, freak shows, and the chance to throw their hard-earned money away at the game booths in hopes of winning a stuffed animal or some cheap drinking glasses.

The air was pungent with the smell of popcorn and frying onions and the hot dogs Luke couldn't resist. Supper had only been cold collards left over from lunch. Alma's church was holding a revival with services every night, so she wasn't cooking much this week. He washed the hot dog down with a Pepsi, then bought a bag of roasted peanuts to nibble as he strolled along the midway.

There was a big crowd. Word had spread about the wreck, and he heard a few people talking about it, but most everyone was too busy having a good time to dwell on tragedy. Tomorrow, to be sure, they would flock to the funeral home, then head to wherever the victims' families were gathered for fried chicken and all the fixings. Funerals in small towns were a social occasion.

Luke didn't have any trouble locating the cooch show. Just like Tootie had reported to Clyde, the line was long. What the men paid to see would be inside, of course, but outside there was a narrow stage for the girls to parade up and down. Wearing filmy baby doll pajamas over skimpy bikinis, the girls did a lazy bump-and-grind routine to the tinny music from a record player while a sleazy-looking guy walked up and down promising the gawking men that the show inside was guaranteed to put lead in their pencils.

Luke saw the girl wrapped in fake fur, and she was, by far, the best looking of the bunch. The others had seen better days, but the men didn't care about their faces. They came to see their bodies and imagine all the unnatural, perverted acts they could do with them. He recalled how last year he had happened along to find Ronnie Turnage behind the stage whacking off in the dark and thought how if he'd done that this year instead of getting drunk and mad at his flirty wife, he'd still be alive. Luke entered the tent. His badge was his ticket.

The hawker rushed up to him to whisper, "Hey, sheriff, cut a little slack, will you? These little gals are just trying to make a living. They don't mean no harm. And they ain't into no funny business after the show, neither. Sure, they get lots of offers for a quickie, but they're exotic dancers, not hookers. So don't pull the plug on us, okay?"

Luke brushed by him. The girls knew how far they could go. So did the hawker.

Boards set on nail kegs provided seating before the raised platform at the front of the tent, and the men were packed in tight. Luke stood to one side in the shadows and scanned the excited faces of the waiting audience and decided the hawker had done a good job in making sure no minors got in. He did, however, spot Burch Cleghorn sitting on the very front row and thought again what a hypocrite he was. If it got out that he had been there, Burch would just claim he had merely been checking it all out for his church because he was a deacon.

The first girl who came out was always the worst. Tonight was no exception. "Tiny Lou," as she was called, was at least fifty pounds overweight, and the men were only mildly interested in seeing her strip down to flimsy underwear. Her prop was a feather boa that she rubbed back and forth between her fleshy thighs, but the crowd never really got worked up.

The next one drew whistles when she was able to swing the red, white, and blue tassles fastened on her nipples in time to the tune of *Stars and Stripes Forever*. The gold foil star between her legs covered her privates.

He didn't care how much any of them bared, just so they didn't go to the altogether. What he was waiting for was one of them to get totally naked, and when the one called Sheena came onstage, she quickly obliged.

After her performance, which Luke found as lewd as Tootie Byrd has reported to Clyde, the tent emptied quickly. Luke made his way behind the curtains to where the girls were lounging around in robes, sipping beer and smoking. At the sight of his badge and uniform, they all started talking at once, saying they hadn't done anything wrong. All of them, that is, except Sheena.

She was sitting off to one side, away from the others. Fixing Luke with an icy glare, she silently puffed on her cigarette. When he started toward her, she said, with a smirk, "What do you want back here, sheriff? A private show?"

"No," he said quietly, "I just wanted to offer you a ride to the bus station."

She stubbed out her cigarette and bolted to her feet. "What kind of bull is this? You can't run me out of town just like that. Hell, I'm willing to tone things down some."

Suddenly a pudgy little man in a shabby suit rushed in. "Hey, what's going on, sheriff? I'm Manny Duncan, and I run this show. You giving my gals a hard time?"

Luke motioned to Sheena. "Just her. She's out of here."

"Aw, come on, sheriff," Manny pleaded. "Give her a chance to work up a different act. She's the best-looking broad I got. The men will pay to see her dance without getting naked."

"It's too late for that. Word spreads. The guys will show up expecting to see a repeat of tonight and get pissed off when they don't and cause a ruckus. Besides, the God-squad will come down hard on me if I don't run her off."

Manny swore and told Sheena, "Just go on to Phoenix City and meet us there. You know where my brother lives. He'll let you stay at his place."

She held out her hand. "I need money to get there. I want my pay."

"Uh-uh, baby. If I give it to you now, you won't show up, and I need you. Phoenix City ain't as hicky as this place. We can make big money there." He shot a glare at Luke.

"Damn it, Manny, if you don't give me some money, what am I gonna live off between now and then? Hell, I don't even have the price of a bus ticket."

Manny took a twenty dollar bill from his wallet. "This will buy your ticket, and Eddie will feed you when you get there."

"Yeah, sure he will . . . if I let him do me when his old lady ain't looking."

"Well, see that she's looking, and you ain't got nothing to worry about." He motioned to the other girls. "Get off your butts. It's time to start drumming up business for the next show."

Sheena turned on Luke. "I hope you're real happy, sheriff. After I buy my ticket, I'll have about five bucks between me and starvation."

"I'll give you something to tide you over."

She raised a brow. "Yeah, and then *I* give *you* something to tide you over, right? Don't worry. I know how to play the game."

"You've got it wrong."

But she was no longer listening, having quickly disappeared behind a dirty, tattered curtain.

Luke went and brought the patrol car around to the back of the tent. He had no intentions of walking her through the midway for everybody to see.

By the time he returned, she was waiting in the shadows with a battered suitcase held together by a rope. She was wearing a raincoat over a skirt and sweater. Her flame red hair was pulled up on top of her head, and if not for the thick layers of pancake makeup, the garish green eye shadow, and lipstick the color of blood, he figured she would be a right nice-looking woman. He already knew she had a damn good body.

She got in and lit a cigarette. They rode along in silence for a few moments, then she asked in a bored tone, "So how long have you lived here, Sheriff?" Not giving him a chance to answer, she continued with a harsh laugh. "I'll bet you were born here and you'll die here, right? Hell, I know how that is. I was born in a jerky little town like this, too, but believe me, I got my ass out of there as soon as I could and never went back. God, I hated that place."

He could have told her she was wrong, that he was living for the day he could escape, but let her ramble on and drove faster than usual to get her to Creech's station. It was closed, as he knew it would be, the lights off. The bus driver would collect the ticket money.

He pulled around back and stopped.

"So we do it here?" Sheena asked, wide-eyed. "Jeez, Sheriff, I figured you for the sort to spring for a cheap motel room instead of doing it behind a gas station, but I don't guess we've got much time. Manny says the midnight bus is the only one out of here till morning."

Luke told her the gas station was also the bus depot. He gave her twenty dollars. "It's all I can spare."

She took the money and shoved it down her sweater and into her bra, then maneuvered off the seat and onto her knees so fast she took him by surprise, and he didn't realize what she was up to till he felt her tug at the zipper of his fly.

He caught her wrist and held tight. "Thanks . . . but no thanks."

She was stunned. "I ain't never been turned down before."

"Well, there's always a first time." He pushed her back, got her on the seat, then reached across and opened the door.

With an oath, she got out, yanking her suitcase from the back seat, then slammed the door and gave him the finger through the window.

He had just pulled away from the station when he heard Matt on the radio. He had sent him to deliver the bad news to the Hendon family and asked if he had found them.

"Yeah, and it was bad. You can imagine. Anything going on at the fair?"

"There was. But I just put her on the bus." Luke told him to take a run out to Junior's place so he'd know they were keeping an eye on him. Then he headed for the Bulldog and the pecan pie he hoped was still waiting. As he was easing into a parking space, Ned Tucker radioed, "We got a ten-eighty out at Rudy Veazey's place."

Luke swore. Ten-eighty was the code for a domestic disturbance, and he hated them. Without a warrant, he couldn't enter the house, anyway, and nine times out of ten, the wife wouldn't sign one. If she did, her husband would either sweeten her up to get her to drop it before court date or put the fear of God in her if she didn't. It was a waste of time and risky, to boot. But most of all, he didn't want to respond to anything connected with Rudy Veazey.

Ned went on to say, "It could be bad. His old lady called in and said he was killin' her, and I could hear Rudy yelling in the background, and then she let out a real loud scream and the line went dead."

Luke quickly backed the car out, hit the siren, and took off with tires squealing.

CHAPTER 9

Luke had radioed Matt to meet him. It was always a good idea to have backup for a domestic violence case, but Luke especially wanted a witness because of the bad blood between him and Rudy.

The house was ablaze with lights. Rudy's truck was around back, his mother's car parked beside it. Luke eased the cruiser in and got out. Matt was right behind him, pointing to Bertha Veazey's car as he said, "Looks like she got word her baby boy was being naughty."

Luke paused to throw down his cigarette and grind it out with his heel. "In her eyes, he's never done anything wrong in his whole life."

"Have you seen Rudy's old lady?" They headed for the back door. Nobody in the country ever used their front doors.

"No. And frankly I'm not anxious to see what somebody dumb enough to marry Rudy looks like."

"Oh, come on. Give the devil his due. Rudy's not a bad lookin' guy. Remember how the girls chased after him in high school? That curly hair of his gives him that little boy look women fall for. Besides, she's not from around here. I heard he met her when he was stationed in Florida."

"You know her?"

"No, but I've seen her at Creech's getting gas. She's right nice-looking. Cute figure, and . . ."

"Just hold it right there." The screen door opened and closed with a loud bang as Rudy stepped out on the porch. He was holding a shotgun, pointed at the ground.

Luke pulled his holster strap open. "Put it down, Rudy."

"My gun. My house. My business. Now you ain't got no right to be here, and you know it."

His speech was slurred, and he was lurching from side to side, obviously drunk. "I'm not telling you twice, Rudy."

"Do what he says, honey." Bertha Veazey came up behind Rudy and put her hands on his shoulders. She was wearing a faded blue chenille robe over a muslin nightgown. Her gray hair, which she normally wore wrapped in a tight bun at the nape of her neck, hung loose down her back.

Rudy, bare-chested, bare-footed, his jeans slung low beneath his beer belly, shook her away. "Stay out of this, Ma."

"There ain't no need for trouble with the law." Bertha stepped in front of Rudy to glare down at Luke and Matt. "You all ain't got no business here. Now git."

"We had a call from his wife, Mrs. Veazey, saying he was trying to kill her," Luke said, not taking his eyes off Rudy and the shotgun.

"So they had a little fight, and she got mad and called the law. So what? They've made up now, so you ain't needed."

Rudy grinned. "That's right. And you ain't got no warrant and can't come inside without one, and if you don't hurry up and get off my property, I'm gonna blow you away."

Luke's eyes narrowed. "I'm telling you for the last time to put that damn gun away."

"Do it, honey," Bertha urged.

Scowling, Rudy lowered the gun to point at the ground.

"Get your wife out here now," Luke ordered. "She's the one that called. We need to talk to her."

"She's gone to bed," Bertha said.

"Then wake her up, because we aren't leaving till we see her."

"Go get her, Ma," Rudy growled. "Let's get this over with."

Bertha disappeared inside the house, grumbling to herself.

Rudy's eyes narrowed as he stared down at Luke. "I've managed not to have a run-in with you since the stupid folks of Buford County elected you sheriff, but I should've known it was just a matter of time till you tried to use that tin badge to try and get back at me for that fight back in high school. Well, you'd best get something straight: I ain't takin' no shit off you, Ballard."

Luke and Matt exchanged smiles, and Luke said, "I have no reason to get back at you for that fight, Rudy, seeing as how I whipped your ass. As for my badge, I didn't need it then to take you on, and I don't need it now. So watch yourself, and you won't have anything to worry about."

Rudy hooted. "Worry about you? Hell, that'll be the day, and . . ."

"Here she is."

Luke watched as Bertha shoved a girl who looked to be in her late teens or early twenties out on the porch. He couldn't tell if Matt was right about her being pretty because she had her head down, and he couldn't see her face. She was wearing white capri pants and a yellow blouse. The sleeve on the right had been ripped away, exposing the big whelp on her shoulder.

"Tell him you're fine, Emma Jean," Bertha said brusquely. "And tell him you and Rudy done made up, so's there no reason for them to be here."

"That's right," Emma Jean mumbled but did not look up.

Luke walked up the steps so he could see her better in the porch light, then cursed to see the red imprint of a hand on her cheek. Her eye was almost swollen shut.

Embarrassed, she made a tiny fist and pressed it to her mouth to hide her torn lower lip, which was oozing blood. He could also see a tiny bald spot on her scalp where a hank of hair had been ripped out.

Whirling on Rudy, he cried, "I ought to rip out your eyes and piss on your brain for this."

Rudy took a step backwards and began to slowly raise the shotgun, but Luke was quicker, yanking it away to fling into the yard as he drew his revolver.

Matt caught his arm. "Cool it. I'd like to blow him away myself, but unless she takes out a warrant . . ."

Luke turned back to Emma Jean, who had backed against the side of the house, her eyes like a frightened doe surrounded by hunters. "You'll sign a warrant, won't you? After what he did to you?"

She turned away, her tiny shoulders quaking as silent sobs racked her body.

"Mrs. Veazey, please . . ."

Bertha cried, "She ain't signin' nothin', sheriff, and you'd best go on and git."

Matt nudged Luke. "She's right. If she won't sign, there's nothing we can do."

But Luke wasn't about to give up. "Think about it, Mrs. Veazey. You don't have to put up with this. Just say the word, and . . ."

Between clenched teeth, Rudy warned, "I'm warnin' you, Luke . . ."

It was a scene Luke had witnessed all too often with other couples. "If you change your mind, call me," he told Emma Jean.

He was about to turn away when he noticed the red stain in the crotch of her white pants. "She's bleeding," he said as her knees buckled. He caught her before she slumped to the floor. Bertha and Rudy both lunged for her, but Matt held them back.

"Take him in and book him," Luke ordered, lifting Emma Jean in his arms. "I'll get her to the hospital."

"You can't do this, damn you," Rudy screamed at Luke as Matt cuffed him and steered him to the patrol car. "I'll sue your bastard ass. I swear I will."

Matt shoved him into the back seat without the obligatory motion of pushing his head down. It smacked the roof, and Rudy cursed all the louder.

Luke was already on his way, siren blaring, as Matt backed out of the drive with Bertha running alongside the car, huffing and puffing as she shouted to her son, "I'll go wake up your pa, and he'll be down there to get you out. Don't you worry none. He'll have you out in no time."

"Aw, to hell with it." Frustrated, Rudy threw his head back against the seat. "I shoulda just yanked the damn phone out before she called the law."

"What I wish you'd have done," Matt taunted, "was keep pushing Luke so he'd blow you away."

"Screw you, Rumsey." Rudy jabbed the air with his middle finger.

Luke paced about the empty waiting room. Emma Jean hadn't said a word during the ride, although he kept trying to convince her to take out a warrant. Otherwise, he couldn't keep Rudy in jail.

He told her he'd known Rudy in school and how he had always been a bully. He said the best thing for her to do was leave him and go back to wherever she came from because it wasn't going to get any better. But she had just sat there, doubled over and clutching her stomach and moaning.

When they got to the emergency room, she was whisked into a treatment room. Luke told the triage nurse he would wait, hoping that after Emma Jean had time to think about it, she'd change her mind.

It wasn't long before he was called to the phone. Matt said Wilbur Veazey was down at the jail raising holy hell about his boy being locked up without a warrant, and Matt wanted to know what Luke wanted him to do.

"The fact that Rudy's wife is being treated because he beat her up is all the warrant I need right now. If Wilbur gets nasty about it, you can lock him up, too."

Luke saw Dr. Soseby, the doctor on call, motioning and put the phone down.

"She's had a miscarriage," Dr. Soseby said. "I've got her scheduled for a D&C first thing in the morning to clean things up. Other than a few bruises, she'll be okay after a few days rest."

Luke did not mourn the loss of a baby sired by Rudy Veazey and hoped his wife had sense enough not to either. "I need to see her. She's got to sign a warrant or I can't hold him."

The doctor shook his head. "Sorry. She was in a lot of pain, so I had to sedate her. Maybe tomorrow."

There was nothing for Luke to do but head home, and by the time he got there it was nearly four o'clock.

One of the first things Alma had done when they bought the little two-bedroom house after he got elected sheriff was to have the back porch closed in to make a room for him. She said it was because he would be working late hours, and she didn't want him waking her up when she had to get up so early to go to work at the mill. He knew the real reason was because she didn't want to sleep with him. Fine. He didn't want to sleep with her either.

He grimaced at the sound of the back door squeaking when he opened it. Alma raised all kinds of hell when he woke her up, and he was too tired to listen to her bitching.

The bed was just as he'd left it when he had crawled out of it at six a.m. the day before. That didn't surprise him. The only time she made it up was when she changed sheets on Saturday morning. Otherwise she only went in his room when she wanted to nag about something. Like now. He groaned to hear her coming and quickly dove into bed and pulled the covers over his head.

In a screeching whisper, she began her tirade. "Luke, it does look like you'd try to be quieter when you come dragging in at all hours. You know I've got to be up for church, and once I get woke up, I can't go back to sleep. And how come you're out so late? Who were you screwing this time? One of those cheap hoochy-coochy girls at the fair, I'll bet. Irene Cleghorn called to tell me you were out there. She said Burch went on behalf of the church to see just how dirty it was and that you were there and left with one of the girls."

He burrowed his head under the pillow to try and shut her out.

"I don't know what to do about you, Luke. I swear I don't."

He could picture her dramatically throwing her arms over her head.

"I try to have a decent home. I keep a clean house that you don't appreciate because you're never here. I cook good meals that you don't eat because you're never here. I get up at dawn five days a week to stand on my feet at the mill all day, sometimes six, and Sundays I take our daughter to church, but you never come with us. I'm a good Christian wife, but our marriage stinks because you don't care, and the least you could do for the sake of appearances is try. You could have some self-respect and do your screwing around where folks can't see you."

She paused to take a breath and sailed in again. "You could at least have the decency to think of your daughter. I mean, my God, Luke, we use the same bathroom, and what if you bring home crabs or some kind of nasty disease from those women you screw? Me and her could catch your filthy crud."

In that moment, Luke thought if Emma Jean Veazey were like Alma, then maybe he could understand why Rudy had lost control and beat the hell out of her. Something told him Emma Jean wasn't like Alma, because *nobody* was like Alma. And he sure as hell wasn't like Rudy and would never hit a woman for any reason, but right then he admitted to being sorely tempted.

Flinging back the covers, he bounded out of bed to tower over her. His face was red, and his breath was coming in quick, hot gasps, and he kept his fists squeezed tight at his sides. "There's a limit to what a man can take, and you're fast pushing me to mine. You don't know what the hell you're talking about. Now get out of here and let me have some peace. I'm dog-assed tired, and I don't need this crap."

Alma stared at him uncertainly. True, he had never hit her, but there was always a first time, and she figured she had made her point anyway. "You just remember what I said about your bringing home your crud," she said in retreat as she backed toward the door. "And I'm going to tell Tammy not to use the toilet after you till she wipes if off with Pinesol."

It was almost ten when Matt called and woke him up. "We gotta do something about Rudy. His old man called that jack-legged lawyer from Childersburg, Steve Lindsey, and he says you got no right to hold Rudy, and if you don't let him go he says he's calling the attorney general."

Luke was worn out. His whole body ached, and his mouth tasted like something had crawled in and died. "Stall him. Tell him you can't get up with me. Meanwhile, I'll go back to the hospital and see if I can talk to Rudy's wife."

He hung up and went to take a shower, glad Alma had gone to church and he had the house to himself. The bottle of disinfectant she had left on the back of the commode got him riled all over again, and he angrily shoved out the window screen and threw it in the yard. The woman was going to drive him crazy.

Shaved, showered, and dressed in a uniform fresh from the

cleaners, his stomach led him to the kitchen. He made a peanut butter and banana sandwich and wolfed it down on the way to the prowler.

Because it was Sunday afternoon, the hospital parking lot was full.

Ramona Whitley, wearing a pink volunteer smock, was on duty at the visitor's desk. Mrs. Veazey was in Room 110, she said, but both visitors' passes were out. She offered to call the room and have someone come out so he could go in, but Luke said he would try later.

He left by the front door, walked around the side of the building, and reentered the hospital via the emergency room. Positioning himself where he could keep an eye on 110, he figured the visitors could only be members of Rudy's family and wouldn't stay long. He was right. Within ten minutes, Bertha Veazey came out with her sister, Pinella.

He stepped around a corner so they wouldn't see him and heard Bertha boasting as they passed, "She won't sign no papers on my boy. She knows he'll kill her if she does."

In a husky cigarette voice, Pinella agreed, "Well, I don't think she will, either, but he shouldn't beat up on her like that. He was drunk again, won't he?"

"Well, she drives him to drink, her and her hoity-toity ways, but that's what he gets for not marryin' one of his own kind. And if she don't learn her place, he's gonna keep on beatin' up on her. That's the way men are. Lord knows, Wilbur smacked me around till I got over my sassiness."

"Well, Ernie's hit me a few times, too, but he's done good by me and the kids. We ain't never gone to bed hungry."

The voices faded away. The ignorant prattle disgusted Luke. He had heard it before from other battered wives. He entered the room and was glad the other bed was empty so he could talk to Emma Jean without anyone hearing.

She was laying on her side facing the wall, her back to the door.

"Mrs. Veazey, it's Sheriff Ballard. I know you probably aren't feeling good, but I really need to talk to you."

When she did not respond, he walked around the bed, wincing to see her bruised and swollen face. "I'm sorry about the baby." It seemed the proper thing to say, even if he didn't mean it.

"I'm not."

He saw that the frightened doe eyes of the night before were now red sparks of anger.

"I don't want his baby."

Her face crumpled like paper tossed into a trash can, and her hands snaked from beneath the sheets to cover her eyes. "I'm sorry. I shouldn't have said that. Please don't tell anybody."

Luke pulled up a chair and sat down. "You don't ever have to worry about anything you tell me. Now I'm going to stick my nose in your business *again,* and tell you *again,* that you ought to leave him and go back to your family. But first I want you to sign a warrant for what he did to you."

"I don't have any family. I don't have anywhere else to go. Rudy is all I've got. And I'm not signing any warrant, so you can leave."

Luke argued, "The warrant will teach him a lesson. He won't go to prison this time, but he'll get a suspended sentence. He's got sense enough to know if it happens again, the judge would throw the book at him."

"He'd kill me."

"I know his mother was just here to scare you into thinking that, but . . ."

"It was my fault."

"And how do you figure that?"

It was like a dam unleashed, as though she had to hear with her own ears some kind of justification for what had happened, even if it meant taking the blame herself. "We were at the dance in Talladega. I didn't want to go, but Rudy made me. He made me dance with Frank Goforth, and I didn't want to do that, either, because I can't stand the way he looks at me when I go in the supermarket where he's the meatcutter. But Rudy was dancing with Frank's wife, Nina, so I didn't see any way out of it. It was a slow dance, too, which made it worse because Frank danced me into the shadows and started rubbing . . . ," she trailed to an embarrassed silence.

"It's okay," Luke prodded. "You can tell me anything."

Finally, she went on. "He started rubbing his *thing* against me and kind of hunching at me. Then he whispered that I should meet him in the alley behind the supermarket sometime, so we could sneak into the storage room and have some real fun." Her face twisted with disgust. "He said he'd give me the sirloin between his legs and, afterwards, he'd give me a pound of hamburger for free to take home for supper."

Luke thought that sounded just like Frank Goforth, who fancied himself a lady's man but had all the class of a pig at a trough. "So Rudy saw what was going on and got mad and took it out on you."

"Not exactly. I told him about it on the way home, 'cause I was so mad at Frank, but he said Frank wouldn't have acted like that if I hadn't given him reason to think he could. One thing led to another, and he started hitting me." She bit her lower lip, then winced because it was sore. "I shouldn't have called the law. He didn't hit me in the stomach till after I did."

If Rudy had walked in the room right then, Luke knew he would have pounded him right into the floor and not given a damn as to the consequences. "Sign the warrant, please."

"I can't." She rolled over on her back and stared up at the ceiling. "You just don't understand, sheriff. I'm sorry I bothered you with this, and I'd appreciate it if you'd just go on now. I really don't feel like talking any more."

Either Bertha or Pinela had left their orange visitor's pass on the nightstand next to the bed. Luke picked it up, took a pencil from his pocket, and scribbled both the number of the sheriff's office and his home phone. He stuck it in her hand. "Keep that where you know where it is and call me anytime you need me, day or night."

He could only hope that she didn't throw the numbers away, because if she kept living with Rudy, sooner or later, she was going to need them.

Back at the courthouse, he told Matt to let Rudy go but make sure he left by the back exit because, if he saw his smirking face, he was going to bash it in.

Matt pointed out, "He's going to want to come up here and use the phone to call his old man to come get him."

"He can walk home or use a pay phone on the street. Now if nothing else is going on, I'd like to hide out in my office and catch a nap." He would have preferred his own bed but avoided being around the house when Alma was there, which he knew she would be on a Sunday afternoon.

"Jubal Cochran wants you to call him. He's left two messages."

Jubal had been a big contributor to Luke's campaign, but Luke liked him for reasons beyond that. He was a good man, and Luke felt sorry for him. His wife of forty-some years had died the past week. "He's probably lonesome. If he calls back, tell him I'll drop by later. I'm really bushed, Matt."

"I know. Once I get rid of Rudy, I'm going to take a snooze myself, but I think I'll call Jubal and let him know you'll be around. He sounded upset. Something about Hardy Moon and his wife's funeral."

Luke was careful not to let his sudden interest show. If Jubal had a complaint about Hardy, he damn well wanted to hear it. "Well, maybe I'll take a run over there now."

He was out the door before Matt could ask why he had so abruptly changed his mind.

Jubal offered what was left of the casseroles and desserts the ladies of his church had brought, but Luke politely declined. The cheese on the broccoli looked like a dirty floor mat, and the pound cake resembled a sour sponge. Besides, he was too anxious to hear what Jubal had to say about Hardy to care about eating.

Jubal settled into his recliner and offered Luke a cigar, which he also declined. Then Jubal lit up his own before explaining what had him upset. "It's about what happened the day Henrietta was buried. Now I know the usual thing is for the family to leave while the grave is covered up and then come back later after the flowers are all in place, but I just felt like I wanted to stay with her till she was in the ground. They wouldn't let me, though—Ozzie and Hank. They said Hardy had a rule against it, and he'd have their heads if they covered her up while I was there.

"I said I was staying anyway," he continued, "and Ozzie, he got real huffy and said if I didn't leave Henrietta would sit right there till I did. They meant it, too. I could tell. So I told 'em to go ahead, and then I made like I was leaving. Only I parked way off down the road and sneaked back."

Luke leaned forward in his chair. "Then what happened?"

"They were too fast. They figured what I was up to and had her buried by the time I got back."

Luke could understand Jubal's disappointment but did not

feel he had a legitimate complaint. "I'm sorry, but there's really nothing I can do."

Jubal flared, "Not even about the flowers? And that's just the least of it."

"What about the flowers?" Luke asked patiently.

"When I went back, I saw that some of the ones that were on wire stands had been taken off and put right on the ground. Now you know there was another funeral the day after Henrietta was buried. Bea Canady, remember?"

Luke nodded, wondering what Jubal was leading up to.

Jubal shook his cigar for emphasis as he said, "Well, I'll just bet the stands for Bea's flowers were the same ones taken from Henrietta's grave. I think Hardy had Ozzie and Hank strip off Henrietta's flowers so Lucy could use them on the arrangements for Bea Canady. He has to buy those, you know.

"And that's not the worst part." He lowered his voice to a near whisper. "I think they switched coffins."

Luke tensed. "Why do you say that?"

The corners of Jubal's mouth began to twitch with rage as he recounted how he had looked for Ozzie and Hank to ask them about the flower stands, and when he had gone to the tool shed, thinking they might be in there, he had seen a white pine coffin standing against the wall. "I was curious," he said, "because it was just like the one I picked out for Henrietta, and I remember Hardy telling me at the time that it was the only one he had like that—white pine with lavender lining and a big purple satin bow on the top like a box of candy. I knew Henrietta would have liked it, only I'll bet my last dollar she's not buried in it."

"Now let me get this straight," Luke said carefully. "You're telling me that Hardy only had one coffin like the one you picked out, and you saw what you believe was that very same coffin in the shed after Henrietta was buried?"

"That's right."

"And now you think that's why Ozzie and Hank wouldn't let you stay because they took her out of the coffin you bought and put her in a different coffin?"

Jubal nodded. "A *cheaper* coffin, Luke. That's why he would've done it. He charged me for the better one, then switched."

Luke was not about to confide his suspicion that Hank and Ozzie had probably not bothered and dumped Henrietta right in the grave and covered her up. "Well, I can only say I hope you're wrong."

Jubal's voice cracked and tears trailed down the wrinkles in his face like water streaming through a canyon. "I think that's the way it was, Luke. And I want you to do something about it. I want her dug up and put in her own coffin, and I want that no-good, thieving varmint to pay for daring to commit such a sacrilege."

Luke got to his feet but motioned for Jubal to keep his seat. "Don't worry. I'll check it out and get back to you, but it may take a few days."

"No hurry," Jubal called after him. "Henrietta isn't going any place."

Luke did not turn around as he let himself out the front door because he did not want Jubal to see how he was smiling. He had good reason . . . because he might have just found a way to bring the hammer down on Hardy Moon.

Chapter 10

"For the last time, Betsy, I am not going to open that coffin."

Hardy was blocking the door to the viewing room and the metal coffin containing the remains of Betsy Borden's nephew, Normie Meese. He had been killed in Vietnam; his body had arrived on the afternoon train from Birmingham. The funeral was not scheduled until the next day, but Hardy was wishing he could send Hank and Ozzie to dig a hole and throw Normie in it then and there. Betsy and her whole weird family were driving him crazy with their demands to open the sealed coffin. They had been in and out of the funeral home all afternoon, and now it was after ten, and they refused to leave.

"He's our kin," Betsy said not for the first time.

Behind her, five heads bobbed to agree. Hardy swept them with a cold glare of contempt. Betsy smelled like the fish she cleaned at the supermarket. He could see little scales on the tattered sweater she wore over a flannel shirt and baggy overalls.

Towering behind her was her dim-witted father, Ebner

Meese, who was just as scruffy as his daughter. The legs of his bib overalls barely stretched to his calves, and Hardy cringed to see bits of food trapped in his bushy gray beard. Betsy's brother, Dougie Meese, and his wife, Frannie, were no better. Normie's mother, Ruth Meese, was likewise disgusting.

Hardy turned away, unable to stomach them any longer. "If you don't leave, I'm going to call the sheriff. I've already let you stay past visitation time."

"You call this visitin'?" Betsy protested. "When all we get to do is stand here behind this little rope and stare at a gray box? Besides, *we* done told *you* for the last time that we can't be sure our kin is even in it till we see for sure."

Hardy again tried to make her understand. "The remains were identified by the government, and they sealed the coffin. Because your nephew was killed nearly three weeks ago. The body isn't fit to view. The smell would be atrocious." *Even worse than you*, he thought, *if that were possible.* "I have no way of opening it, anyway. It would take a crowbar, for god's sake, and the coffin would be destroyed in the process.

"Now I'm telling you one last time," he shook his finger as he spoke, "if you don't leave this instant I'm calling Sheriff Ballard and having you arrested for trespassing."

"I think he means it, girl," Ebner said, tobacco juice running from the corner of his mouth. He swiped at it with the cuff of a tattered sleeve.

Betsy stood there a moment longer, eyes narrowed as she stared at the coffin. "All right," she said finally and thoughtfully. "We'll just have to take the government's word for it that Normie is in there."

"Are you sure?" Ruth asked doubtfully.

Hardy stared at the little stick hanging from Ruth's brown-stained lips. She was a snuff dipper. The stick was a custom of the women of her generation, used to roll the wad of snuff around in the mouth from time to time. He found it even more repugnant than chewing tobacco.

Betsy took Ruth's arm and led her out, whispering something in her ear. Hardy didn't care what she was saying. He didn't care about anything except getting them out of there, locking the door behind them, and having a good, stiff drink.

Outside the funeral home, Dougie and Frannie dutifully crawled up into the back of Ebner's pickup truck and pulled old feedsacks around them to ward off the night chill. Ebner backed the truck out of the driveway. Ruth sat in the middle, and Betsy, by the door.

"So what do we do now?" Ruth wailed. "I just don't feel right about it. That might not be my boy in that box, and till I know for sure it is, I can't say good-bye to him. I'll always wonder if he's alive somewhere, and . . ."

"You don't gotta wonder, Ruth," Betsy said.

"Why not? You heard Mr. Moon."

"That don't matter. Just let me and Dougie handle it, and I promise we'll find out for certain if it's Normie. Now let's get on home. Me and Dougie need a nap 'cause we got work to do later."

It was nearly five in the morning when Betsy and Dougie returned to the funeral home with crowbar and flashlight, parking Ebner's truck two blocks away. They kept to the shadows to stay out of the glow of streetlights. Betsy explained to Dougie that she had checked things out when they were there earlier and noticed that a window in the room next to Normie's coffin was unlocked. "All we gotta do is slide it open real quiet and crawl right in."

The window opened as easily as Betsy had hoped, and in seconds they were inside. Remembering the chair sitting in front of the window, she whispered to Dougie to step down onto it and not trip.

Finally standing before the coffin, she turned on the flashlight. "Now be as quiet as you can. Mr. Moon sleeps upstairs, if you make a lot of noise, he might hear and come runnin'."

In his wilder days, Dougie had done his share of breaking and entering, luckily without getting caught, so cracking open the metal coffin was a piece of cake for him. One quick snap, and the metal twisted beneath his strong hands. "Here goes." He gave a hearty yank. Then, with the air inside the coffin rushing into his face, he cried, "Oh, shit," and gagged as the turtle stew he'd had for supper found its way back up his throat.

"Do it over there, stupid. Not on the floor." Betsy shone the light at a potted plant. Her stomach was stronger, but still she fought against nausea as she turned the flashlight beam down into the coffin.

"What the hell?" She backed away in disbelief, then moved cautiously forward once again. "This is Normie?" She picked up a plastic bag with what looked like rotting chicken guts inside and held it up for closer scrutiny. Then she saw the dog tag. Although it was smeared with body fluids and blood and turning dark, she could make out the name stamped on it, *Borden, Norman Leroy,* followed by a serial number.

She dropped the bag back into the coffin. "It's what's left of Normie," she said, sickened to the core. "Now let's get out of here before Mr. Moon hears us."

But Hardy had already heard noises coming from below and was dialing the number of the sheriff's office. On the other side of the bed, Lucy struggled to wake from a sound sleep. "Who are you calling at this hour?"

"Shut up," he growled, annoyed that no one was answering. "We got a prowler, and I'm calling the law."

Lucy sat up, not at all alarmed. "Well, why don't you go downstairs and look around before you bother the sheriff? It could be the cat. Did you remember to put him out?"

"Shut up," he repeated, harsher this time, for he had pulled the phone line to the window in time to hear the sound of footsteps running down the gravel driveway. Even without seeing anyone, he knew it was the crazy Bordens.

Finally, Ned Tucker heard the phone ringing in the sheriff's office and stumbled sleepily from across the hall where he'd been stretched out on the magistrate's sofa. He listened to Hardy's complaint, then asked, "Did you check to see if anything is missing?"

"No. I haven't been downstairs."

"But you say whoever it was left."

"I heard someone running down the driveway, and I know who it was, too . . . Betsy Borden's looney family. They were here last night till all hours, demanding that I open their nephew's coffin, and . . ."

"Well, you need to go see if anything's missing or disturbed. You don't even know for sure they broke in. They might've been just trying to." Ned yawned, anxious to get back to the sofa. If he could snooze another hour, he wouldn't have to go back to bed when he got off work and could go fishing early and stay all day.

"What I *need*," Hardy roared into the phone, "is for you to send a deputy over here now, damnit. It's not my job to go looking for prowlers."

"Oh, hell, Hardy, I'm trying to tell you that you don't even know for sure you had one. Go check and call me back."

Ned hung up the phone and returned to the magistrate's office and the waiting sofa. When the sheriff's phone rang again, he ignored it.

"It's about time you got here," Hardy snapped at Luke as he opened the door to let him in. "I couldn't get anybody to answer the damn phone in your office till Wilma got there at seven this morning. You oughta fire that worthless piece of shit, Ned Tucker. Now come in here and see what some *other* worthless shit did. You're not going to believe this."

Hardy led the way to the parlor and pointed at the open window. "That's how they got in. Betsy must've noticed it wasn't locked when they were here earlier. Hell, why should I worry about whether my windows are locked or not? Who'd want to break into a funeral home, for god's sake? Only nitwits like Betsy and the Meeses, that's who."

"Now look at this." He went into the viewing room. "But I warn you, it might make you throw up like it did one of them." He nodded with disgust at the flower pot. "I'm gonna have to throw it out—another expense they caused me."

The vomit did not bother Luke, and he registered only mild revulsion after lifting the mangled top of the coffin to see the plastic bag with Normie's remains. Luke had taken his turn in Vietnam preparing the dead for shipment home and had seen plenty of little plastic bags containing only a handful of guts and goo. Claymore mines could do that to a human body. There was no need to use big, clumsy rubber bags. Fill a sandwich bag, add the dog tag, stick it in a metal coffin, and the job was done. Quick and neat.

"I want them charged with breaking and entering and vandalism. So go arrest them."

"You should have just opened the coffin, Hardy, and then there wouldn't have been a problem."

"It was sealed, for god's sake. You can see they had to use a crowbar, and . . ."

"You could have taken the screws out. It's a bit of work, but it can be done."

"Well, it's too late now. They've destroyed it, and somebody is going to have to pay for a new one, and . . ." The phone rang. "Excuse me. I'll be right back."

Luke watched him hurry away. A body might need to be picked up, which meant money, so Hardy wasted no time answering.

Likewise, Luke wasted no time in making his way to the room at the back where coffins were displayed. It had been nearly a week since he had promised Jubal he would check everything out, but there had been no chance without making Hardy suspicious, till now.

He flicked on the light. A dozen or so coffins were scattered throughout the room. He zeroed in on one that fit the description Jubal had given him: white pine with lavender lining and a big purple ribbon stretched inside the lid. Closer scrutiny brought a tight knot of fury to his throat as he saw that beneath it, on two corners, there were tiny little smudges of red clay. Jubal was right.

He could hear Hardy winding up his conversation and quickly went back to the viewing room. "I'll go talk to them," he said when Hardy returned. "Maybe I can get them to confess and scare them into buying a new coffin, but I can't see arresting them. A judge wouldn't put them in jail for wanting to identify their kin, especially when he sees they're nuts, anyway."

Hardy waved him towards the door. "You just tell them they'd better not ever step foot in my funeral home again. Betsy still owes me for burying her husband and kids anyway."

Luke drove out to the Meese cabin. Rusting cars were parked everywhere. Lubie Warsh, who owned the only garage in town and had the only wrecker service around, gave Ebner twenty dollars for each car he let him dump there. Sometimes Ebner made a little selling old parts.

Cats were all over the yard, and a couple of fierce-looking dogs tied to trees barked as Luke made his way up the rutted path.

Ebner was sitting in a rocker on the front porch, carving

what was beginning to look like a rolling pin from a block of wood. "Mornin', sheriff," he said lazily. "What brings you out here? You come to look at Ronnie Turnage's Ford, I'll bet, or what's left of it. If I'd charged two bits a head when Lubie first hauled it out here, I coulda made me some real money. Everybody wanted to see Ronnie's brain layin' in the rear window."

Luke swallowed hard. "Run that by me again, Ebner. You say Ronnie's *brain* was still in the car when Lubie towed it in?"

Just then Ebner noticed that one of the cats was lapping out of the cup of cider he'd set on the floor next to his rocker. He spat a wad of tobacco juice and hit him square on top of his head to send him bolting from the porch. "Dang cats," he grumbled. "Nothin' but trouble. Can't get rid of 'em, and they multiply like flies. Tried puttin' out poison but wound up killin' two of the dogs. I need them to chase off the thievin' assholes who creep around here at night tryin' to steal off the cars." Getting back to Luke's question, he confirmed, "Yep, it was there all right. A big gray glob."

Luke was livid and didn't know who to blame—the rescue squad or Lubie. Death cars always drew the morbidly curious but to leave a brain inside? Jesus. "Is it still there, Ebner?"

"Naw. Ronnie's old man heard about it and came to get it the next day, mad as a wet hen, but it was gone. I reckon the cats ate it that night. I'd been chasin' 'em off it all day."

Luke made a mental note to raise enough hell with those who might have been responsible that it would never happen again.

"I need to talk to Betsy."

"She's inside, washing one of Dougie's younguns' hair. Teacher sent him home again with lice."

Luke walked on up the steps and into the cabin, and promptly felt something squish under his foot. Looking down, he grimaced to see he had stepped into a pile of chicken doo.

"Gotta watch where you're walkin, sheriff," Betsy said from where she had a small boy doubled over a washtub pouring what smelled like kerosene over his head as he screamed bloody murder.

Luke glanced around. There was hardly room to move because of so much furniture crowded in the tiny room: old sofas that vomited stuffing, rickety chairs set around a three-legged table, stacks of newspapers ready for shredding to use in the outhouse, and eight stained mattresses on the floor.

The smell was awful, too, of grease, onions, urine, but maybe the worst was the sight of the chickens picking and cackling, and dropping more doo on the floor.

Betsy saw him staring and shrieked at the hens, "Out! Right this minute."

Luke thought she meant him, then realized it was the chickens she was talking to when she lifted her hands from the water and kerosene to wave at them and yell, "Shoo! Shoo!"

As they began to obediently make their way to the door, she called after them, "You all know you ain't allowed in here when I got company. Now git before you wind up bein' supper."

He was amazed at how they obeyed her, the hens walking out in single file behind a cocky red rooster leading the way.

"Now what you want, sheriff?" Betsy turned back to her task. "Kids," she grumbled. "Send 'em to school and they come home full of nits. I'll be glad when they all turn sixteen so's they can quit."

Luke doubted it would be that long before Betsy's numerous nieces and nephews dropped out. Not a one of the Meeses had ever gone beyond sixth or seventh grade. "Hardy Moon says you and your family broke into the funeral home last night and busted your nephew's coffin open."

"Well, it's his word against ours."

"Did you do it?"

"What if we did?" She jerked the boy's head out of the tub, covered it with a rag, and told him to go outside and dry off.

"Betsy, you can go to jail for breaking and entering. Damaging that coffin is called vandalism."

"Look, sheriff," she talked as she dragged the bucket to the back door and tipped it out to empty the water in the yard. "If'n we *did* do it—and I ain't sayin' we did—it was because that ass Hardy Moon wouldn't let us make sure it was our kin inside that box. We had a right to know."

"And are you satisfied now that it is?"

She grinned. "Uh-uh, sheriff. You ain't trickin' me into sayin' we done it. You gotta prove it."

Luke saw one of her front teeth was missing, and the rotten one next to it didn't look like it would be in her mouth much longer either.

"*Can* you?"

"Betsy, I could take you in for questioning, and if I dig hard enough, and long enough, yeah, I can probably prove it, but I'm not going to, because I can understand how you felt."

She nodded without looking at him.

"Okay. That's settled. Now let's talk about you and your family paying for a new coffin. The government isn't going to spring for two."

"There ain't no need. A bag of guts don't need no box. Me and Pa and Dougie are going to the funeral home this afternoon and get Normie and bury him in the family graveyard up on Crow's Knob. Dougie and our cousin, Lem, are up there now diggin' the hole."

Luke saw nothing wrong with that. Maybe it was bending the law a bit, but he leaned on the theory that sometimes it was best to *go* along to *get* along, especially with people like Betsy and her backwoods family. "I'm going to let you slide by this time, but if you ever pull a stunt like that again, you'll be spending some time in jail. Understand?"

She said she did.

He knew she didn't.

As he left, he paused to scrape the bottom of his shoe against the steps.

Luke was stopped for a traffic light when he recognized Emma Jean Veazey crossing the street in front of his car. She glanced in his direction and quickly ducked her head and pretended not to see him.

She was wearing light blue pedal pushers, white sneakers with no socks, and a beige pullover sweater that had seen better days. Her hair was pulled back in a perky ponytail. She looked like a sixteen-year-old. Luke was amused to think how, even though she obviously played down her looks to pacify Rudy's jealous streak, she could not completely hide the fact she was a damn fine-looking woman.

The light changed, and he turned in the opposite direction toward the funeral home. As he passed, he saw Lucy Moon getting into her car. She waved. He waved back. He liked Lucy. Always had. It was just a shame she was so plain homely she had leaped at the chance to marry Hardy without stopping to think he was only after her money. The funeral home was a gold mine, and Hardy had known it.

Luke made up a story to satisfy Jubal. He said the wreaths had been taken off the wire stands and put on the ground so they wouldn't blow around. This was flimsy, but Luke hadn't bothered to check. He had bigger fish to fry than charging Hardy with scoffing flowers off stands to use again and charge for new ones each time he did.

As for the coffin Jubal had seen in the storage shed, Luke lied and said he'd learned it was just being kept there because of lack of space. He wasn't about to tell him the truth. He was also glad he didn't have to worry about the same thing having happened to his mother because he'd stayed till the grave was covered. Ozzie and Hank hadn't dared tell him to leave.

When he got off the phone with Jubal, Wilma said Rudy Veazey was on the other line. "He says somebody stole his wallet."

Luke told her to let Kirby handle it.

A little while later, Kirby came into his office. "I can't believe that guy. Claims he fell asleep in his car at the grill Friday night, and somebody stole his wallet right out of his pocket. He probably got drunk and lost it."

Luke told him not to worry about it, all the while hoping Rudy wouldn't take his bad mood out on Emma Jean. Then he chided himself for thinking so much about her lately anyway.

A call came about a fender bender out on the Talladega highway and Kirby left. Right after he did, Wilma yelled, "Sheriff, your wife's on the phone."

Luke barely had time to speak into the receiver before Alma started in. "Don't give me no excuses about tonight, Luke. You promised Tammy you'd go to revival with us."

"I didn't promise anything, and you put her up to asking." It really griped him how Alma had started to use Tammy to try and get her own way. "All I told her was that I'd try to go if I wasn't busy, but it looks like I will be."

"Doing what? Luke, damn it to hell, you're never home."

Cupping his hand over the mouthpiece, he whirled his chair around so his back was to the open door to the outer office. "I've told you before. Don't call me down here raising hell. And listen to you cussing like a sailor in the same breath you're talking about going to church."

"Don't you tell me how to talk. Now are you going to go or not?"

"I told you I've got to work. Maybe next time." *Maybe never,* he thought, or at least not unless she outlived him and had his funeral in her kooky church. That was the only way she would ever get him there. "Now I've got to go."

"You can go to hell," she snapped into the receiver before slamming it down.

Luke leaned back in his chair, pulled a cigarette from the pack in his shirt pocket, and lit it. He didn't really have anything to do that night, and, like so many other times, he would probably stay right in his office and read till all hours. It beat going home to Alma.

He decided to have supper at the Bulldog and kill some time there. Mondays were never busy, and Clyde joined him in the booth with a cup of coffee. Luke always enjoyed the chance to talk to Clyde and was annoyed when Ned phoned to report someone had found Rudy's wallet behind the grill. Only there was no money in it, and Wanda was worried Rudy would think she took it since she was the one who found it.

Kirby and Matt were patrolling on opposite ends of the county, so Luke drove out to the grill where Wanda was waiting to swear over and over that the wallet was empty when she found it next to the dump bin when she took the trash out.

"With that temper of his, I don't need him on my back, and I'm afraid he's going to go around calling me a thief."

Luke said he would handle it. Besides, it was a nice evening for a drive in that almost hallowed time between dusk and darkness, when the land seems hesitant, yet poised, to leap into night. The few cotton blossoms remaining in Sid Dootree's fields running along both sides of the road seemed like sprinkles of silver from the half-moon rising in the sky.

A nip of fall was in the air. Luke rolled up the window, but not before catching a whiff of boll weevil poison lingering on the brown cotton stalks since spring. The sweetly acrid smell brought back memories of long-ago summer nights when he would take Sara parking on the backside of the fields. The thought ignited a fire in his loins, not for the woman-wife-mother she was now, but for the recklessness and hot blood of his youth.

He slowed to gaze longingly at the fields. A part of him would always be there. A part of Sara, too, and every other teen who had been there in search of something he, or she, could not understand, knowing only that a hunger was awakening within that begged to be fed.

In times when his memories took him back, Luke always found himself wondering how his life would have turned out if Sara had loved him back. But she hadn't. It had always been Dewey for her. Still, he couldn't help thinking about it, imagining what it would be like to share the kind of love Sara told him she and Dewey had for each other.

Maybe he was meant to be alone. He had said that to Sara once when they were having one of their soulful conversations on her front porch. They only got to do that in the summer when Tim was working a late shift and it was warm enough for them to sit outside. They never went in the house alone, knowing it would cause talk if anybody saw them.

So they visited outside in front of God and everybody. Sara told him that he should never give up hope of finding a true love. Maybe he would have to hide his feelings from the world as she did, but the necessary deceit was worth it.

"There's always an excuse for love," she had said many times. "It would be a real sad life if there wasn't."

Luke's life *was* sad because it seemed his only reason for existing anymore was vengeance. He had no idea what he would do with the rest of his life when he felt like his mother could finally rest in peace. For the moment love didn't seem important, but he still couldn't deny feeling lonely sometimes.

Luke could not tell whether Rudy was home till he drove around back of the house. Seeing his truck wasn't there, he started to leave, but the porch light came on, and Emma Jean appeared, framing her eyes with her hand against the light as she strained to see who it was.

Luke stopped and got out. No need to make her worry over why a patrol car had pulled into her yard. "Evening, Mrs. Veazey," he called as he walked towards the porch. "I've got Rudy's wallet. Somebody found it behind the grill and turned it in."

"He'll be so glad," she said, sounding relieved herself. "All his pay was in there."

"Well, I'm afraid somebody stole that. I'm sorry."

"Oh, no." Her hand flew to her throat. "He . . . we . . . needed that money. The hospital bill and all . . ." Her voice trailed and she glanced away, embarrassed to bring up that humiliating night. "But thanks for coming out here with it. I'll tell Rudy when he gets home. He's working third shift this week."

Luke felt a relaxing wave for not having to worry about Rudy tearing into the drive any second to raise hell about his being there. "Are you doing all right now?"

"Yes, I am. Thank you."

Luke wondered again how anybody could hit something that looked that good. "Well, I'm glad to hear it, and I hope things work out for you."

He turned to go. He didn't want to but knew it was best because looking at her, being so close, gave him a strange feeling he did not understand.

"Sheriff . . ."

He whipped about to see how scared she looked and thought how there was no need to be. Not around him. No, Lord. Never around him.

"I'm sorry I told you what I did."

"About what?"

"About Frank Goforth. I had no right. I mean, a woman shouldn't talk about such things to a man. I've been embarrassed ever since. Please don't tell nobody else."

"I won't. And it's okay that you told me. Besides, I wasn't surprised. Frank is like that. I've seen how he acts around women, especially when he's drinking."

"You have?"

"Oh, yeah." He stepped up on the porch and leaned back against the railing. Folding his arms across his chest, he continued, "To tell you the truth, I think when married folks go to those dances, they're asking for trouble when they dance with other people and get to flirting and all. Frankly, I'm surprised Rudy took you there. I remember in high school he was always crazy jealous over whatever girl he was going with."

"I think he wanted to dance with Inez Turnage. He was real hugged up to her a few times till Bobby Ray Walston cut in.

Then Ronnie got mad and left, and, well, you know what happened after that. Such a shame, all them folks getting killed over what went on at a dance."

"Well, you lost your baby for the same reason." Realizing what he'd said, he was quick to apologize. "I shouldn't have brought that up. I'm sorry."

"It's okay. I told you I didn't care I lost it. Oh, dang it!" She stamped her foot. "There I go again, saying something I got no business saying."

"It's all right."

"What I mean is, I don't feel like I'm ready to have a baby yet, so it's just as well I lost it. I didn't mean I didn't want one by Rudy."

He knew she was lying. "Well, if you feel that way, maybe it was for the best."

She was wearing a dress made from a feed sack. Luke knew because he had been at the Seed 'n Feed the day the truck unloaded the bags with that particular pattern. He had thought it was pretty then, and even prettier now on her. It was a soft plaid, turquoise and gold with a few splashes of tiny white daisies woven into the pattern. She had fashioned it into a neat little dress with puffed sleeves, a sash, and a billowing skirt.

"You sew real well," he said, a bit awkward, because he wasn't sure how she would feel about his complimenting her on something personal like her clothes. But he need not have worried. Not used to praise, Emma Jean was delighted. "Why, thank you, sheriff. Nobody's ever told me that before. Miss Ruby is always criticizing, saying I make things fit me too tight or too short."

"Don't pay her any mind. She's wears her clothes big to try and hide her fat, but you don't have to do that. She's got ugly legs, too. Like a knock-kneed goat."

Emma Jean giggled, and it was a good feeling because she could not remember the last time there had been any laughter in her life. "So have you always lived here, Sheriff?" she asked, sitting down on the top step.

He dropped beside her, keeping a proper space between them. "Yes, except for when I was in the army. And call me Luke."

"Luke," she repeated softly.

He felt a little shiver deep inside. Nobody had ever said his name like that before, like they were stroking it with a velvet hand.

"Okay, and you can call me Emma Jean."

He nodded in acceptance of the new familiarity between them, then felt the need to remind, "I meant what I said, you know, about your calling me if you ever need me."

"Oh, I don't think I'll be doing that again," she said quickly, nervously.

"Then you don't think Rudy will hit you again? I hope you're right, but I've always heard and known it to be true that if a man ever hits a woman the first time, he'll do it again." He boldly added, "I've got a feeling the other night wasn't the first time anyway."

She did not say anything, and he had learned early on in law enforcement that silence usually meant assent. "I thought so," he said. "And I know it's none of my business, but why do you put up with it? Are you that crazy about him?"

The look she gave him was one of horror that he could think such a thing, but it was with careful control that she responded, "I took vows for better or worse."

"Bull!"

She blinked. "You don't believe in keeping your marriage vows?"

"You're just making excuses, and you know it. Either you're crazy or you're a coward with nowhere else to go. Those are the only reasons I can think of that a woman would put up with a man low enough to beat on her. So which is it? You seem to have plenty of sense to me."

"I guess I got nowhere to go."

"Everybody's got someplace to go. Where's your family?"

She met his probing gaze and was struck to think how he was probably the easiest person to talk to that she'd ever met in her whole life, and she had never wanted, or needed, a friend more.

"Would you like some coffee, Luke?" she suddenly asked. "I've got some left over from lunch, and it might not be as good as fresh, but I can heat it up and bring it out here so's if anybody should happen by they won't think nothing about our talking out in the open like this, even if it is nighttime."

How well he knew the reason for such precaution.

He smiled at her, really smiled, for the first time in too long to remember. "I'd really like that, Emma Jean. I'd like it a lot."

CHAPTER 11

"Wait till you hear what went on at Junior Kearney's place last night."

Luke did not look up as Kirby rushed into his office. He was going over the latest "Wanted" posters, not that any big-time fugitives ever passed through town. It was just something to try and keep his mind off Emma Jean. "Yeah, I heard a rumor he's been selling moonshine again. We need to check it out."

"It's worse than that. He made two little colored kids put on a show last night."

Luke looked hard at him then. "What kind of show?"

"A sex show."

"Say again?"

"The way I heard it, Junior caught Rufus Bynum's boy, Wooly, stealing soda and cigarettes at the fruit stand and told him if he'd bring his girlfriend in and put on a show he wouldn't have him arrested."

"How old is this kid?"

"Twelve or thirteen. I'm not sure. Lehman Fuller was there and told it at Creech's this morning. Wooly brought a little girl. Lehman said she couldn't have been over eleven or twelve, and she was crying the whole time."

Luke gritted his teeth. "Who was she?"

"Lehman didn't know, but I figure we've got Junior on contributing to the delinquency of a minor, and no telling what else once you check the statutes. Want me to go pick him up?"

"I'll take care of it."

"Okay. I'll tell Wanda to get the warrant ready."

Luke started leafing through the posters again. "That won't be necessary. I'm just going to have a talk with him."

Kirby's eyes bugged. "A talk? Is that all?"

"For now."

Luke's face was like granite, his voice cold and final. Kirby knew he was plenty steamed, just like he knew he probably had a good reason for not rushing to arrest Junior. But he wasn't about to ask what it was. When Luke was mad, it was best to leave him alone.

Luke had been keeping an eye on Junior for some time. He knew Friday nights were when he drove out to the old logging road to meet his bootlegger. Probably the bootlegger was from somewhere up on Cheaha mountain, but he wasn't after him. Let the revenue boys do their job. All he wanted was to catch Junior red-handed.

It was cold, drizzling rain, and foggy. Luke backed his car off the road into a pine thicket. He was directly across from the rendezvous point, which was a clearing next to the old grist mill and the stream flowing down from the mountain. Kids swam there in the summer. Fishermen came around in the spring. Other than that, there was no traffic because Hampton Mill owned the property and had no intentions of selling. The Hamptons had always been a greedy lot and would have owned everything in the whole damn county if there'd been a way.

He opened a second pack of cigarettes. He'd been chain-smoking since he had got there shortly after signing off to Ned for the night. He just hoped Alma didn't call in looking for him. If she found out he'd gone off duty, she'd accuse him of being with another woman.

He acknowledged as he stared out the window into the fog that there was a time when she would have been right. But he had learned a long time ago that if he was with the same girl more than once or twice, she wanted a serious relationship, and he didn't want to get all tangled up. He wanted to keep his promise to his mother, then leave town and get on with his life.

At least that's how it had been till Emma Jean.

Time had gotten away from them that night on her porch as they had drifted into easy conversation. It was like they had once been old friends, separated for a time, but reunited and anxious to share everything that had happened since.

After the coffee, she had gone inside and made a pitcher of grape KoolAid and found a box of vanilla wafers. They might as well have been drinking champagne and eating caviar at some fancy, big city party because they fell into fun and laughter so easily.

After a while, he said maybe he should leave because somebody might come by and get the wrong idea. She said it was too late for folks to be out, and she wasn't the least bit sleepy and really enjoyed having someone to talk to.

So he stayed, and she chatted on about how Rudy was going to get her an old car but not so she could gad about. He warned her not to even think about that. He wanted her to have a way to get to work at the laundromat that his cousin, Bert Veazey, ran, but only during the months she wasn't working for Mr. Dootree in the fields. Part of the deal when Rudy rented the house was that she'd be available for picking tomatos or any other work in the fields.

At one point, their knees had accidently touched, and Emma Jean jumped and moved away. Luke had self-consciously cleared his throat and said he really ought to be getting home. Then she thanked him for going to see her at the hospital and said she knew he had been right in urging her to take out a warrant against Rudy but just couldn't.

That opened the door to more intimate conversation, and she wound up telling Luke the story of how she had come to marry Rudy in the first place, out of fear of being on her own in a world she never learned to cope with.

He listened and thought he understood and dared to share a bit about his own past: the shame of growing up illegitimate, having to get married when he was still a kid. He did not, however, tell her of his quest for revenge. That was a secret he vowed he would, unlike his mother, carry to the grave. Hardy and Burch and Buddy might wonder, but he was damned if he would let them know that he was aware that one of them was his father.

"Don't you ever wonder who your daddy was?" Emma Jean had innocently asked.

And he had given her the answer he always gave himself when he pondered the same thing: "Nope. Being here is all that matters. How I came to be doesn't."

When they finally called it a night, and he got up to leave, he marveled at what a tiny thing she was, her head barely coming to the bottom of his chin. Lord, how he ached to wrap his arms around her and hold her tight so nobody could ever hurt her again. Instead, he stuffed his hands in the pockets of his khaki uniform jacket and reminded her that she had his number if she needed him.

He saw her a few days later, and, sure enough, Rudy had bought her a car, a 1950 Ford that was a real klunker and blew black smoke out the exhaust pipe. She was proud of it, nonetheless, and waved and grinned at Luke the morning he passed her as she was turning into the laundromat.

He glanced at his watch, saw it was five to eight, and ever since he made it a habit to try to be at the corner at that time every morning. So far, he hadn't missed her a single day and was starting to wonder if maybe she was timing him, too.

He had sense enough to realize he was playing with fire, and it worried him that he didn't care. There was just something about her that warmed a spot in his heart that had been cold for a long, long time, maybe since that day he got the letter in Nam from Sara telling him why she could never return his love.

Suddenly headlights loomed in the distance, coming from town. Luke got out of his car fast, making sure the overhead light did not flash on to give him away. Crouching behind a tree, he waited for the truck to turn into the clearing and saw it was Junior. At the same time, lights approached from the north, from Cheaha, and in a few minutes, a sleek Cadillac pulled in.

Luke stealthily crossed the road and eased into the drainage ditch running alongside so he could be close enough to hear what was being said without being noticed. He recognized Junior's voice.

"You got the ten jugs I asked for?"

"Didn't have that much. Only ran twenty gallons this week and had to send some of that to Coosa County."

Luke was relieved to hear it was Early Raffitt because he had never been known to sell the contaminated whiskey known as rotgut. Rotgut was the result of bootleggers running their brew through rusting radiators or tossing an animal carcass into the mash to make it work faster.

Junior whined, "I told you, I'm all out, and I got to make money on this before the law starts nosing around."

Luke smiled. *The law already is nosing around, Junior.*

"It's the best I can do. Ten bucks a jug."

"Ten bucks? Shit, man, that's highway robbery. How come you went up? It was only seven last time."

"It's getting scarce. And how come you're bellyachin'? You'll sell it for twenty."

"I'll sell it by the drink and make more'n that."

"So quit your bitchin' and let's get this stuff in your truck. You know I do my business fast. You can't never tell who'll come by."

"*No, you can't,*" Luke said as he stepped out of the ditch and into the glow of the Cadillac's trunk light, gun in hand. "Just hold it right where you are, boys."

Early paled. He was already on parole. Arrest would send him back to Kilby prison in Montgomery. He raised his arms in surrender. "Listen, sheriff, this is my first run since I got out. It'll be my last, I swear. Just gimme a break. I've got a family to look after. If I go back to prison, they'll starve."

"You're lying. You've been running shine for weeks."

"Please . . ."

Luke waved the gun for silence and looked to Junior. "And what's your excuse? I let you off last time, remember?"

Junior grinned. "Yeah, because we both know you owe me on account of your momma."

Luke fought the urge to crack him across the face with his gun butt. "That debt is paid. Shut your mouth about it. Now you and Early get those jugs unloaded and then smash them on the rocks over there." He beamed his flashlight on the ditch.

Junior and Early moved quickly to obey, and soon shards of broken glass sparkled in the glow of the flashlight, the air heavy with the sour-sweet smell of whiskey.

When they finished, Luke went to Junior's truck, took the keys from the ignition, and told Junior to get in and sit down. He then went to the front of Early's Cadillac and used the butt of the flashlight to knock out both headlights. Early dared not protest, quaking where he stood. Luke then walked to the back of the car and smashed the tail lights.

"Now," he said finally, "I'm letting you off this time, but don't let me catch you in Buford County again. You got that?"

"Oh, yes, yes," Early babbled gratefully. "You won't see me around here. I swear you won't, and . . ."

Luke cut him off. "You can either start walking or wait till daylight to drive. Either way, get out of my sight."

Early took off running down the road to be swallowed up in the darkness.

Luke walked to the passenger side of the truck, opened the door, and got in. Returning the keys to the ignition, he switched on the dashlights and saw how Junior sat rigidly behind the steering wheel, gripping it tightly, worried eyes staring straight ahead.

"So how much time do you need to get your affairs in order before you're shipped off to Kilby?" Luke asked matter-of-factly.

Junior cried, "You ain't gonna really send me off, are you, Luke? Not after all I did for your ma . . ."

"We talked about that last time, remember?"

"So I slipped up. I won't do it again. I swear. But you can't send me off. You think back what I did for her. I took her in. She had no place else to go. She would've starved if not for me, and you know it."

"Maybe so, but you also treated her like shit, Junior."

"So I'd get drunk once in a while and cranky. But I never tossed her out, did I? Even after you was grown and left home, I let her and your wife and young'un stay there. You owe me, Luke. You know you do."

"And I told you, that debt was paid when I let you off the hook last time. You promised to go straight. You didn't keep your word. Think about that down at Kilby when some big gorilla bends you over a chair."

Junior beat his fists against the steering wheel. "It'll kill me to go to Kilby. I'll never survive. I'm an old man."

"Oh, I wouldn't say that. I hear you moved that new waitress of yours—Reba Lou, is that her name?—into your cabin. I also hear she's a real wildcat in bed. An old man couldn't hang onto something like that, now could he?"

"It don't matter. It don't matter. It'll kill me to go to prison. You gotta let me off, Luke. I swear, it won't happen again."

Luke lit a cigarette, then, with a deep exhale of smoke, said in a mock thoughtful tone, "Well, I might give you another chance if you do me a little favor."

Junior sat up straight, hope surging. "Anything, Luke. You name it, and I'll do it."

"Well, I was just thinking about how you shamed us white boys last night."

Junior gulped. "Huh? What're you talking about?"

"I heard you got some colored kids to screw for the gang at the fruit stand."

"Yeah, but what . . ."

"I also heard they put on quite a show."

"Well . . ."

"The way I see it, we can't have colored folks outdoing white folks when it comes to having sex, now can we?"

Junior wiped his brow with the back of his hand. "I don't know what you mean."

Luke turned sideways in the seat so he could meet Junior's anxious eyes. "What I mean is that I think you owe it to your race to prove coloreds aren't any better that way. So the favor I am asking is for you and Reba Lou to put on a show for the boys just like those colored kids did. You know, show what a man you are, let them bet on how many times you can make Reba Lou pop her cookies. Make a game out of it." Luke chuckled and slapped his shoulder. "I know you can do it, Junior. Hell, you've always been my hero where the ladies are concerned," he added with a chuckle of contempt.

Junior looked sick.

Luke gave his shoulder another pat, only harder. "So how about it? I do you a favor by letting you off, and you do me a favor by showing up the colored kids. Have we got a deal?"

Junior closed his eyes, and his words were barely audible as he spoke around the knot in his throat. "I guess we do."

"Good. You let me know when you plan to take care of it, and if I can't be there, I'm sure I'll hear about it."

He opened the door and stepped outside, then leaned back in to add one last taunt. "I'm sure everybody in town will hear about it, too, so try to put on a real good show."

Luke walked away and could hear the sounds of Junior's rage echoing through the night.

One down.
Another on the way.
Rest in peace soon, Momma.

Chapter 12

Unless she was working overtime at the mill, Alma was usually around the house on Saturdays, so Luke tried to ease out before she was up and stirring. This time, however, he was too late.

He stepped out the back door to hear her cursing and banging around in the shed next to the house where the wringer washer was hooked up. Hurrying, he hoped to make his getaway before she saw him, but just then she came out of the shed.

"Luke, I've got to have a new washer. This one is blown to hell, and it's so old there's no sense in having it fixed again." A cold, brisk wind was blowing. She pulled her sweater tighter and glared up at him like it was his fault.

Despite the way she treated him, Luke felt sorry for her. Having to drag clothes out of the house to the shed in bad weather was hard enough, and with only a week left till Thanksgiving, winter was right around the corner.

"Tell you what. I've got to go to Birmingham Monday. I'll run by Sears and see about having one delivered. All we have to do is rip out one section of kitchen cabinets to make room so you can have it in the house."

"Oh, no. I'll pick it out, because *I'll* be the one to have to pay for it. You sure don't make enough to support us."

She railed on, "And meanwhile what about today's wash? I don't have time to lug it to the laundromat and wait for it, then lug it back and hang it on the line. You're going to have to help out around here for a change."

He pretended to be annoyed. "Well, get everything in the basket, and I'll drop it off and pick it up on my way home."

"Oh, praise the Lord," she cried dramatically, waving her arms over her head. "His royal highness has decided to help out around here. I don't believe it. Will wonders never cease? Jesus, help me hurry before he changes his mind."

Luke was glad to find Emma Jean working at the laundromat. Sometimes she had Saturdays off. Better still, when he carried in his laundry basket, there was nobody else around.

The air was heavy with the mingling odors of bleach and soap powder. Emma Jean was taking a load of wash out of a dryer. When she saw him, he hoped it wasn't wishful thinking, that her face really *had* lit up like a sparkler on the fourth of July because she was so glad to see him.

She rubbed her cheeks with the back of her hand like she was afraid there might be dirty smudges. "Well, good morning, Luke. What brings you here?" She saw the basket. "Uh-oh. The washer died, right?"

"Afraid so. It's been on its last legs for a while now. Guess we're going to have to get a new one." He walked over to the row of machines and set the basket on the floor. "Would it be a bother for you to wash these for me? I can run by at lunch and take them home for Alma to hang on the line."

"Why not let me dry and fold them, too?"

"You sure you don't mind?"

"Mind? Well, it's not like I'm doing it for free, mister," she said with mock indignity. "You'll have to pay me a quarter."

"That'll be fine."

They melted into an awkward silence, eyes locked, neither knowing what to say and both not wanting the moment to end. Luke was being needled by the awareness that his attraction to her was not just because he wanted to go to bed with her, which he did. Being around her made him think of things kids did when they were in high school: smooching in the back row at the movies, sharing hot fudge sundaes and walks along the creek bank holding hands, having picnics up to Cheaha Mountain on a Sunday afternoon.

But he was no kid, and they were both married, so what the hell was he doing standing there trying not to get a hard-on because she was standing so close he could feel her heat? He told himself to grow up and murmured, "Well, thanks a lot. I'd better get along."

"Say, would you like some pop before you go? Bert let the Pepsi man put a machine in yesterday, but he's not done yet, and it isn't locked. He left some for me to have free till he comes back Monday."

"Free Pepsi? Can't turn that down." He followed after her, eyes riveted on her swinging hips. "How are things going? You like it here?"

"I sure do. The work isn't hard, and I enjoy being around folks." She made a face. "About the only place I ever get to go is church with Miss Bertha. She rolled her eyes and said, "Good grief, talk about a bunch of nuts."

He took the frosty bottle of soda she removed from the machine and popped the cap off in the opener above the coin slot. "Yeah, I've heard about it. Real Holy Rollers. Talking in tongues, stuff like that. I've also heard they handle snakes. One of these nights I'm going to sneak out there and find out. Have you ever seen them do it?"

"No, but I hear they only do it on Wednesday nights. Miss Bertha says I can't go then because only *born-agains* can go, that unsaved heathens like me aren't welcome. I plan to keep it that way as long as I can, even though she digs a bruise in my side with her elbow every time the preacher gives his altar call at the end of service. She doesn't like me, anyway, because I'm not from around here. She's always saying Rudy shouldn't have married a city girl. That's why we don't get along. She says I've got high-falootin' ways and think I'm better than anybody else. And she doesn't care that he beats me, either, except she didn't want him to go to jail. She said I deserve it. Only thing was, she wished he hadn't done it when I was pregnant and made me lose the baby. She wants a grandbaby real bad."

"Why, when she'd like to see you bust up?"

"Oh, she don't want that. She says what's done is done, and we have to stay together, no matter what. We've got to have babies because that's what a woman is supposed to do, have babies and keep her mouth shut so she won't make her husband beat her."

Luke drained the bottle and put it in the rack. "Well, like I've said before, it's none of my business, but I don't understand why you don't leave him."

"*Leave him?*" she hooted, putting her hands on her hips and staring up at him like he had lost his mind to suggest such a thing. "Why, if I leave him and don't work here anymore, who's going to fold your clothes and give you free pop? Think about that."

She gave him a good-natured cuff on his chin, and Luke fought the impulse to grab her hand and press it to his lips. What was wrong with him, damn it? He'd never in his life thought about kissing a girl's hand. "Yeah, you're right. Now I guess I better go so you can get back to work."

She looked beyond him to the window beyond. "Uh-oh. Here comes *plenty* of work."

Luke followed her gaze and saw Lucy Moon getting out of her car with a big basket.

"She called yesterday and said she'd be dropping off the slipcovers from the chairs in the parlor if they didn't have a *call*, as she put it—meaning a dead body—before today. She and Mr. Moon are going to Atlanta for the weekend to a funeral directors' convention."

Luke knew it was the chance he had been waiting for, and the wheels in his head started to spin.

"Sure you've got time to do my things?" he asked as she walked with him to the door.

"For you, I'll make time. You're my friend, Luke. Probably the only real one I've got in this town."

Lucy Moon had left one basket outside the door and gone back to get another from the car. Ordinarily, Luke would have done the gentlemanly thing and given her a hand, but instead he savored the last moments alone with Emma Jean.

"You've listened to me," she continued. "For the first time in so long I can't remember, I haven't felt like I was wrong all the time, that everything I do isn't stupid and everything I say isn't dumb, you know?"

He knew. Alma sometimes made him feel that way, too.

"You're my friend," she repeated solemnly.

Suddenly, he knew he had to get out of there before he did or said something he might later regret.

"Luke, you don't think I'm awful, do you? Rudy would kill me if he heard me talk like this. He'd say I'm acting like a strumpet, saying such things to a man."

"You could never act like a strumpet, and I could never think you're awful. What we say to each other is nobody's business, anyway. We're friends, remember?"

The smile he gave her came from a place in his heart he had thought was sealed forever.

That night, Luke entered the funeral home the same way Betsy and her family had, through the unlocked parlor window. He found nothing out of the ordinary in the office. Lucy did most of the paperwork, he'd heard, and things were neat and clean. Going through the files, he found the one he was looking for ... Henrietta Cochran. He scanned the bill for her funeral and saw the charge for the white pine coffin had been eight hundred dollars.

Deciding there was nothing else to be found there, he went down in the basement where Hardy did the embalming. The windows were painted black, so he turned on the lights.

It was like a chamber of horrors: the metal table with the trough running down each side to catch blood and send it on to the lidless toilet under the hole at the end for flushing to the sewer; the rubber hoses, still blood-stained at the ends from being attached to a cannula in the carotid artery; and the embalming pump, with its big glass jug filled with pink formaldehyde next to a tray with all kinds of instruments used for pickling a corpse.

Again, he found nothing out of the ordinary till he spotted a curtain in one corner that hid a door. It was locked, but he had brought a ring of skeleton keys. He took one look inside, then stumbled back a few steps, for within was the *real* chamber of horrors.

Emma Jean was so far over on her side she was almost falling off the sagging mattress. She did not want to touch Rudy when he came to bed, especially when she was feeling all warm inside, like her tummy was filled with hot, buttered biscuits. Thinking about Luke made her that way as she thought back to that morning and every word he had spoken and how he had looked at her like he could eat her.

She had been telling herself all day she had to be crazy. Luke was married, just like she was, and there was no need in starting something that could get both of them killed. Still, there was no harm in dreaming, was there? After all, it might help her through the bad times, till she could finish the correspondence course and get a job at the mill in the steno pool. She had learned to type before she quit school.

She was confident Rudy would let her do it, too, when he found out how much she would make, $1.50 an hour. He only made $1.80 on the line. Then, when she had some experience, she could find a job as a stenographer anywhere, maybe even as a private secretary. She could run away and make a new life. Till then, the only thing she could do was bide her time and try not to make him mad enough to hit her.

It was nearly two in the morning. The grill had closed at midnight. That was the law. No beer sold on Sundays in Buford County. Rudy hadn't come in yet, which meant he and some of his low-life friends had a bottle of whiskey and were riding the back roads drinking. They wouldn't come home till they ran out of whiskey or the sun rose, whichever came first.

She was starting to relax, daring to hope he would be out all night. Hugging the pillow, she pretended it was Luke. He wasn't so big and gruff as he made folks think. He could be gentle as rainwater. She just knew it. And he liked her. She could tell.

Headlights turning in the drive flashed across the bedroom windows. Emma Jean let go of the pillow and sat up. Brakes squealing. Laughter and loud talking punctuated with filthy language. A door opening and closing. An engine roaring. Tires squealing into the night. Rudy was home.

The kitchen door opened with a bang, and she heard him bump into the table, which was right in the middle of the floor like it always was. He hadn't remembered that because he was drunk.

She squeezed her eyes shut, pulled the sheet up over her head, and got very, very still. He gave the dangling overhead cord a yank, and the room was flooded with light. She could hear him taking off his clothes.

Please, God, let him be too drunk to do anything.

The covers were yanked off her.

Don't move, Emma Jean, she commanded herself, teeth ground tight together. *Maybe he'll think you're so dead to the world, he won't . . .*

"Hey. You ain't asleep, bitch."

She forced herself to do what he wanted, and dreams of Luke faded as she surrendered to the wretchedness of her life.

Chapter 13

Leaning back in his chair, Luke stared moodily through templed fingers. The door to his office was closed, which meant he was not to be disturbed except for an emergency. He could hear the phone ring now and then, the sounds of people coming and going. But he wanted no part of that world now, for he was lost in thoughts of another world, one that was not only disgusting but also illegal.

What he had seen in Hardy's closet four nights ago had turned his stomach, and not because of the gore. He could handle that. It was some of the items in Hardy's collection that repulsed. Collecting eyeglasses and false teeth was one thing, but it took a real sick person to harvest a fetus from a female corpse. Hell, if Hardy had gone that far, he shuddered to think what else he may have done to her. And, sweet Jesus, there had even been a penis and testicles among the glass jars filled with formaldehyde.

But, aside from Hardy and his macabre hobby, something else was crowding his mind . . . Emma Jean. When he had returned to the laundromat Saturday afternoon, his laundry was neatly folded and stacked in the basket, the ticket on top. Bert was there to collect the money, and Emma Jean was busy with a customer. So Luke had left without talking to her, figuring there was no need to give Bert ideas that something was going on between them. He had been wondering ever since if maybe there actually was. He kept telling himself they were just good friends, yet there was no getting around the reality that what he was starting to feel for her had nothing to do with being buddies.

She had not been at work Monday or Tuesday. He knew because he had driven by.

Forcing himself to stop thinking about her, he tried to concentrate on Hardy. He knew he had to have a good, solid case against him. The first step was to hide and watch what happened after old Minnie Plummer's funeral, scheduled for that afternoon. He heard that morning that Minnie's son, Virgil, had bought the most expensive coffin Hardy had because a sideline of Hardy's was selling burial insurance. Since he had sold Minnie a huge policy several years before, Virgil intended to use every penny of it. It was a perfect setup for another coffin switch, and, if it happened, Luke intended to get proof.

His stomach gave a rumble. He looked at his watch, almost twelve-thirty. He hit the intercom switch. "Wilma, I'm going to lunch. Do I need to return any calls?"

"No, I took care of everything," she said, "Except a call from Emma Jean Veazey. She wouldn't say what she wanted."

Luke felt a quickening in his gut. "What did she say?"

"Nothing. I told her you were busy, and she hung up."

He switched off the intercom and pulled on his heavy jacket. It was cold outside, the sky gray and overcast. He hoped it didn't start sleeting because he was going to be outdoors for no telling how long.

He went into the front office. "Did she sound upset?"

"Who?" Wilma blinked, confused. She had already forgotten what they had been talking about.

"Emma Jean Veazey."

"Oh." She thought a second. "No. It was like I said. Why?"

"I thought she might be calling about her old man beating her again."

"She didn't sound like anything was wrong, not that I could tell, anyway."

"Well, if it's important she'll call back. I'm going to the cafe."

Instead, he drove straight to the laundromat. Emma Jean was folding clothes. At the tinkling sound of the bell over the door, she glanced up, gave a shy smile of recognition, then nodded ever so slightly toward a woman sitting near a chugging machine to let him know she was not alone.

Luke nodded politely to Sadie Perkins, one of the biggest gossips in town.

Emma Jean raised her voice so Sadie wouldn't miss a word. "Sheriff, thanks for dropping by. I wanted you to check the new lock on the back door and see what you think. Bert's afraid now that we've got a drink machine somebody might break in to steal the money out of it."

"Sure. Lead the way."

When they got to the storage room where the back door opened to the alley, Luke started to inspect the lock, but Emma Jean quickly whispered, "That's not really why I called. I wanted to give you this." From her apron pocket she took a black sock. "This was left in the dryer Saturday." She was not about to admit she had purposely overlooked it so she would have an excuse to call him. Neither was she going to tell him how she had pressed it to her cheek too many times to count when nobody was looking.

He stuffed it in his pocket, thinking how she could have given it to him out front but pleased she hadn't. "I thought maybe you weren't working here anymore. I didn't see your car yesterday or the day before."

"I wasn't feeling good." It was not altogether a lie. Rudy had slapped her so many times Saturday night that she'd had a blinding headache and couldn't get out of bed.

Luke noticed her heavy makeup and couldn't remember her ever layering it on like that before. Then he noticed the dark place on her cheek, like a bruise. "Did he hit you again?"

She forced a shaky laugh. "Yeah, but it wasn't so bad."

He swore under his breath. "Maybe I'd better have a talk with him."

"No, don't, please," she was quick to protest. "It would just make things worse."

"They sure as hell aren't going to get any better, and you're a fool if you think they are."

"It'll be okay."

"No, it won't. You think it will, but it won't."

"I shouldn't have called you over here. I thought I had the bruise covered so's you wouldn't notice."

He put a finger under her chin and forced her to look at him. "What's the real reason you called? It wasn't the sock. That could have waited. And you say you didn't want me to see the bruise. So what *did* you want?"

"I guess I just wanted . . . *needed* . . . a friend. I don't have anybody to talk to in this town, and . . ."

He felt a heated rush and before he realized it, his hand was on the back of her neck, and he was drawing her face toward his.

"Emma Jean, I need change for the dryer."

At Sadie's annoyed screech from out front, they sprang apart.

"Coming," Emma Jean called. She smoothed back her hair, pulled at her apron, as though by so doing her emotions would be checked. But it didn't work, and she and Luke looked at each other as they pondered the meaning behind what had almost happened, and where it was all going to lead.

"Emma Jean!"

"Yes, ma'am."

Luke followed as she returned to the front.

"Thank you, sheriff," she said, hoping Sadie couldn't see how her heart was jumping around like a frog in her chest. "I'll tell Bert you said the lock was okay."

"Yeah. He doesn't have anything to worry about."

Luke wished he could say the same about himself because it struck like a thunderbolt that he couldn't remember ever in his whole life wanting to kiss anyone so bad.

Calling in to Wilma that he would be out of service for a few hours, he drove past the cemetery and parked in a grove of pecan trees. It had started sleeting, and he didn't relish a mile walk, but he was not about to chance his car being spotted.

He pulled his jacket collar around his neck as high as it would go and jammed his hat down on his head. Then he entered the woods bordering the cemetery, skirting the edge till he spotted the familiar green and white Taylor-Moon tent that marked Minnie's grave.

He positioned himself behind a clump of evergreen bushes where he could hide and still peek out and see what was going on. The dirt from the grave had been neatly covered by a green carpet. Ozzie and Hank were nowhere around.

In the frosty mist, it looked like every setting he'd ever seen in a scary movie. He wouldn't have been surprised to see a ghost crawl out of a grave or a ghoul step from behind a headstone. He was getting stiff from the cold when he finally heard cars approaching. Slowly the hearse came into sight, followed by Hardy's black Cadillac, which he used to transport the family.

But not for me, Luke recalled with a bitter taste in his mouth. *I wouldn't ride in your shitty car to my mother's funeral, Hardy. I drove my own and didn't give a damn if folks wondered why.*

There was another car carrying pallbearers and only a few more after that because the bad weather was obviously causing some people to skip the graveside service.

The family stayed in the Cadillac while Hardy guided the pallbearers to slide the coffin with its floral blanket from the hearse and position it on the grave rollers. Then the Methodist preacher, Paul Whitsett, took his place at the head of the casket, and Hardy ushered Minnie's family to the folding chairs lined up under the tent. Luke noticed Ozzie easing his truck to the curb. Hank was sitting next to him.

The service didn't take long. Paul said a few words and a prayer, then shook hands with those under the tent and left. The others wasted no time leaving, either, for the wind had picked up, and the sleet had changed back to rain and was coming down harder.

When the last car was out of sight, Ozzie and Hank leaped out of the truck and ran to join Hardy under the tent. Over the roar of the wind and the pounding of the rain, Luke could not hear what was being said, but he didn't need to. What he could *see* was more than enough.

After Hardy removed the blanket of carnations, Ozzie and Hank lifted the coffin off the rollers and placed it on the ground. Hardy then lifted the lid to reveal Minnie dressed in a blue gown. Ozzie grasped her shoulders, and Hank took her feet. Hardy supported her torso, which wasn't necessary, because the embalming fluid had left her stiff as a board. Quickly, they hoisted her from the coffin and dumped her in the grave.

Ozzie and Hank then took the empty coffin and practically ran with it to the hearse, shoved it inside, and slammed the doors. No doubt they had not had time to do that with Henrietta Cochran's; instead they were forced to stow it in the shed, anticipating Jubal would be sneaking back up the road and might see them.

While they were moving the coffin, Hardy was busy putting some of the flowers in the back seat of the Cadillac, no doubt planning to have Lucy dismantle the arrangements and return the flowers to the refrigerator in case there was an opportunity to reuse them for the next funeral. With the coffin stashed, Ozzie and Hank got busy covering poor Minnie in her raw grave.

Luke knew, at last, that he had Hardy dead to rights. He could arrest him and send him away for a long, long time. But jail was too good for him because what Luke had in mind was much worse.

Luke went home to change out of his wet clothes and was cleaning out his pants pockets when he found the sock Emma Jean had given him. Again he wondered if she had really overlooked it or kept it to have an excuse to call him. She sure hadn't pulled away when he'd been about to kiss her, so maybe she was feeling for him what he was feeling for her, which could lead to trouble. But while that thought didn't scare him, he wanted to make sure it wasn't all one-sided and make a fool of himself.

After a hot shower, he put on a fresh uniform, then drove to Creech's station where there was a phone booth just outside. A married man using a pay phone around town was said to be a dead-giveaway he was calling his girlfriend, but Luke wasn't thinking about that just then.

He dialed the laundromat, counted six rings, and looked at his watch. It was half past four. He wasn't sure what time the place closed, but he guessed not before five or six.

At last she answered, out of breath. "Bert's Laundromat."

"It's me—Luke. Can you talk?"

"Yes. We aren't real busy right now. Just a few people using the dryers, because it's too bad outside to dry on the line."

He could hear the soft whooshing sound of the big machines and faint conversation in the background.

"I have to ask you something." He sucked in his breath, mustering his nerve. God, he hadn't batted an eye at plunging into hand-to-hand combat with the Vietcong, but now his knees were like jelly. It wasn't too late. He could still turn around, just hang up the phone and put her out of his mind.

Yeah, right.

"Okay," she said softly.

"It's about what almost happened between us this afternoon."

"Uh-huh."

He could just picture her, pressing into the corner next to the storage room, her hand cupped about the phone's mouthpiece to make sure no one would overhear.

He plunged ahead. "If what almost happened *had* happened, would you be sorry?" *God, he felt like a teenager with his first crush.*

"I don't think so. What about you?"

He started to relax and laughed softly, "I was the instigator, remember?"

She laughed, too. "I remember all right."

"Well, I'm going to stick my neck out and say that ever since that night on your back porch I've thought about you a lot, but I don't want to make things worse for you than they already are."

"You might not understand, but having you for my friend makes it all better."

He understood, all right, because having her made things better for him, too, like when Alma was screaming at him. He would think about Emma Jean, and it made the misery easier to bear. "I know," he said finally, "but it could get a little complicated."

"What do you mean?"

"I want us to be more than friends."

There was silence, and just as Luke started to worry she had hung up, he heard her voice, as soft and wispy as a feather in the air.

"I want that, too. I honestly do. Only we have to be real careful."

"We will be." He felt like singing.

CHAPTER 14

Luke had to attend a meeting for law enforcement officers in Mobile for a few days. It was Saturday when he got home, and Alma came running out the back door the second he turned in the drive. She was wearing jeans rolled up above her knees and one of his old flannel shirts. Her hair was tucked into a red bandanna, and she was still holding the wet mop she'd been using on the kitchen floor.

She waited till he got to the bottom step before shrieking like a crow chased from a corn field. "So you finally sobered up to remember where you live, eh? Well, it's about time, damn you."

"Cut it out, Alma," he yelled, throwing up his hands against the spray of dirty water from the mop she was shaking at him.

"I called the sheriff's office in Mobile and found out the meetings were over yesterday. So where the hell have you been since then?"

He could have told her the truth, that he had spent the night with Jim Burkhalter, an army buddy from Nam, and how he'd had a real fine time with Jim's wife and kids. He might also have shared how they grilled hot dogs and watched Jim's slides and talked about the old days and even described Jim's nice house on the water and how he was now a lawyer with his daddy's firm, proving that life does go on after wars and people do get married and live happily ever after. Only Alma wouldn't have believed him, and she wouldn't have cared, anyway, so he didn't say anything except that he was tired from the drive and wanted to take a nap before checking in at the office.

He started by her, and that was when she raised the mop, intending to whack him on the side of his head, but he saw in time and snatched it away to send it flying across the yard to land with a thud against the wood shed. She spat the words like a cat hissing at a dog. "Damn you, Luke. You ain't worth shit." He went on in the kitchen. Tammy glared at him from where she was beating what looked like cake batter in a big bowl.

"Sorry, baby," he murmured, not exactly sure what it was that he was sorry for unless if was having had anything to do with her being born to parents who couldn't stand each other.

"Why do you have to upset her all the time?" Tammy's voice was as cold as her eyes.

"I didn't do anything but come home, sweetheart. Did you hear me say one word to her out there before she started in on me?"

"You were supposed to be back yesterday."

"I told your mother it would be yesterday or today. I didn't say for sure." Jesus, he was getting it from both of them now. Forget the nap. He could doze in his chair at the office. There would be no peace here.

He turned on his heel and bumped into Alma, who was right behind him.

"*Now* where do you think you're going?"

"To work."

"It's Saturday."

"I don't care. I'd rather be anywhere than here when you're acting like this."

"You can spend some time with your family for a change."

"You mean spend time listening to you nag."

Tammy threw the bowl into the sink. "I am so sick of this," she cried, bursting into tears. "All you two do is fight. I can't stand it . . ."

She ran out, and a few seconds later the front door slammed.

Alma smirked. "Well, I hope you're happy. You ran your daughter out of her own house."

Reminding himself that trying to reason with Alma was useless as teats on a boar hog, Luke stepped around her and bolted down the steps.

She chased after him. "Don't you forget you're supposed to go to the pancake supper at church tonight."

"I have work to do." He got in the car.

"You said you'd go."

He probably had in a weak moment. Anything to get her off his back. "Maybe next time."

"Maybe never. You don't care, Luke. Not about me. Not about Tammy. All you think about is yourself. What I can't figure out is why you came back here, anyhow. I'd hoped you'd settle down and care about your family and the respectable position you've got in the community. But no. All you care about is . . ."

Her last words melted in the sound of squealing tires as he escaped.

Such times made him wish he had never come back, despite his promise to his mother. Avenging the misery of her life was robbing him of his own, which he needed to get on with before it was too late. So he had to start concentrating on what he had to do and not let anything get in his way—like Emma Jean. Just thinking about her soothed like a shot of bourbon as he realized he was doing fifty in a twenty zone and quickly slowed.

What was the harm, he argued with himself, in both of them taking a little pleasure in each other to escape the way things were at home? She was smart enough to know that's all it would be—a diversion. Nothing serious.

As he stopped for a red light before turning the corner to the courthouse, he saw Matt and Kirby standing on the sidewalk. He could see they were excited about something from the way they were laughing and waving their hands as they talked. They were good guys, and they had made damn good deputies. Even the rednecks, the ones always getting arrested for being drunk, speeding, brawling, whatever, treated them with respect, and, so far, there had been no complaints. Sure, they ran around on their wives. It was, Luke supposed, part of that southern male culture, the country side of it, anyway, that adhered to the notion that a man wasn't a real man if only one woman could satisfy him.

"It's like eating Moon Pies," a beer-bellied redneck had once remarked to him. "They're sweet and good and you enjoy 'em, but you don't want 'em all the time. Every once in a while, you need a Twinkie or a bag of pork skins just for a change."

If Luke had never left the backwoods of the south, he might have had the same kind of weak mind-set, but he had learned sex could be real good and satisfying with one woman when things were in sync, like with himself and Coquina.

He'd had no reason to try a Twinkie.

He'd been happy with his Moon Pie.

The only wrinkle was knowing he could never love her, that all they'd ever have was a lot of different ways of doing it, like with strawberry body paint, whipped cream, and chocolate-flavored condoms. He supposed it was like eating for taste and to hell with nutrition.

Still, he could remember long nights in Nam, laying in a muddy ditch in the warm, steaming rain and staring up at the sky and wondering if he would ever find his place in life, his reason for being. And to take himself away from the misery of the moment, he would think about what it might be like to be married to a woman who loved him as much as he loved her and how great the sex would be because of their love. They'd have kids, a home, a life. He would find out what it was like to live normal. Silly, soppy dreams he'd never share with anybody but there just the same.

The light changed.

One day, he promised himself as he made the turn. One day and, *someday*, things would be different.

As soon as he stepped out of the car, Matt and Kirby were on him like yellow jackets after spilled soda.

Matt was grinning from ear to ear. "Wait till you hear. Oh, man, just wait till you hear."

Kirby was actually bouncing up and down on the balls of his feet in his eagerness to convey the news, "Junior Kearney's been laughed out of town."

Luke played dumb. "What are you talking about?"

They proceeded to take turns telling him how the night before—Friday—Junior had gathered some of his buddies out back in the closed-up-for-the-winter fruit stand to watch him and his girlfriend, Reba Lou, have sex, and it had turned into a circus. Junior couldn't keep an erection, and, after a while, everybody felt so embarrassed for him they got up and left. But one of the last to go said Junior, had finally given up and curled up in a ball right there on the floor and started crying, and Reba Lou was yelling she was leaving town because she could never face people again.

Kirby said, "I drove out there this morning to see if he'd just totally lost his mind and needed to be locked up, but there was no sign of him."

Matt reported, "Tommy Creech said when he opened the station Reba Lou was there waiting for the early bus. Maybe Junior's gone for good, too."

"I doubt we'll be that lucky." Luke figured Junior would go off a few days to sulk, then realize he had no choice except to return and face the humiliation he would never be able to live down.

As they walked on toward the office, Kirby added, "They say the only thing Junior said was that he wanted to prove he could outdo coloreds, so it must have had something to do with his making those kids do it the other night."

"Probably." Luke said absently, like he didn't care.

"But can you imagine pulling a stunt like that? He'll be a laughingstock for years to come."

"Yeah. Just imagine"

On to number two, Momma.

The day was brisk and cold with storm clouds hovering, but bad weather would not deter the golf nuts headed to the course at Lake Martin for the afternoon, including Hardy Moon.

Luke parked in front of the post office, just down the street from the funeral home and waited. He knew Hardy would be playing with Burch and Buddy. A real threesome they were. Golf together on Wednesday and Saturday afternoons. Breakfast every morning at the Bulldog. Once upon a time they had gotten together, gang-banged a young girl, and ruined her life. Real pals they were, shared everything, and if Luke had anything to do with it, they were going to share a living hell, as well, and *he* was going to be the one to jab them on their way with a pitchfork, one at a time.

When Hardy finally left, Luke continued on and pulled into the drive. No other cars were around, the hearse was backed into the shed at the rear, and he hadn't heard of anybody dying lately so it was a good time to talk to Lucy.

He stepped up on the porch as a rude burst of wind sent leaves dancing around his feet. Rockers where mourners passed time during the summer were turned about and neatly propped against the wall like kneeling soldiers. A conservative wreath with a white bow, the only hint of Christmas, hung primly on the door. He rang the bell and could hear the mournful sound echoing through the big, rambling house.

After a few moments, Lucy opened the door. "Oh, don't tell me we're about to have some more business. I hate it when someone passes away close to the holidays."

"Miss Lucy, you know I would've called if that were the case. I'm here to see you about something else."

"Well, come on in. It's nippy out here." She cast a wary eye skyward. "Maybe we'll have a white Christmas. You ever seen one, Luke?"

"No, but if one comes, those sleds down at the hardware store covered with years of dust will sell like hotcakes." He followed her as she led the way down the dimly lit hall and wondered, not for the first time, why she didn't sit some of those bottles around with the wet, green, slimy things sticking out of the neck—air wicks, they were called—to try and tone down the smell of the place.

She took him into the office he had rummaged a week earlier.

"I was just having a cup of tea. Would you like some?"

"No, thanks. I'm not much of a tea drinker, I'm afraid." He sat down in one of the velvet-upholstered chairs that had seen better days. Jesus stared down at him complacently from a calendar advertising a casket company in Baltimore. Gray light filtered through the frosted glass of the one and only window.

It was a depressing room in a depressing place, and as he scrutinized Lucy to see if she appeared at all nervous, he thought how she fit right into the scene like a piece in a jigsaw puzzle. Her salt and pepper hair was pulled back in a severe bun at the nape of her neck, giving her face the look of a peeled onion. She had clear blue eyes behind round spectacles that forever slipped up and down on her pointed nose. Her lips were perpetually turned down at the corners like an inverted "U," but Luke supposed if he had to live with Hardy Moon, he'd look pissed all the time, too.

He wondered if she had ever owned more than two dresses in her life because, in all the times he'd seen her through the years, she was wearing either a brown or wine color with a high peter pan collar trimmed in white lace, the sleeves tapered to the wrist, and a straight waistline with the skirt hanging just to the tops of her black leather, high-top, pointed-toe shoes. Her jewelry was always the same, amethyst earbobs edged in silver and a tiny pin that was actually a watch hanging upside down she could tell the time without turning it around.

Lucy's brow furrowed with concern. "Luke, is something wrong?"

He leaned back and folded his arms across his chest. "You know there is, Miss Lucy. Suppose you tell me about your part in it."

She avoided making eye contact, which, to Luke, being a lawman, signified discomfort that most of the time translated to guilt.

She licked her lips nervously. "I'm afraid I don't know what you mean."

"I believe you do. Now if you feel uncomfortable talking about it, I can go ahead and order the funeral home books audited. At the same time, I can do an inventory of the stock."

She had been lifting her tea cup but suddenly set it back down with a loud and nervous clatter against the saucer. "Why on earth would you want to do all that?"

"To prove that more coffins have been sold than bought. Then there's the matter of flowers being stolen off graves to use at the next funeral. But that's small potatoes compared to snatching coffins, wouldn't you say?" He watched her as he spoke and saw how her mouth changed from the upside down "U" to a thin line, the edges of her teeth pressing against her lip as her jaws began to twitch.

"I'm afraid . . ." she paused, then unleashed the plea like air from a leaking tire, ". . . that you will have to talk to my husband. It's not my place . . ."

"Your place isn't in jail either, Miss Lucy, but I'm afraid that's where you're headed if you don't cooperate with me on this. You see . . ." he uncrossed his legs, pressing his knees against the desk as he spread his hands on the top, "last week I saw

Hardy, Ozzie, and Hank take Minnie Plummer out of her coffin and dump her in her grave, then put the coffin back in the hearse."

Lucy drew back into her chair as though sucked by a giant vacuum cleaner. Her first attempt at speech failed, lost among the knots jumping in her throat like a child's game of ball and jacks. Then, finally, she was able to croak, "That . . . that's not true."

Luke sighed, disappointed she was not breaking as fast as he'd hoped. Lucy was a mouse, otherwise she would never have put up with Hardy's shenanigans. "If you don't want to cooperate then you leave me no choice but to place you under arrest."

"But if I tell you, then you *will* arrest me . . ." Her hands flew to her mouth. "Oh, God," she whispered through her fingers, horrified to realize she had just as good as confessed.

He shook his head. "Not if you help me on this because I know you could never condone what your husband did."

"Oh, heavens no, Luke. Heavens no. I hated it."

"I don't imagine Hank and Ozzie liked it much either."

"Oh, they didn't. Ozzie was all the time talking to me about it, worried that sooner or later somebody was going to find out. He even told Hardy he didn't like being involved, but Hardy said if he and Hank didn't go along with it, he'd fire them and swear it was because he caught them stealing jewelry off the bodies."

"Well, I'm not going to mention this to them. Hardy is the one who has to be punished."

"Will he go to prison?"

He smiled. "Oh, I've got something else in mind that he'll find a lot worse."

"I don't understand."

"He's going to stay right here under your thumb and toe the line, while you see he operates this place like it should be. He's also going to get rid of that weird collection of horrors he's got stashed in the basement."

She turned even paler. "You know about that, too?"

"Oh, yes."

"Look, I want you to understand that I've not had a say about anything that goes on around here since my father died."

"Well, that's all going to change now."

She gave a nervous little laugh. "You don't know my husband very well, do you? He doesn't take orders from anyone, especially me."

"When I get through with him, he'll sit up and beg for dog biscuits if you tell him to. You're going to run things around here, Miss Lucy. After all, your family started this business, so it's fair you should have a say.

"Only from now on," he added with a wink, "You're going to be the one doing *all* the talking."

Doubt was melting from her eyes like frost in sunshine, her acquiescing nod firm and positive. "Luke, I swear to you I've never approved of the way he's done things. Sometimes I think that's why he married me, anyway, so he could take over."

Luke did not pick up on that. Hell, she didn't *think* it, she *knew* it. But why twist the knife?

She started to lift the tea cup, but her hands were shaking too hard. "I want you to know I did argue with Hardy about it. But he said it didn't matter whether the body was in a coffin or not, that sooner or later it was going to decay, anyway. I was always glad when the family bought a vault because it had to be in the ground before the funeral, so that meant the body was at least buried inside that and not just put down in the raw earth."

Hesitantly, she continued, "I know the bodies will have to be dug up and reburied proper in coffins. I'll be glad to pay the cost, and . . ."

"No, that would only cause the families more grief to find out about it, and there'd be no way we could keep him out of jail once they did. There would also be lawsuits that would send you into bankruptcy."

"I'm so sorry, Luke. So very, very sorry. I know you think I'm a coward, a weakling, but you don't have to live with Hardy. He can be real mean when he wants to be."

And mean men rape helpless women, Luke thought with a flash of anger.

"I'm ready to make atonement for my sin of neglect," she said with finality. "Just tell me how I can help."

In the privacy of his office, Luke dialed the laundromat. Emma Jean answered on the first ring, and he wondered if she had been waiting for him to call since he hadn't been around for several days. Not bothering with preliminaries, he asked if she could talk.

"Yes. But just for a minute. Bert took the trash out. He'll be back any second."

"Can you see him?"

"Yes. Through the window. He just got to the barrels."

"I wanted to see how you're doing." *I wanted to hear your voice.*

"I'm fine. But where have you been?"

"I had a meeting out of town, and I've got to leave again to take care of some business and probably won't be back till late tomorrow. What shift is Rudy working next week?"

"Graveyard, eleven to seven."

"Can you meet me someplace Monday night?"

"I don't dare. He checks my mileage."

"I can run it back."

"I don't know. I'm scared. I mean, what if somebody sees me out that time of night? It might get back to Rudy."

"You're probably right."

There was silence as they pondered the situation, then Emma Jean suggested, "Could you come by? You know, pull around back after midnight? We could sit on the porch and talk like we did before."

"Sure, but I think it's only fair to warn you I've got something on my mind besides sipping KoolAid."

Suddenly, she hung up, and he was left to wonder whether someone had walked up on her or if what he had said had scared her off. Maybe, when it came right down to it, she was afraid to fool around. And he couldn't blame her if she were. He just wished she hadn't led him to believe otherwise because, not only did he feel like a fool, he also realized just how much he had been looking forward to being with her. But there was no time to dwell on it now. It was payback time for Hardy Moon, and there was work to be done.

Chapter 15

Luke could tell Lucy was nervous by the way she glanced all around to see if anyone was watching as she crossed the street to where he was parked.

"Don't look so scared," he said when she stood next to the open window on his side of the car. "We've been speaking to each other for years. No one will think anything about it."

"We've never talked about anything like this." She shuddered. "I feel so awful. I want it over with, Luke."

"After tonight, it will be. Are there any bodies at the funeral home now?"

"No. It's been real quiet, praise the Lord."

"Let's hope it stays that way. Now, like I told you on the phone, I want you to go to bed early and ignore anything you might hear later tonight. Understand?"

"I wish you'd tell me what you plan to do."

"It's best you don't know. Just do as I say, and everything will be fine."

As she walked away, Luke wondered if it were his imagination or if she actually had a little spring to her step. Maybe she was thinking how decency was about to be restored to her family heritage. It was Tuesday afternoon, and he had just come back to town. He knew he was going to catch holy hell from Alma so he was in no hurry to go home.

He stopped by the office. Kirby had left for the day, but Matt was still there and asked about the deep-sea fishing trip. That was the story Luke had made up for leaving so sudden, how his friend in Mobile had called to say he'd had a last minute cancellation on a planned outing and, if Luke could get down there fast, he could take the guy's place. Luke didn't care whether anybody believed it or not. He had to go, had to get everything ready to *bring the hammer down.*

"Didn't catch a thing," Luke said. "So were things quiet while I was away?" He began to shuffle through the mail: wanted posters, law enforcement journals.

"Afraid not. Rudy Veazey and Buck Haynie got drunk and had a fight at the grill, and Rudy laid Buck's head wide-open with a tire iron."

"Did you lock him up?" Luke was quick to ask. He shuddered to think of Rudy going home to Emma Jean till he sobered up.

"Yeah, but I had to let him go the next morning because Buck didn't press charges. You know how these rednecks are. They like to settle things their way. Maybe they'll wind up killing each other."

"We'll never be that lucky."

"That wife of Rudy's was sure scared. She was shaking like a dog caught pissin' on the rug. She calmed down, though, when she saw I was gonna lock him up. Guess she was afraid he'd continue the fight with her."

Matt was heading for the door. Luke pretended to be focused on the mail as he casually asked, "Do you know where they'd been?"

"Probably the VFW dance in Talladega."

"That's a breeding ground for trouble. A lot of affairs get started there, husbands dancing with other men's wives, flirting and making plans to meet on some back road."

Matt laughed. "What do you care? You don't ever go there."

"And I don't plan to, either," Luke retorted gruffly.

"So what are you so fired up about?"

"I'm not. It doesn't matter."

But Luke knew it *did* matter, a lot, only he wasn't going to let Matt know that. Neither was he going to confide how it burned his guts to think that blasted dance was what got Rudy stirred up to beat Emma Jean so bad she'd lost her baby. That had been a blessing in disguise because she had no business having a baby by that jerk. Hell, she didn't have any business being married to him at all. Just like he didn't have any business being married to Alma, except for Tammy, who would grow up and leave home, and then what was he going to have? Not a damn thing.

So he needed to hurry up and do what he had come back to do and get the hell out of Hampton, Alabama, once and for all before he wound up in bed with Emma Jean Veazey and then had to kill Rudy if he ever found out about it.

"Luke, are you okay?"

Luke shook his head to clear it from the demons tormenting. "Yeah, I'm fine. Take off."

Luke waited till Ned arrived, then decided to go home and face Alma and get it over with. He had a few hours to kill, anyway, because he didn't want to go to the funeral home till late.

With his hands gripping the steering wheel, he told himself not to drive by the laundromat but, at the last minute, yielded to temptation.

She was coming out the back door, and he slowed at the sight of her. There were no other cars around, no customers. The "closed" sign hung at a front window.

She saw him and froze.

Their gazes locked in question.

Time seemed to stand still, then she motioned he should follow her. She got in her car, drove to the corner, and turned in the opposite direction of the way she usually went to go home.

He stayed a discreet distance behind till she got out of town and turned off on a little used road. He then hit the switch to send the blue light on the top of the patrol car swirling.

Obediently, Emma Jean eased onto the shoulder of the road. He pulled in behind her and got out, trying to look very official should anybody pass by. It was taking a chance. If Rudy heard she'd been pulled over, he'd wonder what she was doing at this end of the county. But right then Luke didn't care because all he was thinking of was how they were going to have a minute alone together.

By the time he got to her car, she had rolled down her window and was waiting to tease, "Oh, officer, I didn't realize how fast I was going. You aren't going to give me a ticket, are you?" She batted her eyelashes at him and giggled.

Luke played along and pulled his ticket pad out of his hip pocket. "I'm afraid I might have to, miss, unless you'd like to pay it off now."

"Pay it off?"

"Yeah. You can do it here instead of at the magistrate's office. What do you say?"

"Well, it depends. What's it going to cost me?"

"This."

He leaned down and touched his mouth to hers, parting her lips with his tongue to plunge deep. She responded with a fervent hunger of her own, reaching out to clutch his shoulders and pull him closer.

Finally, breathlessly, he pulled away to swear, "Damn, you tear me up, woman."

"That's what I want to do," she admitted with candor, "and I don't care how wrong it is, Luke. The way I see it, I've got a right to a little happiness."

He saw the glimmer of tears in her eyes and knew she had

not acted out of mere impulse. Like him, she'd given it a lot of thought. "Then why did you hang up on me the other day?"

"Bert came back inside. I got to listening to you and wasn't watching, and if I'd said another word, he'd have heard me."

"I thought maybe it was because of what I said."

She blinked, not remembering.

"About wanting to do something besides drink KoolAid."

Her soft, warm laugh was like a caress. "I don't have a problem with that, sheriff. I don't have a problem at all."

Glancing up and down the road to make sure no cars were coming, he opened her door. "Only God knows how bad I want you, girl." He began to move his lips over her face, her neck, licking the salty sweetness of her. She smelled of lint and dry cleaning fluid and soap and water softener, and he gloried in it.

"And I want you, Luke, like I've never wanted a man before in my whole life. Tell me it's not wrong," she begged. "I mean, I know we're both married, but I can't help feeling like I do about you. You've been such a friend . . ."

"I always will be."

"Rudy goes to work at eleven tonight. Can you come by?"

"Yeah, but it might be real late." He took out his handkerchief and rubbed her lipstick off his mouth. He'd have to throw it away.

Emma Jean knew what he was thinking and took it from him. "I'll wash it at work tomorrow."

He snatched it back. "No, you won't. Rudy might find it and see it's not his." He kissed her one last time. "I'll see you later on tonight. Keep an eye out for me because I'll kill my lights as soon as I turn off the road."

She watched in the mirror as he returned to his car, loving the way his uniform pants cupped his rear end. He probably had the cutest butt she'd ever seen on a man. She pressed her fingertips to her lips. He could kiss good, too.

And she knew from eleven o'clock on, she'd be perched in a window like an owl in a tree, waiting for him to show up. She just hoped nothing happened to keep him away, or that he wouldn't change his mind. But he'd be there. Luke Ballard was a *cockhound*. That's what Wanda Potts had told her the day she brought her waitress uniforms in to wash, and Emma Jean had managed to bring up Luke's name without looking obvious because she wanted to know if he messed around any at the grill.

"He's good looking, all right," Wanda had said dreamily, a cigarette hanging from the corner of her mouth. "I've had my eye on him for a long time, but I guess he don't want to jump another man's claim."

Emma Jean had given her a bewildered look.

Wanda had laughed, "Oh, don't look so shocked, honey. It's no secret me and Matt Rumsey have had a thing going for years."

"That long?"

"Yeah. Sure." Wanda had exhaled and sucked the smoke back up her nostrils, French inhaling, it was called. "It works out good for both of us," she had continued. "We both got kids, and besides, the way I see it, if you divorce one man to marry another, you're just exchanging one set of problems for another. So why bother? We see each other now and then and have us a time, and it makes the bad times with my old man easier knowing somebody out there gives a damn about me, you know?"

"But if Matt cares about you like you say, how come you want to go off with the sheriff?"

Wanda had rolled her eyes and giggled. "What girl in her right mind wouldn't? Damn, Emma Jean, take a good look at him sometimes. He's so, so . . . I don't know." She had caressed herself, running her fingertips up and down her arms as she mulled the question. "Rough, I guess you'd call it. You know, like he could make love so strong it hurt, but you'd love every minute of it, 'cause he'd be so good at it."

A dryer buzzer had sounded, and Emma Jean had emptied it and piled the clothes on the table for folding. Wanda had sauntered over to a chair and sat down and begun to leaf through an old magazine. No one else was around so Emma Jean had dared ask, "Do you know anybody he's been with?"

"Sure he has. He's a cockhound."

Emma Jean had repeated the unfamiliar word.

Wanda had laughed. "Don't you get it? Cock, like a slang word for sex, and hound, like in bloodhound, always sniffing around looking for something.

"But," she had gone on to say after taking one last draw on her cigarette and grinding it under her heel, "I think he's gotten choosy, 'cause I haven't heard of him messing around with anybody in a long time. Now that's not to say he don't still do it. He might just be extra careful these days."

Maybe, Emma Jean mused as she watched his car disappear around a curve. But if things worked out like she hoped, he wouldn't be messing around with anybody but her, by golly.

It was after midnight, and Luke had been hiding inside Milburn Smith's azalea bushes watching the funeral home for the past two hours. The lights had gone out at ten-thirty, but he wasn't taking any chances on moving too fast. He wanted Hardy to fall sound asleep.

Luke did not like the feeling that he was spying on other people, like Milburn's 14-year old daughter, Sharon. Girl Scout, honor roll, a member of the Youth choir at First Baptist, she seemed like a little Pollyanna. But after what he'd just heard going on in the gazebo between her and Wiley Lansky, the preacher's son, *Lolita* had nothing on Sharon.

Then there was Murline Pruitt, the Smiths' next door neighbor. She always rode to her Monday night bowling league with the town pharmacist, Dennis Blum, because he only lived a few doors down the street and picked her up, but from the way they were necking before Murline got out of the car, it was obvious they shared a whole lot more than a ride together.

At last, he felt the time was right and darted across the street, keeping to the shadows. He found the same window unlocked and slipped inside. Carefully making his way in the darkness from memory, he proceeded to the casket display room. Only after closing the door behind him did he switch on his flashlight.

Down in Mobile, Jim Burkhalter had introduced him to an undertaker who had told him what to look for—a steel coffin with a short metal tube protruding from each corner. Spotting one just inside the door, he opened both the top and bottom lids. From the small satchel he'd brought with him, he took the confession Jim had typed and a pen for signing, but, perhaps most important of all, was the Dictaphone Jim had loaned him. Quickly, he set it up.

Stepping back into the hallway, he shone the light around till it fell on a fern stand with a rather ugly vase on top. He gave it a light shove and the vase toppled to the floor and broke with a loud clatter.

From above came the sound of feet hitting the floor, followed by Hardy's sleepy growl, "What the hell? I'll bet you forgot to put the damn cat out again. So help me, Lucy, this time I'm going to kick him so far he won't be able to find his way back."

Luke switched off his flashlight and got in position beneath the stairs. Hardy turned on the lights and came clomping down, muttering to himself all the way. As he reached the bottom, Luke's hand snaked out to close about his neck. From his Green Beret days, Luke knew exactly how hard and how long to press on the carotid artery to cut off oxygen to the brain to render a man first immobile, then unconscious, without causing brain damage . . . or death.

Hardy went limp. Luke slipped his hands under his armpits and dragged him into the display room. He was heavy, but with a great heave, Luke was able to get him up and into the coffin without turning it over. Staring down at Hardy's face, Luke resisted the impulse to hit him. No matter that the snotty little creep could be his daddy. He slammed the lid down. Through the .18 gauge steel, Luke thought he heard Hardy moan softly. It was almost time for him to wake up.

Then there was no doubt. Hardy *did* moan. Loud. And when he realized he was lying flat on his back in a dark, close place, and it began to dawn exactly what that dark, close place was, he started shouting, "Hey, what the hell is going on? This isn't funny. Let me out, damn it . . ."

Luke took the crank from his pocket that Jim's undertaker friend had given him and fitted it into the metal tube on the corner closest to him and began to turn. The undertaker had given him a demonstration of what would happen, how turning the crank would send the two horizontal metal rods beneath the rubber gasket on the front side of the coffin to meet each other. When they were in place, a vertical rod would automatically move down from the lid to lock between.

The sound was ominous.

Kah-lank. Kah-lank. Kah-lank.

Hardy fell silent and went stiff with terror.

Kah-lank. Kah-lank. Kah-lank.

Hardy knew what it meant, he was in a *sealer*, and comprehending this, his cries were swallowed by hysterical gasps. Had he been placed in any other coffin but a sealer, he knew he could have lasted maybe twenty-four hours or longer with air seeping in around the seams, but with each turn of the crank, each maddening *kah-lank,* death loomed ever closer. "Why are you doing this to me? Who are you? Please . . . let me out . . ."

Luke stopped cranking and plugged in the Dictaphone, then placed it on top of the coffin right over Hardy's head. Hardy's confession might not be audible, having to come through the steel and all, but he had to try. Besides, Hardy wouldn't know if it wasn't because the tape would be locked in a safe deposit box, and only Luke would have the key.

"Please, don't do this . . ." Hardy was sobbing now, punctuating each agonized word with a futile pound of his fists against the lid. "I'll give you whatever you want. Please, I can't breathe . . ."

"Stop screaming and save what air you've got."

Hardy fell silent as he tried to place the familiar voice amidst the panic that held him in a smothering cocoon.

"Just what are you willing to do to get out of there, Hardy?"

The voice, so familiar. But who—?

"Answer me, Hardy. You don't have much time, and you know it."

It couldn't be, *or could it?* "Luke Ballard?" he asked with a flare of hope. "Is that you? Let me out. Quick. Somebody played a terrible trick on me, and . . ."

"It's no trick, Hardy. I put you in there."

Rage overcame fear. "Luke? Come on. Open up. This isn't funny, damn you."

"Neither is robbing corpses of their coffins."

Hardy felt his guts wrench. "I don't know what you're talking about."

"Oh, yes, you do, and you're going to tell me all about it."

"The only thing I'm going to tell you is that if you don't get me out of here, I'll have your badge. You can count on it."

"But *you* can't count on *anything,* Hardy, because according to what I've been told about this kind of coffin, you've only got maybe another twenty-five minutes or so of air left, depending on how panicked you are. And from what I'm hearing, you're *real* panicked, Hardy, and you might not even have that much left. So I suggest you cut your bullshit and admit what you've been doing."

Hardy's mind started whirling. Somehow Luke had found out about the body dumping, but he was bluffing about letting him die. He was just trying to scare him, that's all, and up till then he had done a real fine job. But no way was he going to let himself be bluffed into making a confession that would send him to prison. "You're crazy. Now stop kidding around and open this coffin."

"I saw what you and your half-wit helpers did to Minerva Plummer."

"Well, if you think you saw something, what do you need me for?"

"I want to hear about *all* of them."

"People in hell are going to want ice water, too, you bastard. Oops . . ." Hardy gave an exaggerated giggle . . . "poor choice of words. Sorry."

Luke brought both his fists slamming down on the lid—hard. God, how he ached to shout the truth about how he knew all about that long ago night of hell inflicted on his mother and how it was the reason for what he was doing, but he couldn't. Hardy would tip off Burch and Buddy. Most of all, though, he didn't want any of them to think he had any inkling that one of them was his father. He didn't want to give them the pleasure by damn.

"I'm losing patience, Hardy. Now let me hear it."

"The only thing you're going to hear is me telling you to kiss my ass."

"Wrong. In about fifteen minutes I'm going to hear you gasping your last breath."

Hardy was sure Luke was bluffing. All he had to do was wait.

Luke leaned back against the coffin directly behind him. It was expensive, cherry mahogany. Most of all, it was sturdy, and it was sitting on a steel casket standard, not like the flimsy kind his mother's had been on, which he would never, to his dying day, forget having turned over. He folded his arms across his chest and waited. Five minutes passed.

Hardy felt his pajamas clinging to his skin as nervous sweat oozed from every pore. "Luke," he yelled, then coughed and gasped. The air was getting thin, *real* thin. "Luke, cut it out, boy. I can hardly breathe."

"Then you better start talking."

"Luke, come on now. You don't want to fry for murder."

"You know I'm too smart to get caught. They won't know who did it. You'll just be found dead, but even that will take a while. Nobody will think to look in there. You'll start to smell before . . ."

Hardy was starting to hyperventilate and warned himself to calm down, but it was too late. "Please let me out of here."

"As soon as you talk, Hardy. As soon as you admit everything."

Luke prepared to switch on the Dictaphone, figuring Hardy was ready, and he was, words firing like angry bullets. "All right. All right, so I admit it. I dumped bodies out of coffins and right into the ground and then resold the coffins. But it's no big deal. And it helps keep the overall costs of funerals down for everybody, so nobody really gets hurt. Besides, they don't need a coffin, anyway. Hell, even the Bible says 'ashes to ashes, dust to dust.' It's a waste. Everybody and everything eventually rots."

"How many times have you done it?"

"A couple of dozen. I'm not sure. It doesn't matter. What's done is done. And I'll never do it again. I swear."

"What else have you done that was unethical or illegal?"

"Flowers . . ." his chest was hurting as his lungs fought desperately to suck in the last of the air. "Stole flowers from one grave to use for another funeral. Won't do it again either."

"What about the babies you've cut out of female corpses, Hardy?"

"Oh, shit. You know about that?"

"I know everything."

"Okay. Okay. But what's the harm? Everybody collects things. Stamps. Spoons. So I'm different. So what? My profession is unique. But I promise not to do that again, either. I'll . . . I'll burn it all."

"I have everything in a safe place," Luke said. Actually, he didn't, not yet. But he would before the night was over. If Hardy ever started backsliding, or Lucy died, Luke intended to make sure he would always have the goods to send him to prison, no matter where he, himself, happened to be at the time.

Hardy moaned again, but this time it was barely distinguishable. Luke knew the air was almost depleted. "Everything you have said has been recorded on a Dictaphone."

Right then, Hardy didn't care. He just wanted to *breathe*.

"I also have a typed confession for you to sign when I let you out. And don't get any funny ideas about refusing once you are, because I'll put your sorry ass right back in there. Understand?"

Hardy understood a lot of things. He understood that he hated Luke Ballard's guts. He understood that he was capable of killing him with his bare hands and never feel a second of remorse. And he also understood that he had no choice but to do everything the bastard told him to.

"Do you?" Luke prodded, louder, harsher. He was tired of fooling around. The night was wearing on, and thoughts of Emma Jean waiting for him made him all the more anxious to finish with Hardy.

"Yes, yes, I do. Send me to jail. I don't care. Just let me out of here . . ."

Luke chuckled. "Oh, you aren't going to jail. Not in the real sense, anyway."

He moved to the end of the coffin and began to turn the crank once more.

This time, with each methodical *kah-lank*, Hardy's panic diminished a little. He didn't give a damn what he had to sign or what he had to do. He just wanted out of there.

Lucy stood midway on the stairs listening to their confrontation, clutching the collar of her bathrobe around her neck. She was shaking, but not with fear. Oh, no, not fear at all. Fear was now a thing of the past.

No longer would she have to listen to Hardy's taunts over how ugly she was and how appreciative she should be that he had spared her from being an old maid. Never again would he bully her into doing anything she didn't want to do. Hugging herself with delight, she turned and ran back up the stairs. Life, at last, was going to be very good, for her, anyway.

Luke cut the headlights as soon as he left the pavement. The nearest house, Leonard Letchworth's, was a half-mile away. It was nearly two o'clock, so everybody there would be asleep. He hadn't passed a car driving from town. One of the benefits of being sheriff was that, if he were seen at an unusually late hour, folks thought he was still on duty.

The house was L-shaped, the bend at the back off the

kitchen, where he could park his car so it wouldn't be seen should anybody happen to turn around in the drive.

Emma Jean had been sitting on the steps watching for him. As he started walking across the yard, she struck a match to light a candle she'd stuck in a Pepsi bottle on the porch railing.

He took the steps in one bound and wrapped an arm around her tiny waist. "Did you give up on me?" He brushed his lips against her forehead and felt her tremble at his touch.

"No. I didn't even doze off. I've been sitting right out here, wrapped in a blanket, because it's so cold, and . . ." She giggled nervously, "Listen to me. I'm supposed to play hard to get, and here I am letting you know right off the bat how eager I was to see you."

"That's fine, 'cause I've been counting hours and minutes, too."

She opened the screen door and beckoned him to follow. Her eyes were glowing in the candlelight, her long hair flowing down her back. She was wearing a short cotton dress that came just to her knees, and Luke thought she looked like a little doll baby.

"I've got a surprise." She set the bottle with the candle down on the kitchen table, then crossed to the kitchen sink. Opening the cabinet door beneath, she reached for the bottle of cooking sherry she had hidden behind the Ajax and Clorox. "I thought we could celebrate our first time. I managed to get this through the checkout at the supermarket without Nonnie Bynum saying anything, because it was a real busy day, and she was swishing stuff by like turkeys on parade, and . . ."

He took quick strides to sweep her into his arms and crush her against him. "That's nice, honey, but all we need is this . . ."

CHAPTER 16

Luke had stayed with Emma Jean till nearly dawn. He hadn't dared go home. Instead, he went straight to the office. Ned had been asleep in the magistrate's office, as usual, so Luke had curled up in his chair behind his desk to catch a few winks. Later he claimed he'd fallen asleep around midnight and didn't wake till morning.

It had been two weeks, and he couldn't stop thinking about her. He knew things shouldn't go any farther regardless of how he felt about her. She wasn't the type for an occasional tumble in bed, and he had enough problems just wanting to complete his vendetta and get on with his life. So as bad as he wanted to, he had not called her as he had promised he would and hadn't gone anywhere near the laundromat. She'd be hurt, even mad, but eventually she would get over it.

Now, however, it was New Year's eve, and there was no way he could avoid seeing her because he was responding to a fight at the Moose Lodge. There was a big dance there, and he had seen Rudy's truck parked outside when he had passed by earlier, which meant he and Emma Jean were there.

Luke pulled into the lot with blue light flashing and saw that Matt and Kirby had already arrived to break up the fisticuffs between Cliff Meyers and Jobie Bushnell. Tension was still thick as molasses as supporters of the two men shouted challenges back and forth, but things calmed down as soon as Luke appeared.

He instructed Matt and Kirby to lock up Cliff and Jobie for the night so they'd cool down. He was about to drive off when he saw Emma Jean. She was standing outside with some other folks and looking at him with those big eyes of hers like a puppy that had been kicked and didn't understand why.

Suddenly Ned came over the radio. "Base to twelve. Base to twelve. Come in, sheriff. It's a 10-43."

That meant a chase . . . but who was doing the chasing? He and his deputies were here.

He pressed the mike button. "Say again."

"Sheriff Mosby just radioed that he and two of his deputies are in pursuit of a car he believes is running 'shine and wants you to know they didn't stop at the county line. They're on the back road to Cheaha, and he needs assistance."

"He's got it." Luke hit the blue light again and spun gravel leaving the parking lot. As he did, he caught a glimpse of Emma Jean in the rear view mirror, staring after him with that same whipped-puppy look on her face. He was grateful for the chase, grateful to have something else to focus on. Hell, he wouldn't care if Buford County all of a sudden had a mass murderer to worry about. Anything to get his mind off Emma Jean. He also wished he could hurry up and figure out a way to nail Burch and Buddy so he could hit the road.

Just before he got to the spot where he had caught Junior meeting his bootlegger, Luke heard on the radio that the chase had ended. The runner had lost control of his car and smashed into a tree.

"He lost it going into the curve. He's dead," Sheriff Mosby told Luke when he arrived on the scene. "Sorry we had to cross into your bailiwick without letting you know we were coming, but there was no time, and I've been after this runner for months."

"It's okay." Luke walked over to the car. The driver was dead, all right. Probably killed on impact. He radioed Ned. "Call Hardy and tell him to bring the wagon." He lit a cigarette and leaned against his car to wait.

Ralph Mosbey joined him. "I've been meaning to call you, Luke. I'm hearing reports the Klan is stirring around in my county."

"Are they causing any trouble?"

"Not yet. But you never know. They've got a place out in the boondocks where they rally every so often. I try to keep an eye on 'em, and all they've done so far is shout about how the country is going to hell in a hand basket thanks to the negroes and the commies, and then they burn a cross and that's about it. But I don't like it, and I wish I could drive 'em out like you did."

"It was easy for me, Ralph. The man I beat for sheriff was a Klan member. When he went, so did their support." Luke had also knocked a few heads together, but that was beside the point.

"Yeah, I know, but I thought you'd be interested to know that we spotted a plate from your county at a rally last week. You might want to run a make on it." He took a slip of paper from his wallet and gave it to Luke.

Luke very definitely *did* want to run a make because, if someone from Buford County was going to a Klan rally in Coosa County, it probably meant that either the old bunch was going to start stirring again and wanted to brush up on what the Klan was into lately, or they needed help with a problem they couldn't handle due to the breakup of their own group.

He called the Highway Patrol headquarters in Montgomery as soon as he got back to the office. It wasn't long before he had the name the car was registered to—Cubby Riddle, a supervisor at the mill. It was also known he was Buddy Hampton's right hand man. The only reason he would've been at the rally was because Buddy sent him. And Luke intended to find out why.

"I saw how you was dancing with Frank. When are you gonna learn I don't put up with that shit? You might've screwed around before, but them days are over."

Emma Jean stood on the other side of the kitchen table, trying to keep distance between them.

"I asked you a question, woman."

Rudy took a step, and she backed away.

He had started railing at her in the car on the way home from the dance. She had kept quiet, hoping he would let up, but the minute they walked in the door, he started chasing her around the table.

"Rudy, you got no cause to be mad. I didn't do anything wrong."

"That's what you call rubbing yourself all over a man? Nothin'?"

His eyes were wild, and his mouth was twisted with rage, and she wondered how she could ever have been stupid enough to think he was cute and want to marry him. But she'd been so confused back then, and he was a totally different person now. He hardly ever bathed and had a sloppy beer gut that hung over his belt. He didn't brush his teeth either, and she had to fight to keep from gagging when he kissed her. He was crude, too, farting whenever he felt like it. Once he'd done it in bed, and she'd complained, so he had held her head under the sheet and made her smell it, laughing like it was the funniest thing ever.

"Answer me, bitch."

Terror began to snake up her spine. When he started calling her names it meant he was getting madder and not about to back off. She knew she had to try and pacify him quickly, or he was going to beat her. She didn't want that, didn't want to be laid up in bed two or three days unable to go to work for the bruises and welts. She had to go to the laundromat, had to be there in case Luke called. Only the good Lord knew how it was killing her that he didn't. She'd told herself maybe it hadn't meant anything to him, that he was exactly what Wanda Potts had said he was—a cockhound, and she was just another notch in his *thing*. Only he sure as hell hadn't made her feel that way that night, and the look in his eyes when she'd seen him earlier wasn't how a man looked at a woman that didn't mean jack shit to him. He cared. He cared, by God. Only he was scared, and she had to find a way to make him see he had no reason to be, that she wasn't asking a damn thing from him except to give her some pleasure once in a while, and she'd give the same to him, as good as she could. He'd enjoyed it. She knew he had. But now she had something more important to think about.

Sucking in a deep breath, she attempted reason. "Look, Rudy, you've got to believe me. I didn't do anything. It's Frank." She lowered her voice, embarrassed, "He's the one who pushes his *thing* at me. You need to fuss at him, not me."

"You think I didn't?" he yelled. "You think I didn't say something that other time, too? Yes, I did, by damn, and he swore up and down he'd never do nothing like that to another man's wife, especially mine, 'cause he knows I'd kill him or anybody else who tried to mess with you. He says it was you, that you probably had too much to drink. But I know different. I know it didn't have nothing to do with liquor. You were a whore when I met you, and if you get a chance, you'll be one again. It's how you are. It's how all women are if you don't watch 'em. Now you better come here 'cause you're really pissin' me off."

She saw how he was clenching and unclenching his fists at his sides. Fear was a hot lump in her throat, making it hard to plead around it. "Rudy, you've got to believe me. Frank is lying. And you *made* me dance with him, remember?"

She continued to retreat as he continued to advance. "He came to the table and asked me to dance, and I said no, and then you said I shouldn't be so unsociable and to get out there."

"So? That didn't give you permission to rub all over him."

"Rudy, I didn't."

"You callin' me a liar? I saw you with my own two eyes, Emma Jean. Now you stop runnin' from me."

He lunged, but she was quicker and pulled a chair out to block him. He stumbled and almost fell, hitting his toe, and yelled with the pain. "Now you done it, bitch. I'm gonna teach you who's boss around here."

He picked up the chair and threw it at her. She ducked and it hit the pie safe, shattering one of the glass doors.

"See what you made me do? My momma gave us that pie safe."

He lunged again, and this time Emma Jean was not fast enough. He caught her arm and twisted it painfully. She whimpered, "Rudy, don't hit me. I've gotta go to work, and if you bruise me up, I can't."

He let go of her arm and grabbed her face with his hands to squeeze in a viselike grip. Taunting that she looked like a fish with her mouth all puckered up, he kissed her, forcing his tongue so far and so deep in her mouth that she gagged when he let her go.

"Oh, I ain't gonna mess you up, sweetie pie. I want you to go to work. I want you to make that measly buck an hour my cheap-ass cousin pays you till summer gets here and you can start makin' real money pickin' tomatos. So you ain't gotta worry about me leavin' no bruises as long as you do what I say, which is get your sorry ass in there on that bed right now."

He had been dragging her to the bedroom as he spoke and finally gave her a push that sent her sprawling backwards across the mattress.

She watched with panic creeping as he stripped off his clothes to tower over her naked.

"Now strip, damn you," he roared.

There was no point in resisting, and she began to quietly sob as she worked the buttons on the front of her dress with shaking fingers. Her only solace was knowing it would not take long. When he was drinking, he came quick, if he was able to at all. It would end, and he would slump against her and fall into a deep sleep.

She could then roll out from beneath him and slide from the bed to run into the living room and cry and cry and wonder what she was living for. She had dared to hope lately it was for Luke Ballard. Now hope was a dead thing, as dead as her body that refused to offer the slightest sign of life for the man pummeling into her so brutally.

He had pulled the light cord when they had come into the room, and the bare bulb spotlighted her stricken face.

"Don't like it, huh?," he grunted, staring down at her. "But you don't mind flirting with other men, trying to turn them on, do you?"

He raised his hand to hit her, and she threw up her arms to fend him off. "Please, don't . . ."

"*Please, don't,*" he mimicked. "I'll do anything I damn well please, and I please to do this . . ."

~~~

January passed beneath a shroud of gray clouds spitting icy rains and blowing chilling winds, and February dawned with not much promise of anything better.

Emma Jean went to the bathroom constantly in hopes of finding blood stains on her panties, but with each passing day her fears increased. She was about to miss her second period, and, if she was pregnant, there was no way of knowing whether the baby was Rudy's or Luke's. And what if it *was* Luke's? Would anybody be able to tell after it was born? Rudy would kill her *and* the baby if he thought it was somebody else's.

She had tried everything she had ever heard of that was supposed to make a woman's period start: blackberry brandy, soaking in scalding hot water, running, jumping. She had even swallowed castor oil till it made her so sick she could hardly stand. She took heart, however, to recall that when she was pregnant before she'd had morning sickness only a few days after she missed her first period, and there'd been none of that. Maybe it was nerves. She sure as heck had enough to make her a basket case, what with having to constantly be on her toes to try and keep Rudy from getting riled.

She decided to try whiskey. One of the girls she had worked with in Florida had told her any time she was late she'd get drunk and it would make her come around. She said something about the whiskey heating up the blood, and Emma Jean was desperate enough to try anything. Rudy was working third shift, so it was a good time.

By her fourth drink, she was dizzy and had convinced herself in her stupor that the baby could only be Luke's. That was nicer than Rudy's, regardless of the consequences. She loved Luke. She was sure of it. She had loved him even before that night she would remember forever. But he was never going to love her back. Not her or any other woman. He had a wife, a daughter. He just wanted to *cockaround.*

No, she thought blearily, that wasn't what Wanda Potts had

said. *Cockhound.* That was what he was. She was a *cock,* and he was a *hound,* and he'd *hounded* her, and she'd *cocked* him.

Cockhound.

She giggled.

Staggering and stumbling, she returned to the kitchen and tried to find the bottle of bourbon but couldn't because the whole world was spinning. She reached out to steady herself but fell, knocking the bottle over at the same time. It shattered when it hit the floor, and her arm landed on the jagged glass.

"Oh, Lord, oh, Lord, oh, Lord." She struggled to her feet by hanging onto the back of a chair. Staring at the blood gushing from her arm, she hiccupped, then giggled to say, "I'm bleeding, but not from the right place."

She fumbled around and found a dish towel and wrapped it around her arm, then watched in horror as the towel turned crimson. So much blood. The towel began to drip with it.

Dizzy, she knew she had to get help but froze after picking up the phone. Who could she call? Not Miss Bertha. She lived too far away. And not an ambulance. She'd be embarrassed to death to go riding up to the hospital in an ambulance, and she didn't dare risk driving herself because the room was spinning faster, and she felt like she was going to throw up.

Hating to do it but unable to think of anybody else, she dialed the party line code to make Myrtle Letchworth's phone ring. Myrtle sleepily answered on the third ring, and by then Emma Jean was so scared she started babbling that she was bleeding to death and needed to go to the emergency room right away.

Once it dawned on Myrtle it was Emma Jean, her first thought was that Rudy had beaten her again, and she didn't want to get involved. "I'll call the law for you," she yelled into the phone.

"No, don't do that . . ." Emma Jean protested, just before the floor came up to meet her face.

It had been a long night, and Luke was exhausted and anxious to get home and go to bed. He was almost out the door when the phone rang but hesitated as Ned took the call.

Ned listened, then said, "I'll get somebody over there right away, Miz Letchworth." He rolled his eyes at Luke. "Yeah, yeah,

I know. I don't blame you. Nobody likes these kind of things. You just go on back to bed. We'll see it's taken care of."

He hung up, checked the roster to see which member of the rescue squad was on duty, then started dialing as he told Luke, "That was Myrtle Letchworth. She said Rudy Veazey beat up his old lady again, and she thinks she needs to go to the hospital. Matt and Kirby have already signed off, so I guess you'd better run out there. I'm calling Jimmy Ledbetter. He's got the ambulance tonight."

Luke felt like slamming his fist into the wall. Damn it, he would not, could not, get involved, not unless Emma Jean agreed to take out a warrant so he could arrest Rudy. Otherwise, if she wouldn't leave Rudy, then she'd have to stand the consequences, no matter how damn much he cared.

"Hell, no," he said finally, angrily. "I'm not going to waste my time. That's what she gets for staying with the son of a bitch."

"Well, don't you think somebody needs to check it out?"

"Why? It's the same old shit. She won't press charges. He'll say he's sorry and won't do it again, not till he gets drunk. So why worry about it? It's her problem."

His chest was heaving, and he wanted to kick himself for blowing up because Ned was looking at him like he had lost his mind. Maybe he had. Hell, he didn't know anything anymore except that he wished he were anywhere but Hampton, Ala-bama. He walked out with Ned staring after him and went to the cafe.

Hardy Moon was sitting at the counter, but at the sight of Luke called to Clyde, "Hey, cancel that burger. I don't think I should eat this late after all. It'll give me heartburn. See you." He slid off the stool and rushed out the door.

Luke no longer felt like going home. He knew he would never get to sleep, anyway, not when he was sick to the core thinking about Rudy beating Emma Jean so bad she needed to go to the hospital. It was all he could do to keep from finding the little piece of shit and beating him into the ground.

He managed to make small talk with Clyde, all the while wondering just how bad she'd been hurt. When Jimmy Ledbetter came in an hour or so later, he struggled to hide his anxiety as he asked how she was.

Jimmy snickered. "Well, it wasn't her old man that put her in the hospital this time. It was whiskey." He took the lid off the donut plate and helped himself. Around mouthfuls, he described the scene when he got to the house. "She was laying on the kitchen floor, drunk as a skunk and blood all over the place. Looks like she dropped the whiskey bottle and then fell on top of it. Cut her arm real bad. I took her to the emergency room. The doc said he'd sew her up and let her sleep it off."

But Luke wasn't buying that story. Maybe Rudy had cut her and then run. If so, he didn't need a warrant to arrest him. "I think maybe I'd better have a talk with Rudy."

Jimmy helped himself to another donut before calling after Luke as he walked towards the door, "Oh, he ain't home, sheriff. He's at work. She managed to tell the doc that, and the doc said he'd wait till morning to call him since he was gonna keep her a while."

Luke was relieved, but it needled him to think she'd been drinking so heavily. He hadn't got the impression she was the type, but then what did he really know about her?

"Funny thing, though," Jimmy added as he licked chocolate off his fingers. "She kept moaning she was bleeding from the wrong place. Hell, is there ever a *right* place?"

He glanced at Luke to share a laugh; only Luke wasn't laughing.

"Don't make sense, does it, sheriff?" Jimmy remarked.

No, it didn't, Luke thought with a jolt, *unless she wanted to be bleeding from somewhere else so she'd know she wasn't pregnant. And if that were the case, then maybe she had actually tried to kill herself.*

Luke swallowed a groan seeing Maude Dupree on duty in the emergency room. She had a big mouth, and the story about Emma Jean would be all over town.

Maude gave him a hard time. "She's asleep. You'll have to wait till morning to ask her anything, but I don't see the need, anyhow. All she did was get drunk and fall down and cut herself." She gave a scornful sniff. "Besides, Matt was here a while ago. I told him the same thing, but he insisted on sitting with her for a spell."

So Ned had decided to send a deputy to check things out, anyway. Good. He shouldn't have acted like such a hard case when he first heard about it and gone himself. Without a word, Luke brushed by Maude and located Emma Jean in the last cubicle. Drawing the curtain closed after him, he was a tornado of emotions.

Her face was white as the pillowcase. A sheet was pulled up to her chin, and her injured arm, thick with bandages, rested on a rolled-up towel at her side. He saw that her brow was furrowed, like she was hurting, and he wondered if it was because of her injury or the reason behind it. He did not know, but he cared a lot. He didn't want to, but he did, and no matter how much he argued within himself, he could not help it.

He touched her cheek and whispered her name. He waited a few seconds, then gave her shoulder a gentle shake.

"I never want to wake up," she mumbled.

"Sorry, but I have to ask a few questions."

Her eyes flashed open. "What are you doing here?"

"I want to know how you got hurt."

She turned her face to the wall. "I fell. That's all."

"You were dog-assed drunk. Why?"

"It's not important."

"It is to me."

"Why?"

The words slipped out before he realized it. "Because I care."

She turned to glare at him. "Well, you could've fooled me. I haven't heard a word from you since that night six weeks ago."

"I thought it was best for both of us."

"For you, maybe. Not for me." She turned away again before adding, "I feel like such a fool to think you could have cared anything about me, anyway, since you're nothing but a cockhound."

"A *what?*"

"Cockhound. That's what Wilma Potts said."

"Wilma Potts doesn't know beans about me, and neither do you or you'd have realized I stayed away because I do care about you, Emma Jean. I don't want to. God knows I've tried not to. But I do." *Oh, Lord, what was he getting himself into? All resolve had scattered like a dandelion in a summer breeze.*

He reached for her hand and squeezed, all the time telling himself he was messing up big time and should get the hell out of there fast. His feet might as well have been planted in concrete.

Slowly, she faced him, a glint of hope in her eyes. "Do you really mean that, Luke?"

He drew a breath of resignation. "Yes, I do. But you've got to understand it's a dead-end street. I'm married. You're married. It can't go anywhere. *We* can't go anywhere."

She did not speak for a moment, mind spinning, then said, "But we can be *together*, you know, whenever we can, when we have a chance. I wasn't expecting more than that. I know how it is." She paused to swallow. "I was just looking for a little bit of happiness. That's all. I thought that's what you wanted, too."

"I did, and I do. But we both have to understand it can't ever be more than it is."

Suddenly her world seemed brighter, and she was able to quip, "Which is a quickie, right?"

He grinned. "I seem to recall we had a *longie*." Glancing around to make sure the curtain was still closed, he brushed his lips against hers. "We're going to have to be real careful."

Her head bobbed up and down. "*Real* careful."

"We can't take any chances."

"Absolutely not."

"And we won't be able to see each other as much as we might like to."

"I know."

She withdrew her good arm from beneath the sheet. She had to touch him, had to be sure she wasn't still drunk and only imagining he was there because she so desperately wanted him to be. She touched his cheek. "You *are* real."

He caught her fingers and pressed them to his lips. "I'm very real. Now how about telling me why you were drinking so heavy."

"I was worried I was pregnant."

He tensed. "Are you?"

"No, thank goodness. I remember telling the doctor I might be, but I didn't let on that I didn't want to be. I just said I wanted to make sure so that he didn't give me anything for pain that might hurt the baby, so he examined me and said it looked like I was fixing to start my period.

"Well, it would've made Rudy happy if you were."

"Not if it was yours."

"Did you think it might be?"

A tear slipped down her cheek. "God forgive me, Luke, but I was hoping so. I don't want a baby by him. Not ever."

"And you can't have one by me, so as soon as we can work it out, I'll take you to Birmingham and find a doctor to fit you with one of those diaphragm things."

"Oh, Luke, that would be so wonderful. I've wanted to do that but just never had the money. It'll be great. Rudy won't know I'm wearing it." She reached to pull him close enough to give him a quick kiss before happily exclaiming, "It's going to work out for us. You'll see. And nobody will ever find out. We'll be extra careful. We need each other, Luke. Because just knowing you're out there thinking about me, caring what happens to me, will help me through the bad times."

"And I will be," he promised, knowing then and there he could no longer fight it. He had to have her, had to be with her whenever he could.

"I've got to go," he said reluctantly. "Or prune-faced Maude Dupree in her orthopedic shoes might get suspicious."

"I'll have to work tomorrow even though my arm is hurt. Bert's out of town. Will you call me?"

"You bet."

CHAPTER 17

Again Luke was hiding in Milburn Smith's azaleas, but this time he wasn't there to spy on the funeral home. Instead, he was waiting for Dennis Blum to bring Murline Pruitt home from bowling. Her driveway ran alongside Milburn's hedges, giving Luke a good view. When they arrived, Dennis switched off the headlights before turning in so Murline's husband, Thurman, wouldn't know they were out there.

Luke could hear everything going on because the car windows were down. Murline was giggling. "Oh, Dennis, you're such a bad boy. You know we can't do it here. Thurman might see the car."

"He didn't the last time."

"But . . ."

"Didn't you tell me he stays so glued to the television he wouldn't hear a freight train going through the yard? Now come on, sugar pie. You've been teasing me all night long, shaking that cute little bottom of yours when you got up to bowl, 'cause you know it drives me crazy . . ."

It got quiet, except for sounds of heavy breathing, then fumbling noises as they maneuvered for just the right position. Dennis cursed when he jammed his butt against the gear shift, and Murline complained he was breaking her neck by pushing her so hard into the door.

Luke's eyes were adjusted to the darkness, and he was able to see one of Murline's feet sticking out a window. Something hit the ground, and she said, "My shoe fell off."

"Get it later."

The car was rocking, Dennis was grunting, and Murline was moaning. They were too lost in each other to notice Luke as he crept through the hedge to retrieve the shoe. Never in a million years would he have thought Dennis was ballsy enough to screw Thurman's wife right in the man's own driveway. Square from the word go, everything about Dennis was straight-laced. He was pushing forty, had never been married, and lived with his widowed mother. His clothes were dull and plain, he combed his hair back slick, and his glasses were thick as the bottom of a Coke bottle. He had never missed a day's work behind the pharmacy counter at Dixie Drugs. His only recreation was bowling every Monday night, and, so it seemed, humping Murline Pruitt.

Luke was also surprised at Murline because there had never been so much as a breath of scandal about her that he knew of. They had gone to school together, and all he remembered about her was that she always made the honor roll. He couldn't recall her ever going out with anybody, but it stood to reason she and Thurman, who was dull as she was, would wind up together. He ran a radio and TV repair shop. They had one kid, a boy around six. They attended the First Methodist Church where Murline sang in the choir and Thurman was a deacon. She was active in the PTA, and he went fishing a lot. They were the picture of a wholesome, happy family, except . . .

As part of the Hampton family's effort to appear magnanimous to the common folk, the mill awarded a scholarship to a business college in Birmingham every year. Murline had been one of the winners and had gone to work in the steno pool at the mill after graduation. Eventually she worked her way up to become Buddy Hampton's private secretary, and, thus, the reason Luke was now interested in her personal life.

The car was still rocking, and the groaning was getting louder. At last, the car stopped moving, and so did Murline and Dennis. Luke heard them gasping, then Murline said, "I'll bet I look a sight. I hope Thurman fell asleep in his chair. I don't want him to see me like this."

"Just comb your hair, and you'll be all right."

"I've got to find my shoe. Help me look for it."

"Honey, I don't have time. Momma will be wondering why I'm so late. I've got to go."

Silence.

Probably kissy-kissy goodnight, Luke figured.

The door opened and closed, and there was a brief flash from the dome light.

"Don't forget Saturday," she said, adding, "*if* I don't have to work. It'll be so nice to have an afternoon in a bed, Dennis. We can go to that little motel on the other side of Birmingham. I always feel safe there."

"Yeah, *if* I don't have to take Momma shopping."

"But you only get one Saturday a month off. It's the only day we can sneak off together."

"Yeah, well, it's not always my fault when we can't. Buddy makes you work a lot of overtime."

"I know. But try, won't you?"

Dennis sighed. "I've really got to go, Murline."

"Well, promise you'll tell your mother you've got plans of your own."

"I don't know. She really likes to go to Birmingham on Saturday." He backed out of the driveway but waited till he was farther down the street before turning the headlights on.

Murline walked around for a time, swinging her feet about in the grass in search of her missing shoe. She finally gave up and went inside, no doubt planning to return at first light to try and find it.

No need, Luke smiled to himself as he crept away and into the night. He would see she got it.

Saturday morning Luke was sitting in his patrol car on the shoulder of the Birmingham Highway, sipping coffee from a paper cup, when Dennis Blum drove by. His mother was in the car with him, so that meant Dennis would not be meeting Murline for afternoon delights in a motel room. Luke tossed out the rest of his coffee and hurriedly drove back to town.

First he made sure Thurman Pruitt's truck was parked in the alley behind the repair shop. He spotted his kid through the window, which meant he was spending the day at work with Daddy. Good. Murline would be home alone, unless she had found something to do to ease the disappointment of playing second fiddle to Dennis's mother, which she hadn't. Her Ford was there, which meant so was she.

She met him at the door with that *wonder-what-I've-done* look on her face that people instinctively get when they see the law coming. She was dressed to go out, probably for shopping: skirt, blouse, jacket, high heels, gloves, and hat. No makeup except for lipstick. Hair swept back in a French twist. So prim and proper. He had to swallow a laugh to remember her foot hanging out Dennis Blum's car window.

"Why, what on earth brings you here, Luke? I hope nothing's wrong."

"Everything's fine, Murline. I just need to talk to you a minute. Can I step inside?"

"Of course. Come on in." She stepped back for him to enter. "Would you like coffee? There's some left over from breakfast, but I can make a fresh pot if you like."

"No, thanks." He glanced around the small living room, crowded with furniture, and spotted the sofa Thurman had been snoozing on while his wife humped another man in his driveway. "Let's sit down."

"Well, sure . . ." Her eyes searched his face for some hint of his purpose. "Are you sure there's nothing wrong?"

"I just need your help, Murline. That's all."

She relaxed a little. "Well, if I can, of course."

"I'll get right to the point." He leaned forward, elbows on his knees, and stared her straight in the eyes. "You're Buddy Hampton's private secretary, right?"

A shiver of apprehension made her sit up straight. "Yes, I am."

"And you probably know everything about his business."

"I suppose."

"Both business *and* personal. You have access to all his files, and you know his comings and goings."

Her eyes narrowed. "What's this all about?"

"Cubby Riddle's car was seen a few weeks ago at a Klan rally over in Coosa County."

Trained to be observant, he saw how her face paled ever so slightly.

"So what does that have to do with me?"

"I think Buddy sent him there, and I think you know why."

"But I don't."

Luke saw her squeeze her hands together in her lap and how her lips began to twitch. "Cubby is supervisor over the whole mill. Everybody knows he's Buddy's number one man. Now tell me why Buddy sent him to the rally."

She dropped her gaze to her hands. "I told you I don't know. Mr. Hampton doesn't tell me all his business, and . . ."

"Cut the bullshit, Murline."

Her eyes snapped to his once more, and this time there was no hint of mere pale. She had gone chalk-white.

"You know exactly what's going on. Is it the union wanting to come in again? It's about time for them to be trying."

"Luke, I can't . . ."

"You can . . . and you will. Now talk to me, Murline. It's a known fact Hampton Mills has fought for years to keep the union out. Next year it's going to be time for another vote, and I think Buddy sent Cubby to the rally to ask for the Klan's help. He wants to scare the pants off anybody in favor, and he figures the Klan can do it."

She picked at a thread on the hem of her skirt. "I wouldn't know anything about it."

"All right. Then maybe you know something about this."

He reached inside his jacket and took out her shoe.

"Oh, God." She swayed, eyes going wide.

"I believe this is yours," he said quietly. "It fell off your foot, which was dangling out the window of Dennis Blum's car the other night."

For a few seconds, her lips worked silently, and then she managed to croak a denial and an indignant little squirm. "No. No, that's not so. I don't know where you got it, but . . ."

"Like I said, Murline. Cut the bullshit. I was there. I saw. I heard. Now either you cooperate with me, or the whole town finds out about your affair with Dennis, including Thurman. I wouldn't want to do it, and believe me, I don't like putting you on the spot, but for reasons I can't go into, it's very important."

She looked like she was going to be sick. "You . . . you wouldn't."

He persisted. "You're the only one who can help me. Cooperate, and you get your shoe back, and I don't say a word to anybody. Otherwise . . ." He shrugged.

She bolted from the chair and ran from the room.

He heard her throwing up, the toilet flushing, and a few moments later she returned, a wet washcloth pressed against her brow. She sat down, leaned her head back and closed her eyes. "All right," she whispered feebly, faintly. "I'll do whatever you want."

Chapter 18

Burch Cleghorn, with his flabby jowls and thick neck, had always reminded Sara of a bulldog, which, she felt, was grossly insulting to bulldogs. He had broad shoulders, a big belly, and beefy arms. He wore tortoiseshell horn-rimmed glasses, which did not do enough to hide his beady little snake eyes. His bushy brows reminded her of caterpillars. He gave her the creeps.

On Sundays, when it was his turn, as one of the deacons, to stand next to Reverend Whitsett to say good-byes at the end of service, she dreaded having to shake hands with him because he squeezed hard and tried to hold on longer than usual. She could not stand him.

And now he was sitting in her living room. If only she had thought to peek and see who it was when the doorbell rang, she could have pretended she wasn't home. She had thought it was Sudie from next door, who sometimes came to visit when Tim was working the three to eleven shift. It was only when she opened the door and saw Burch standing there grinning like a loonie that she remembered Sudie had told her she was going to sit with her sick mother for the night.

Burch immediately grabbed her hand, all the while pushing

his way in as he said, "It's church visitation night, Sara, and I got to thinking how it's been a while since I called on you and Tim."

He glanced around the living room expectantly, then asked, feigning disappointment, "Where's Tim? Oh, goodness, I hope I didn't miss him."

"He's at work." She bit her tongue. She should have said he'd gone to the store for cigarettes and would be back any minute, but she hadn't thought quick enough.

Burch sat down on the sofa, stretched an arm across the back and flashed a smile to show off his expensive tooth caps. "Well, you and I will just have a nice little visit then. So how have you been?"

"Fine. Just fine." She was trapped and could only hope he wouldn't stay long. She took the chair across from him and saw the caterpillars wiggle as he frowned. No doubt he'd hoped she would sit next to him on the sofa, but no way, buster.

He led the conversation, first blathering about the weather, then said he was glad March was just around the corner and how everyone was looking forward to the church's homecoming picnic in April. He said he hoped she would think about teaching a Sunday school class next year. She said she didn't think she'd have time. Timmy would be in first grade, and she had promised to be a room mother.

He touched on the church budget and commended her and Tim for how they were honoring their tithes. Then he spoke of the missionary fund in the Philippines. "It's a lovely place. I was stationed there for a short time after the war, and I'll always be grateful I had the chance to get to know the people and their culture."

She politely agreed that it must have been a nice experience, all the while thinking of so many things she could be doing instead of listening to him prattle on. She only hoped Dewey didn't call. Sometimes when Tim was working late shift, he would drive to the store near his farm and use the pay phone to call her.

Her mind continued to drift. She needed to pick out the pattern and material for Bonnie's Easter dress, wanting to get started on it soon to have time for all the intricate handiwork. And she had promised Nell Porter she'd make two cakes and some cookies to sell at the Library Guild's bake sale next Saturday. There were still plenty of pecans out in the storage room. She'd need to crack and pick at least two cups if she wanted to make her special cookies that always sold well. She could start tomorrow after fixing Tim's lunch, and . . .

She snapped to the present, eyes blinking furiously, throat suddenly tight, as her mind argued that no, she could not have heard him right. She absolutely, positively, could not have heard Burch Cleghorn, lawyer and church deacon, talking about the size of his penis.

But she had.

"The women marveled at the width of it, too," he was saying proudly, beady eyes sparkling. "They said they'd never seen one so big. I've heard their men have small ones, but don't take my word for it, *I* certainly didn't witness anyone's erections other than my own, to be sure. But I can tell you, the women had a fit over it. Now remember . . ."

He leaned forward, face slightly flushed by his own heat, "I wasn't married then. I was just a young man sowing my wild oats, as the Good Book says. So for me, it was not a sin to go to bed with a woman. But can you imagine how I felt when they treated me like some kind of god? I swear, Sara, they made an icon out of my penis."

"I think I hear the children." She bolted from the chair and ran from the room.

In the kitchen, she leaned against the wall as she commanded her heart to slow down. Had the man lost his mind? How dare he talk to her that way? But maybe she was overreacting. After all, she'd never been any farther from home than Birmingham, and Burch Cleghorn had probably been all over the world. Maybe it wasn't unusual to talk about such things in a foreign country, and he, forgetting her naivete, did not realize how uncomfortable it made her feel. But she should tell him, so he could apologize, and she would say there was no harm done and how it was nice he had stopped by but she really had to say good-night because she had some chores to do. He would leave, and that would be the end of it.

She sucked in a deep breath, walked back into the living room . . . and nearly fainted.

He was naked from the waist down, having taken off his trousers and underwear, which were neatly folded on the chair where she had been sitting. His right leg was pulled up to his chest, his foot propped on the cushion beneath him. He was gently stroking his very erect penis.

"Wh . . what are you doing?" she managed to croak.

He smiled, eyes shrewd and predatory. "I could tell you didn't believe me, so I wanted to prove it. Big, isn't it? Long and thick."

"P . . put it back. I mean . . ." Oh, why did she have to sound like a ninny? He was obviously crazy, and if she didn't do something, he might become violent and attack. She struggled above the bubbling hysteria to sound angry and forceful rather than scared and confused. "I *mean* that I want you to get your clothes on and get out of this house this instant. How dare you?"

He smirked and continued to rub himself. "How *dare* I? Is *that* what you said, my dear? How *dare* I? Well, I think I should ask you the same thing. How dare *you* pretend to be insulted when you're nothing but a hypocritical little tramp?"

She was astonished. "I . . . I can't believe any of this."

He sneered. "You always act so holier-than-thou. Faithful churchgoer. Loving wife. Doting mother. The picture of respectability. And it's all a lie. You put on such a front for the world, when actually you're no better than a prostitute, Sara, and you know it."

She rallied from shock to point at the door. "You get out of here right now, or I'm calling the sheriff."

"Why not call Dewey instead so we can have a threesome?"

Sara felt like she'd been kicked in her chest by a mule.

He smirked at her reaction. "Oh, yes, I know all about you and Dewey Culver. He pays you, doesn't he? Why else would you fool around with an old geezer like him? But don't worry. I'm willing to shell out, too. Even more than him, depending on how good you are, of course.

"As for the sheriff, he's a waste of time. He doesn't make a whole lot, so you don't want to waste any on him, do you?"

It was like she had swallowed an ice cube as a chill spread throughout her body, but somehow she managed to muster the strength to try and deny. "You don't know what you're talking about. You're sick . . . perverted . . ."

He winked. "Only in bed, my dear, and I know lots of ways to make you moan and groan."

She covered her ears with her hands. "Get out of here!"

"Oh, stop acting. Now how much do you want? Twenty bucks? No problem. And don't worry. I won't tell Dewey if you think he'd be jealous.

"You two are real clever, by the way," he continued. "I only found out by accident when I happened to be out that way one day and saw you and him in his truck turning off the road toward that old abandoned barn. I was curious, so I sneaked up on you and saw what you were doing. I tell you one thing, he didn't have anything like this." He wrapped his hand around his stiffness and shook it at her. "His looked like a little Vienna sausage."

She turned and ran down the hall and into the children's room, slammed the door and locked it, grateful they were both sound sleepers. She didn't want them scared . . . didn't want to have to try and explain what was going on.

She began dragging furniture in front of the door in case he tried to force the lock. Sooner or later he would have to give up, and then she would call Tim at work and tell him. He'd take care of the old lecher. He'd make him sorry he had ever unzipped his pants.

Her hands fell away from the dresser she was struggling to push towards the door as quietly as possible. If she told Tim, he would immediately confront Burch, and Burch would say he would never have made a pass at her if not for having seen her with Dewey. Tim wouldn't believe him at first, but sooner or later, it might all come out.

Many, many lives would be destroyed. She would be shamed and disgraced forevermore. Her family would turn their backs on her. Tim would divorce her and take the children. And poor Dewey. It would ruin him, too.

"Sara?"

Tears streaming down her cheeks, she pressed her face against the door and whispered, "Please don't wake my children. Please go away and leave me alone."

"Sara, I have my clothes on now. I know I frightened you, but come out so we can talk about it. It's the smart thing for you to do, you know. You'll have extra money, and you'll enjoy it more with me than with that old fart."

She turned and slid down to the floor and whimpered, "No. I can't. I can't do what you want me to. I can't. I'm not like that. I'm not."

"You know I'm not lying about seeing you with Dewey Culver. And I've been watching you ever since. I see you go off to meet him."

"Please, leave me alone."

"No, I won't. I've always had an eye for you, always thought you were the sexiest little thing around. And I can be good to you. I can make you a lot happier than Dewey. Let me prove it to you."

"No, no, no . . ."

"Well, you'll change your mind. You're just upset. But don't worry. I won't say a word to anybody unless you make me. It'll be our secret. And once Dewey gets used to the idea, he'll understand. He has to accept that he's old, and you need a real man who can satisfy you. But if you want to keep seeing him, too, that's fine with me. I'm not the jealous type. Besides, I've got a feeling you're a real little fireball. You can take care of all three of us—me, Dewey, and Tim."

She could not speak. She was crying too hard.

"Ahh, you're really upset, aren't you? Well, I tell you what. I'll leave you now to think about it, but understand this, Sara, I intend to dip into that honey hole, too. Or I swear I will see it gets all over town about you and Dewey. And you can take that promise to the bank, girlie."

He kicked the door for emphasis.

"I think it's awful about Matt and that Veazey woman."

Luke had just speared a French fry, and it was almost to his mouth, but his hand froze. "What did you say?"

They were having supper—burgers and fries, and Alma was having a hard time getting catsup out of the bottle. She repeated herself, each word punctuated by a slap of her hand against the bottom of the bottle. "I said—*I think it's awful about Matt and that Veazey woman.*"

When he could only gape at her, too stunned to respond, she snapped, "Well, don't pretend you didn't know about it. He's your deputy, and you know everything that goes on down there.

"Anyway," she went on, "I know it's been a while, but I hadn't heard about it till Maude Dupree told it at my church circle last night. She said Emma Jean Veazey was brought to the emergency room drunk, with her wrists slashed, and it had to have been over Matt because he came running in to check on her. Probably he told her he wasn't going to leave his wife for her, the little tramp, and she wanted to do something to get him shook up and made like she tried to kill herself."

She glared at Luke. "Maude also said *you* were there later, so you had to know about it. I think you should fire him. He's got no business running around on his wife, and you, as sheriff, shouldn't tolerate it, because it makes the whole department look bad."

"Whoa!" Luke laid his fork down. "First of all, she didn't try to kill herself. She just had a little too much to drink and fell and cut herself. Second, there's nothing between her and Matt, and this is how stories get started. Busybodies like Maude jump to conclusions and run their mouths.

"And Matt went to the hospital," he added, "because he was dispatched there."

She sniffed. "A waste of taxpayer's money. Who cares what happens to white trash?"

"Who says she's white trash?"

"Well, decent women don't get drunk and fall down."

"It has nothing to do with decency, Alma. God, but you're self-righteous."

"Don't use the Lord's name like that. It's a sin."

"That's the pot calling the kettle black, or don't you feel it's wrong to spread gossip that can wreck marriages? And I think I'd better speak to Maude. She knows better than to tell what goes on in that emergency room."

"Don't you dare. She'll be mad at me."

"Well, *I'm* mad at *her*."

Tammy suddenly pushed back from her chair so hard it fell backwards as she leaped to her feet. "I can't stand it. All you two do is fight." She ran from the room.

Alma glared at Luke. "Now see what you've done? You've ruined the child's supper and driven her from the table, all because you can't control that temper of yours."

"Not when you're spreading lies about my deputy." He wasn't about to let on it was Emma Jean he was concerned about. If Rudy heard gossip about her and any man, all hell would break loose.

"Don't blame me. Matt's the one who's got folks talking. And your traipsing to the hospital to see her doesn't look nice, either. Why did you have to stick your nose in?"

"I'm the sheriff. I check things out, and I was satisfied with what she told me."

"Which was?"

"Like I said, she had too much to drink and fell down and cut her arm. So let it go, Alma. Doesn't that preacher of yours ever preach against gossip?"

"What do you care? You're going to hell, anyway."

"I hope so. I sure don't want to spend eternity with you and those old biddies who call themselves Christians."

She hit the bottle too hard and catsup spurted all over her plate. "Oh, see what you made me do? You and your blasphemy."

He started to leave, but he was hungry, and she did make good French fries, maybe because they were fried in pure lard. So he ignored her and finished a big helping, along with a thick hamburger smothered in onions. She could cook good when she wanted to, which wasn't often.

He allowed thoughts of Emma Jean to take him away from the misery of the moment and wondered if she could cook but really didn't care. As long as he could be with her, he'd be happy living on peanut butter nabs and bologna sandwiches.

He wished they could be together more often, but in the month since she'd hurt her arm, they'd only managed to see each other once or twice a week. He had managed to get her to Birmingham right away to a doctor, though, and now she had her diaphragm.

So far, they had spent what time they were together making love. He sneaked into her house at night on occasion but preferred she meet him on a back road somewhere. He knew a few out-of-the way places for daytime meetings, too. They were careful. They confided in no one. They took no chances. He was determined they would not be found out.

He forced himself to take one day at a time and not worry about the future because he didn't want to think about Emma Jean no longer being a part of his life. But more and more lately, he had begun to wonder if maybe it would really have to be that way, if he would, in fact, have to leave her behind when he finally got the hell out of town. But he never said anything, never wanted to lead her to hope for something that might never happen.

"I made dessert," Alma said grudgingly, as though wishing she hadn't bothered after they'd wound up having a fight. "Banana pudding."

He figured he might as well have a bowl since he had time. It wasn't quite eight o'clock, and Emma Jean was meeting him at nine behind the cemetery. They wouldn't have long. Rudy got off work at eleven, but it was better than nothing.

"Maybe I'll take a bowl in for Tammy and eat with her," he said, thinking outloud and wishing his daughter didn't resent him so. Alma had done a good job of turning her against him.

"She don't want any. She's watching her figure. Says if *she* don't watch it, the boys won't, either."

"She's got no business thinking about boys at her age. She's not even twelve, yet, for pete's sake."

"Well, it doesn't do her any harm to flirt a little, Luke. All the girls do it."

"Not my daughter."

The phone rang. Alma turned from dipping the pudding to answer. "Yeah, he's here. Who is this?" She listened, then yelled, "Well, if you don't want to say, you aren't talking to him."

Luke knocked the chair over in his haste to lunge across the room and snatch the phone. "Sheriff Ballard."

Alma tried to wrest it away as she protested, "I'm not having women call my husband and not say who they are."

She continued to rail, and Luke turned away, straining to hear who was on the phone.

"Luke? It's me, Murline. I didn't mean to cause any trouble, but I didn't want Alma to know it was me. She'd wonder why I called, and you promised you'd keep me out of all this."

"And I will," he reassured. "And it's okay. Now what's going on?"

"I'm working late. Mr. Hampton needs some letters typed before he goes out of town tomorrow, and I just noticed he left his personal file drawer unlocked. If you can get here fast enough, I can let you in while the guard's gone to supper. We can worry about your getting out without being seen later."

Luke felt an excited rush. He had instructed Murline to let

him know if Buddy left anything unlocked because she didn't have keys to his desk or file cabinet. He had been planning to sneak in and jimmy them open but hadn't got to it because he was so intent on being with Emma Jean every chance he got.

"I'm on my way."

"I've also got something to tell you about Cubby."

"Great. I'll see you in a few minutes."

He hung up the phone and turned to meet Alma's blazing eyes. "So who is she, Luke? Who are you screwing now?"

"Grow up, Alma." He pushed by her and started for the door.

"Damn you, Luke, for the whore-hopper you are."

From experience, he knew what would happen next and ducked just in time to keep from getting hit by the bowl of pudding. She was always throwing things at him, and seeing the globs of meringue and bananas splattering against the wall, he felt like wiping her face in it.

"One of these days I'm gonna take Tammy and leave you," she shrieked. "Just you wait and see."

He kept on going. Long ago he had given up trying to reason, trying to make a go of a marriage that never should have been. All he could do for now was endure the misery and give thanks Emma Jean had come into his life to make it a little easier to bear.

He was almost to the car when he heard the phone ring again but kept on going. An instant later, Alma ran out on the back porch. "It's another one," she screamed. "This time it's your old girlfriend."

He almost said "Sara?", knowing that's who she meant, but instead yelled back, "I don't know who you're talking about."

Alma spat the name as though it tasted vile and bitter upon her tongue. "Sara Daughtry Speight."

Luke got in the car and slammed the door. Sara had been having trouble with somebody stealing her newspaper off her porch. She said she'd call him if she had a clue as to who might be doing it, but there was no rush. He would take care of it later. "Tell her I'm in a hurry, and I'll call her first chance."

Alma stared after him, thinking he had to be the world's biggest fool if he thought she was going to make it easy for him to chase around. She went back to the phone and told Sara, "He says he hasn't got time to mess with you now, and if you've got a problem to take it to one of his deputies. And I'd really prefer that you not call here. I don't like you chasing after my husband."

Sara hung up.

Alma gloated to think she'd bested her this time but still wondered why Sara was crying, why she'd sounded so *scared*.

"Luke, aren't you done yet?" Murline stood just outside the open door to Buddy's office, knees shaking because she was so nervous.

Luke, caught up in what he was doing, did not respond.

She glanced at her watch again. "It's almost ten-thirty, and I've never stayed this late before. I'm afraid the security guard might come barging in wanting to know why."

He raised his eyes from the Western Union receipts in his hand to look at her long and hard before asking in a don't-bull-shit-me tone, "What do you know about these?"

She entered the office to see what he was talking about, and then her face paled as it had when he had shown her the shoe she'd lost out the window of Dennis Blum's car. Backing away, she began to stammer, "Uh, I . . . I really can't say."

He shook them at her. "Your signature is on every single one of them, and they go back for the last twenty years. Five hundred dollars a month, sometimes more, wired from the Western Union office in Anniston to the name *C. Swain* in Birmingham. So what's the story?"

"I don't know. I swear I don't."

"But you sent them."

She leaned against the door frame, closed her eyes momentarily, then looked everywhere but at him as she admitted, "Yes, I did, but I don't know anything else about them."

"Well, it's easy enough to figure out Buddy was trying to hide something, but why did he have you send them from Anniston?"

"I'm always going there. My parents moved there right after I graduated from high school when my dad changed jobs. Buddy told me to send the wires when I visited them around the first of the month."

"Are you sure you don't know who C. Swain is?"

"I swear I don't. I just do what Buddy tells me to. I don't ask questions. Maybe that's why I've managed to keep my job all this long." She spread her hands in a pleading gesture. "Please. Don't make me get fired. Thurman doesn't make much in his repair shop, and we've got a lot of bills. He was sick in the hospital a few years ago, and we're still paying for it."

He sensed she was close to tears, and he didn't need her going to pieces. "Help me, Murline, and I promise you won't have anything to worry about." Hell, he'd even see to it she got a raise, she and anybody else at the mill that he named. All he had to do was get something to hold over Buddy, and Buddy would dance to his tune forevermore, like Junior Kearney and Hardy Moon. "But you can't just feed me bits and pieces along. I have to find all the skeletons in Buddy's closet at one time because, if he figures out I'm onto him, he'll start covering his tracks, destroying evidence, like these receipts . . ." He shook them at her again.

She was twisting her hands nervously and starting to sniffle. "But I just don't know anything else. He gives me the money in cash the first week of every month, and I wire it like I've done for years. I never ask questions. I just do it. I had no idea he even kept the receipts."

"Maybe somebody is blackmailing him."

She could not resist a sarcastic comeback. "Like the way *you're* blackmailing *me*?"

He gave her a dark look. "Call it what you will, but if you don't keep working with me on this, I promise Thurman will find out it wasn't Cinderella's foot hanging out Dennis Blum's car window when a shoe fell off."

She sank into the nearest chair in defeat. "I just don't like snitching, Luke. I've always minded my own business and let anything I hear go in one ear and out the other because Buddy has been good to me. I make more than any of the other secretaries, and . . ."

He cut her off to remind, "You said on the phone you've got something to tell me about Cubby Riddle."

"It's like you thought, about why Buddy sent him to the Klan rally. I forgot my gloves the other day and came back to get them, and Cubby was in here. They didn't know I was around, and I heard Cubby say there was nothing to worry about, that the Klan had promised to deal with anybody who started stirring up support for the union."

"Did they mention any names?"

"Just one—Ocie Rhoden. But I probably could have told you that without overhearing Cubby. Everybody knows Ocie is for the union. He's been very outspoken, handing out leaflets, talking it up."

Luke remembered the first year he was sheriff, Ocie had gotten his discharge from the army and told him how the only job he could find was at the mill and that he hated how the coloreds were mistreated. They didn't make minimum wage, and their working conditions were terrible. They had to use the outdoor toilets because indoor facilities were for whites only. The same was true of water fountains. If the coloreds wanted water, they had to wait till lunch break to get a drink from an outdoor spigot. Ocie also confided that the supervisors cursed and yelled at them. He likened the situation to slavery, except for the small pittance they received.

So it came as no surprise to Luke that Ocie would get involved in the struggle to bring the union into the mill if it meant fair wages and decent working conditions for him and his people.

Luke pointed a warning finger at Murline. "You don't want anything to happen to Ocie Rhoden and have me think that you knew something and didn't tell me beforehand. Understand?"

She managed to shake her head, worried she was going to be sick again. The boiled pork and peas she'd gulped down for supper were rolling around in her stomach.

"I want you to keep your eyes and ears open, and if you hear even a whisper that Buddy is about to sic the Klan on Ocie, you better tell me quick."

She pressed her hand against her mouth and spoke through her fingers. "Yes."

"How often do Buddy and Cubby have private meetings?"

"Often."

"Well, sooner or later they're going to talk about Ocie again, so I'd suggest you start forgetting your gloves every day, so you can be listening outside that door when they do."

She tasted boiled pork and peas. "I'm sorry . . ." She leaped to her feet and ran from the room.

Glancing around to make sure he'd left no clue that he'd been there, he thought of Emma Jean and wondered how long she had waited behind the cemetery before giving up on him. He hadn't meant to take so long going through Buddy's files, but then he never thought there would be so many.

He left as he had come, without being seen. He was done. Now all he had to do was figure out why Buddy Hampton sent money to Birmingham every month and hope he had scared Murline into keeping him informed of anything else he might find useful.

He drove by Emma Jean's house. The lights were on in the kitchen. Rudy would be home, and she was probably fixing him something to eat, and then they'd go to bed, and . . .

He slammed his hands on the steering wheel and cursed himself for fretting because it was a danger signal he was getting too involved. Hell, he'd known for weeks he was getting in over his head, but what to do about it was bugging him badly. He drove on through the night, the air sweet and loamy from fresh-planted crops as he took back roads, not only through the countryside but also through his mind. So many landmarks to ignite memories. Some good. Some bad. But all there, indelibly stamped in his brain.

He wondered if maybe it didn't get worse as a person got older, the years stretching out behind and leaving a trail in the dust like drops from a leaky oil tank, making more and more memories to hurt and sting and prod wishes for having done things differently. But it was called life, and there was no getting around it. Face it. Feel the hurt. Mull the disappointments. Keep on going, and try like hell to leave some good drops along with the bad.

CHAPTER 19

Spring came to Alabama.

Dogwood blossoms dotted the woods like popcorn, and cotton plants strained to burst forth from the earth. There had been some heavy rains and a few small tornadoes, which was not unusual for this time of year, but the sweet fragrance of gardenias wafted from front porches banked by red and pink and white azaleas. Lawns were greening, and birds were nesting.

It was a most glorious season, and, for the first time in his life, Luke welcomed and enjoyed it because, in the past, springtime hadn't meant anything to him. Maybe that was because he had never had anyone to share it with. And now he did—Emma Jean.

Lord, that woman had a hold on his heart he didn't want to think about. Every time they were together, he fell harder and counted the days and hours till next time.

He had been especially looking forward to the day ahead because Bert Veazey, the old skinflint, was being forced to close the laundromat long enough to install two new dryers after the old ones finally gave out and couldn't be fixed. So Emma Jean was off while Rudy was on day shift.

It wasn't quite nine o'clock. Luke was picking her up on the road a little ways from her house at a spot where she could duck into a thicket of wild plum bushes and hide if anybody happened along before he did. He had a blanket in the trunk and knew of a real isolated spot by a creek below Crow's Knob where he'd played as a kid. Nobody ever went there anymore.

He stopped by the store and picked up a couple of ready-made sandwiches, a can of pork and beans, a slab of hoop cheese, two Moon Pies, and a couple of sodas. They would have a picnic on the creek bank . . . *and a picnic in each other's arms.* Yes, it was going to be a mighty fine day, and he was whistling when he turned into Creech's station.

He got out of the car as one of the attendants started filling the tank, intending to go inside and catch up on any gossip from the men hanging around in there. Then he saw Sara drive up to a pump and remembered it had been several weeks since that night she'd called and Alma got her back up about it.

He walked over. "Sorry, I haven't had a chance to call you, Sara. Is somebody still swiping your papers?"

"It wasn't about the damn newspapers, Luke."

"Oh?" He put a hand on the roof of the truck and leaned closer. "What then?"

She turned her head, but not before he saw tears in her eyes. "Tim hasn't found out about Dewey, has he?"

She was curt. "No."

"Then what's wrong?"

"I'll handle it myself."

"Okay, so you're mad at me because I didn't get back to you, and I'm sorry. Now tell me about it."

"Not here." She darted anxious glances about. "God knows, Luke, Alma was so mad about my calling you I half-expected her to come running right over to my house that night to tear my hair out."

He felt a rush of peeve. "Don't worry about her. Just tell me what you wanted."

"Not here," she repeated, looking at him again, this time in desperation rather than anger. "I've got to get back to the field. Dewey is setting tomato plants, and I've got to stop at the store to get sodas for the hands. Follow me, and we can talk there."

The store was in the opposite direction from where he was supposed to meet Emma Jean in ten minutes. If he followed Sara, he'd be delayed at least a half hour, maybe longer. Emma Jean wouldn't know what was keeping him and give up and go home. There was no way for him to contact her, and the day would be ruined. "Look, Sara, I can't right now. There's some place I've got to go. But later . . ."

"Oh, forget it." She turned the ignition key to start the engine.

"Hey, Sara," Leonard Creech yelled. "Hang on. I'll be right with you."

"Never mind," she yelled back. "I've got enough to do me."

She shifted gears, preparing to drive away, and Luke tried once more. "Maybe late this evening I can give you a call, and we can meet then."

"Tim will be home. I said I'll handle it myself."

She fixed him with an icy scowl before squealing tires as she tore away from the gas station. Had it been anybody else, he would have jumped in his car and hit the blue light, pulled them over, and written a ticket for reckless driving. But this was Sara, and something had her really agitated, so he let her go.

Leonard walked over to grumble about impatient women, but Luke wasn't listening. He was too engrossed in wondering what had riled Sara so. He had never seen her like that. However, by the time he signed the charge slip for the gas and drove away, she had slipped from his mind, pushed away by thoughts of Emma Jean.

"This is what heaven must be like." Emma Jean twined a weeping willow frond about her fingers as she stood marveling at the clear, cool waters of the creek and the velvety green banks.

Luke laughed and pointed to a limb hanging out over the stream. "I doubt heaven will have any rotten ropes."

She followed his gaze. "What on earth is that? Was somebody hanged here?"

"No. It's a swing rope. We used to come here in the summer when we were kids, and we'd grab hold of it and back off for a running start and then leap from the bank to swing right about to there." He pointed to a wide spot in the creek. "And then we'd let go. But I guess kids nowadays spend all their time watching television instead of playing outside."

He had taken off his shirt. She threw herself against him, wrapping her arms about him as she pressed her cheek against his chest. "I can't think of anything in the whole world I'd rather do than play outside with you."

He cupped her chin and lowered his face to hers. "I feel the same way, honey. I've never had so much fun as I do when I'm with you."

He kissed her, leaving them both shaken when he finally let her go to quickly spread the blanket beneath the weeping willow.

"Are you sure nobody ever comes along here?" she asked nervously as she began to unbutton her blouse. She folded it carefully, along with her shorts, so she wouldn't have to explain wrinkles or grass stains.

"There's nothing to worry about," he assured, peeling out of his khaki uniform trousers and laying them neatly beside his shirt. "There used to be a little church nearby, but it burned back in the fifties. I heard the county eventually took the land over when the taxes weren't paid, so here it sits. It's so far out nobody wants it."

"I'd want it. I'd want a house right up there on that little knoll. And I wouldn't care how far out it is because, if you and me were living here, I'd never want to go anywhere, and . . ." She fell silent, suddenly embarrassed. They never talked about being together that way, and here she had made it sound like she was living for the day when he'd divorce Alma and marry her. Oh, Lord, why couldn't she keep her mouth shut?

Luke pulled her into his arms once more. "I'd like that, sweetheart. I really would."

They collapsed to the ground in a frenzy of heat.

Afterwards, Luke rolled to his side. Propping on an elbow as he tenderly gazed down at her, he toyed with one of her nipples, liking the feel of it rolling between his thumb and fingers. "Plump like a strawberry. I envy the baby that nurses on you, Emma Jean."

"Well, I don't reckon there'll ever be one. Not as long as I'm married to Rudy if I can help it." She stared up into the swaying fronds, the tender moment spoiled by thoughts of her wretched marriage.

Not about to let a shadow fall over their day, Luke scrambled to his feet, pulling her up with him. "How about a swim?"

She resisted. "My hair will get wet, and it might not dry by the time I get home, thick as it is, and Rudy will notice and start asking questions."

"Tell him you washed it."

"On a Wednesday? He'd never believe that. He knows I only shampoo on Saturdays. That's when we heat water on the stove for our baths."

"Then we'll just go in up to our necks."

And so they did. Afterwards, they feasted on the picnic Luke had brought, then walked along the creek bank in search of four-leaf clovers. They held hands and talked, eventually broaching the part of their lives that caused them the most grief, their marriages.

"Wasn't there ever a time when you thought you were in love with Alma?" Emma Jean asked as they sat on rocks, their feet dangling in the water. She had put her bra and panties back on, and Luke was wearing his shorts.

He scoffed at the question. "No, there wasn't. Like I said, it was a quickie in the back seat that made a baby, and I had to do right by her, at least, that's what my momma made me believe."

"You loved her a lot, didn't you, your momma?"

"Yes, I did, because she was the only person I ever felt loved me. She was all I had."

"But what about your little girl? Aren't you close to her?"

"Alma's done a good job of making her think all our problems are my fault. I gave up on her long ago."

Emma Jean's heart went out to him, and, as she placed her hand on his knee in a gesture of comfort, longed to tell him he was wrong, that his mother wasn't the only person who had ever loved him. But she said nothing, keeping her secret. They had agreed only to have fun together, not to get serious, which could lead to complications. She feared if he realized she had fallen for him, he would stop seeing her, and she could not bear the thoughts of that. He was the only reason she had to live in an otherwise cruel and lonely world.

Luke looked at his watch. It was nearly three o'clock, and Emma Jean cried, "Oh, God, Luke, I'll never make it home before Rudy. I've got to walk home from where you drop me off, and then wash off, and . . ."

"And you'll make it." He grabbed her arm and steered her along the creek to where he'd left the car. She laid down in the seat, her head in his lap so she would not be seen by anyone they passed as he drove as fast as he dared on the curving roads. Reaching her drive and making sure Rudy's truck wasn't there, he let her out. No time for a kiss, just a hurried promise to be in touch when he could. Emma Jean scrambled from the car and ran all the way to the house.

The stove clock read 3:10, which meant she had about ten minutes to get herself looking normal and start supper. Rudy liked to eat early when the days were warm and getting longer. It gave him more time afterwards to spend at the grill with his drinking buddies. With cold water from the sink, she quickly soaped and rinsed and had just pulled on clean shorts and a top when Rudy drove his truck into the yard. A few seconds later, he walked in, set his metal lunch box on the table with a thud, glanced around, then snarled, "You ain't started my supper yet, woman? I shoulda known you wouldn't do nothin' on your day off 'cept sit on your ass."

"I'm sorry, Rudy." Frantically, she looked in the refrigerator for something to fix. She had been looking forward to seeing Luke so much she'd forgotten all about grocery shopping.

"You gonna stand there with the refrigerator door open and let all the cold air out? Don't you know that runs up the light bill? But you don't care about that, do you?" He came up behind and gave her a hard slap on her backsides. "You don't pay the damn light bill, so why should you give a shit?"

"I . . . I help with the bills," she could not resist reminding. "I give you my pay every week, Rudy."

"And anything else I want." He hit her bottom again, then squeezed. "Gettin' a little fat, ain't you? But in the wrong place. I want to see some fat here." He moved his hand to her flat stomach. "Only you ain't gettin' knocked up, and you know why?"

He spun her around to face him, and she smelled his sour breath and knew he'd had a beer on the way home.

"Cause I don't never get any, that's why."

Ordinarily, Emma Jean would not dare protest, but in the afterglow of being with Luke, the thought of doing it with Rudy just then swept her with revulsion.

Pushing him away, she said, "I need to go to the store. I'll get some pork chops, and . . ."

"*This* is your pork chop," he gave a nasty laugh and shoved his pelvis against her so she could feel his erection.

"Rudy, don't . . ."

"*Rudy, don't . . .*" he mimicked, grabbing a handful of her hair and twisting to make her scream.

Maneuvering her to the table, he turned her around and shoved her, face forward, across it. "You don't never tell me don't do nothin', you hear me, bitch? You're my wife, and I take what I want, when I want, and I reckon I want it now . . ."

As he was talking, he had unzipped his jeans and yanked down her shorts and panties. She bit her lip to keep from screaming again because it only made him all the rougher when she did. She tasted blood and closed her eyes and ground her teeth together and prayed it would soon be over.

When he was done, he yanked her up and gave her a shove. "Now you fix my supper and then get ready for prayer meetin'. Me and Ma have decided it's time you got saved. She says then you'll get pregnant."

He took a beer from the refrigerator, and Emma Jean watched, trembling, till he'd drunk nearly half of it in one long gulp before she dared to say, "I don't like that church, Rudy. They do crazy things, talking in tongue and rolling around on the floor, and . . ."

"Oh, shut up. They do what they believe in. Besides, it don't look good for me to have a wife that ain't saved. All women get saved. Ma says God gives 'em babies then."

"You . . . you don't really believe that, do you?" she asked cautiously.

"No, but if it makes Ma happy, I'm not gonna say different. You just make sure when the preacher gives the altar call tonight you march your ass up there and get born again, understand? 'Cause if you don't, I'm gonna give you a beatin' you'll never forget."

"Rudy . . ."

He had started from the room but spun about, one hand clenched in a fist of warning. "You gonna talk back to me, woman?"

She shook her head wildly from side to side. "No. No. If that's what you want, Rudy, I'll do it for you. It's just that . . ."

"Just what?"

She swallowed hard. "When you get born again in that church, they make you handle the snakes."

"So? If you haven't done nothin' wrong, you got nothin' to worry about. The snakes won't bite." He took a step forward and she instantly cowered. "But if you do something, like run around on me, it won't matter 'cause I'll kill you myself. You hear me?"

She heard, all right, and when he left the kitchen, she closed her eyes and tried to fill herself with the solace of remembering how Luke had held her and kissed her. He had to care something about her to be so tender, and if he did, then he'd find a way to save her from the snakes. She had to think that way . . . or go crazy worrying.

CHAPTER 20

November, 1969

Alma was bored stiff. Shifting in her chair in hopes of finding a more comfortable position, she wished she were anywhere but the hospital.

Luke had survived the ambulance ride to Birmingham, as well as the delicate surgery to remove the bullet from his brain. But he had been in a coma ever since, and the doctors had no idea when, or if, he'd come out of it. So all anybody could do was wait and see what happened.

Well, she wouldn't have to be keeping such a vigil, Alma angrily thought, if not for Sara. No matter how many times Alma had cussed her out and told her to stay away, Sara kept trying to sneak in to see Luke. The hussy just wouldn't give up.

The door opened, and Alma frowned as a nurse came in carrying a pan of water and the fixings for Luke's bath. "Don't ask me to give it to him," Alma was quick to say. "Like I told all them other nurses, I'm not washing him."

The nurse regarded her coldly. "They told me you refused, but it seems to me since he's your husband, you'd rather bathe him than have a stranger do it. And we are terribly busy today."

Alma returned her glare, not about to be put down by her or anybody else. "I don't care. You're getting paid to bathe him. I'm not. So you do it. I'm gonna go have me some lunch."

The nurse stared after her, then shifted her gaze to Luke in pity. If that was all he had to wake up to, she thought, then maybe he'd be better off if he just kept on sleeping.

Chapter 21

Spring, 1969

Billy Saulston's country store was like hundreds of others that dotted the rural back roads of the south in the sixties. A square wood building, the covered porch was a gathering place for farmers to wile away summer nights complaining about crops or sharing idle talk, till winter drove them inside to the warmth of the pot-bellied stove.

Out back on Friday nights someone usually cooked a stew in a big black cauldron over an open fire—turtle, squirrel, but mostly fish, with potatoes, onions, eggs, and catsup.

Nearby, at the edge of the corn field bordering the store, an outhouse leaned precariously to one side. Inside the store, the floor was rarely swept, red clay thickly imbedded between the worn planks. Wood shelves, buckling from the weight of dusty cans, lined the walls from floor to ceiling. No one ever bought real groceries, but Billy kept a small selection anyway, just in case. His primary stock was in cigarettes, chewing tobacco, snuff, sodas, candy bars, and peanut butter crackers called

"Nabs" because a company called Nabisco made them. Billy also sold ice cream bars, sandwich bread, hoop cheese, penny cookies, pickled eggs and pickled pig's feet, along with small cans of pork and beans, sardines, and Vienna sausage.

Normally, during the farming months, the store was deserted during the day, except for people rushing in to buy sodas and sacks of candy and Nabs for the field hands' mid-morning break. It could get crowded quickly, as Sara discovered when she drove up in Dewey's truck to fetch treats for his workers. She had to park in the rear and went in the back door.

Standing last in line, she scanned her shopping list: twelve RC colas, seven Tabs, three root beers, a dozen Moon Pies, six Nabs, three Baby Ruths, and a Powerhouse candy bar. She only hoped Billy didn't sell out of root beer before it was her turn. The boys wanting it could get real crabby, and she was running late. When she'd gone to get in the truck, Dewey just happened to be there, and with nobody else around to see, they'd tarried for a little kissy-kissy, touchy-feely, and she felt a delicious shiver in her tummy to think about it.

That was what was so wonderful about her and Dewey, she mused dreamily as she waited in line. They didn't have to go to bed together to be happy. All she really needed was a kiss now and then and a hug. And, oh Lord, how she loved his big, smothering bear hugs. After all, he was nearly sixty-two years old and liked to tease that he wanted sex as much as he always did, *just not as much of it*. So, lots of times they were content to slip off and be together without it. A warm, hand-holding kind of love. That was how she'd tried to describe what they had to Luke.

She was suddenly needled to think how strange Luke was acting lately, like he was in a world of his own. Maybe he and Alma were getting along worse than usual, but then he was always saying it just couldn't *get* any worse. Sara had started wondering if there might be another woman.

Besides, she was daring to hope maybe she wouldn't need his help, after all. It had been a while since Burch Cleghorn's disgusting visit, and he hadn't bothered her since. Oh, there'd been a few times when she answered the phone to hear heavy breathing and nobody would say anything. She thought it was him, but if that was all he intended to do, she could put up with that.

In those first, nerve-wracking days afterwards, she'd been

tempted to tell Dewey but thought better of it and now she was glad. He'd have been so mad there was no telling what he might have done. He hadn't been feeling real good lately, either, complaining about his stomach and gobbling Tums like they were Lifesavers. If *she* were his wife, she knew she would get him to the doctor one way or the other, but Aunt Carrie stayed so busy around the farm and with her church work that she paid him no mind.

"What'll it be today, Sara?" Billy asked when it was finally her turn.

She handed him her order. "About the same as always."

He got everything together, except for the root beer. "Sold out five minutes ago. Sorry. Can't seem to keep enough on hand. I substituted RCs. Hope that's okay."

"Well, they won't like it," she said as she opened her own bottle of pop to sip on the way back. Sweat was running down her face, and it felt like every stitch she had on was wet.

There were customers waiting, and Billy said, "If you can wait a minute, I'll carry all that out for you."

"It's okay. I can make a couple of trips."

"Oh, no need for that," a voice spoke from behind. "I'll carry the sodas. You take the candy and other stuff."

Sara whirled about to stare in horror.

Billy not seeing her reaction, said, "That's real nice of you, Mr. Cleghorn," then turned to the next person in line.

Not about to make a scene for everyone to wonder about, Sara picked up the sacks, the paper rattling noisily because her hand was shaking so. "Thank you," she managed to murmur, wishing she had been able to park in front of the store, where there were people coming and going. Nobody was out back except her.

Hurrying, she opened the door to the truck's cab and slid inside, tossing the bags on the seat. "Just put it in the back." She stuck the key in the ignition, turned it, and the motor sprang to life.

Burch smirked at her through the open window. "Well, now, Sara, honey," he drawled. "I'm real glad to see you. Didn't dream I would when I stopped by for a cold soda. But now that we've met up, how about you taking these drinks where they need to go and then meeting me someplace?"

"Not a chance." She gunned the motor. "Now please put them in the back. I'm in a hurry."

His smirk did not waver. "So am I, *to get in your britches*."

"When hell freezes, damn you. Now load those drinks before I yell for Billy."

The smirk disappeared, and his lids lowered to hood his eyes in malice. "You're going to be sorry, you little tramp." He slammed the bottles down.

She backed out with a fury, tires spinning as she switched gears to send the truck hurtling down the road toward Dewey's farm. It wasn't going to get any better, and she was a fool to think it might. Burch was going to keep after her, and sooner or later something bad would happen. She had to have Luke's help to make him stop.

The day passed with agonizing slowness, and finally she was on her way home, stopping at the pay phone at Billy's store to call Luke. She did not dare use the one at Dewey's house because of his party line.

Wilma put her straight through to Luke after Sara said it was urgent. As soon as she heard his voice, she blurted, "I've got to see you right away. It can't wait."

"What's wrong?"

"I'll tell you when I see you. Name the place, and I'm on my way."

"I was fixing to take the jail laundry to the laundromat."

"I'll be there in ten minutes."

Luke set the basket on the floor, relieved nobody else was around. When Emma Jean came out of the storage room, he felt like his mouth was going to crack at the corners from grinning at the sight of her.

"I've got a good mind to drag you back there and show you just how much I've missed you, woman."

"I don't think that would be a good idea."

He saw how her lips were trembling, her eyes brimming with tears. He started toward her. "Baby, what's wrong?"

"Don't!" She nodded towards the window behind him. "Somebody's coming."

He turned and saw it was Sara and quickly explained that

she had wanted to meet him there. "But it can wait till you tell me what's got you so upset."

"Snakes," she said with a shiver. "It's the snakes, Luke. They're going to make me handle them tonight."

He felt like he'd been kicked by a mule. "No, hell, you aren't."

"I have to. After Rudy made me go to the altar to supposedly get saved, Miss Bertha says I have to be purged to make sure I'm truly cleansed of sin." She gave a little snort. "Oh, yeah. I'll get cleansed all right. Those snakes are going to eat me alive, and we both know it." She ran her hands up and down the goosebumps on her arms. "Miss Bertha says the reason I haven't gotten pregnant again is because I haven't been right with the Lord, so she's insisting on all of this, 'cause she wants a grandbaby so bad."

"Well, it's not going to happen," he said fiercely, furiously. "It's against the law. I'll raid the place."

"If you do, it'll make everybody wonder how you found out it was going on."

He ran his hands through his bristly crew cut. "That's nothing to fret about. I've always known those crazies play with snakes but haven't done anything about it. I figure it's their funeral, and I've got more important things to do. But this is different. Now you just go on like you're supposed to, and I promise me and Matt and Kirby will be there in time to break it up before things get started, okay?" God, he wanted to take her in his arms so bad it hurt, but Sara was out there, sitting in her car, no doubt watching through the window and wondering what was keeping him.

Emma Jean protested, "I need your help, but there has to be another way. Rudy hates you. He's always saying so. If he hears you broke it up, he might start wondering, and God help me if that happens."

"I can't let you take a chance on getting bit."

"Maybe I won't," she said, braver than she felt. "Miss Bertha says I just have to be careful and not make the snakes feel threatened."

"Hell, they're going to be stirred up by all the drums and cymbals and folks screaming before you even pick one up, so it's not going to matter whether you stroke it like a baby or croon it a lullaby."

"But Miss Bertha says she handles all the time, and so do a lot of other folks, and they don't get bit."

He rubbed his hands through his hair again, feeling desperate. A dryer buzzer sounded, and they both jumped.

"You'd better go on out there and see Sara," Emma Jean said, walking toward the dryer. "And you forget about raiding that church."

"I'll think of something, Emma Jean. I swear."

She had never seen him look so worried. "I know you will, Luke, and I love you for it."

Quickly, she turned away, not wanting to see his face, because she had never mentioned love to him, not in any way, and she was afraid of his reaction to her having done so now.

Luke's palms were sweating as he walked out to meet Sara, but not from the weather. The heat was in his heart. *She had said she loved him.*

"I love you for it," she had said, which meant she loved him for promising to help.

But maybe it actually meant something else, something he dreamed about, fantasized about, but wouldn't let himself seriously consider happening. They couldn't fall in love with each other. In *lust*, okay. Even friendship. But love meant problems. Love meant thinking about tomorrow and the next day, forever and always. And they couldn't do that.

Could they?

His mind jerked to the present, realizing he was standing by the window of Sara's car, and she was staring up at him.

"You look funny," she said.

"Uh, I'm okay. Just busy." He was struggling to abandon thoughts of Emma Jean for the moment and concentrate on Sara, but his mind refused. Prayer meeting started at seven. It was nearly four-thirty. He didn't have long, and the idea he had in mind was going to be taking a chance, anyway, but it was the only one he had. Otherwise, he'd have to go against Emma Jean's wishes and raid the church. Rudy and everybody else could think what they wanted to, and . . .

Sara's tone was sharp, "If you still don't have time to listen to me . . ."

He leaned so he could fold his arms on the window, face

inches from hers. "I've just got a lot on my mind. Now, what's up, doc?" He wiggled his nose like Bugs Bunny to try and cheer her up, only it didn't work, and he said, "Hey, you don't look so good."

"I'm not good. Nothing's good." She gave her head a wild toss and gripped the steering wheel and felt like butting her head against it. "I've got trouble, Luke. Big trouble. It's Burch Cleghorn."

She had his attention then, and he listened intently. By the time she finished, she was in tears. "I just don't know what to do, Luke. He's threatening to see Ted finds out about me and Dewey if I don't do what he wants."

"Have you told Dewey?"

"Of course not. He'd pitch a fit and try to tear him apart. I can't tell him or anybody else. Just you. And you've got to do something, Luke. Talk to him. Make him leave me alone and warn him about running his mouth and saying anything about me and Dewey. So many people would be hurt. I might lose my kids, and . . ." She shook her head at such a heartbreaking thought and rubbed her eyes with the back of her hands.

Luke glanced up as Emma Jean came out of the laundromat, locking the door behind her.

She waved to Sara, and, in a genial voice only Luke knew was forced, called, "I'm going to prayer meeting tonight, so I'm closing a little early. Did you need anything, Sara?"

Sara answered, "No, but thanks."

Time was wasting, and there was only one chance he could find a way to protect her besides raiding the church.

He had to find the snake man.

As the story went, Elmer Bruce Cribbes earned the name by virtue of having been stricken as a child with some kind of strange skin disease. His grandmother, not believing in doctors like so many of her generation, concocted a salve that not only destroyed the disease but also Elmer Bruce's skin. It had shed and come off, *just like a snake.* When it grew back, it was in shiny, scaly patches of gray and black with yellow flesh on the undersides, *just like a snake.* The other kids had taunted and made fun of him, and, as he grew up, Elmer Bruce retreated into his own world, a world filled with snakes. He collected them, made pets of them, and, when he was old enough, had gone to live with them in a tar paper shanty in Thunder Swamp, which he built himself out of scraps he hauled from the county dump.

Eventually he got himself saved at the Thunder Swamp Pentecostal Holiness church and went on to become one of its biggest handlers. There wasn't a snake big enough or mean enough to scare Elmer Bruce. He would pick up a rattler or a cottonmouth and coil them all around his face and neck and arms without batting an eye. Rumor said he had been bitten a time or two and nearly died, but nobody would say for sure. Secrecy was very important to snake-handlers, and that was why those bitten sometimes died. They were afraid to seek medical help for fear of bringing the law down on the church. They were also ashamed to have it get around they had been bitten, for it made them look *un*annointed and in disfavor with the Holy Spirit. It was only natural that Elmer Bruce would wind up being the snake-keeper for the church, and, accordingly, Luke figured he was the one person who could help him now.

Suddenly, Sara could not stand Luke's inattention any longer. "Damn it, you're staring off into space like you haven't heard a word I've said, and I don't have anybody else to turn to but you."

Luke was aware that Sara's problem could ultimately prove to be a way to bring the hammer down on Burch, but he needed time to think about it. "I heard you, all right, and I'm mad as hell, believe me. But I need a few days to figure out the best way to handle it."

"I may not have that long. He's crazy. There's no telling what he might do. Luke, me and Dewey have been seeing each other for over fifteen years, and nobody has ever suspected a thing."

"Maybe, but you can't be sure. People might have noticed and not said anything where you would've heard it. You have to remember not much goes on in this town that doesn't eventually get found out. It's the chance you take when you fool around."

Irritated that he was not being the instant hero she'd hoped he would be, she could not resist the barb, "Like the one you're taking with Emma Jean Veazey?"

He forced a laugh. "What kind of nonsense is that? What have you heard?"

"Nothing." She waved her hand, wishing she hadn't said anything. "I'm just being shitty because you aren't helping me."

He decided if she did suspect, she'd never say anything. He didn't have time to worry about it right then, anyway. "Hey, you just hit me with this, remember? I can't jump off and do something that might make things worse. Besides, you blew up and told him off today, when the other time you just cried. So maybe he'll leave you alone now."

"Maybe," she agreed, deciding he had a point. She really hadn't stood up to Burch before. "But be thinking about it, okay?"

"I will. I promise. And meanwhile, if he does anything else, you call me, and I'll get right on it, okay?"

With a nod, she backed out of the parking lot and drove away.

Luke looked at his watch again. He only had a little over two hours left to try and keep Emma Jean from getting bit. He jumped in his car and headed for Thunder Swamp and the snake man.

"When are we gonna move on these nuts, Luke?"

Luke held a finger to his lips, even though it was unlikely they could be heard over all the racket inside: pounding drums, shaking tambourines, dancing, stomping, yelling. Everyone was up and moving around. Except Emma Jean. She was sitting on the front row with her hands clasped beneath her chin. Her face was the color of bread dough, and tears were streaming from her eyes. Luke wished he could just leap through the window, grab her, and run.

The church, built of pine boards and tar paper, was just one small room with benches and a plywood stage at one end. Surrounded on three sides by dense swampland, it was pretty isolated, which discouraged anyone except members from coming around. Snake-handling churches did not encourage visitors.

Luke and Matt were watching through a window. Since it was pitch dark, they would not be noticed. He had brought Matt in case something did happen, like Emma Jean getting bit, which would cause him to expose his presence. Matt being with him would make it look like an official surveillance. After all, the state legislature had passed a law against fooling around with poisonous snakes back in 1950. It was a felony, could get somebody one to five years in prison, but the believers didn't let that possibility dissuade them.

"Hear the word, children," the preacher was shouting. "Hear the holy word of Mark 16: *'They shall take up serpents, and if they drink any deadly thing, it shall not hurt them . . .'*

"Have the faith," he cried, pacing rapidly back and forth, "Have the faith, and no harm will come to you. God will prove you are saved and pure in heart . . ."

"Oh, man," Matt whispered. "Look at that."

A man had thrown himself on the floor spread-eagled, and another was leaping over him holding a snake stretched between his hands. The snake looked bewildered, hypnotized, almost, by all the hysteria, which, Luke knew after talking to Elmer Bruce, was the key to a handler not getting bit.

"Ahi-lai-wanna-gwum-heeny-heeny," the man on the floor cried as he thrust his pelvis up and down like a fifty dollar hooker. "Yeemah! Yeemah! Allywannayamma Yeemah!"

Someone else pointed and screamed, "He's got it! The Holy Ghost! He's filled with the spirit. Oh, praise God, Wally's got it!"

As best Luke could tell amidst the delirium, three snakes were being passed around. One was a canebrake rattler, fat and a yellowish gray color. He knew the snake by Elmer Bruce's description, just as he recognized the two copperheads, bronze and gold in the overhead lights. Elmer Bruce said the copperheads were the least likely to bite if they were handled right and had promised not to use the eastern diamondback rattlers, which were the most dangerous. Neither would he bring out the timber rattlers, which were used most often.

Bertha Veazey, knees jerking up to her big belly as she stomped in cadence to the drums, danced her way to Emma Jean and tugged at her arms. Luke bit the inside of his jaw and tasted blood. It was taking every shred of self-control he could muster to keep from charging in.

He tried to focus on Elmer Bruce's promise that he would bring only old snakes tonight. He'd also said he'd see to it they were well-fed with barn mice beforehand so they'd be real lazy and not care much what was going on. All this, of course, had been extracted from Elmer Bruce after Luke had matter-of-factly assured him that, if any harm came to Emma Jean, he would kill him without any qualms whatsoever and make it look like an accident.

Luke's pulse quickened as he saw Bertha wave toward a man dancing with a canebrake to bring it over. He didn't want Emma Jean handling that one, damn it. It was too alert, whipping his head from side to side, forked tongue flicking in menace. But then Elmer Bruce suddenly appeared. Like Bertha, he was keeping time with the drums, his worn ankle boots clopping up and down. Without breaking his rhythm, he lifted a copperhead from a man who seemed to be having some kind of a spell, eyes rolled back in his head and spittle running from the corners of his mouth. He didn't seem to notice when the snake was taken away from him.

Elmer Bruce held the serpent out to Emma Jean, his head bobbing up and down to her in a silent, secret message that it was all right. She had nothing to fear. But she had no way of knowing it was a set-up deal, that Luke had put a deeper fear into Elmer Bruce Cribbes than the Holy Ghost or Satan had ever been able to do, and that before he'd let her be bitten, he'd take the snake's fangs in his own flesh.

Luke, on the other hand, had no way of knowing that Emma Jean had put all her faith in *him* for the night instead of God. He had said he would think of something, and she believed him because she loved him and dared to hope he might love her, too.

The snake was testing the air with his tongue, and Elmer Bruce put his finger in front of his mouth, letting him touch it. Then he pressed his face against the snake's, and the two seemed to be watching each other for a few seconds before the snake finally drew back and flicked at the air again.

Bertha managed to pull Emma Jean, whose horrified gaze was locked on the snake, to her feet. Elmer Bruce gave her a lopsided smile, trying once more to secretly convey she had nothing to worry about, because he had given his word to the sheriff. Though the sheriff had not said why he wanted her protected, Elmer Bruce could guess. But it was none of his business. All he cared about was keeping his promise because he was firmly convinced the sheriff would surely keep his if he didn't.

Very slowly, very carefully, he held the snake high above his head, then brought it down to drape over Emma Jean's forearm, the rest of its cold, scaly body stretching around her wrist and hand. Emma Jean gagged as the snake began to move in and around her fingers as bits of his skin fell to the floor. Luke saw the snake and knew it was shedding. Elmer Bruce had said he thought he had a copperhead that was, which was a good thing, because they were even more docile. It was like they were too busy reinventing themselves, making new out of old, to be concerned with biting anybody.

Emma Jean made eye contact with the snake, and Luke just knew she was going to faint and hoped to hell she didn't because Bertha would only make her go through it all over again, and he wanted this night to be it.

"Stay with it," he muttered under his breath, unaware he was evoking a curious look from Matt. "Stay with it, baby. You can do it."

Elmer Bruce fastened his hands around Emma Jean's wrists and was guiding her paralyzed limbs toward her face. She swayed as the snake's tongue flicked across her nose. For an instant, Luke thought that was it, that she was going down. But, miraculously, she was able to stand there, to get through it, and Elmer Bruce, bless him, was not about to push a good thing and quickly took the snake away.

Bertha Veazey then bellowed so loud that the drums and tambourines stopped playing and everyone around her froze. "Praise Jesus. Oh, Praise God. The sinner is saved. She's been anointed by the Holy Spirit. And now she's pure in heart, and us Veazeys'll be havin' us a baby in the family a'fore long."

Those not still lolling on the floor or in the throes of a self-induced seizure began clapping their hands and surged toward Emma Jean to hug and congratulate.

"All right. Let's go." Luke moved from the window.

Matt had been watching him curiously. He'd had his suspicions about Luke and Emma Jean, even shared them with Kirby and his Aunt Wilma. Now he was sure she had told him she was going to be made to handle a snake tonight, and that's why they were there, to be around in case she got bitten and needed to get to a doctor quickly.

Okay, Matt allowed. It was Luke's business, just like his screwing Wanda Potts was his, but at least her husband wasn't a hot-tempered nut like Rudy Veazey. If Rudy ever found out, it wouldn't make a hill of beans that Luke was the sheriff. Rudy would do his best to try and kill him.

Still, even though he now knew Luke's motive, Matt could not resist asking, "So how come we drive all the way out here and stand in the mud and mosquitoes for hours just to turn around and leave? You saw them handle. You can arrest every one of 'em and close down that looney bin. So why don't you?"

They were making their way back through the woods to where the patrol car was parked, perhaps a mile or more away, and Luke glanced at Matt in the scant moonlight filtering down through the branches of the trees overhead. He smiled. "Maybe I believe in freedom of religion."

"Then why'd you want to come out here?" Matt persisted.

"To see what was going on."

"So you saw they were breaking the law . . ."

"And I decided not to arrest anybody, okay?"

"Yeah, sure." Matt knew when to back off, and they made their way on through the night in silence.

Just as they neared the car, Luke quickened his pace at the sound of the radio crackling. He knew it had to be important because he had told Ned not to try and raise him unless it was.

He reached through the open window and grabbed the mike. "Sheriff here. Go base."

Ned did not waste time with codes. "It's bad, Sheriff. Real bad. The Klan got Ocie Rhoden tonight. Beat him up something awful. Slapped his wife and kid around. Burned a cross and then set his house on fire."

Luke hit the siren, rubber burning the highway as headlights burned holes in the darkness.

※

Lily Rhoden stood before the smoking skeleton of what had been her home. Charred bones stretching toward the night sky danced eerily in the swirling remnants of smoke from the dwindling embers, the acrid odor stinging her nose and throat and making her cough and choke on her sobs.

Luke touched her shoulder. "Lily, are you all right?"

She did not respond.

A valiant, charred beam lost its struggle and fell crashing into the rubble, the momentary flash of sparks illumining her face, and Luke could see the rising welts on her cheek. Her left eye was swollen shut. Between clenched teeth he asked, "Did they hurt Patti Sue?"

"No, thank God, but she'll have nightmares the rest of her life. *The devils!*"

"Do you feel like talking about it now or would you rather wait till tomorrow?"

"It doesn't matter. I can't tell you anything, anyway. They were wearing hoods. I couldn't see their faces."

"Did you recognize a voice?"

"No. It all happened so fast. We were listening to the radio, and all of a sudden the door flew open and they rushed in and started hitting Ocie, hitting me. Then they dragged Ocie out, and that's when I saw the cross burning, and . . ." Her voice broke, but she managed to go on. "They let me go. They said, 'take your pickaninny and run, nigger, or we'll fix you, too'."

She turned to throw herself against him as she sobbed, "I thought they were going to kill Ocie, and there was nothing I could do but grab Patti Sue and run for help."

"You did right," he said. "And I'll make them pay, Lily. I promise."

It was after midnight when Luke got to the emergency room. Volunteers were helping Matt and Kirby scour the crime scene for any clues that might help identify those responsible. The state police had been notified, which was protocol whenever the Klan was thought to be involved in a crime. Later, the FBI would probably be called in.

The night was hot, humid, and sticky. Thunder rolled over the Cheaha mountain range, and now and then lightning split the sky like a blazing fork angrily thrown from the gods. It was spring, and it was Alabama, and Luke knew the weather could quickly turn dangerous.

Dr. Campbell reported that Ocie was being readied for transport to Birmingham where orthopedic surgeons at the big hospital there would try to repair the extensive damage done to his right arm.

"Can I talk to him?"

"You can try, but he's heavily sedated."

Pushing aside the curtain, they entered the cubicle. Luke went to Ocie's bedside and gently said, "I know you don't feel like talking, but I need your help to find the ones who did this to you. Did you recognize any of them?"

Ocie's "No" sounded more like an anguished moan than a word.

"Not even a familiar voice?"

Again, the wretched sound.

"Did they say why they were doing it?"

"Union. They said . . . maybe now . . . I'd leave th' union alone . . ."

It was the motive Luke suspected, but there was no time to probe deeper because just then a nurse poked her head through the curtain to tell Dr. Campbell, "He's got another visitor."

He shook his head. "Not now. We're getting him ready for transport."

"But it's Mr. Hampton."

Dr. Campbell nodded. "Send him on back." To Luke, he said, "It's kind of hard to say no to the chairman of the hospital board, you know?"

Luke knew, all right, and he gave himself a silent pep talk to keep his cool, not to give himself away. To do so would throw a kink in all his plans, and he'd come too far to screw up now.

A few seconds later the curtains swished open and Buddy breezed in, his face a mask of deep concern.

With a curt nod to Luke and Dr. Campbell, he leaned over Ocie and said, "I'm so sorry, and I want you to know you don't have anything to worry about. The mill takes care of its own, and you'll have a job waiting for you no matter how long it takes for you to get back on your feet."

Ocie grimaced. "They say I won't have no more use of my arm. I can't work no line."

Luke felt like cramming his fist down Buddy's throat when he patronizingly said, "Don't you worry, boy. We'll find something you can do if it's only pushing a broom."

And pushing a broom would likely pay all of fifty cents an hour, Luke silently fumed, and everybody who saw Ocie would be reminded of what happened to anyone who dared speak out against injustice at the blasted mill.

There was a pay phone in a corner of the waiting room. Making sure no one was around to overhear, Luke dropped a coin in the slot and dialed.

Fortunately, Murline answered. If she hadn't, Luke would have asked to speak to her and not given a damn as to what explanation she'd give Thurman about a man calling her in the middle of the night.

He did not mince words. "You were supposed to keep me informed, remember?"

Sleepy, groggy, Murline fought to bring her senses to life. "Who . . . who is this?"

"Wake up, Murline," he snapped. "It's me, Luke Ballard. The Klan hit Ocie tonight. They terrorized his little girl, slapped his wife around, and beat the hell out of him. He may lose the use of his right arm. They also burned his house down. Why didn't you tip me off so I could've tried to stop it?"

At that, she was wide awake and gasped, "I didn't know. I swear I didn't."

"I think you did. Just like I think there's lots you haven't told me."

"No . . . I, there's nothing." He heard her gulp.

"You're lying, *Cinderella*," he said coldly, "and your fairy god*father* is getting real pissed."

With that, he hung up the phone.

Chapter 22

Luke was anxious to drive over to Coosa County and talk to Sheriff Mosby about the Klan, but the phone kept him busy all morning. News spread fast about Ocie, and folks were worried it might mean racial trouble was brewing. Wilma fielded as many calls as she could but most demanded to speak directly to Luke.

He managed to sneak a call to Emma Jean to make sure she was all right. She broke down and cried when he told her what he'd done to ensure her safety. She begged him to come by after dark since Rudy was working a double shift. Luke promised he'd try.

Finally, he told Wilma he was leaving, but just then the phone rang again and it was Sara. She was nearly hysterical wanting him to do something about Burch.

"He called a little while ago. He said he was tired of waiting, and if I don't do what he wants, he'll see to it Tim finds out about . . . you know." She drew a ragged breath and let it out on a sob.

Luke felt guilty not to have done something about the situation sooner, only he had been so tied up with Emma Jean he hadn't made it a priority and now wished he had. "I'll see him today, Sara, I promise. I'll get him off your back, okay?"

"Can't you do it now? This very minute? Dewey called off work in the fields because it's raining, so we've got a chance to be together, but I'm afraid Burch will be watching and follow me."

"Don't worry. I'll find him." It meant further delay getting over to Coosa County, but an hour or so wouldn't make much difference. For the time being, he decided to just warn Burch he'd had a complaint from Sara that he was trying to blackmail her and if he didn't back off, he'd be arrested. Later, Luke would think of something stronger, maybe make it a part of the *hammer*, the stipulation that he would get off her back forevermore.

"I'm out of here," he said as he breezed by Wilma's desk. "Take names."

The phone rang again, and he hurried down the hall and was almost to the steps when Wilma called after him. "There's something funny about this one. You might want to take it."

He kept on going and shouted, without turning around, "I told you to get their name."

"But that's the funny part. She says her name is *Cinderella*."

When Luke took the phone, Murline had immediately admitted he'd been right, that she did know something she hadn't told him. "And I can't keep it to myself any longer. God forgive me, I wish I'd told you sooner."

She said she'd called in to work sick and was home by herself. He hurried right over, parking in the alley that ran behind her house.

She was waiting at the back door, crying into a shredded tissue. Gripping her shoulders, he gave her a little shake and said, "Look, we don't have time for you to go to pieces. Now get hold of yourself and tell me what you know."

He pulled out a chair for her at the kitchen table, and, with an obedient sniff, she sat down.

He turned the one next to her around and straddled it. "You knew they were going after Ocie last night, didn't you?"

She tossed the soaked tissue aside and snatched up a paper napkin from the table and began nervously twisting it. "Yes. I overheard Buddy and Cubby Riddle talking yesterday when I came back from the supply room. Buddy must have thought I'd gone to lunch. I didn't hear all that was said, but I thought maybe they were only going to try and scare him, anyway. I never dreamed they'd do what they did."

"So what, exactly, did you hear?"

"Something like, 'I want you and your boys to teach him a lesson. Do it tonight and get it over with. The damn union's not coming into my mill.' I can't remember word for word. I just wanted to get out of there before they saw me."

"And you didn't call me," Luke said in disgust.

"Luke, I was afraid to get involved."

He hit the table with his fist, and she jumped.

"I might have been able to stop it, Murline," he cried, all the while wondering how on earth he would have managed that with having to be at the snake-handling to look after Emma Jean. But he would have tried, by damn.

"I just feel so bad."

"You should feel bad. Real damn bad. Hell, I hope you can't sleep at night."

"I'm going to ask my church to start a fund for him. I can get them to. I just know it. Ocie and his family will need a place to stay, and money to live on, because he won't be able to work, and . . ."

Luke's smile was bitter. "Oh, Buddy has very generously promised him a job, once he learns how to push a broom with his left arm." He recounted Buddy's visit to the emergency room the night before. "I wanted to strangle the son of a bitch. Now is there anything else you haven't told me?"

He did not miss the guilt mirrored in her eyes as she mumbled, "No, nothing."

"So help me, if I find out you keep anything else from me, I swear I'll drop your damn shoe in Thurman's lap."

She knew he meant it. "All right. I know who C. Swain is. His name is *Carl* Swain, and he used to work at the mill. I also know why Buddy has been sending him money all these years."

Luke felt excitement rip through his backbone as something told him he was about to discover the nail for his hammer, by God. "Swain was blackmailing him?"

"Not exactly. His daughter is Buddy's mistress."

Luke was disappointed. Buddy having a mistress was no big deal. If his wife found out, she would raise hell, but she likely wouldn't divorce him and give up all the goodies that went with being the wife of the wealthiest man in the county. "So he's been keeping a woman and her father for twenty years. He must care a lot about her, but evidently he doesn't intend to toss out his wife for her. I need something more than that."

She placed her hands on the table and stretched the tear-moist napkin between her fingers. "No, he'll never marry her, but he isn't exactly keeping her up. He's supporting his son."

Luke gave a half-laugh. "She had his kid?"

"Yes. And maybe there was a little blackmail involved back in the beginning. After all, Juanita—Carl's daughter—was only fourteen at the time, and . . ."

"Fourteen? That's jail-bait. He could have done time."

"You aren't going to arrest him, are you? I mean, it was a long time ago. The boy's grown. It would hurt so many people, and . . ."

"No, I won't arrest him. Don't worry."

"He cares about her," Murline said quietly. "I think he maybe even loves her because he's taken care of her all these years."

A thought struck. "How come Buddy let you know all this? How come he isn't worried you'll blackmail him like his girlfriend's father?"

Her laugh was soft, cynical. "Maybe it's the other way around."

"I don't follow you."

"Maybe you aren't the only one who holds something over me."

"You mean he knows about you and Dennis? But Dennis has only been living here a few years, and . . ." His eyes narrowed, "Are you saying you had an affair with somebody else, and Buddy knows?"

"Yes." She said so low he had to strain to hear. "With Buddy. I was young and foolish, and I believed him when he said he loved me and would leave his wife and marry me. It lasted nearly three years, and by that time, Buddy's father had died and Buddy took over the plant and made me his private secretary.

"But," she continued dully, the bitterness of long ago buried deep within, "he was tired of me by then, and he was actually very up-front about it. He said he'd keep me on as his secretary, but it would be strictly business. It was later I found out he'd fallen for Juanita."

"So how could he blackmail you when you had as much over him as he did you?"

She bit her lip and stared up at the frosted light fixture above the kitchen table, struggling to hold back fresh tears as she mustered nerve to tell the rest of her story. "I used to have a nice figure, Luke," she said, almost shamefully. "You couldn't tell because my mother was very strict. She made me bind my breasts and wear full blouses and skirts. But I did have a good shape, and Buddy made me feel like I was a goddess or something. He talked me into posing for some, you know, sexy pictures. He still has them. That's the hold he has on me. He told me he'd say he came across them by accident, that he found them in some worker's locker."

Misery and shame pooled in her limpid eyes. "That's his weapon, but he doesn't really need one. I make a nice salary and have the security of a good job as long as I want it because he trusts me. So it hasn't been all bad. In fact, I hadn't even thought about it in a long time . . . till now.

"You've got a shoe," she concluded sardonically, "and he's got pictures. So you've both got a piece of me, don't you?"

Luke felt sorry for her, but it was, after all, a bed of her own making, as his mother would have said. He still needed her help and wasn't about to back off now.

He pressed on. "Do you think he's in love with this Juanita?"

"Oh, yes. And he's crazy about his son, too. He talks to me about them sometimes. Archie, that's his son, just graduated from college this spring, and Buddy was disappointed he couldn't be there to see him get his diploma. I'm the only person he can talk to when he's feeling down about it all, you see."

"How nice for him," Luke murmured sarcastically. Then he said, "Maybe he'll give him a good job at the mill. He doesn't go by *Hampton*, does he?"

"Oh, no. He wouldn't dare. Buddy told me Juanita has never put pressure on him about anything, and she's never asked him for money, either. It's her father. But Buddy doesn't care. He just says he's glad he can afford it and that he's got me to see that it gets to her every month."

Luke stood, pushed the chair back under the table, and went to stare out the window over the kitchen sink. "Is there anything else?"

She hesitated too long, and he knew she was lying when she finally said, "No. That's it. And I'll call you if I hear anything at all I think you should know about. I really promise this time, Luke."

He frowned at the gathering clouds. They were thick, heavy, and seemed to press and hold the heat close to the ground, almost smothering with the pressure of the humidity.

Thunder rumbled in the distance, but it was the little tit-like appendages from the clouds that gave cause for concern, for that was the first sign a tornado was forming. Tiny gray fingers would dangle along the bottom of the clouds, and suddenly one would dip down and start spinning to finally take a dreaded funnel shape to wreak a path of havoc and destruction. Alabama, after all, was part of what was known as tornado alley, and it was the time of year when conditions were ripe for a major twister.

Finally, he said, "Remember, don't hold back on me, Cinderella, 'cause I'm afraid you'd have a hard time convincing Thurman that shoe belonged to your sisters."

"Maybe so," she said out loud to the empty room after he had gone, "but for me, there's no Prince Charming, either."

Sara saw Dewey's truck coming and stepped from where she had been crouched in a plum thicket beside the road. Her car was hidden nearby. They were going to his old deserted barn where nobody ever went. He kept blankets there, and it was real cozy. Tim was at work, her mother had the kids, Aunt Carrie was visiting her father in the nursing home in Childersburg, so the day belonged to her and Dewey. She didn't care how bad the weather got as long as they were together.

Dewey leaned across the seat to open the door for her, love shining on his leathery face. "You doing okay, honey?"

She glanced up and down the road one more time. There was no sign of Burch. "I'm fine," she said with a smile, scrambling in and snuggling against him. "And we're going to have us a wonderful time despite the rain."

He drove a little ways farther before turning down the long, winding path to the barn.

Neither saw the silver Cadillac ease from a grove of trees to follow slowly after them.

Dewey spread a blanket on the hay-littered floor of the barn, and they laid down and wrapped their arms about each other. The barn trembled in the ever-increasing fury of the wind, and Sara worried aloud, "Do you think we're safe in here?"

Dewey was unbuttoning her blouse and raining kisses over her face. "This old barn's been here longer than you and me, punkin. My granddaddy built it. I'd say we're probably safer here than anywhere else. Besides, it's just a summer storm. Nothing to worry about."

When they were naked, Dewey got on top of her and pushed himself inside her. The rain coming down in torrents on the old tin roof sounded like a thousand nails being pounded. It had gotten real dark, and over Dewey's head she thought she could see the rafters moving ever so slightly, but she told herself it was her imagination.

Dewey's mouth was against her neck, and she hoped he didn't leave a hickey, because if he did, she'd have to wear a scarf or try to cover it up with makeup so it wouldn't show.

"Well, now, isn't that sweet?"

A voice boomed above the thunder, and Dewey froze as Sara screamed at the sight of Burch Cleghorn stepping from the shadows.

"What the shit . . ." Dewey rocked back on his heels, stunned and out of breath.

Sara rolled to her knees. Snatching up her blouse, she tried to cover herself as Burch towered over them.

"You don't need to do that, Sara, baby. I'm going to see you naked any time I want to from now on, and it's time he learned how it's gonna be." He glared down at Dewey, who was wheezing, his face beet red. "Get out of the way and watch a real man put it to her."

Dewey came alive and staggered to his feet. "You son of a bitch! You touch her, and I'll kill you."

"Oh, I'm gonna do more than touch her, Dewey. I'm going to pork her like she's never been porked before, and when I'm done, you can bet she's not going to want that little weenie of yours anymore." He pointed to Dewey's now flaccid penis and taunted, "Looks like one of them Vienna sausages you shit-kickin' farmers eat for lunch."

Sara sprang and shoved him backwards. "Leave him alone! Get out or . . ."

"Or *what?* Just what are you going to do about it, you little slut?" He unbuttoned his belt and tugged at his zipper. "If either one of you tells about this, I'll see that the whole county hears about your dirty little affair. Now you just lay back down there and get ready for the best you've ever had."

"No. Don't you touch her." Dewey stumbled forward, one hand against his chest. "I'll kill you . . ."

Burch gave Dewey a shove with his foot, knocking him flat on his back.

Sara screamed and tried to get to him, but Burch grabbed her arm and flung her to one side as he growled, "I told you to lay down, you strumpet."

Dewey tried to get up again, but, with both hands to his chest, his face purple as a plum, he gave one garbled, choking cry, then went limp. Crying his name, Sara crawled to him on her hands and knees as Burch watched, suddenly uneasy.

Cradling Dewey's head, she leaned to press her ear against his nose and mouth. "He's barely breathing. We've got to get him to the hospital. Help me get him to your car, quick."

Burch zipped up his pants and buckled his belt. "*We* aren't doing anything. I've never been here today, understand?" He began to back away.

Sara stared at him in terror, dizzily thinking how the rain sounded like rocks being slammed against the roof, then realized it was hail. But what did that matter when Dewey might be dying? "You can't leave. You've got to help me get him to the hospital."

"I can't afford to get involved." He pointed a finger at her as he reached the door. "And don't you dare tell anybody I was here, or I'll fix you good, understand?"

He disappeared in a gray swirl of rain, hail, and flying

leaves. A tree fell and crashed nearby, and thunder rolled and lightning flashed.

Dimly, Sara was aware of the faint sound of an engine starting up above the din as she gave Dewey a little shake and wailed, "Don't you die on me. You hear? I'll get you out of here. I swear I will . . ."

Gently lowering his head to the floor, she dressed quickly, then dropped to her knees beside him once more to see if he was still breathing. When she heard the rattling sound in his chest, she dared to hope he was rallying, sucking air into his lungs.

She got behind him and took him by his shoulders and tried to drag him toward the door. If she could get him to the truck, she knew it would take quite a heave to get him all the way up in the cab but she had to do it. Only she was not having much luck even getting him across the floor. He was a big man, over six feet tall, and weighed around 220. She wasn't quite five-four and weighed 110. There was no way she was going to be able to get him out of the barn and all the way to where the truck was parked, especially with the furious wind against her. She would have to leave him and go for help.

"I'll be back. I promise." She kissed his blue lips and tore out into the wind.

She was all the way to the truck before she discovered the keys were not in the ignition. Out of habit, Dewey had stuck them in his pocket. Leaping down from the cab, she was almost to the barn door when there was a great roar, followed by a cracking sound, then busting glass, and she whirled about to see that a tree had fallen on the truck. A terrified moan escaped her lips when she realized that, had she not gone back for the keys, she would have been in that gnarled and twisted mess of glass and metal.

Leaves slapped her face. A piece of tin blown from the roof struck her leg. She cried out from the pain and saw blood, but she staggered onward into the storm in the direction she hoped was the path to the road beyond. It was at least a mile back to where she'd left her car, then a couple more to Billy Saulston's store and a telephone, if the lines weren't blown down. She lost count of how many times she fell in the mud. Part of the way she had to crawl on her hands and knees for the force of the wind was such that she could not stand against it.

After what seemed hours, she reached her car, and, slowly, the wipers fighting to free the windshield of leaves and trash, Sara maneuvered through nature's relentless assault. The rain was coming down so hard she could barely see. She dared not drive fast for fear of running off the road and into the ditches that bordered each side. At last, like a giant tombstone rising from a mist-shrouded graveyard, the store came into view. Drawing closer, she saw it was deserted.

She got out of the car and fought the wind to reach the porch. The door was locked, but she knew she had to get inside. The phone lines, as best she could see in the downpour, were still up. Billy's house was on down the road, but there was no time to go any farther. She had to get help, had to call Luke. He would know what to do. Picking up the largest rock she could find, she ran around to the side and smashed a window, then grabbed another rock in a frantic attempt to clear glass shards from the frame so she wouldn't be cut to pieces when she hoisted herself through it.

With a grunt and a heave, she pulled herself up and in, wincing as a piece of glass sliced into her hand. Her leg was still bleeding from the piece of tin roof, and now blood dripped from her palm, but she kept on going.

Grabbing up the phone she screamed, "Thank God," at the blessed sound of a dial tone. Too hysterical to remember the number of the sheriff's department, she stuck her finger in the "O" slot and gave the dial a spin. When the operator answered after what seemed forever, she begged to be put through at once. "It's an emergency. Oh, hurry, please . . ."

Blood dripped to the floor, and she fought to keep from fainting while the walls of the plank-sided store began to sway precariously as the storm mustered fury for a final assault upon the land.

In the sky to the west, the great billowing cloud seemed to take the shape of a giant hand, and from it came a long, thin finger, pointing to the earth to touch and spin, giving birth to a deadly tornado.

CHAPTER 23

The whistle at the mill blew continuously, the ominous signal a tornado had been sighted. While everyone else raced for cover, Luke and his deputies prowled the tree-littered streets by car, checking for anyone needing assistance as well as for downed power lines. If they saw the funnel swooping down, they, too, would make a beeline for refuge.

Luke was two blocks from the courthouse when Wilma's voice came over the radio, barely audible because of the static, wind, and hail pounding the windshield. "You've got to speak louder," he said. "There's a lot of noise out here."

"Where are you?"

"Elm Street. Has anybody reported seeing the funnel touch down?"

"Not yet, but Sara Speight just called from Billy Saulston's store screaming her head off and said for me to find you as quick as I could and tell you to get out there and not to send anybody else."

"Did she say what was wrong?"

"Nope. She just kept yelling for you, and then I heard a noise like a freight train and the line went dead."

. . . like a freight train.

There was no better way to describe the sound of a tornado. "I'm on my way."

Apprehension was an icicle, stabbing his spine as he drove as fast as he dared through the flying debris of broken limbs, rolling garbage cans, and anything else not battened down against the storm's relentless fury. Once in the country he saw several houses with shingles blown off but no evidence of the kind of damage that would have been left in the wake of a whirling, sucking tornado. The closer he got to the area where Saulston's store was located, the situation worsened. Johnny Taylor's barn was blown away, along with most of his house, but Luke knew Johnny had a good storm cellar and would have taken refuge with his family down there, so he kept on going, hell-bent to get to Sara.

He cursed himself for not being much of a friend to her lately. He needed to deal with Burch Cleghorn and would get right on it as soon as the present crisis was over. When he got through with him, Sara wouldn't have to worry about him ever again. If not for the storm, he would have kept his promise to her to find him that very day, by damn.

He saw her car in the littered parking lot of Saulston's store and turned in. The building was still standing, but the front porch was partially smashed by the weight of the tree that had fallen against it.

"Sara, are you in here?" Luke climbed over broken tree limbs to get to the door. "Sara, answer me . . ."

She appeared and leaned against the frame for support. Her face was the color of chalk, and she was holding her bloodied arm against her chest. He could see her leg was also injured. "Hold on. I've got a first-aid kit in the trunk . . ."

"There's no time. We've got to get to Dewey. I think he's had a heart attack. He's at the old barn. I had to leave him. I tried to carry him, but I couldn't . . ."

He closed the door behind her, heard it lock, then lifted her in his arms. "You're bleeding bad, Sara. We've got to take care of you."

"No," she argued as he struggled to carry her through the debris to the patrol car, "I'll be all right. We've got to get Dewey to the hospital. He might be dying."

"We aren't going anywhere till I get a pressure bandage on these cuts."

He put her in the back seat and thought that if Dewey had really suffered a heart attack, he was most likely dead by now, anyhow.

He got the first aid kit and began binding her wounds. "Looks like you've still got glass in your arm."

"I did that breaking a window to get in the store."

"They'll have to take it out at the hospital. Now tell me what happened."

She quickly did so, culminating with the angry denunciation: "It was all Burch's fault. And then he just walked out and left me and wouldn't help and said if I told anybody he'd been there, he'd fix me good. Now Dewey's going to die. I just know it." She grabbed the front of his shirt. "You've got to save him, Luke. You've got to."

As she had been talking, he had methodically wrapped gauze around the calf of her leg, tight enough to slow the bleeding but not enough to cut off circulation. Rage had been building with each word she spoke, but he told himself that the seriousness of the situation demanded calm. He could not yield to knee-jerk reactions. "Listen to me, Sara, and listen good. I know it's bad, and believe me, I want to help Dewey, and I will, but you've got to remember we can't let anybody know you were there. So what I've got to do now is take you to the hospital, then I'll go back and get him."

"No!" She tried to get out of the car, but he held her back. "He'll die."

"And how will you explain being at that old barn with him, Sara? Can't you see the gossips would have a field day speculating? Are you ready for everybody to guess the truth about you two? Do you think Dewey wants that? Think of the consequences, damn it, and calm down and let me do it my way."

Knowing he was right, the fight went out of her.

"That's better." He let her go. "Now tell me, where are the kids?"

"At Tim's mother's."

"Well, she's got sense enough to know work would have been canceled in the fields because of the weather, but what had you planned to tell her you were doing all this time?"

"That I decided to take advantage of being off and drove to Birmingham to shop for the kids' school clothes."

"Okay. Then here's your story: you were on your way home when the twister struck, and you took shelter in the store and called me, because you couldn't get through to anybody else."

He got in the front seat, leaving her in the rear, and started the car.

"Okay for me, but what about Dewey?"

"After I leave you at the emergency room, I'll just say I was looking for storm victims and found him. No one will question it, even his being at the old barn. They'll think he was checking for damages or something."

"Right now I don't care what anybody thinks. I just want to get him to a hospital."

"Believe me, honey, Dewey would want us to handle it this way."

"And what about Burch?"

"Leave him to me, Sara," he said, teeth clenched. "Just leave him to me."

After dropping her off at the hospital, Luke checked in with Wilma on the radio as he headed back into the country.

"Looks like the worst is over," she said as Luke heard the mill whistle sound the all-clear signal. "We're getting the most damage reports from out where Sara was. Matt and Kirby have gone out there since we haven't had any serious calls from town."

"I'll follow the twister's path and see what I find," he said, setting the stage to discover Dewey in the old barn. As he neared the path leading back to it, he began to worry that he would not be stretching the truth, after all, because it appeared the tornado had moved in that direction. It had stopped raining, and a patch of blue was beginning to show at the ragged edge of the retreating storm clouds. The wind had died down, but the air was still thick and humid. It was impossible to drive all the way up to the barn because of all the debris blown around, so he parked and walked. The cab of Dewey's truck was crushed, like Sara had said, but the barn was miraculously still standing.

Inside, he found Dewey and knew, without having to check for a pulse, he was dead. His lips were a grayish blue color, and his face had already taken on the waxy hue that death brings so quickly. His eyes were open, staring sightlessly at the cobwebbed rafters above. Luke would later close the lids and take pennies from his pockets to lay on top for weight to keep them shut. The first order of business was to get some clothes on him. Dewey could not be found naked.

Maybe it wouldn't have made any difference if Burch *had* gotten Dewey to the hospital, but that wasn't the point. He should have *tried*, damn it. So now Burch had two sins to answer for, by God, which meant the hammer was going to come down twice as hard.

He called in the death report to Wilma and told her to have the rescue squad transport the body to the funeral home.

"Oh, I'm so sorry," she wailed into the radio. "I always liked Dewey. He was a dear old soul. A lot of folks loved that man."

And so did Sara, he sadly thought, and that was why he wanted to be the one to tell her, so she wouldn't go off the deep end and let something slip if she heard it otherwise.

He instructed Wilma, "Tell the rescue boys to keep it quiet till I can get word to the family."

"Will do, Sheriff."

When Luke arrived at the emergency room, Dr. Campbell had just finished stitching Sara's wounds, and she was resting on a cot in one of the treatment rooms. No one else was around. She took one look at his face and burst into tears.

He pulled her against him, his whisper at her ear harsh and rapid, "You've got to get hold of yourself and act grieved at the death of a family member and nothing more. And you have to keep telling yourself over and over it's how he'd want it."

She continued to cry but after a few moments finally drew back to tremulously ask, "Will you see me through it, Luke? I don't have anybody else to lean on."

"Of course, I will. I'm just sorry I let you down, honey. If I'd dealt with Burch when you first asked me to, maybe this wouldn't have happened. Now I've got to live with the guilt."

"Dewey wouldn't want you to feel that way, and neither do I."

"Well, Burch will pay for what he did, Sara. Count on it."

He saw how she stiffened and knew that rage was beginning to wage a war with grief and would eventually take over. That was good, for anger would make her strong. It sure as hell kept him going.

After breaking the news of her husband's death to Carrie Culver, who calmly reacted with the pragmatic declaration that it was God's will, Luke spent the rest of the evening checking on the tornado's aftermath.

It had not gone in the direction where Emma Jean lived so he was satisfied she would be okay. Still, he ached to see her. Maybe it was feeling sorry for Sara that made him long to be with someone he felt close to, because he dreaded going home to Alma and her nagging.

It was still a couple of hours before Rudy got off work, so back in the privacy of his office Luke dialed Emma Jean's number and let it ring twice, the signal he was coming by, and hung up.

He was almost to the highway when Ned radioed with a report of suspected looting at Saulston's store. "Billy says somebody stopped by his house to tell him they saw some kids prowling around over there. He's scared if he catches 'em he'll wind up killing somebody, so he wants you to handle it. He thinks it's the Scroggins boys. He's had some trouble with them in the past."

"Who hasn't?" Luke fired back irritably. He wanted to see Emma Jean, not deal with smart-mouth punks like Rossie and Ollis Scroggins trying to steal cigarettes and beer.

He'd had run-ins with them in the past. The whole family was nothing but white trash. Old man Reuben Scroggins was a drunk and hell-raiser from way back and had been in and out of prison all his life for one thing or another. His wife, Nina Lou, was currently doing time at the women's penitentiary in Montgomery for stabbing a woman she had caught sleeping with Reuben. Then there were two teenage daughters who had never been married and had half a dozen kids between them and lived on welfare.

Luke arrived at the store just as it appeared the boys had gathered the nerve to go in and start loading up. Rossie was climbing through the same window Sara had cut herself on. Ollis saw Luke and yelled and tried to run, but Luke felled him with one blow from his flashlight.

"We ain't doin' nothin'," Rossie yelped as Luke jerked him down out of the window. "Just lookin' around, that's all. Makin' sure there ain't no damage. Tryin' to do a good deed," he added with a smirk, dusting the front of his shirt as Luke let him go.

"Yeah, that's right," Ollis said from where he was sprawled on the ground, blood oozing from a slight cut over his ear.

Rossie saw his brother's injury and roared at Luke, "Hey, what'd you do that for, you asshole? You didn't have to hit him." He turned toward Luke in menace, fists clenched.

Luke did not back away, merely slapped the flashlight rhythmically in his open palm. "You want some, too?"

Rossie backed off but continued to smirk. "You'd like me to jump you, wouldn't you? Well, when I do, you won't see me comin'. You can bet on that."

Luke nodded to the patrol car. "Get in."

Rossie demanded to know where Luke was taking them, angrily protesting that he hadn't actually caught them stealing anything and couldn't disprove their story of merely checking things out.

Luke said not to worry, he was only giving them a neighborly ride home, they both tried to get out of the car, but they were locked in.

"You can't do that, man," Ollis cried. "If our old man is there, and you tell him you think we was gettin' ready to loot Billy's store, he'll beat the shit out of us."

"And if he's drunk," Rossie added in rising panic, "He'll do worse. You let us out of here, you bastard."

Rossie saw how that needled Luke and zeroed in to twist the knife even deeper, "Bastard," he repeated. "That's what you are, for sure. Your momma didn't even know who your daddy was. My momma said so. She said . . ."

Luke flung his right arm out to slam the flashlight against the wire cage, and they recoiled like monkeys in a pen. "If you don't want me to stop this car and beat you myself, you'd best keep your mouth shut, boy."

Ollis jabbed Rossie with his elbow, and Rossie reluctantly leaned back in sullen silence. A few moments later, Luke turned into a yard void of grass and littered with beer cans, whiskey bottles, and old tires. In the middle of all the trash sat a rusting, dilapidated trailer, most of the windows broken out, and a bent television antenna hanging over the side.

The trailer door opened with a bang, and Reuben Scroggins, bare-chested and wearing stained trousers, appeared. He was holding a beer and swaying from side to side as he wondered what the law was doing in his yard. Then he saw his sons in the back seat and bellowed, "You little shits. What've you done now?"

He began tugging at his belt as he stumbled down the steps.

Rossie hissed at Luke, "I'm gonna get you for this, you bastard. I swear I will. You're gonna pay."

Luke got out of the car and opened the back doors. The boys took off running, but Rossie slipped and fell. Before he could scramble to his feet, Reuben brought his belt zinging down across his back. Then, holding him down with his foot, he angrily demanded of Luke, "Tell me what they done, damn it."

Luke explained that while he had caught them about to loot Billy Saulston's store, he didn't have enough evidence to arrest them but wanted Reuben to know about it.

Reuben stomped on Rossie's head and whacked his buttocks with his belt. "I told you I ain't puttin' up with that kind o' shit. I ain't raisin' no thieves . . ."

Rossie screamed and railed at Luke, "You son of a bitch . . ."

Reuben Scroggins whacked him again. "Shut your mouth. The sheriff's just doin' his job."

But Rossie kept on yelling. "Maybe I'll just go piss on your whore-momma's grave, sheriff."

"I'll beat you till you bleed, boy." Reuben hit him again, this time across his face.

Rossie shrieked and grabbed Reuben's ankle and twisted, knocking him off balance, then scrambled to his feet to escape to the woods with his brother. Luke got back in the car and drove away.

Rossie and Ollis would eventually get the beating Reuben intended, and Matt and Kirby could finish checking out the storm damage. He had more important things to do, like get to Emma Jean's to spend the precious few hours before time for Rudy to get off work.

Emma Jean was waiting when Luke turned into the yard, and since it was dark and no one could see, she threw herself in his arms the second he got out of the car. She would not let him go, even when he tried to unwrap her arms from around his neck.

"Just kiss me," she laughed, pressing her mouth against his.

He obliged till they were breathless, then held her tight against his chest, his chin resting on top of her head. He wanted to feel her warmth, smell her sweetness, and, most of all, experience the wonder of having someone who cared about him so very, very close.

Emma Jean had never known him to act that way and finally pulled back to ask, "Is something wrong, Luke? You seem so . . . I don't know . . . so sad, somehow."

He admitted he was and told her why, knowing he could trust her not to tell anyone and confident Sara would not mind that he had if she knew how things were between them.

Emma Jean was horrified. "Oh, that's awful. Just awful. Oh, Lord, Luke, after all these years of them loving each other, and she's got to act like he's no more to her than her uncle. I feel so bad for her."

"I probably shouldn't have told you, but . . ."

"Stop it." She pressed a finger against his lips. "I want you to always tell me when you're troubled, Luke. We're best friends, remember? We tell each other everything. Lord knows, I've cried on your shoulder plenty of times."

She was wearing shorts and a blouse with the hem knotted under her bosom. Her hair was braided into pigtails with bows, and he thought how sometimes she seemed like just a little girl, all baby powder and ribbons, yet he knew she was a woman who could satisfy him like no other ever had.

Only it was not desire he felt for her this night. It was closeness and friendship and all the wonderful things that make a relationship between a man and woman mean more than sex. It was what made life tolerable, that special feeling that somebody else gave a damn.

"I've got us a beer hid under the sink. It's not cold, but . . ."

"It doesn't matter. We'll drink it, anyway."

So they sat on the back steps in the dark and shared a warm beer and listened to the constant churr-churr-churr of the tree frogs, watched fireflies dancing, and slapped at mosquitoes, all the while reveling in the joy and contentment of just being together.

"Look!" Emma Jean suddenly cried, pointing skyward. "A shooting star. Did you see it?"

Luke had caught the tail end of it. "Yeah, I sure did. That's one thing I always liked about Alabama—the falling stars."

"We're supposed to wish on it." She closed her eyes briefly, brow furrowed in deep concentration, then opened them and said, "You tell me your wish, and I'll tell you mine."

"We aren't supposed to," he said, not about to confide his wish that he never had to go home, that this was actually their house, and he had the right to take her inside to bed and make love to her and fall asleep afterwards and wake up in the morning with her head on his shoulder.

When he did not say anything, she prattled on, as was her way. "I think I know what Sara must be feeling, because I'd be the same if anything happened to you. I mean, what would I do if some crook shot and killed you? I'd have to do my grieving in private or else Rudy would figure out why I was so upset. Then he'd kill me, and you wouldn't be around to help me, and . . ."

"I may not always be around, anyway, Emma Jean," he felt the sudden need to make clear.

"What do you mean?" she asked, frowning as she absently tugged at one of her pigtails.

"I mean that maybe I'll decide to leave here one day."

She was quiet for a moment, then murmured, "Well, I guess folks do what they've got to do, but I'd miss you."

Suddenly uncomfortable, he downed the rest of the beer, feigned a yawn, and got to his feet. "Well, for now, I'd better just leave from *here*. It's almost time for Rudy to get home."

She followed him to the car. "You go home and get some rest, you hear? You've had a really rough day. And I'll bet you haven't had time to eat supper, have you? Well, Alma probably saved it for you. So you eat, you hear?"

His chuckle was bitter. "She always has supper ready at six and throws it out if I'm not there by seven. She says she's got other things to do besides cater to my being so inconsiderate and maybe throwing it out will teach me to get there on time."

Emma Jean flared, "That's awful. I'd never treat you like that. I'd have a hot meal ready for you no matter what time you got home if you were my husband, Luke."

He had no doubt she would but was feeling more ill at ease by the second. Things were getting complicated. *Real* complicated. And thinking about how Sara now faced a lonely, bleak future after losing the warm, hand-holding kind of love that had been her breath of life since she was practically a child filled him with a strange kind of desolation.

CHAPTER 24

Dewey's coffin had been placed in the parlor of the farmhouse where he and Carrie had lived since their marriage forty years ago. Carrie sat nearby with her six grown children in a row of metal folding chairs that Hardy had brought from the funeral home. As a seemingly endless procession of people filed by to offer condolences, no one noticed Luke and Sara, who stood together in the shadowed hallway just outside. Casseroles and cakes covered the dining room table along with sandwiches and potato salad. A large galvanized tub, filled with fried chicken, sat on the floor. Another tub held ice and bottles of sodas.

Luke spotted Betsy Borden moving along the food line stuffing sandwiches and chicken into her large handbag. Betsy never missed a wake, and it didn't matter whether she knew the deceased or not. She came for the food, but no one ever said anything because there was always plenty to spare. Southerners, Luke knew, believed the balm for grief was having plenty to eat.

Sara made a face as Burch came in. Luke reminded her he was a deacon, and it was only natural he'd show up at the wake.

"But look at him," she said bitterly, "how he's shaking Aunt Carrie's hand and oozing sympathy. I wonder what everyone would think if I just marched right in there and told how he ran off and left poor Dewey to die."

"They'd be too busy wondering how you knew that to care."

"Well, I can't help it."

"You'd better try because I've got a plan to fix Burch's ass for all time, only you're going to have to be quite a little actress if we're to pull it off."

Her eyes flashed with interest. "Tell me."

"I will later. Meanwhile, just try to be friendly to him. *Real* friendly."

"Are you crazy? If I were Bette Davis I couldn't act friendly to that monster."

"You have to if you want revenge."

"It won't work. He knows I hate him."

"Maybe, but remember he never stopped to think you and Dewey loved each other. He figured your motive was money, and it's only natural you'd be looking for a new sugar daddy so you're willing to forgive and forget."

"That's disgusting."

"To you, but not Burch. So do as I say, and I promise he'll be so miserable he'll wish it was him instead of Dewey in that coffin."

She looked doubtful. "Well, I just hope he doesn't come near me tonight. God knows, I'm dying inside."

He gave her a gentle pat on the back. "Dewey would be proud of how you're holding together. I know *I* am."

She leaned into him. "I don't know what I'd do without you. It was bad enough all these years, anyway. Sort of like living between heaven and hell, having to sneak and lie, when all I ever wanted was to belong only to him, have his babies, wake up with my head on his shoulder every day for the rest of our lives. Now I can't even mourn him properly. I have to hide in the shadows like I'm ashamed of what we had, and I'm not. It was beautiful and good and . . ."

"You're on the edge, sweetheart," Luke spoke in her ear. "And you're making me have to stand too close to you in case anybody is watching to remind you of that fact, so calm down before you get both of us in trouble."

"I'm sorry. I really am. You just don't know what its like."

"Oh, yes, I do."

He hadn't meant to say it, but he had, and she turned to look up at him with wonder splashed on her face. "Why, Luke, I really believe you do. I've suspected it, but I wasn't sure."

"And you still aren't, so forget I said anything." He glanced around to make sure no one was paying any attention to them. "Look, I've got some business to take care of. Are you going to be all right without me?"

"I think so."

He had turned away but paused when she called softly, "I'm happy for you, Luke. I really am."

He kept on going, all the while thinking what a big mouth he had, but he could trust Sara. If suspecting he had something serious going with somebody took her mind off her troubles, then maybe it was a good thing.

───

Cubby Riddle unzipped his trousers, took out his penis, and peed on the ground next to the back door. Janie Sue always bitched about him doing it, claiming it drew flies. He argued that her chickens dumpin' all over the place was what did it, not him taking a piss because he didn't feel like going inside and walking all the way down the hall to the toilet. Hell, he'd been pissing in the yard his whole life and no woman was going to tell him what to do, anyhow. He started up the steps, felt a hand close about his throat and immediately lost consciousness.

Luke quickly dragged him across the yard through the chicken droppings and behind the barn where he'd earlier managed to park the squad car without anyone hearing. He opened the trunk, tossed Cubby inside, and closed the lid.

He waited a moment to make sure no lights came on inside the house, then took the car out of gear and pushed it all the way out to the road before jumping in to start the engine and drive away.

All the preparations had been made early that morning, just before dawn. Now it was nearly midnight, and he had been waiting for two hours for Cubby to come home from playing poker and boozing with his buddies. He had signed off to Ned. Alma thought he was working, and Ned knew better than to tell her he wasn't if she called looking for him. He had decided the logical place for Cubby's confession should be at the Klan's meeting place in Coosa County.

The Klan burned a cross at every rally, igniting kerosene-soaked rags that had been wrapped around the wooden cross bars. But they never let it burn completely to the ground, probably, Luke figured, because they didn't want to go to the trouble of building a new one for the next gathering.

That morning he had brought a saw and cut the cross down, leaving a six-inch base, which was where Cubby would awaken to find his penis pressed tightly and held firmly in place by a thin chain. He had positioned Cubby with his legs straddling the base, ankles tightly tied to stakes. His left arm was bound to his side; his right was free.

Luke sat cross-legged on the ground approximately twenty feet away, holding the end of a rope that ran along the ground to the base. Both rope and base had been soaked in kerosene.

First, Cubby began to twitch, then he groggily lifted his head to glance about in the darkness, no doubt wondering where he was and what was going on. He tried to move, then realized his arm was the only limb not secured at the exact same instant Luke struck a match to the small torch he was holding.

"Evenin', Cubby," he said lazily.

Cubby's eyes went wide. "What the shit?" Then, anger rising, "What's goin' on? How come you got me hog-tied, and . . ." He looked down and saw his shackled member. "Hey, what have you done? You let me go, damn you . . ." With his free hand, he tugged at himself, only to shriek in simultaneous pain and rage to realize it was no use. He was held fast.

"Shut up and listen, Cubby."

Cubby beat at the air with his fist. "You let me go. I'll have your badge, you asshole. Who th' hell do you think you are trussin' me up like this? You hurt my dick, and I'll kill you, I swear . . ."

Luke smiled. "Smell anything?"

Cubby sniffed and unleashed a fresh round of screams. "Oh, God! Kerosene! You done soaked me in kerosene!"

"Not *you*, Cubby. Just the base of the cross you creeps use so profanely, as well as the rope tied to your ankles. All I've got to do is light the end I'm holding, and . . ."

"Don't. Oh, don't. Please, Sheriff. Don't light it. What'd I ever do to you that you want to kill me? I've never give you no trouble, ain't never done nothin' to you . . ."

"That's right," Luke said matter-of-factly, "You've never done anything to me, Cubby, but you did something real bad to a friend of mine the other night."

"No. Not me. I ain't done nothin' . . ."

"You and your friends dressed up in your sheets and hoods and paid Ocie Rhoden a visit, only it wasn't a neighborly visit, was it?"

"No. I didn't. You got it all wrong."

Luke held the torch closer to the rope.

Cubby yelped, "Don't do it, Sheriff. Don't . . ."

"Is that what Ocie said to you when you set fire to his house? Did he beg you not to do it? And what about his arm when you busted it? Did he cry and beg like you're doing now?"

"Oh, you got it all wrong. It won't me. I won't there. It was the Klan, all right, but . . ."

"You're lying. And it always pisses me off when somebody lies to me, Cubby."

Luke touched the flame to the end of the rope. He had carefully chosen a hemp that would burn slowly.

"Oh, no. Don't. Don't do it. I'll burn to death."

"Not if you tell me what I want to know. I know you were there, Cubby. Ocie recognized your voice," Luke said adding the lie to his growing list of sins.

At that, Cubby surrendered in a panic, his eyes on the smoldering rope. "Okay. Okay. I was there. But there were others. It wasn't just me."

"I want names."

"There was . . . there was five of us."

"Names, Cubby. Give me names, and I'll give you a chance to save yourself. I'll turn the others over to the FBI for prosecution and leave you out of it."

Cubby's eyes were transfixed to the rope, which had burned about two inches so far.

"Talk to me, Cubby."

Luke was deliberately not asking who had given the order. He did not want Buddy Hampton mentioned. Otherwise, Cubby would think it odd when he was not eventually charged. He might even say as much to Buddy, which would put him on guard.

Sure, Luke knew he could put Buddy away for his Klan involvement, but time in prison was not enough. He had bigger things in store if his suspicions about Murline holding information back proved true, and, so far, his intuition regarding her had been justified. While he had no idea what he would ultimately discover, his gut instinct told him to hold on, that bigger rewards were in store if he were patient.

"But they'll know I told," Cubby whined.

"You can leave town. You won't have a home anyway, once the Klan figures out you turned them in. They'll likely burn you out like they did Ocie. So you'll have to run fast and far, but it's up to you. You can stay here and burn to death instead."

Cubby hit the base of the cross with his right fist as tears streamed down his cheeks. The fire was creeping ever closer, and he knew he had no choice. He would squeal on his friends, then run home and pack what he could in his truck and take off. All he had to do was recite four names. "Hank Pugh, Rooster Grice, Mackie Coombs, and Wiley Wooter. Now let me go, damnit."

Luke calculated that it would take about three more minutes for the rope to reach the kerosene and engulf Cubby in flames.

He stood and took a knife from his pocket. "I didn't say I'd let you go. I said I'd give you a chance to save yourself."

He tossed the knife in front of Cubby and watched as Cubby eagerly cut the rope binding his feet and his left arm. Then he tried to get up and shrieked with pain as the chain tore into his penis.

"Use your knife, Cubby."

"It won't cut a chain," he wailed in terror.

"It'll cut something else."

Cubby lifted horror-stricken eyes as reality struck. "You . . . you're gonna make me cut my dick off. Oh, god, no . . ."

Luke shrugged. "It's your choice, Cubby, which is more than you gave Ocie Rhoden." He tossed down the towels he had bought the same day as the knife. "I saw a soldier get his cut off in Nam. A Vietcong was torturing him when our patrol came along to save him. He didn't bleed to death because we wrapped him good. We were a half hour's walk to medical aid. You're about twenty minutes from the nearest house where you can get help. I checked it out earlier. Then from there maybe ten more to a doctor. You'll make it."

As Cubby pleaded for him to come back, Luke began walking to where he'd left his car. He was almost there when he heard the scream that made the hair on the back of his neck stand up.

CHAPTER 25

Luke turned the names Cubby Riddle had given him over to the FBI. All four men broke under interrogation and confessed everything. They were brought to swift justice, tried and convicted within a month, and sentenced to twenty years in Kilby prison. Luke sent them each a jar of petroleum jelly without explanation. Soon enough, they'd find out what it was for.

Meanwhile, Cubby Riddle was the topic of much conversation. Word spread how a farmer in Coosa County had opened his door in the middle of the night to find Cubby standing there, hands pressed against his bloody crotch. The farmer got him to a doctor right away, then hung around long enough to confirm that Cubby's penis had been severed, but Cubby refused to say how it had happened.

The doctor stitched him to stop the bleeding and told him he needed to be in the hospital for repair surgery, but Cubby refused and dropped out of sight for nearly a week, then resurfaced long enough to throw his clothes in his truck and disappear again. His wife said he had refused to tell her anything, either, but when a cross was burned in their yard he couldn't get out of town fast enough.

Folks speculated that Cubby had told the law about his accomplices in exchange for his own freedom, and, as a result, the

Klan was after him. Some even said maybe it was the Klan that had mutilated him. This theory was reinforced when the story got out about the discovery of some strange goings-on at their meeting site. Ocie, Luke felt, had been properly vindicated and no one suspected his part in any of it.

In addition, because of Murline's guilty conscience, which no one knew about except Luke, of course, a tidy sum of money was raised for Ocie and his family. Once out of the hospital, Ocie used the funds to move his family to Birmingham and make a new life there. Luke then turned his attention to the last two nails to be pounded into the ground by his hammer of vengeance, Burch Cleghorn and Buddy Hampton.

Summer was over, fall was in the air, and other than his gnawing need to be with Emma Jean and his desire to finish taking revenge for his mother, Luke felt his life was running pretty smoothly. He was unaware, however, that Sid Dootree had spotted him and Emma Jean easing down to the creek behind her house at the far border of Sid's property and that whispers of gossip about them had begun to spread and smell like raked manure in a vegetable garden.

All Luke knew was that he loved her, and he worried more and more that when the time came to leave her he wouldn't be able to. At least tomato picking season was over, and she had gone back to work at the laundromat, which meant he could see her occasionally during the day.

Luke was relieved there were no cars in the parking lot, thinking he would have a moment alone with Emma Jean, but, as he approached the door, it opened, and he saw Sara standing there.

"Hi," she said dully. "My washer's on the blink again."

Every time he had seen her in the months since Dewey's death, she looked ready to cry. He decided it was time they had a talk. "When I'm done here, I'd like a few words with you."

"Sure." She went back and sat down next to the dryer where her clothes were tumbling.

Emma Jean was trying not to look as though she were about to pop with joy and motioned Luke to the room in the back. "Boy, am I glad you're here, Sheriff. I've got a cabinet stuck that I can't get open. You mind giving me a hand?"

He set the bags down and followed her, and once they were inside and out of sight, grabbed her and kissed her till they were dizzy.

"Tonight," she whispered excitedly. "Rudy's on night shift. We can be together till dawn."

He said that sounded wonderful, and right then he couldn't think of anything that would keep him from being there but added, "I can't stay out all night, sugar. I don't know what's got into Alma lately, but she's watching me like a hawk. Every time I work late, she calls the office a dozen times trying to find out where I am and what I'm doing. She's driving Ned crazy."

Emma Jean did not want to talk about Alma. She didn't even want to think about her. "I'll take whatever time you've got. Just make it quick as you can once it gets dark. Promise?"

He promised, kissed her again, then wiped his lips with the back of his hand in case there was lipstick, but she grinned and said she had seen him coming and rubbed off as much as she could.

"I wish I could stay and talk to you, but Sara's here."

"It's okay. I'll see you soon."

Walking back to the front, he motioned to Sara to go with him outside. They were almost to the door when the phone rang, and Emma Jean answered and quickly yelled after them, "Sheriff, it's for you."

It was Wilma to tell him there had been a wreck on the Talladega highway between a truck and a school bus. There were no serious injuries reported, but a lot of parents were hysterical and converging on the scene. Matt and Kirby were afraid things were getting out of hand. He hurried out, leaving Emma Jean staring after him to wonder what was going on and hope whatever it was would not spoil their plans.

Sara was standing next to his car, and he paused long enough to grasp her by her shoulders and look deep into her eyes and say, "Look, honey, you've got to snap out of this."

"I know. It's just so hard."

"Are you ready to take revenge on Burch?"

For the first time, she showed spirit. "You know I'd give anything to make that devil pay."

"Okay then. I think we've waited long enough. If you'd given him the come-on right after it happened, he might have gotten suspicious. So fix yourself up and go to prayer meeting tonight and see how he acts. Flirt a little. Make him think you're real wild and horny. Make him think you like to do it different ways, different places."

She recoiled, brows raised. "Are you crazy?"

His smile was grim but assuring. "Trust me. There is method in my madness." He patted her arm, then got in the car and leaned out the window to add, "I'll call you tomorrow and see how it went."

Then he was gone in a spray of gravel.

Sara turned to go back into the laundromat, but just then Irene Cleghorn drove in. Flipping a white-gloved hand absently in Sara's direction as she got out of the Cadillac, she breezed inside. Sara followed after her, thinking how Irene was the only woman in town who dressed every day like she was going to church. Today she had on a green and white flowered silk dress, and high-heeled black patent leather shoes. She was even wearing a hat.

Pushing the door open, Sara heard Irene snapping to Emma Jean to go out to her car and bring in her laundry. "The maid didn't come today," she said, "and she'll be out all week, and I can't stand having dirty clothes smelling in the hamper. Get them done and drop them by my house before you go home."

"Well, we don't deliver," Emma Jean said apologetically.

Irene looked at her like she was something stuck on the bottom of her shoe. "Well, you do now, or I'll complain to Bert." She snapped gloved fingers together, "You'll lose your job, just like that."

Emma Jean murmured, "Yes ma'mm."

Irene acknowledged Sara. "So, how are you? I haven't seen you in church lately, and you haven't been to circle meeting either."

"I . . . I haven't been feeling well," Sara managed, fighting the impulse to scream that she'd be feeling just fine, thank you, if Irene's horny, worthless, piece-of-shit husband hadn't caused the death of the man she loved.

"Well, you don't look well, either. Maybe you should see a doctor." Irene glanced at her Bulova with the diamond band. "My, my, I've got to run along. Emma Jean, go on and get my laundry now. I'm having my bridge club tonight, and heaven only knows what I'm going to do without Loweezy to make those darling little finger sandwiches of hers."

Emma Jean doggedly obliged and, once Irene was gone, exploded, "I swear, that woman's voice sets my teeth on edge like nails dragging a blackboard. She sounds like a cat with a head cold." Placing a hand on her hip and bending her other at the wrist, she began to sashay around the room, imitating Irene's voice. "Whatever will I do without Loweezy's little finger sandwiches? If I have to make them myself, I'll get mayonnaise all over my gloves. Oh, my, my, my."

Sara burst out laughing. "I swear, you sound just like her."

"Do I? Well, I have to admit I've been mimicking her ever since I started working here. She comes in when Loweezy doesn't show up, which is often. Can you imagine what it'd be like to work for that woman? And Mr. Cleghorn probably has it rough, too, and . . ." She noticed Sara's expression. "Oh, I'm sorry. I shouldn't have said anything about him."

Sara's eyes narrowed suspiciously. "Why not?"

Emma Jean was truly flustered. "Well, because I know how you must hate him on account of Dewey, and, oh, Lordy, I should learn to keep my big mouth shut."

"You know, don't you?" Sara sank into the nearest chair. "That means the whole town does, too."

Emma Jean could not let her think that and dropped to her knees beside her. "Oh, no. It's not like that at all. Nobody else knows. Luke told me, you see, and . . ." It dawned suddenly that now she had really messed up because Sara would wonder why Luke would confide in her and might guess the truth. She frantically tried to cover and stammered, "I . . . I mean, he . . . he's the sheriff, and sometimes he tells me what's happening around town when he drops by. We . . . we're friends. Nothing more. And I don't want you thinking . . ."

"It's all right," Sara said, waves of relief washing over her. She had suspected Luke was involved with Emma Jean, only now she was sure it was much more than that. Otherwise, he would not have trusted her enough to tell about her and Dewey. "It's all right," she repeated. "Luke deserves some happiness. I probably know better than anybody what a miserable life he's had, especially since he married Alma. And you don't have to worry. I won't say anything. We'll just keep each other's secrets."

Emma Jean was beaming as she got up to sit next to Sara. It

felt so wonderful to be able to talk about her love, at last, and the words poured out of her as she confided just how much Luke meant to her. They bonded quickly as they bared their souls to each other, for Sara was likewise grateful to have someone else to confide in.

"I just worry where it's all going to lead," Emma Jean bemoaned. "I mean, if Rudy ever found out, he'd kill me. And I'm scared of Alma, too."

"And you've every reason to be. Oh, she pretends to be born-again, but she's a hypocrite. I despise her for the way she treats Luke. I wish he'd leave her. It's just a shame she got pregnant or he'd never have married her."

"I kind of thought that's how it happened."

"Yes, because Orlena Ballard was not going to see her grandchild raised a bastard. Not after the misery she'd suffered over the same thing. She saw to it Luke married Alma real quick."

"Did they get along in the beginning?"

Sara laughed. "They didn't even live together till after Orlena died, and he moved back here to be sheriff. He quit school and joined the army and only came home on leave. If you ask me, I think he's been miserable from day one, and I know for a fact he never loved her."

Again, with her usual candor, Emma Jean asked, "Did you think Dewey loved you?"

A glow spread across Sara's face to remember. "Oh, yes. He loved me with all his heart. And he still does." She crossed her arms over her bosom and whispered, "Sometimes it's like I feel he's with me, holding me tight."

"And that's why Burch has to pay for what he did," she ended with a rush of anger.

"How will you do that?"

Sara stared at the dryer, the clothes tossed and tumbled by the drum as recklessly as the emotions surging within her. "Luke has a plan. He hasn't told me what it is, but I've got to get busy setting Burch up for it."

The dryer clicked off, and she raced towards it and began stuffing her clothes in her basket.

"Hey, everything will be wrinkled," Emma Jean protested.

"It doesn't matter. I've got to hurry home and get ready for prayer meeting tonight. I've got to wash and roll my hair and get a bath and fix my face and try to look really nice." She was talking more to herself than Emma Jean as she planned how to look enticing for Burch without being obvious.

Emma Jean elbowed her away from the dryer. "Here. Stop it. I'll fold these and leave them on your porch on my way home from work. You go ahead."

Sara stared in grateful surprise. "You'll do that?"

"Of course, I will. Thanks to Irene Cleghorn, I've got a delivery service going." She began to mimic her again. "Now you just run along, my dear, I've got to get busy making little finger sandwiches for my bridge club."

Laughing, they walked outside together, pausing to look across the street where Betsy Borden was rummaging in a garbage can.

"That poor woman," Sara said. "She ought to be put away somewhere."

Emma Jean agreed. "She's a weird one, all right. Rudy's had to run her off a couple of times when she was trying to sleep in the roost house." She couldn't help but giggle as she added, "When he asked her why she didn't go sleep in her own, she said she liked to visit different chickens in the neighborhood."

"Sad," Sara murmured. "So very, very sad."

Sara felt Burch's eyes on her all during worship service. He was sitting directly behind her, and she didn't think that was by accident. There were a lot of empty pews. He was alone, too, because Irene was playing the piano.

Sara had purposely chosen a spot away from everyone else, and Burch had played right into her hands. The service ended, everyone rose, and she turned automatically, as though to greet whoever was nearby. Feigning surprise, she knew she had missed her calling as an actress, for she was able to paste on a smile and exclaim, "Oh, Mr. Cleghorn—Burch—I didn't know you were there. Good evening to you."

She stepped into the aisle, but he moved quickly to get in front of her, lips spread in his best *deacon-greeter* grin. But it was not his usual patronizing routine. Instead, with voice lowered against anyone possibly overhearing, he said in a rush, "You aren't still mad at me, are you, Sara? I mean, it was an accident. You know that. He was old. It wasn't my fault. And I had to get out of there. I couldn't afford to get involved. I'm just glad you managed to get away, too. I should've taken you with me, doggone it, but I'm ashamed to say I was just too damn scared at the time to think straight."

Sara marveled over how she was able to appear so composed when she was itching to rake her nails down his lying face. "Well, it was a bad situation. I hope you aren't going to say anything about me and Dewey. I mean, it's over. There's no need to hurt anybody."

He made his eyes go wide, as though stunned she could even suggest such a thing. "Why, Sara. Don't you know that's the last thing I want?"

He put a big, beefy hand on her shoulder, and she gritted her teeth against the impulse to fling it off. She made herself stand there as he leaned into her face and said, "But you must be lonely, and I can take care of that if you'll let me. I'll make it worth your while financially, too, just like Dewey did. You keep me happy, and I'll keep you happy, understand?"

"I . . . I'll think about it." Her jaws were aching from having to keep her phony smile in place. "I guess we'd better be going. People will wonder what we're talking about."

"No one ever wonders about a deacon talking to a church member. Now when can we get together?"

"I . . . I'm not sure," she stammered nervously. "I have to think about it."

As though sent by her guardian angel, she saw Irene coming towards them.

"Don't take too long," Burch snapped, stepping away from her and changing his tone to continue loudly, "Well, it's great to see you here tonight, Sara. I hope you'll be back Sunday."

He put his arm around Irene as she joined them.

Beaming at Sara, Irene proudly exclaimed, "It was my little talk with you today at the laundromat that brought you out tonight, wasn't it, dear? Well, I'm glad you took it to heart." She patted her arm. "I'll expect to see you at circle meeting next month, too."

Irene told Burch they had to go, and Sara doggedly followed after them but kept her distance.

Whatever Luke had in mind, she hoped he moved fast because she didn't know how long she could keep up the charade.

Burch wasted no time in calling the next morning. "So when can we meet?"

Sara gritted her teeth. "I want more than a little fling, Burch. Dewey and me were together a long time." God, she hated talking to him about Dewey. It was a sacrilege.

"Dewey was just a farmer," he coldly reminded, "and now you figure you've got a chance to latch onto a rich lawyer for your new sugar daddy. Well, I need to see how good you are first."

She swallowed the bile that rose in her throat. "I want it to be special. Not just a quickie in the back seat."

"How about meeting me at a motel in Birmingham?"

"That's not special enough."

He bit out each word like he was chewing up the side of a pork rib. *"Then what do you want?"*

She had talked to Luke late the night before, and he had told her what to say. "Will you meet me anywhere I want? Do anything I want?" She made her voice husky. "I like to do kinky things, Burch. I'm very playful."

His whispered "Oh, my god," was barely audible, but she heard and stifled a gag.

"You name it. Oh, babe, if you're as good as you're trying to make me think you are, we're going to be together a long, long time. And I'll treat you real good. You'll see."

Luke had also instructed her to string him along, and now the time had come for the showdown. "Call me this afternoon. I'll let you know then."

"Why can't we make a date now?"

"I need to make some arrangements." *Luke* had to make arrangements.

"Okay. But I warn you, make a definite date or that's it. I'll start the gossip rolling and, within a week, Dewey's widow will be spitting on his grave, and Tim will wring your neck for the two-timing whore you are."

She hung up, then dialed the sheriff's office, praying Luke would be there. He was, and she rushed to tell him Burch was playing right into her hands.

"Great. Meet me at the post office in half an hour. It'll look like we just happened to run into each other. I'll give you all the details then."

Forty minutes later Luke told Sara his plan, and she was so astonished she had to steady herself by leaning against the hood of his car. "Are you serious? You really want me to make a date to meet him in the *church?* Luke, I know he's lower than whale shit. But he *is* a deacon, and surely he'd balk at doing it in the church."

"Don't be so naive. He'd do it on the altar if he had to and not bat an eye. Now when does Tim go on three to eleven again?"

"Monday."

"Perfect. Today's Friday. When is Burch supposed to call again?"

"This afternoon."

"Good. Tell him to meet you at the church Monday night at seven. Tell him to walk, so his car won't be in the parking lot. If he asks how you plan to get in when the doors are locked, tell him you have a key because you do some volunteer work in the office once in a while. He won't question that. He's probably got one, too. And don't worry. You won't have to go all the way with him, but you may have to go pretty far."

"Why can't you just take him out in the woods and beat the hell out of him and tell him if he says one word about me you'll kill him next time? Why do I have to be involved at all?" She shuddered. "God, Luke, when I think about him putting his hands on me, I want to throw up."

"Trust me. If my plan works, and I believe it will, his life will be hell forevermore, but it's best you don't know the details till Monday night. I don't want you stewing about it."

"I'll be stewing enough thinking about having to let that creep paw me."

"Just keep telling yourself it's revenge for Dewey."

"I'll try," she said miserably. "Dear Lord, I'll try."

Yielding to the urge to see Emma Jean, Luke circled the laundromat several times waiting for Irene Cleghorn to leave. Emma Jean saw him through the window but couldn't hurry Irene.

"No way would I give up," he assured as they stepped into the back room for a quick kiss. "But why was she here so long? Don't tell me she was actually doing her own laundry."

"Oh, no chance of that. Her maid didn't show up again, and

she's all to pieces worrying her good linens won't be ready for her bridge party this evening."

Emma Jean went into her routine of mimicking Irene, then fell silent to see how Luke was staring. "What's wrong? You don't think I'm being mean to make fun of her, do you?"

"No, it's okay. Do some more."

"More?"

"Yes. Talk like her some more. Say, 'I'm having a surprise party for Ramona Hampton'."

"Why? That's silly."

"Just do it. Please."

She did, and Luke laughed out loud and slammed a fist into his open palm. "Perfect. Just perfect. I didn't know till this minute how I was going to pull it off, but you just solved everything . . . if you'll do it."

"Anything," she said without hesitancy. Lord, if he asked her to jump off a cliff, she wouldn't bat an eye.

He explained in detail what he wanted.

She looked doubtful. "I don't know. It doesn't make sense, calling all those people and making them think I'm Irene. What happens when she isn't at the party? Won't folks wonder? And what about when she hears somebody pretended to be her?"

He put his hands on her shoulders. "You let me do all the worrying, okay? You just make the calls. You can start this afternoon. Have you got enough dimes for the pay phone?"

"Sure. The dryers take dimes. I always make sure I've got plenty for folks who need change."

He pressed his lips against her forehead. "You saved the day, honey."

Basking in his praise, she said without thinking, "Well, I'm surprised Sara didn't tell you how I could do Irene, especially since that's the time I messed up and let her know you told me about her and Dewey. I didn't mean to, mind you, but I was poking fun at Mrs. Cleghorn and said something about how I felt sorry for her husband, and Sara looked hurt. Then I remembered what you told me, and I apologized and said too much and she figured out I knew everything."

"You mean you told Sara that I confided that to you? Then she must have wondered why . . ."

"She did," Emma Jean said without guile. "And I just went

ahead and told her, 'cause I knew she'd guessed it, and she said she had, but we don't need to worry. She's such a good friend to you, Luke."

"I know that." Then, because of the seriousness of their situation, he felt compelled to prod, "You haven't told anyone else about us, have you?"

"Of course not. You and Sara are the only friends I've got in this town. And I don't see any harm in her knowing. She won't tell. And who knows? We might need her some time as a go-between. You know it's awful hard sometimes for us to get word to each other when we need to."

"I guess you're right." He put his arms around her, and she winced and drew back. "Has he hurt you again?" he asked sharply.

She tried to pass it off. "Oh, you know Rudy. He gets a little bullish sometimes and shoves me harder than he realizes. It's nothing. Now get along with you. I need to catch up on everything so I can start making those phone calls."

"I wish it didn't have to be this way. When I think of him hurting you . . ."

"Oh, it's not so bad," she lied, wriggling in his grasp. "Now let me go before somebody comes in."

He released her and swore, "That damn redneck is going to hurt you bad one day, and then I'll kill him."

Flustered, because he was standing so close, and she wanted so badly to throw herself in his arms, she feigned annoyance to hide what she was actually feeling. "Well, what would you have me do, Luke? Hit him back?"

"Leave him. I've told you that before."

If I left him, I'd be leaving you, and I don't want to do that."

Luke, also waging an inner war of his own, lashed out, "You can't plan your life around me, Emma Jean. You knew how it was when we started this thing. We can't let it get away from us, so you better think of yourself and what kind of life you're going to have if you stay married to Rudy."

She was on the verge of tears. "If you're around to be my friend, I can stand it."

"Well, maybe I won't always be."

"Then I guess I'll have to manage somehow, won't I?"

Their gazes locked in mingled anger and pain.

"I'd better get going," he said finally.

He was almost to the door but turned and saw how she was staring after him like the last mourner before a coffin lid closes.

Chapter 26

It was almost dark when Luke entered the church through a rear door. Once inside, there was enough light yet filtering through the windows that he could see his way around. He was in the storage room, situated directly behind the baptismal pool which was sandwiched between velvet curtains. Choir robes hung on a rack along one wall with hymn books stacked neatly on shelves beneath.

The pool was flush with the floor, steps on each end. It was bigger than most, ten feet long, six feet wide and four feet deep. It was said the wife of Cleve Hampton-the-second, who had built the church, weighed over three hundred pounds and wanted to be the first person baptized in it. She had insisted on making sure it was large enough for her.

The pool stayed empty unless it was needed, so Luke turned on the valves to start water running. While it was filling he made sure the curtain on the other side behind the altar was tightly closed. He then entered the sanctuary through a side door and hurried past the neat rows of pews and up the red carpeted center aisle to switch on one light in the foyer. It would be enough that the ladies could find their way to a seat.

If Emma Jean followed all his instructions, the ladies would know to park a good distance away and walk to the church, slip inside, and be as quiet as possible as they waited for the party to begin. Even Reverend Lansky, who lived right next door, would not notice anything going on.

Luke had called Emma Jean just before she closed the laundromat. All the women she had called, while pretending to be Irene Cleghorn, had said they'd be there.

Satisfied the stage was set, he hurried to the storage room in time to let Sara in the back door before she panicked and thought he hadn't arrived yet.

"It's pitch dark in here," she whispered uneasily. "I can't see my hand in front of my face."

"Just relax. I'll tell you everything you have to do."

When he finished, she groaned, "Oh, Luke, I don't know . . ."

"You have to. Otherwise he'll carry out his threat."

"But how will I know to time things to happen?"

"I'll be standing in the far corner, and when you hear what sounds like a hoot owl, you'll know it's time to start getting him in the pool. The rest is up to you. I'll be listening, and when he's in position, I'll yank the curtains open at the same time I turn on the light over the pool. The switch is close enough I can hit them both before Burch realizes what's happening.

"Now the second that light flashes on," he continued, "I want you to already have your back turned to the sanctuary and ready to pull yourself out of the pool. I'll move fast to get behind the curtain and pull you under it. There won't be time for you to get your clothes back on because we've got to get out of here fast. Go ahead and take them off now, and I'll have them bundled and ready by the back door."

"Now?" she echoed uncertainly.

"I can't very well gather them up in the dark later, and if you try to afterwards, somebody is liable to come tearing back here and recognize you. Besides, you're going to be wet, remember?"

"But . . ."

"Just do it fast. He might walk in that door any second."

"But won't it look funny if I'm standing here naked? Won't he be suspicious if I look too eager?"

"He's so arrogant he probably expects you to be, but just in case . . ." He snatched a choir robe off the rack. "Put this on. He'll think it's sexy."

"Sexy?" she yelped, holding up the white robe. "Good grief, Luke. It's sick. Me in a choir robe acting like a slut."

"He'll love it. Hell, tell him it's your idea of being a virgin for him, the first time you're having him and all that kind of stuff."

"I still say it's sick. And it's also sacrilegious."

"Well, so is he."

Luke was pleased to hear her giggle.

"It's terrible, but the more I think about it, the better I like it."

"I knew you would once you stopped being so scared. Now hurry and get undressed."

She giggled again. "You've been waiting years for this, haven't you?"

He laughed. "You don't know how many times I froze my ass in a cold shower over you, woman."

She peeled out of her dress. "Well, you're more mature now. I think I can trust you. She yielded to impulse, "Besides, I understand you've got somebody else to blame for cold showers now."

Luke wasn't sure how to respond, then decided to hell with it. She already knew, and it was pretty bad if he couldn't trust her, of all people. "Yes, I guess I do."

"Well, I'm real happy for you, Luke, but please be careful."

"We have been, and we will be, and I don't believe she'd have said anything to you if I hadn't told her about you and Dewey. I was with her that night after it happened, and I was so bummed out I just had to unload."

"I know the feeling, and it's okay. I just don't want you to get hurt. She's a sweet girl, and I know her life has to be hell married to Rudy, but it's a one-way street. You know that. So don't get in too deep."

"Maybe I already am," he admitted.

"I was afraid of that." She had taken off her slip and bra and panties and was totally naked but too intent on what was about to take place to be embarrassed or self-conscious.

Luke rolled her clothes in a bundle and placed them next to the door while she put on the robe. "Okay. I'm going to get into position. The rest is up to you." He found her in the darkness and hugged her. "I know you can do—for Dewey and for yourself."

She hugged him back. "I want you to know how grateful I am you're doing this for me."

"I'm just sorry I didn't take care of it sooner. If I had . . ."

She pressed a finger to his lips. "Shush. I don't want to hear it. You're keeping me from being blackmailed into having to be that creep's whore for the rest of my life, and I'll never forget it."

He thought how he was not doing it solely for her, only she would never know that.

Burch opened the door slowly and instinctively reached for the light switch, but Sara was ready, as Luke had instructed, to stop him.

"I want it dark," she said, her hand covering his as she once more fought an impulse to gag. "I told you, honey child, this is gonna be a special night."

He laughed throatily and reached for her, then, feeling the billowy garment, paused to ask in wonder, "Hey, what is this?"

"A choir robe. I'm wearing it because it's white."

"Yeah," he scoffed. "Like you're a virgin."

"It's my first time with you, so that makes me a virgin *for* you."

"Yeah, I guess . . ." he groped for her breasts. "So you've made your point. Now take it off. I want to see what I'm buying."

She felt like spitting in his face but instead managed to coo, "Now I told you, Burchie, baby, it's got to be special, and you aren't going to see me till I say so."

"Okay, I'll play your stupid game, but get that thing off so I can feel you up good."

"And you get undressed. I want to feel you, too, sweet thing." She fought to keep from gagging.

"Yeah, I will. Hurry . . ."

He fumbled with his clothes, then grabbed her again, but, realizing he was still wearing his undershirt, she held him at bay. "Not till you've taken everything off."

He pulled the undershirt over his head, then roughly drew her into his arms and began covering her face with hot, wet kisses. Sara willed herself to let him, reminding herself over and over it was revenge for Dewey, and also to ensure her children would not be taken from her, that they would not have to grow up in a broken home. And when this was over, she was going to concentrate on being the best mother she could be. She was also going to get a real job, maybe in the new drapery plant rumored to be opening up next year. She would save every penny she could so when the children were grown she could strike out on her own and make a new life. She would not, by God, continue to live in a loveless marriage after they left home.

He had been there less than five minutes, and Sara wasn't sure she could take another second of it but knew she had come too far to turn back. She also knew how disappointed Luke would be if she failed. Emma Jean, too, because he had told her if not for Emma Jean, they couldn't have pulled it off, that she had used her talent to imitate Irene Cleghorn to make those women she had called think they were being invited to a surprise party for Ramona Hampton.

Luke had been thorough in his planning, too, not allowing for any chance that word might get out. *Emma Jean-Irene* had made each lady she called promise not to tell her husband, not to tell a soul, for fear it might somehow get back to Ramona.

As for why the party was being held in the sanctuary instead of the church fellowship hall, Luke had come up with a believable explanation. He just had *Emma Jean-Irene* say that the special treat she had planned could only be held there.

But no presents were wanted, *Emma Jean/Irene* had emphasized. The reason was that Luke did not want paper rattling when the ladies came down the aisle, afraid Burch might hear. *Emma Jean/Irene* had explained that Ramona would like it better if everyone contributed a few dollars each to buy a needed electric skillet for the church kitchen in her name. But, most important, *Emma Jean/Irene* had instructed, they all had to be very quiet and sit in the dark till the big surprise happened.

"Come on," Burch was snarling at Sara's ear as he clutched her buttocks and thrust himself at her. "I want a quickie now. We can play later."

Luke could hear every word and knew Sara was having a rough time holding Burch off. They were still by the door, far away from the pool, so he stealthily picked his way to the curtain separating the pool from the sanctuary and opened it just a crack. The soft, sparse light from the foyer behind them was sufficient to frame the women seated on the front row. He counted ten. One was missing, Irene Cleghorn, the purported hostess.

Emma Jean was to have called her at the very last minute and pretend to be the maid of one of the other ladies, apologizing for her mistress because she had not been invited to the surprise party. She was also to convey the explanation that her mistress had been so busy getting everything together she thought she had already invited her and was so embarrassed when she realize she hadn't. Irene's feelings would be hurt, but she would, of course, rush to the church.

Burch was trying to push himself inside her, and Sara twisted away. "No," she whispered, remembering despite her rage to keep her voice down, for the *guests* had probably begun to arrive, though it was doubtful they would be able to hear from such a distance. "I told you, we have to do it special."

"And I want it now."

"And you're going to have to wait."

"Hey, I think you better get something straight." His hand shot out to twist her hair and yank. "I'm boss here. Always. I say how we do it and when. Not you. Now get on the floor and . . ."

"I won't."

He yanked harder.

"Listen," she hissed between clenched teeth because he was hurting her, "If you want just plain, ordinary sex, man on top, woman on bottom, then you aren't half the man my Dewey was."

"Oh, yeah? And what made him so damn special? I saw his pecker, remember?" He snickered. "Or maybe I should say his *weenie*. Feel of this, bitch." He grabbed her hand and pulled it against his erection. "It's big. Real big. You saw it before. You're feeling it now. And Dewey Culver, the old fart, never saw the day he was half my size."

Sara's knee was actually starting to twitch from wanting to slam into his balls, but she managed to hold back and continued to goad, "I'm not talking about size, Burch. I'm talking about being adventuresome. Now I told you I wanted tonight to be special because it's the first time. If you aren't willing to play, then okay, we do it your way. I'll take your money and screw you whenever you want, and it'll be as boring to me as it probably is for your wife."

He gave her hair one last yank and let her go. "Okay. So what do you want to play? I'll stand you on your head if that's what you want. And you can bet your sweet bippie when this night is over, you'll know you've been had by a real man, damn you."

"Talk, talk, talk," she said, swinging her head from side to side.

"I said tell me what you want."

"Okay. Why do you think I asked you to meet me here at the church?"

He thought a minute. "Hell, I don't know. Maybe you're just a nut. It doesn't matter to me where we do it, but I'm ready right now."

"Silly." She managed a giggle. "I want to play in the pool."

"The . . . pool?" he sputtered. "You . . . you mean the *baptismal* pool?"

"That's right. And I've already filled it with water." She put her arms around his neck, rubbed her breasts against his chest and heard him suck in his breath. "I think it'll be fun. Then, every time it's used from now on, you'll think of us doing it there, and if I'm in church that day, I'm going to look at you and smile, and I'll bet it makes you hard."

"It . . . it probably will," he whispered, digging his fingers into her buttocks and trying once more to pump against her, only she wriggled away from him.

"And what we can do then," she went on to arouse him even more, "is sneak into that Sunday School room upstairs that's got the little cloakroom and have a quickie 'cause everyone will have left. Now won't that be fun to think about while you're watching all those folks getting dunked in the water?"

"Oh, yeah, yeah, yeah . . ."

He was running his tongue over her face, and Sara mustered all her willpower to keep at him, wanting to get it over with, desperate to end the madness.

"I'm going to get in the pool, real quiet. And I want you to stand at the top of the steps on the other end, and when I call you, you come in and try to find me. You know, like a submarine firing a torpedo.

Mercifully, at that instant, Sara heard Luke's signal, a hoot owl, so very, very faint. She stepped away from Burch and into the shadows. "Think you can find me in the dark, you big bad submarine?"

"Oh, I'll find you, all right. I'll . . ."

"Shhhh. No noise. It's part of the game. You have to find your way to the pool, and I've got to be real quiet so you won't know where I am."

She could tell by the lilt in his voice he was getting into the spirit of what he thought was going to be the wildest sex he'd ever had. "That pool's not all that big. I'll find you, all right."

"But you can't use your hands to reach out for me because I'm going to be waiting with my legs spread wide open, and I want to see if you can find me in the dark and plunge right in, and then we'll have at it, big guy."

"Big guy," he echoed proudly. "Oh, yeah, I'm big, all right. Hell, I don't think I've ever been this big. You've got me so hot I don't have enough skin left to blink my eyes."

Sara found the curtain and parted it as she whispered, "This way. You stand right here. Feel with your toe for the water, so you'll know where the steps begin. I'm going on in, okay? Now remember to be real quiet so you can hear which way I'm going."

"So what happens if I don't find you the first time I try?"

"Then you lose."

"What does that mean?" He was beginning to wonder if it were going to be as much fun as he'd thought.

"You don't get any tonight."

"Hey, that's not going to happen."

"We'll see."

She stepped into the water and immediately moved to the side to position herself for a quick exit, aware at any time the overhead lights would flash on, the curtain to the sanctuary would open, and she would have maybe two seconds to hoist herself out of the pool and shimmy on her belly to disappear beneath the rear curtain. She only hoped Luke moved fast to pull her up so they could get out of there.

Pressing her hands, palms down, on the floor behind the pool, Sara took a deep breath and readied herself. It would be over any second. All of it. Burch would be ruined forevermore, and she could get on with her life, satisfied that Dewey had been avenged.

Suddenly, Burch let out a roar that would have made Johnny Weismuller proud and yelled, "I'm gonna fire my torpedo. Me and my big torpedo are gonna . . ."

The lights flashed on. The curtains opened. And ten women plus Irene Cleghorn gasped in unison at the sight of Burch standing on the top step into the baptism pool pumping his penis up and down as he tried to make himself even harder in anticipation of launch.

Those who could tear their astonished, horrified gaze away from Burch caught only a glimpse of a woman's bare ass as she slipped beneath the curtain with all the ease and grace of a seal sliding along ice. No face was seen. Not even the color of her hair was noted. It all happened too fast.

Burch, still holding onto his penis, which was rapidly shrinking, threw himself into the pool, for, in the midst of the horror of realizing he had an audience, heard Luke's hasty, whispered warning from behind the curtain.

"Say it was Sara, and I swear I'll kill you and make it look like an accident."

Burch hit the water so hard it splashed up and over the sides and across the altar and all the way to the front row to soak the women who had managed to get to their feet.

Irene fainted. The other ten women, their gasps having changed to hysterical shrieks, ran into each other in their mad haste to exit. One fell and her ankle snapped when someone stepped on it. Another slipped in the water spilling from the pool and split her head open on the edge of the altar. The rest made it to the door and burst onto the wide marble steps outside to scream at the top of their lungs and wake the whole town.

And all the while, Burch floundered in the pool. He was still there when Reverend Lansky, hearing the commotion from the parsonage next door, arrived on the scene moments later to help him out and put yet another choir robe to use covering a naked body.

Meanwhile, Luke and Sara escaped without being seen.

"Good job," Sara gave him a hug and a kiss before turning her gaze toward the heavens to solemnly declare, "I did it for you, Dewey. Rest in peace, my love."

After she had gone, Luke also looked to the stars. "You rest, too, Momma," he murmured.

Chapter 27

Leaning back in his chair, feet propped on the sill, Luke stared out the window through templed fingers. It was October. The air was crisp and cold, with trees rattling in the wind and leaves scudding down the street.

Two months had passed since Burch was caught, literally, with his pants down in the baptismal pool at the First Baptist Church. The town could not have been rocked more had a dynamite blast at the marble quarry gone awry.

Burch disappeared for a few days, finally creeping back home when he realized he had no place to go. He was ruined, socially and professionally, and all he could do was hang his head and hope the talk would eventually die down.

Everyone knew, of course, that the party for Ramona had been a ruse and Irene had not made the phone calls. No one knew why Burch had been set up and didn't care, anyway.

As for the woman's identity, folks had no idea whose face went with the bare fanny seen emerging from the baptismal pool.

To ensure that Burch didn't yield to temptation once the initial shock wore off, Luke had phoned him at his office and bluntly repeated his threat. Burch had actually broken down crying as he promised over and over that his lips were sealed. And Luke had smiled and whispered into the phone, "Cry me a river, Burch. Cry me a river."

So now Luke had only one swing of the hammer left—Buddy Hampton, but he was starting to worry that he might not succeed in getting anything on him, after all. Sending him to jail for being involved with the Klan was not what Luke had in mind for retribution, and it would be hard to convict him, anyway. Buddy had money, connections, and would probably find a way to weasel out of it. As for his having a mistress and an illegitimate child, he could handle that kind of scandal, too.

Murline had promised to let Luke know when Buddy sent her to Talladega to wire money again, but he hadn't for the past couple of months. It wasn't unusual, she assured Luke. Sometimes when he went on a business trip, he would take care of it himself because she suspected he took an extra day or two to spend with his girlfriend.

The phone rang in the outer office. Luke hoped it wasn't for him. He was a maelstrom of emotions lately. Besides the hunger to get something on Buddy, he was stewing about Emma Jean and what she would say if he asked her to run away with him. He was pretty sure she cared about him, but he was leery of giving her the opportunity to use him as a scapegoat to get away from her misery if she didn't. Yet he knew that unless he got up the nerve to ask, he might never know because so far they had both stuck to their agreement that neither would expect anything permanent, that what they had was for today only and to hell with tomorrow. And maybe he should leave it at that. Maybe it wasn't too late to take that job as a mercenary. He could make plenty of money, and if he didn't get killed, he could retire at an early age and spend the rest of his life on a beach in California with some hot-blooded babe like Coquina. Only he didn't want Coquina, or anybody like her. He wanted Emma Jean and was going to have to make up his mind what to do about her.

Wilma called, "It's for you. A woman. Won't tell me her name."

Luke took the phone and waited for Wilma to hang up the extension before saying, "Sheriff Ballard here."

"I can't talk but a second. He's gone to the restroom."

Hearing Murline's voice, Luke felt a rush of excitement. "What's up?"

"He's sending me to Talladega this morning to wire money to Birmingham. You said to let you know."

"When are you leaving?"

"In about half an hour."

"Do you think Swain knows it's being sent today?"

"Probably. I got here a little early this morning and happened to spot Buddy going into the cafeteria. I was curious, so I peeked in and saw him on the pay phone. I suspect he was calling Juanita to tell her. I've never known him to call her from his office, even on his private line. He just doesn't take any chances, like I'm doing now," she added grimly.

"I wonder . . ." he said slowly, thoughtfully, "why I get the feeling that you could save me a lot of time if you wanted to, Murline."

"What . . . what do you mean?"

"I mean that I think you've got all the answers I need, but you're making me dig. How come?"

"I . . . I don't know what you're talking about," she stammered. "You said to call you the next time he asked me to wire money, so I did."

"It's just a feeling. I hope I'm wrong."

He hung up and pulled on his jacket, thinking how he had planned to sneak in to see Emma Jean that night because Rudy was working the three to eleven shift, but now he was going to Birmingham to see if he could find out for himself what Murline seemed scared to tell him. Since there was no way of knowing how long it would take, he needed to let Emma Jean know he might not make it, after all.

"Is the jail laundry ready?" he asked as he stepped into the outer office.

In a hurry, he did not notice how Kirby and Matt looked at each other as Wilma, brows raised in surprise, reminded him, "You took it yesterday."

He remembered, felt sheepish, then quickly recovered. "Oh, yeah, well, I guess it's ready to pick up then. I'll get it on my way out of town."

"Out of town?" she echoed.

"Birmingham. I've got to check on some things." He hurried on his way, not giving her time to ask more questions.

The laundromat was so busy Luke could only have a hasty, whispered exchange with Emma Jean as he picked up the basket of clean, folded linens for the jail. He murmured he had urgent business out of town and might not get to see her that night. He stopped by his house long enough to change into civvies, glad Alma was at work so he didn't have to go through the usual inquisition, then drove to Birmingham.

The Western Union office was located in the heart of the big industrial steel town. He parked his car a few blocks away and walked back to the office. Giving the bored-looking agent a fictitious name, he asked whether a wire for him had arrived yet.

"Nothing this morning," the clerk said without having to check. He had been on duty since seven and was aware of everything that had come in.

"I'll wait then."

"Suit yourself." The clerk went back to reading the morning paper.

Luke settled into a chair and picked up an old copy of *National Geographic* and absently leafed through it. Glancing at the wall clock often, he watched the time creep to noon. Finally, a bell tinkled as the door opened. Luke saw it was a negro man and continued flipping magazine pages. He hoped C. Swain, *Carl Swain*, would hurry up. He didn't want to spend all day in Birmingham. He wanted to get back to Hampton, catch up on all his work, and make ready for a nice, quiet evening with Emma Jean. He'd rather take her to a motel, though. He didn't like making love to her in Rudy's bed, but she said it gave her good memories for the times when . . . Luke shook away the thought of her and Rudy in bed.

"Count it yourself, Carl. It's twice as much as usual."

Luke's head snapped up.

"Oh, I trust you, suh," the old negro responded. He stuffed the money into his pocket, signed the receipt the agent shoved across the counter, then left.

The agent met Luke's inquiring eyes with a snicker. "Yeah, I know. That's a lot of dough for a nigger, but it's been rolling in ever since I've been working here."

Luke strained to keep his voice even, to hide the excitement he felt bubbling from deep within. "And how long is that?"

"Nine years now."

"And he gets money every month?"

"Most of the time."

"Wonder where it comes from."

"The office in Talladega. Me and the agent there have talked about it from time to time. He says a white woman brings it in, but she never says nothin', just pays the fee to wire it."

"Well, maybe he works for white people and picks it up for them."

"Naw. I don't think so. But it's sure funny."

"What's his last name?"

"Swain. Why?"

"No reason. Just curious." Luke stood, stretched and forced a yawn. "Well, evidently my ship's not coming in today. I'll check tomorrow."

"I'll be here," the agent said in dismissal.

Luke burned up the highway and was in Hampton in time to change back into his uniform before Alma got off work. Then he drove straight to Murline's house but was not surprised she wasn't home yet. She was taking advantage of her day off after going to Talladega. He radioed Wilma to let her know he was back in service, then spent the rest of the afternoon just cruising around town, frequently checking to see if Murline had returned.

Around four, he finally saw her car parked in the driveway. He pulled in and started to get out, then reached under the seat where he had stashed her shoe and stuffed it in his pocket in case she needed reminding. He walked right up to the front door but did not have to knock. She was waiting for him, her face pale and drawn, stepping back as he entered.

"Are you alone?"

She nodded, twisting her hands together in that way she had when she was nervous. He told her to sit down, and she did. Then, barely able to contain his rage, he grasped the arms of the chair and leaned right into her face. "Why didn't you tell me Buddy's mistress is colored?"

She tried not to meet his fiery gaze, but his eyes were mere inches from hers. "I . . . I couldn't," she said feebly. "It . . . it wasn't my place."

"And you were hoping I'd eventually give up and not find out, weren't you?"

"Yes. Because I didn't want Juanita or her son hurt."

"And you thought I'd do that?"

"I didn't know, especially when you kept digging even after you found out Buddy was involved in the Klan. Why couldn't that have been enough for you?"

With a sudden wave of bravado, she lifted her chin to irately demand, "Good Lord, Luke, what *do* you want? And why are you after Buddy, anyway? What's he ever done to you that you hate him so much?"

"That's my business." He moved away from her but did not sit down. Instead, he turned to the window to stare out at the falling leaves.

Murline persisted. "Well, whatever it is, please don't hurt Juanita. Her relationship with Buddy has been a secret all these years, but if you . . ."

He cut her off. "What about her son? Does he pass for white or colored?"

"Why . . . why colored, of course."

"Does he *look* colored?"

"Yes, he does. Buddy showed me a picture of him in his cap and gown when he graduated. He's a handsome young man, and he definitely passes for colored."

At that, Luke whirled about to explode, "Damn the hypocritical asshole! He's involved with the Klan big-time. He gives the order for colored people to be beaten, maybe even killed, and yet he proudly shows off a picture of his half-colored son?"

"He's not proud," Murline was quick to dispute. "If he were, he wouldn't hide it, would he? No, he's not *proud*, Luke. He just loves his son's mother. And his son, too, I suppose. But society and circumstances dictate he has to keep them both secret, and that's how they'll stay unless you tell, and if you do . . ."

Her voice trailed hesitantly, and Luke challenged, "Go on. Finish."

"I'll believe you really are a bastard."

He almost winced but didn't. He could understand her fear that innocent people would be hurt for whatever his motive. "You don't have to worry."

Her sigh came from her very soul. "Thank you."

"So what is the boy going to do now that he's through with college?"

"He's got a job lined up in Detroit. Buddy said he was sending extra money this time so he can buy some nice new clothes and get set up in an apartment. He also said Juanita was upset over his leaving home, but they both know there really aren't any good job opportunities for negroes around here. He's a bright boy, too. Made the Dean's List all through college. He should do real well up north."

Luke laughed softly and shook his head to think about Buddy Hampton bragging about his half-negro son's college grades to his ex-mistress when all the while he was one of the biggest racists in the state of Alabama.

Murline ventured to ask, "What are you thinking?"

"I'm thinking," he said, reaching into his pocket, "how I'd rather be a bastard than a hypocrite."

She took it the wrong way and cried, "No. You promised you wouldn't . . ."

"And I won't," he was quick to assure. "Thanks for everything, Murline. And you can stop worrying. Your fairy godfather said so."

He dropped her shoe in her lap and walked out.

Luke eased the patrol car around back. The house was dark, and he thought maybe Emma Jean had given up on him, but then she came running from the shadows where she had been waiting.

"How come no lights are on?" he asked as he hugged her. "I

told you it has to look like I'm here on official business, because something scared you, and you called the law."

She giggled. "I *did* get scared that you wouldn't come. But you're here now, and everything is all right." She tugged at his arm. "It's almost ten o'clock. We don't have long."

"Yeah, but first we're going to turn on some lights."

They went inside, and he switched on first the porch light, then the kitchen. "If we hear anybody, we'll come back in here real quick."

In the bedroom, Emma Jean unbuttoned his shirt while he unbuckled his holster. He protested when she tugged at his trousers. "I'll have to leave them on, sugar, and just unzip."

"You took them off before."

"Well, it's best I don't as late as it is."

"That's not fair," she teased. "Look at me."

She opened her robe, and in the light spilling from the kitchen, he saw she was completely naked.

His breath caught in his throat. "Lord, woman . . . ," and gently, quickly, he pushed her down on the bed to fall on top of her. His hands were everywhere at once as his mouth devoured hers.

"Oh, Luke," she moaned, "I wish it could be like this all the time."

He drew back so he could see her face in the light. "Do you mean that?"

She became still, puzzled by his expression. "Why . . . sure I do. You've told me how you and Alma never do it, how she never liked to, and how much it's meant to you that I'm always ready. And I've told you I'd never refuse you, that I know what it means to a man to get it when he wants it, and . . . ."

"But that's not what I'm talking about. I . . . ," he floundered, trying to decide if he was ready to talk about it —*them*—here and now and get it over with. She meant giving him sex when he wanted it. He was thinking about just being able to be with her, damnit, and not have to sneak and worry about getting caught, and . . .

Emma Jean prodded. "What?"

"Baby, I . . ."

They both heard the sound and sprang apart.

Panicked, she cried, "Oh, God. It's Rudy. I know his truck."

Luke was yanking on his shirt at the same time he stuffed his feet in his shoes. "Get some clothes on. Quick."

In the faint light she found jeans and a shirt and put them on while Luke zipped his pants and buckled on his holster. Then, desperate and thinking fast, he drew his gun and rushed to the window to smash a lower pane with the butt.

Emma Jean yelped, "What'd you do that for?"

"Never mind. Just let me do the talking and back up anything I say. Now let's get to the kitchen."

Emma Jean gave the top sheet one quick yank and ran after him. By the time Rudy jerked open the screen door, red-faced and furious at having seen the patrol car, Luke was casually leaning against the refrigerator. Emma Jean was standing on the other side of the room, arms folded across her bosom and looking appropriately scared.

"It's okay, Rudy," Luke said breezily. "Whoever it was got scared off when your wife screamed."

"Huh?" Rudy, fists clenched at his side, looked from Luke to Emma Jean, then back at Luke. "What the shit are you talkin' about?"

Luke feigned surprise. "Didn't the office call and tell you there'd been a prowler here? I figured you'd rush right home. I've been waiting for you. She was scared to death, and you can see she's still upset."

Rudy snapped, "Ain't nobody told me nothin'."

Emma Jean, having gathered her wits enough to realize what Luke was doing, how he was trying to bluff their way out of it—was able to innocently ask, "Isn't that why you came home early?"

His eyes hooded. "Woman, ain't you learned by now you don't ask me nothin' about what I do and when I do it?"

Luke gritted his teeth, knowing if he hadn't been there, Rudy probably would have hit her.

"I come home 'cause I ain't feelin' good," Rudy said to Luke. "And I don't mind tellin' you it made me mad as hell to see your car in my yard. How do I know you aren't here trying to make my old lady?"

Luke gave an exaggerated sigh. "I don't give a damn what you think, but you can go look for yourself. The window's broken. The prowler tried to jimmy it open, I guess. I looked around outside but didn't see anything. Like I said, her screaming probably ran him off."

Rudy glowered at Luke as he brushed by him to go into the bedroom.

Luke was glad he had thought to switch on the overhead light. He looked at Emma Jean. Her face was white as lard, she was shaking all over, and he decided he had better wrap things up quick before she really went to pieces.

"Satisfied?" he asked Rudy, who was staring at the broken glass on the floor.

Rudy returned to the kitchen before answering. "Yeah, I reckon."

"There's nothing else I can do," Luke said, walking to the back door. "I suggest, though, that you get that window fixed right away." He turned to Emma Jean, "Make sure you keep it locked."

"Oh, I will, Sheriff. I will." Her head bobbed up and down.

He stepped onto the porch and Rudy slammed the door after him.

Rudy waited till he was sure Luke had driven away, then walked over to Emma Jean and backhanded her so hard she bounced off the refrigerator. She cried out and tried to dart past him, but he grabbed a handful of her hair and painfully twisted as he pulled her face close to his. "You listen to me, bitch. If I ever find that son of a bitch in this house again, I'll kill him and you, too. You got that?"

She tried to nod but he was twisting her hair too tight.

"Yes, Rudy, yes. Please, let me go . . ."

"I'll let you go when I'm good and ready. Now you listen to somethin' else. Don't you never talk to me in front of nobody like that again, you hear me? I thought by now you would've learned your place, but you keep runnin' that big mouth of yours, don't you?"

She tried again to nod, to agree, to do anything to get him to leave her alone so he would stop hurting her, but he held tight.

"I hate that son of a bitch," he railed on. " 'Cause that's what he is and everybody knows it. I've hated him my whole life, and if I ever thought there was something goin' on between you two, I swear I'd kill him."

He released her so abruptly she stumbled and fell to her knees. "Now clean up that mess in there before I step on some glass."

~~~

Luke had difficulty seeing through the angry red haze that clouded his eyes. He did not report back in service. Ned was off for the night. Bailey Albritton was covering for him—an old fart Luke had little use for—but he was Ned's cousin and Ned whined he needed the extra money so Luke let him work. Bailey liked to yak on the radio, and Luke did not like idle chatter, especially now, so he stayed ten-seven as he cruised around the county, sticking to the back roads as he tried to sort his jumbled thoughts.

Yeah, Rudy would hit her, all right, probably right after he left. But Emma Jean would cover any mark with makeup to try to keep him from finding out. Luke knew there were lots of times Rudy beat her that he didn't know about. And now she was probably huddled in a corner crying her eyes out and, maybe, if she wasn't hurt too bad, she might even be wondering what it was he would have said had Rudy not come home when he did.

Only Luke wasn't sure himself, at least not for many long hours that night. He drove and thought, and thought and drove, nearly running out of gas at one point and had to go unlock the pumps at the county garage to fill the tank. And still he drove.

He stopped a couple of times, wearily leaning his head back against the seat, but sleep would not come, not when his brain was on fire, along with his heart, as he tried to figure out what he was going to do about the one woman who had truly brought sunshine into his life. He knew he did not want to leave her. That thought rang clear as the sunrise that broke in the east as he found himself on top of Cheaha Mountain all the way over in Talladega County.

He watched the ash-colored sky turn to pale pink, then peach, as the first creeping fingers of dawn reached from the horizon to snatch away the last vestiges of night. And finally he knew. He was not going to leave without her.

He had to go home. He hated to, but he needed a shower, shave, and clean clothes. First, however, he stopped at the diner in Childersburg on his way back from Cheaha for eggs and grits and bacon, because his rumbling stomach kept reminding him he'd been too preoccupied to remember to eat supper the night before. He also downed cups of strong, black coffee as he tried to brace himself to face the day ahead.

It was nearly eight o'clock when he pulled around back of his house and groaned out loud to see Alma's car. She should have left for work a long time ago. Maybe she was sick. If so, she'd be in bed asleep, and he could get in and out without her hearing.

No such luck. He no sooner stepped up on the back porch than the door flew open and there she stood, eyes wild, hair flying around her face, clutching her bathrobe to her throat with one hand, a cigarette in her other as she exploded, "Damn you for the tom-cat you are, Luke Ballard. You've been screwing around all night with some whore and now you've got the nerve to come dragging in here to wash off your filth and germs . . ."

He shoved her back into the kitchen and shut the door with his foot. "Stop it, Alma. You want the whole neighborhood to hear you? I've been working . . ."

"You've been screwing some whore," she cried, her face twisting with rage. "I know, because I called the office at midnight last night, and Bailey Albritton said you'd been off duty since before ten o'clock."

Silently, he raged, *Great going, Bailey.* Everybody else knew how to deal with Alma when she called.

"Bailey Albritton doesn't know his ass from a hole in the ground. I was over in Coosa County. He knew that. I was helping bust up a still."

"Like hell you were."

"Alma, I'm tired." He turned toward his room, but she quickly moved to block his path.

"You think I'm not?" she shrieked. "I've walked the floor the whole night thinking about your running around on me."

Making sure he was very gentle so he could not be accused of abusing her in any way, Luke put his hands on her shoulders and pushed her out of his way. "I have to change and get back to work, Alma. Now please, get off my back . . ."

She struck like a snake, her nails raking his face. She was about to slap him when Luke caught her wrists. "Damn it, woman! Have you gone crazy?"

He flung her away from him, wheeled about, and tried to flee, but she threw herself at him, leaping up on his back, arms going around him as she dug at his face again. She was straddling him, and the only way he could get her off was to bang her against the wall. Screaming, she finally let go and fell to the floor, and he rushed out, knowing if he didn't get away fast, he might lose control and do something he'd later be sorry for.

Wilma's eyes bugged when he walked in the office. "What on earth..."

"Don't ask." He stormed past her. "Just get me some alcohol and cotton and when the cleaners opens, go pick up one of my uniforms."

Mouth agape, Wilma stared after him. His face looked like it had been gone over with a rake. Curious, she went to the door and peered into his office. "I want to know what happened. You look awful."

He repeated the lie he had told Alma about being over in Coosa County but embellished, "I was arresting a moonshiner, and his wife attacked me."

Wilma crept closer. "Some of those scratches are deep. You could get blood poisoning."

"Not if you get me the alcohol like I asked you to, Wilma."

As soon as she left, he reached for the phone.

Hearing his voice, Murline protested, "I thought it was over, that you didn't need me anymore."

"One more time. That's all. Today's Wednesday, and Buddy will be playing golf down at Lake Martin this afternoon, won't he?"

"Yes, but I hope you don't want to get into his files again. If he locks them, there's no way I can open them."

"Nothing like that. I just need to know when he leaves the mill."

"Usually around twelve."

"Call me the second he does."

When she did not immediately agree, he prodded, "Come on, Murline. I need this one last favor, and then I won't bother you again, I promise."

"Okay," she said finally, "but please, keep me out of it. I need this job, and if he ever found out..."

"You don't have to worry."

It came at ten past twelve. Wilma put the unidentified female caller through to him, rolling her eyes thinking it was Emma Jean Veazey. There had been some rumors going around.

Luke took it, heard only two words: "He's left." He hung up, and rushed out the door.

There was a section of road between the mill and town where there were no houses, just an old barn used for hay storage with farmland on either side. Luke and the deputies sometimes hid their cars behind it to catch speeders. This day, however, Luke was waiting for Buddy Hampton, and as soon as he breezed by in his red Thunderbird, Luke pulled out right behind him, blue light flashing.

When Buddy promptly eased over to the shoulder of the road, Luke parked behind him and purposely waited a few moments before getting out of the car.

Buddy rolled down the window. "What the hell is this about? If you make me late for my golf game, I'm going to be real pissed." Seeing the claw marks on Luke's face, he grinned. "Looks like I'm not the only one you've pissed off lately."

"No need to be concerned about being late, Buddy. You aren't going to show at all."

Buddy's grin quickly faded. "Who the hell do you think you're talking to? And where do you get off calling me Buddy? It's *Mister Hampton* to you. I'll have your badge, you insolent asshole. You seem to forget who you're dealing with."

"Oh, I know, all right." Luke enjoyed seeing Buddy so steamed. His face was red as a beet, and his eyes were actually bugging out of his head. "Now I want you to follow me."

"You're crazy. I'm not following you anywhere, and you've no call to give me a ticket. I wasn't speeding. He jabbed at the air with his finger. "I warn you, boy, I can have your badge snatched off that pompous chest of yours in a matter of minutes. All I've got to do is call Hardy Moon. He's the coroner, and I shouldn't have to remind you that under Alabama law a coroner has the power to fire the sheriff. All it will take from me is one phone call . . ."

"One phone call," Luke lazily echoed with a smirk. "Yeah, that's all it will take, *Buddy*." He emphasized his words to irritate. "Just one phone call to the Klan to tell them all about your negro mistress and the son you had by her, and that should take care of everything."

Buddy's face changed from red to pasty white. "I . . . I don't know what you're talking about," he said feebly. "This isn't funny."

"The Klan won't think so, either. Tell me, do you think they'll stop at burning a cross in front of your house?" He scratched his chin thoughtfully, then shook his head. "Nah. I think they'll do more than that. After all, we both know you're real big in the Klan, and they won't take it lightly. Uh-uh. Not at all. They might do to you what folks say they did to Cubby Riddle."

Buddy's hands dropped protectively to his crotch. "Oh, no, please don't tell anybody."

"No one has to know as long as you cooperate."

Buddy's head snapped up. "What do you want? Money?" he asked, excitement flashing. "Listen, you name it. Any amount, and . . ."

Luke was quick to burst that bubble of hope. "It's not about money. When we get where we're going, I'll explain what you've got to do to keep your skeletons in your closet."

"I . . . I don't have a choice," Buddy said, more to himself than Luke.

Luke nodded and smiled. He had been waiting a long time for this moment. "That's right. You don't. Now let's go."

Luke had driven out to Hampton Pond many times since the night his mother told him everything. He would park for long hours in the weed-choked drive, chest tight with pain as he thought of how horrible it must have been for her on that cold night back in 1939.

Buddy had eventually bought a vacation house over on Lake Martin, and the old cabin had fallen to ruin. Kudzu vines, which would not let go till the first frost, had covered everything with a thick, green shroud. The boarded-up windows were barely visible. One end of the porch roof had collapsed, and the rest looked like it might give way any time.

"Why did you bring me here?" Buddy called nervously as he got out of his car and hurried towards him.

"It's deserted . . . a good place for us to talk." Luke stood in front of the cabin, thinking how his mother had probably screamed over and over that night, and now the echo of her torment was burrowed deep within the rotting timbers. There had been no one to hear her then except her attackers, just as there was no one to hear Buddy's screams now should he decide to dig his thumbs in his throat and squeeze till his eyeballs popped.

"Please . . ." Buddy clamped a hand on his shoulder. "A lot of innocent people will be hurt if you . . ." He trailed to a groan of pain as Luke carefully, slowly, wrapped his fingers around his wrist in a paralyzing grip.

"Inside. Now." He gave him a shove, and Buddy began running toward the cabin, stumbling as he looked back over his shoulder, his face a mask of panic. Picking his way across the rotting porch, he tore at the kudzu in a frenzy as he pleaded, "You can't tell the Klan. You just can't. Please . . ."

He tried to open the door, but it was locked. "We can't get in," he said shrilly. "I don't have a key."

Luke walked up on the porch, shoved Buddy aside, and, with one powerful kick, broke the door down. Grabbing Buddy by the nape of his neck, he shoved him inside. Buddy went tumbling across the room to slam against the table and fall to his knees but quickly recovered to scramble back up.

Luke pushed him into a rickety chair next to the table. Towering over him, he accused, "You gave the order to have Ocie Rhoden's arm broken, didn't you?"

Buddy's head swung like a pendulum. "No. No, I swear."

"Don't lie to me."

Perspiration beaded Buddy's forehead. He licked his lips, tried to find his voice and finally squeaked, "Yes, but I had to do something to shut him up. He was pushing for the union."

"You're going to pay for what you did." Luke bit his tongue to keep from saying that he was also going to pay for something else. But Luke did not want Buddy, or *anybody* else, to find out he knew about his mother's rape. "You're also going to pay for your hypocrisy, for all the years you've been part of the Klan, pretending to look down on negroes when all the time you were sleeping with one . . . fathering a child."

Perspiration beaded Buddy's forehead. "What do you mean?"

"The mill has problems even the union will have a hard time fixing, and something has to be done about it."

Again, Buddy shook his head. "I don't understand."

"I'm talking race relations, and I think the person to fix things might be your son, Archie Swain. And what better choice? I understand he graduated from Tuskeegee after four years on the Dean's list. So you're going to hire him and give him a title like, oh, Senior Vice-President for Labor and Race Relations, something like that. And he'll have an irrevocable mandate from you to bring management of the plant into the 20th century. Not only will you give your blessings to the employees voting on the union if that's what they want, but you're also going to give your son free rein to have equal treatments for the coloreds. Equal pay for equal work. No more separate water fountains. No outdoor toilets.

Luke leaned so close Buddy could feel his breath on his face. "And all the while, you are going to stay on as President. But, of course, you'll see to it Archie eventually gets controlling stock or whatever it takes for him to have his share after you've gone to hell."

Buddy's stomach lurched. He put his hand to his mouth, feeling sick. "I . . . I don't think I can do that. I mean, what will people say? My wife? My family?"

"Oh, I'm sure you can come out of this smelling like a rose, Buddy. You can make yourself look real magnanimous, paving the way for equal opportunities for all races. I'm sure you can carry it off."

Buddy's eyes narrowed as it dawned, and anger swept the fear away. "It was Murline, wasn't it? She told you. It had to be her."

"No, I've been following you for months. Oh, I tried to worm stuff out of her in the beginning, but she was tight as a tick, claimed she didn't know a thing about your personal life." His brow furrowed in a mock frown. "Now it pisses me off to know she lied. Maybe she's in the Klan, too."

"No, no, believe me, she isn't," Buddy all but shouted as he suddenly felt the need to protect her. "She never knew anything, I swear it. I just thought maybe she'd been in my papers or something."

Luke squinted as he pretended to consider that Buddy might

be telling the truth, finally conceding, "Well, she did sound awful convincing.

"Anyway," Luke said, walking towards the door, "You can think about how you're going to get the wheels in motion while you're walking the five miles or so back to your car."

He gave a little salute and disappeared among the kudzu vines.

PART III

Chapter 28

Late November, 1969

Luke moaned, ever so softly. Alma frowned. She was making a stitch picture of a garden scene, and the French knots in the center of the daisies were very difficult. She kept cutting the thread too close to the fabric, snipping the knot itself and having to start over. Every time Luke moaned, it made things worse. The doctors said it was normal for somebody in a coma to make noises once in a while, but it really got on her nerves.

She had been there since early morning, having relieved Violet Bradley. The ladies in the church had been real good about sitting with Luke during the night, but Alma suspected they weren't altogether motivated by Christian goodness. Instead they were probably hoping they'd be there if he woke up so they could hear whatever he might say. She wanted to do the same, which was why she'd taken a leave of absence from work to stay all day. She'd have liked to also stay nights, but that was just too much. Tammy needed her, too.

Alma was glad Burch Cleghorn, who'd been appointed Emma Jean's lawyer by the court, was going to plead her guilty. He told the Veazey family at first he thought about sending her off for testing to see if she were crazy. If so, he would have her plead not guilty by reason of insanity. But he said Emma Jean didn't want to drag things out, that she had known what she was doing when she killed Rudy and was ready to take her punishment. He said he thought that was best because the longer the case dragged out, the longer it would be till the family could start getting over it.

Everybody liked Burch for that, including Alma. He could have run up his bill to the county but instead was thinking of Rudy's family and the taxpayers. Now lots of them were saying maybe the awful thing that happened in the baptismal pool wasn't really his fault. Maybe somebody wanting revenge for him having beat them in court had somehow drugged him and set him up.

He had come to the hospital one day to ask Alma how she felt about things. She hadn't minced words, declaring she hoped the little whore fried for what she did, murdering her own husband, trying to murder *hers*.

Luke made another noise, like a sigh. Alma glanced at him, thinking how she despised him and when all this was over with, and he was back on his feet, things were going to be different. Licking the end of the thread, she ran it through the needle's eye after the third try. First off, he was going to give up being sheriff. After all that had happened he'd never get reelected, anyway. And Matt was doing a good job of taking over. There was talk of him doing it permanently. So Luke could just get a job at the mill.

He moaned again, and Alma gave up and tossed her embroidery aside. She leaned back and closed her eyes and thought about how the weeks since the shooting all seemed to run together: trips to and from Birmingham, people coming and going from the church, food eaten off paper plates, drinking awful coffee from a machine.

Mr. Hampton had been real good about giving her time off, but sooner or later she'd have to return to work. The insurance might not cover all the hospital and doctor bills.

Luke made another sound, louder this time, like he was trying to say something.

"Oh, Lordy," Alma cried, bounding to her feet to realize he was awake and looking at her. "Oh, dear Lord. I gotta get somebody."

She rang the call bell for the nurse, then ran to fling the door open to yell, "Somebody get in here quick."

Sara had been sitting outside the door and stood to fearfully ask, "Oh, no. Is he worse?"

Alma glared at her. "It's none of your business, and what are you doing back here, anyway? I told you, you aren't going to see him."

"And I told you—Luke is my friend, and sooner or later I *will* see him."

"I've had it with you, bitch." Alma slapped her, and, for an instant, Sara could only stare at her in astonishment. Then her own rage took over. She was about to return the blow when firm fingers wrapped around her wrist, and she twisted about to see a man in a white coat and a stethoscope draped around his neck.

"What is going on here?" the doctor asked, looking from

Sara to Alma in angry disgust. "This is a hospital. Take your cat fights outside."

"Don't pay her no mind, doctor," Alma grabbed his arm and drew him into the room, closing the door in Sara's face. Pointing at Luke, who now lay very still with eyes closed, she whispered so Sara wouldn't hear, "He was awake a minute ago. He opened his eyes, and it sounded like he was trying to say something."

He made a phone call, and soon nurses and more doctors arrived.

Outside, it did not take Sara long to figure out what was going on. Luke was waking up, thank God. But Alma was determined not to let her anywhere near him. The ladies who sat with him at night stood fast, also. But still she tried, hoping he would come around so she could find a way to let him know Emma Jean desperately needed his help. Sara didn't believe for one minute she had shot him. As for her killing Rudy, that had to have been self-defense.

Several times Sara had tried to visit her at the jail, only to be told she refused to see anybody. Matt had taken her there straight from the emergency room. Burch hadn't asked for bail, claiming she wouldn't be safe if she were released on bond, because of Rudy's family.

A nurse came to ask Sara to leave, saying she was upsetting the family. Sara took her purse and went to the end of the T-shaped hall and found a bench where she would be out of sight of Luke's room. She would have to play Johnny-jump up to keep an eye on things, but that didn't matter. She had to be around to take advantage of any opportunity to try and slip into his room when nobody was around. She also had an ulterior motive besides helping Emma Jean, because, without Luke around, Burch would go back to blackmailing her and making her life miserable.

The day wore on. She ate the pimento cheese sandwich she'd brought from home. She wished for a Coca-Cola to wash it down but the snack bar was in the basement, and she wasn't about to leave and go down there. It was bad enough when she had to go to the bathroom, always worried she would miss a chance to see Luke.

She felt her first stab of hope when Matt arrived. He had been real good about keeping her informed how Luke was doing when he visited, not that there'd been much to report.

After a half hour or so, he came out. Sara followed him, waiting till he was in the parking lot before grabbing his arm to ask in a frenzy, "Is he really awake, Matt? Is he talking? What did he say? And did you get a chance to tell him about Emma Jean?"

"Hey, hold on," he said, startled. "And calm down, Sara."

"I have to know how he is."

"He's waking up, but it's going to take a while for him to come around completely."

Sara was trembling in her desperation to make him understand. "Matt, we're running out of time. He's the only one who can save Emma Jean."

He ran agitated fingers through his crew cut. "Sara, we've been over this again and again. Emma Jean is not on trial for shooting Luke."

"And I've told you," she persisted, "He can testify how Rudy beat her, and then everybody will know she did it in self-defense."

"And *I've* told you," he said, "she admits she did it. I've also tried to make you understand it's best to leave Luke out of this for the sake of his family. There's been enough gossip."

"You know she didn't shoot Luke."

"No, and I'm hoping when he wakes up he can tell me who did. But I want you to stay out of it. The trial is set for next week. Let's hope it's over with quick so the healing can begin for everybody."

"That soon? But why?"

"Burch pushed for a quick trial date for the sake of everybody concerned."

"No. He did it for his sake, because he's hoping by sacrificing Emma Jean when everyone is screaming for blood they'll forget about him in the baptism pool, the hypocritical son of a bitch."

Matt had never seen her so mad. "Gosh, Sara, what's got you so riled? Why do you care what folks think about Burch?"

"You wouldn't understand. Now will you help me get in to see Luke so I can tell him about Emma Jean?"

Matt shook his head. "I can't do that, Sara. Alma just asked me if she can get some kind of restraining order to keep you away from the hospital. I had to tell her I'll see what I can do. Sorry."

"Thanks a lot," she quipped sarcastically. "And I guess you're going to continue to keep me from seeing Emma Jean, too."

"How many times do I have to tell you. She told Burch she didn't want any visitors."

"Well, I don't believe she told him anything except that she's innocent. The lying son of a bitch is going to see she's convicted because he thinks it will make him some kind of hero. And I can't believe you're helping him, Matt. You're as disgusting as he is."

She turned on her heel and walked away.

Sara waited till well after midnight to leave the house. The children were sound asleep, and Tim was working night shift. She parked in the alley behind the Bulldog Cafe, so her car would not be noticed if anyone was riding around at such an hour.

She saw the lights were on in the third floor of the courthouse. Floyd Dixon, the part-time jailer and also married to her second cousin, was also working. He was there because of Emma Jean, and so was Sara. She was determined to see Emma Jean this night come hell or high water.

Entering the courthouse through the basement, she made her way upstairs. Floyd was asleep behind the desk, snoring loudly. The door to the narrow corridor between the barred cells was open. Stepping inside, she closed it after her.

"Emma Jean," she called softly. "It's me, Sara."

There was no answer, and she walked past the cells to the one on the end, next to the window. A street light cast eery shadows, but she could make out a narrow cot against one wall, a toilet, sink, and, sitting on the floor staring up at the barred window was Emma Jean.

Sara used the back of her wedding right to tap on the bars. "Emma Jean, are you all right?"

The voice that responded was wispy as a dandelion. "Go away."

"Not till you talk to me. You're in big trouble, Emma Jean, because Burch wants you to go to prison for killing Rudy, but I know it was self-defense. And that's what you've got to tell them, and . . ."

"I don't care," Emma Jean whipped her head about to say defiantly, "and I just want to die. Now leave me alone."

Emma Jean looked like someone gone mad, her eyes dark and sunken, hair matted and wild about her stricken face. "My God, what have they done to you?"

"Nothing. They haven't done nothing. They leave me alone like I want you to do." She turned away.

"I can't understand why you've given up. What about Luke? Don't you care about him, anymore? Good grief, honey, folks say you shot him, and I know you could never do that. He started waking up today. Alma won't let me in to see him, but I'll find a way. When he hears about you, he's going to want you to fight, and . . ."

Sara's voice trailed as she saw Emma Jean slowly, shakily, crawling toward the bars, one hand extended like a starving beggar groveling for a bread crumb.

"Luke is going to live? But they said he never would . . . that the doctors couldn't get the bullet out of his head, that he was going to die . . ."

Sara dropped to her knees so they were facing each other. "They did get the bullet out. He's been in a coma, but I think he's going to be fine. And so are you, if you'll fight this thing." Rage boiled like water in a tea kettle as she demanded, "Who told you that?"

"Mr. Cleghorn. He said the doctors told him there was no hope. And he also said everybody thinks I shot him because he wouldn't leave Alma for me. But that's not so. I'd never hurt Luke. God knows, I wouldn't. I love him, Sara." She began to cry.

Sara patted her back, wishing she were inside to hold and comfort her. "I know you do. And you know why Burch lied? He doesn't want you to fight. He wants you to give up so it will be easier for him. With everyone thinking you're a homewrecker and a cold-blooded murderer, it makes him a kind of hero to help put you away. Then they'll start forgetting about what he did. That's what he's after. He doesn't care about you."

Emma Jean wailed, "Oh, Lordy, Sara, what am I going to do? I thank God Luke is going to live, but there's no hope for me. I *did* kill Rudy. Don't you see? I stabbed him with a butcher knife."

"But he was beating you, wasn't he? It was self-defense. He'd beaten you before, and you couldn't take it, anymore. That's what you can say, and with Luke to back you up, the jury will believe you."

"No, they won't. They'll say he's only doing it because we've been sleeping together. But maybe they would if Matt would take up for me, too. After all, he was there that time I lost the baby. He saw me all bruised up, and . . ." Noting Sara's expression, she asked fearfully, "What's wrong?"

"He won't get involved. Nobody would dare to except for me and Luke. I won't be any good as a witness because I never saw Rudy beat you or any sign he had. Now your trial starts next week, and if you let Burch plead you guilty it's going to be cut and dried. You'll be sentenced right away, unless you stand up for yourself and say it was self-defense."

"But he won't let me."

"He can't stop you. And you don't even have to let him know ahead of time you plan to do it. The judge will ask how you plead, and you just shout out 'not guilty' and then explain how you did it in self-defense. You can say Rudy was beating you like he'd been doing for a long time, and something snapped and you couldn't take it, anymore."

"I . . . I could do that," Emma Jean said, spirit beginning to stir. "I could tell everything that happened that night and hope and pray they believe me."

"Tell *me*," Sara prodded. "Tell *me* exactly what happened. Every single detail. Don't hold anything back."

Emma Jean pulled herself up to sit next to the bars. Swallowing hard, she tried to think of how to put the horror into words. Finally, with a deep, ragged breath, she told her story.

He had entered the bedroom carrying the butcher knife, bellowing his fury.

"You been screwin' around with him, you little whore. It took me a while, but I finally figured out that damn window was busted from the inside. Not the outside. There weren't no burglar that night. I caught you two, only I didn't know it then."

Emma Jean shrank away from him, whimpering in terror. "No, Rudy, no. It's not like that. You've gotta believe me."

He backhanded her so hard lights flashed before her eyes as she was knocked against the wall. He hit her again with his open palm, making her fall sideways. Another backhand sent her reeling the other way like a pendulum.

"Rudy, please, don't . . ." Blood ran from the corner of her mouth.

His fist slammed into her belly, and when she rolled into a fetal position, he yanked her off the bed and threw her to the floor and kicked her. "I told you if I ever caught you screwin' around, I'd make you sorry you was born. I should've known you'd never change. You was a whore when I met you, but you're gonna learn no woman cheats on me. I'm gonna teach you a lesson you won't never forget.

"Now get back on that bed." He grabbed a handful of her hair and twisted, painfully pulling her up to her feet.

Emma Jean was howling with pain. Again, he made a fist and hit her in her chest. She was struggling to breathe, wheezing sounds coming from deep in her throat.

Rudy began stripping off his clothes. "I'll give you something to cry about, you little bitch." Yanking his leather belt from his trousers, he brought it down viciously across her back. "Now lay there and take what you got comin' and don't you make a sound."

She was laying on her stomach, ears ringing. Through the misting anguish that blurred her vision, she saw the knife he had laid aside on the orange crate table next to the bed. Fingers clawing at the sheets as he shoved himself painfully into her from the rear, the thought came to her that she would rather cut her own throat than endure another second of tormented degradation. She loved Luke. Deeply and truly she did. But he was not free, and neither was she and never would be. There was no place for her to escape the madness except the grave.

Slowly, her hand snaked out for the knife. Lost in his perverse lust Rudy did not notice. Her trembling hands closed about the handle, and she began sliding it towards her. It would be over soon. A quick, sharp slash to her throat, and she would quickly bleed to death. She only prayed that Luke would escape Rudy's wrath. Surely, with her dead, he would leave Luke alone. It would be over.

Suddenly, Rudy flipped her roughly over on her back. "You're gonna finish it for me, whore. I'll bet you do it for him all the time, don't you? Well, you won't do it again, 'cause I'm gonna cut his dick off before I kill him. Oh, yeah, I'm gonna kill him. I'm gonna make him squeal like a pig on butcherin' day."

Like the puncturing fangs of a rattlesnake, Rudy's threat against Luke ignited rage and rebellion unlike anything Emma Jean had ever known before. She bit down. Hard. Twisting, pulling, tearing. She tasted blood but did not let go.

And in her hysterical insanity, she plunged the knife into him again and again.

Emma Jean slumped to the floor, sobbing quietly.

Sara was also crying and murmuring, "It's okay, honey. You aren't to blame."

But Sara feared a jury might think differently, even if Luke was able to testify about Rudy's beating her in the past. It had been a brutal killing, and only someone who had experienced such cruelty and humiliation could empathize. It would, sadly, be a hard case to prove, especially with a lawyer who was secretly sacrificing his client for his own gain.

Sara sat with her until Emma Jean quieted, then said she was going to see what she could do to help.

Emma Jean asked her to please try to sneak back and let her know how Luke was doing. "And tell him I love him. I never told him that before, and it's important he know."

"I'll tell him," Sara managed a smile. "But I think he already does."

Sara drove through the night but did not want to go home just yet. Finally, as it started getting light, she felt the need to go to the Veazey house to see where it had happened. There was a wreath, signifying a death in the house, tied with string through holes in the screen door. The flowers were dried, the leaves crumpled, and the ribbon hung limp. She tried the door. It was locked.

She turned away, not knowing what she had been looking for, anyway. Walls could not talk. Neither could the chickens, who were beginning to come out of the hen house. Someone, probably Sid Dootree looking out for things since he owned the house and the land, had filled the feeder with mash, and the chickens were migrating toward it, cackling softly among themselves as the rooster crowed to herald the dawn.

Sara turned toward the car, but, out of the corner of her eye, she saw something or someone emerging from the roost house. She whipped about in time to see a woman run around the side to disappear behind it. Sara's heart quickened. Maybe there was someone who might be able to help Emma Jean after all.

Chapter 29

"Come on, Luke, tell us who did it," Matt asked, not for the first time. He and Kirby stood on opposite sides of the hospital bed. It had been nearly a week since Luke had awakened, and it was the first time the doctors felt he should be questioned.

The bed was rolled to a sitting position. Luke was sipping a cup of coffee. "Like I said. I'll take care of it myself."

Kirby argued, "But you aren't going to be out of here for a while. We need to go ahead an make an arrest. Just give us the name."

"There's no hurry," Luke said quietly. "They aren't going anywhere."

Matt and Kirby looked at each other, then Matt said, "So there was more than one."

"Of course there were. Now stop yammering at me about it and tell me what's been going on." He longed to ask about Emma Jean but didn't dare. He wondered where Sara was, why she hadn't been to see him. She'd not only fill him in but also get a message to Emma Jean. Since waking up, he'd had little to do but lay there and think. And what he thought about the most was how he wanted to get out of the hospital so he could make plans to leave town. And he was taking Emma Jean with him, by God. All the hammers had struck, his mother now rested in peace, and he could, finally, get on with his life.

Again, Matt and Kirby exchanged glances, but Luke did not notice.

"Well, actually, nothing's been going on," Matt said. He had promised Alma he wouldn't tell Luke about Emma Jean murdering Rudy, how she was going on trial, none of it. Alma said the doctors had told her Luke wasn't up to handling anything stressful for a while. It made sense to Matt. Besides, Luke couldn't do anything about it, anyway. Better to get it over with. He'd be plenty mad later, but Matt figured that was Alma's problem. He was just cooperating.

Kirby chimed in, "Yeah, the only thing folks talk about is you, wondering who did it, and . . ."

Luke interrupted, "One of you do me a favor and call Sara. Tell her I'd like to see her. Don't say anything to Alma. You both know how she feels about her."

Matt said, "Yeah, sure." He motioned to Kirby. "We'd better get going. Remember they said we couldn't stay long. Tires him out."

Being in bed so long had left Luke weak. He could neither stand nor walk by himself. A physical therapist was due to start working with him soon, but the doctors had said he'd be in the hospital for several weeks yet. But he could stand all that, could stand anything, if only he could get a message to Emma Jean and tell her to hang in there, that he loved her more than anything in the world, and as soon as he was able they were taking off. And Sara would do it for him. He had no doubt about that.

"Don't forget to call Sara," he reminded as Matt and Kirby walked out.

Alma was waiting outside and heard. "Don't you dare call that little bitch," she whispered viciously once the door closed after them. "I mean it. I don't want her anywhere around him."

Matt had never cared for Alma, but she was, after all, Luke's wife. "Don't worry. We agree he doesn't need to know what's going on. He's not well yet by any means."

"That's right. Next time you visit just tell him you couldn't reach her."

"We probably won't be back any time soon," Matt said. "We were only able to come today because Judge Barrett gave everybody a day off because the court reporter is sick. She'll be back tomorrow, and we're hoping they'll finish jury selection. It's keeping us real busy."

Kirby looked worried. "Yeah, Rudy Veazey's kin have filled the courtroom every day, and those that couldn't get in made so much noise in the hall we had to run 'em off. It'll turn into a circus if we aren't careful."

Alma sniffed and said, "Well, I don't see why there even has to be a trial. I mean, after all, Burch says she's pleading guilty. Why not be done with it?"

"Oh, it won't take long," Matt assured. "Once the guilty plea is entered, all that's left is for the jury to deliberate and decide the sentence."

Alma brightened. "Well, I hope she gets the electric chair."

Kirby shook his head. "Don't count on it. She'll probably get life instead, and that's when we expect the Veazey clan to go nuts."

"Can't say as I blame them. What she did was unforgivable." Alma wanted her to be executed so Luke would eventually forget her, which wouldn't happen as long as she was sitting in the women's prison down in Montgomery. She told Matt and Kirby good-bye and went back into Luke's room.

He was awake, and he saw the "No Visitors" sign for the first time. "How come nobody can see me?" he asked, annoyed.

"You need your rest," she said sweetly. "But don't worry. In a few days, you can have all the company you want."

Because, she smiled to think, in a few days, it wasn't going to matter.

⌒⌒

"Don't you feel a little bit guilty about not calling Sara for Luke?" Kirby asked as Matt eased the patrol car into a parking slot behind the courthouse. "I mean, they've always been close, and I think Alma is off-base thinking there's more to it than friendship."

Matt switched off the motor and leaned back to give Kirby a look that plainly told him he thought he was off his rocker. "I can't believe I have to spell it out for you. Alma doesn't want anybody visiting Luke that might tell him about Emma Jean going on trial. She was there when I found Emma Jean holding a knife and covered in blood. Alma was there because she thought Luke was there. Somehow she found out about him and Emma Jean.

"So," he continued, "she wants Emma Jean to go to prison to get her out of Luke's life. She's also afraid that if he hears, he might try to do something to stop it, like get up and testify how he thinks Emma Jean did it in self-defense. He knows how Rudy used to beat her."

"Hell, you could testify to that."

"I'm not getting involved, and if you're smart, you won't, either. Listen, Luke's my friend, but he got himself in this mess with Emma Jean. I can't see risking my reputation in this town by stepping into a hornet's nest, which is what I'd be doing if I got up and said she had a right to kill her old man 'cause he slapped her around a time or two."

"I don't know," Kirby said doubtfully. "It just don't seem right."

"Since when is minding your own business not the right thing to do? We've got families, you know? And they've got to live in this town just like we do. I say we stay out if it."

Kirby thought a minute, then nodded in concession. "I guess you're right. And if Luke raises hell with us about it when he finds out, well, we'll just say we were doing what his wife asked us to."

"Exactly." Matt started to open the door, then turned as someone called his name.

Buddy Hampton was crossing the street from the cafe. "How's the sheriff?" he asked with what he hoped was an expression of genuine concern. "I hear he's awake."

Kirby headed on toward the courthouse while Matt explained Luke's condition for the moment, how he was on the mend but terribly weak and could not have visitors.

"Such a shame, such a shame," Buddy clucked mechanically, all the while thinking about his waning hopes that Luke would die, and his troubles would be over. "Has he told you who shot him?"

"No. I wish he would, but he says he's going to take care of it himself."

Buddy murmured, "Yes, he has a way of taking matters into his own hands, doesn't he? Well, keep me informed." With a tip of his hat, he went to his car and got in.

As each day passed and Luke had not awakened, Buddy had dared to hope Luke would die. But now, hearing that wasn't going to happen, he would have to follow orders and slowly put Luke's plan into motion. When he could put it off no longer, he would make the announcement that a young negro named Archie Swain was being appointed to the newly created position of Senior Vice-President for Labor and Race Relations. That would, of course, follow explanation of the mill's new policies, not only in regards to racial issues but also in support of voting in the union as well. It made him gag to think about it.

And, once again, he cursed the shooter for missing his mark.

Even though it was the second day of December, the weather was warm and humid. Betsy had dragged her table out of the fish cleaning shack because there weren't any windows, and the supermarket folks were too damn cheap to buy a fan. She was covered in scales from head to toe, and as she reached to push her hair back from her face, a piece of fish gut smeared across her cheek to leave a bloody streak.

She was wearing baggy overalls and no shirt beneath. No underwear, either, if the truth be known. She was standing barefoot in a puddle of melting ice from the fish boxes, as well as blood and entrails . . . and more scales.

Glancing up at the sound of a car in the alley, she saw it was Sara Speight. Betsy knew everybody in town. She went to a lot of funerals and church picnics, anywhere there was free food. She fished in the pocket of her overalls for the good-sized cigarette butt she had found in the alley that morning. It still had a few puffs left, and she had a box of penny matches, too. Lighting up, she took a deep draw and said, as Sara drew closer, "You can't buy no fish back here. You gotta go in the store. But they ain't got no fresh in there yet and won't have till I clean 'em. Gonna be good, too. Got a nice catch of bass."

Sara tried not to wrinkle her nose at the revolting scene, as well as the smell. If she had been in a buying notion, her mind would have changed real quick. "I came to talk to you, Betsy."

"What for? I ain't done nothing." Betsy eyed her warily. She could not think of any business Sara Speight might have with her. Sometimes she picked through the trash in her neighborhood, but she never stole anything that wasn't already thrown away. Sara had good scraps, too. Once she had found three nice pieces of fried chicken.

Sara tried to put her at ease. "I didn't say you had. I just want to ask you a few questions."

Betsy frowned. "What kind of questions?"

"You sleep in roost houses sometimes, don't you?"

Betsy shrugged. "So what if I do? You ain't got one, so what's it to you?"

"Emma Jean Veazey saw you coming out of hers one morning."

Betsy took one last drag on the cigarette. She tossed it into the puddle at her feet. "How does she know? She's in jail." Slicing open the fish's belly, she ran her fingers inside and drew out the contents.

Sara winced, glancing away as she said, "It was a long time ago."

"Yeah. I been there. She's got some nice hens. Real friendly. I like her rooster, too. And the perch is good. More comfortable to sit on than most others because the poles are wider." She tossed the fish entrails to the cats hovering about. "What's this all about? I don't bother nobody."

"I know you don't," Sara assured, then, with a breath as deep as the one Betsy had taken to suck in the last of the cigarette, she got to the point. "But I was wondering if you ever heard Rudy Veazey beating Emma Jean."

Betsy's expression changed, ever so slightly, but it was enough that Sara saw it and drew closer, despite the muck and blood.

"Did you?" she pressed. "Did you hear him hitting her, Betsy?"

Betsy tossed the fish into the box that would eventually be taken inside the supermarket for packaging and sale. Picking up another, she attacked it with a vengeance. "I don't repeat nothin' I hear. If I did, folks wouldn't let me sleep in their roost house. I go and come and don't make trouble, and they let me, and that's the way I want it. So if I had heard anything goin' on out there, I wouldn't tell you."

"Not even if it could save her life?"

"I don't know what you're gettin' at. Me sleepin' in her roost house ain't gonna change the fact she killed her old man. Hacked him with a knife, too." Betsy looked up at her and grinned almost maniacally as she brought hers down on the fish's head, severing it with a sickening crunch.

Sara grimaced but managed to continue. "If you were there the night she killed him and heard him beating her and would testify that you did, the jury would see it was self-defense and set her free."

"And what makes you think I care what happens to her?"

"Because of Sheriff Ballard. He would want you to help her."

Betsy hooted. "I don't know what the shit for. She tried to kill him, too. And that's a shame. Sheriff's a good man. Helped me lots of times, he did. Chased off them assholes that scared me to death on Halloween with their blasted sheet, makin' me think it was a ghost. That was the same night he was shot, but I hear he's gonna be all right, praise the Lord."

"That's true. And it's also true Emma Jean didn't shoot him. She couldn't have, because she loves him, and he loves her. But I've got an idea you know all that because you probably saw him sneak into her house late at night sometimes, and . . ."

Betsy angrily cut her off. "And I told you I don't repeat nothin' I hear or see."

Sara pleaded, "I'm not asking you to say you saw him at her house. I'm asking you to say that you heard Rudy beat her on the night she killed him and all the other nights as well. Please, Betsy. You've got to help her. And if Luke were standing here, he'd be begging right along with me."

Betsy stared at her long and hard before saying, "Well, I won't there that night. Like I done said, I was at my own roost house on Halloween. I still keep some hens there, even though I live with my pa. So I won't at Emma Jean's. Not that night."

"But did you ever hear him beat her the nights you were?"

Betsy decided there was no harm in admitting she had heard the beatings since Sara seemed to know, anyway. "Yeah, I guess I did. Lots of times. Once she tried to get away from him and ran out the back door. The porch light was on, and I could see through the slats in the roost house when he caught her and dragged her back inside by the hair of her head. I heard him hit her that night, too, 'cause they was in the kitchen. He was smackin' her real good. Beat the shit out of her, he did."

She had finished cleaning another fish and tossed it into the box. "So he probably deserved to die 'cause he was one mean son of a bitch. I can't tell you he was beatin' her when she killed him 'cause, like I said, I won't there that night."

"But would you be willing to testify to what you saw and heard the nights when you were there?"

"Are you crazy?" Betsy lopped off another fish head so viciously Sara jumped. "Me get up in that courtroom in front of all them people? No thank you, ma'am. Not me. She shook the bloody knife at Sara. "I done told you I won't there when she killed him, so what difference does it make if I saw him beat her before? She didn't kill him those times."

"No, she didn't, but your testimony would make the jury see that in all probability he was beating her *that* night, and she just couldn't take it any more. Maybe she even killed him to keep *him* from killing her. Self-defense, Betsy. That's what we're talking about."

"What we're talkin' about is how you're gettin' on my nerves." She shook the knife again. "And I'm startin' to get pissed off. Now you get on out of here, and if you want some fish, you go inside. I ain't sellin' you none."

Sara saw a funny look come into Betsy's eyes. She had heard it said she sometimes drifted away into a world of her own without warning.

"Besides," Betsy took out another fish and this time began scaling it with an almost tender stroke of the blade. "I'm a'gettin' married soon. Gonna have me a new life, I am."

"Well, I'm happy for you," Sara said uneasily as she began to back away. "And I wish you the best."

Dreamily, Betsy said, "Why thanks a whole bunch. I know I'm gonna love Tennessee."

"You're moving to Tennessee?"

Betsy glared defiantly. "Said I was, didn't I? How else you think I'm gonna be able to marry Elvis Presley if I don't move to Memphis? You think he'd want to live in this shitty little town? Hell, honey, if God ever decides to give the world an enema, he's gonna stick the nozzle right here in Hampton, Alabama, but me and Elvis ain't gonna be here to see it. No sir, we're gonna be up in Tennessee. Now if you ain't gonna buy some fish, get the hell out of here. You've wasted enough of my time."

By the time Betsy finished her tirade, Sara had backed all the way to her car and could not get out of there fast enough. If she was willing and could stay rational long enough, Betsy could have helped with her testimony on past beatings, but Sara knew there was no hope.

She drove a block further to the courthouse but could not find a parking space. Out-of-county tags meant lots of curiosity seekers were coming in for the trial. Parking at the supermarket, but in front and nowhere near the alley and Betsy with her knife,

Sara hurried back to the courthouse. She was relieved to find the county prosecutor, Melvin Parker, still in his office. They had been in school together. He was two classes ahead, but she had known him well enough then to call him by his first name now. "Mel, I've got to talk to you about Emma Jean Veazey. I want to know if I can testify in her behalf."

He was putting papers in his brief case but stopped to look at her in wonder. "What on earth for? What could you possibly . . ."

Sara replied, "I know Rudy used to beat her. I think he was beating her that night, and that she killed him in self-defense."

His smile was that of indulgence conveyed upon a precocious child. "Then let her plead self-defense and testify on her own."

"But why can't I testify, too?"

"Were you there that night? Did you see what happened?"

"No, but . . ."

"Have you ever seen him hit her?"

"No. But if you'll let me explain . . ."

"Then you can't testify."

"But Luke told me Rudy had beaten her. He told me he even caused her to have a miscarriage. If the jury hears that . . ."

Mel shook his head. "That would be hearsay evidence and not admissible. Besides, this is something you should be talking about with Burch Cleghorn, not me. He's her attorney. My job is to prosecute her for first-degree murder on behalf of the state."

"But she did it in self-defense. Rudy brought the knife into the bedroom threatening to kill her. Then he started beating her and raped her. Emma Jean was ready to cut her own throat to end her misery but wound up stabbing him instead in self-defense, damn it."

Mel threw up his hands. "I don't want to hear this. Talk to Burch."

"I can't. Because he won't let her tell how it happened. Good grief, Mel, he won't even let her have visitors, wouldn't let her get out of jail on bond. Don't you see? He wants to put her away."

"That's a serious accusation, Sara." Mel's lips were a thin, condemning line. "Granted, Burch may be guilty of personal indiscretion, but he would never stop a client from pleading however they wanted to, much less deliberately try to have them convicted. You should be ashamed of yourself for saying such a thing."

"Please, Mel. You've got to help me. Burch isn't going to. Just postpone the trial for a few weeks until Luke is well enough to tell what he knows. He can see to it Emma Jean gets a new lawyer, too, and . . ."

He waved her to silence. "I suggest you stay out of it before you find yourself in very deep shit. Don't you know Burch could sue you for slander? Now I've listened to all of this I'm going to."

He shoved her aside and walked out. Sara stared after him, feeling like she had been kicked by a mule.

Kicked, bruised, but not down because she had not even begun to fight.

CHAPTER 30

Jury selection had been completed on Thursday. The Judge declared a recess till Monday. That left Sara only three days to find a way to see Luke. She feared that, even if she succeeded, he'd be in no condition to help. Her motive was not only to save Emma Jean, but also herself. If Burch succeeded in his scheme, he would regain some of his stature in the community, which would make him cocky enough to carry out his threat to expose Sara's affair with Dewey. And if Luke didn't fully recover, he'd be unable to carry out his threat against Burch.

Tim went to bed early that night. Sara curled up on the sofa pretending to be engrossed in a movie. As soon as she heard him snoring, she was out of the house and on her way to Birmingham. Forty-five minutes later she turned into the hospital parking lot. She entered through the emergency room which was busy, as she had hoped. No one noticed as she casually walked through the waiting area to drift into the hall leading to the vending machines. Beyond was a stairway, and when no one else was around, she hurried up to Luke's floor. The halls were quiet, the lights dimmed. Visiting hours had ended long ago. Nurses had made their bedtime rounds and were at their station, busy making notes in patients' charts before shifts changed at eleven.

Sara looked up and down the hall. Finding it clear, she emerged from the stairwell, just as a nurse came out of a patient's room to recognize her.

"You!" The tray of medication she was holding rattled in her anger. "You know you aren't allowed on this floor. It's after hours, anyway. I'm calling Security."

Sara backed away. "No, it's okay. I'm leaving, honest . . ." She ran back to the stairwell and all the way down to the basement. She didn't know where she was going, only that she was not leaving until she saw Luke.

"Where'd she go?" someone yelled in the distance. "Did she make it all the way down here?"

Another called back, "I don't know. We'd better check and see."

There was a door on her right, and she pushed it open without reading the sign: *Morgue—No Admittance.* As soon as she saw the white mounds on stretchers lining a far wall, she realized with a jolt where she was.

The sound of running footsteps grew closer. There was no time to shiver in the 42-degree temperature of the morgue nor to be afraid of its occupants. She had to find a place to hide, and ran into the shower adjacent to the autopsy room. Drawing the curtain closed, she held her breath.

The outer door opened.

"I don't see her in here."

"Then let's go. This place always gives me the creeps."

Even after they had gone, Sara stayed where she was. It was too soon to risk leaving. She just wished it weren't so quiet, for it made her all the more uneasy, like expecting to hear one of the bodies breathe, cough, or show some sign of life. By her watch, an hour passed. It was after midnight. They should have stopped looking for her, and a new shift of nurses would have taken over.

Once again, she crept back up the stairs. Again, a nurse came out of a patient's room. This time, Sara managed to duck into a supply closet before she was spotted. In her haste, she bumped into a bucket of dirty water that sloshed over her bare legs.

She smelled the odor of heavy disinfectant at the same instant her legs began to sting. Groping about in the darkness for a light switch, she couldn't find one. Neither could she locate a sink, which explained why the janitor had left the dirty water. He was too lazy to take it wherever he was supposed to dump it.

Long moments passed as she pranced from one foot to the other in a dance borne of anguish. She bit her lip till she tasted blood to keep from crying out and wondered how much longer she could stand feeling like her flesh was on fire.

―――

Slowly, methodically, Luke held on to the triangle-shaped bar and pulled himself up and down. It hurt like hell, but he had to get his strength back if it meant working day and night. Bad enough that the physical therapist didn't think he was ready to be wheeled down to the gym to work with weights. He wanted to *walk*, damn it, wanted to get his legs going again. Sure, he'd had it all explained to him that, after over a month of being flat on his back, his muscles had begun to atrophy, but that didn't ease his anxiety to return to normal.

It didn't help, either, to have a feeling people were keeping something from him. Alma was pissed off, too. He could tell that easy enough, but he didn't really care what had her riled. What bugged him the most was not having a phone. He'd asked for one, but Alma said he needed his rest and shouldn't be talking a lot. What he *needed*, he thought with a painful grunt as he pulled himself up again, was to talk to Emma Jean, to see her, hold her, and ask what he'd been planning to ask the night he got shot, which was if she loved him enough to run away with him. Hell, he knew she had to be nervous as a cat having kittens after all this time not seeing him, and as soon as he could walk, no, *crawl*, he was going to find a phone and call Sara. Maybe she could sneak her in the hospital. Where was Sara, anyhow? Why hadn't she been to see him? She would tell him what was going on, by God. He was angry with Matt and Kirby, too, for not calling her like he'd asked.

The first days after he woke up had been hazy. He had drifted in and out of consciousness as doctors poked and prodded. Finally, he was able to gather his wits enough to start asking questions, only to be told he needed to rest. God, he was sick of that word. He had too damn much to do to keep laying there because right after he got things straight with Emma Jean, he was going after the SOB that shot him. He'd had but one glimpse of his face as the flashlight swung, but it was enough.

He was also going to make sure Buddy Hampton followed his orders to put his son to work at the mill. Only then could he do what he'd longed to for so very, very long, which was to put Hampton, Alabama, in his rear view mirror on his way out of town, hopefully never to return.

He was exhausted, arms aching, but he managed to pull up a few more times before calling it a night. Since he'd refused to take sleeping pills he'd probably lay awake till morning, anyway, but he didn't care. He felt like he'd slept enough for a lifetime. Besides, about every fifteen minutes for the past hour or so, someone had been poking their head in the door to look around without explanation.

He pressed the button to roll the bed to a sitting position and reached for a magazine. He was hungry. All they would give him at night were crackers and juice. He longed for a beer and a burger.

He thought how relieved he'd be to begin his new life. Taking revenge for his mother, as well as Ocie, had taken its toll on him. He didn't relish making folks suffer, even if what he'd done was justified. Still, he looked forward to peaceful times and decided that, even if Emma Jean didn't go with him he could always go into police work out in California, a desk job, maybe, anything to avoid stress and confrontation. He might even reenlist and be assigned to train soldiers for combat. There was a whole world waiting, and he was anxious to join it.

His eyelids grew heavy. He put the magazine aside and was about to roll the bed back down when the door opened.

He had turned to one side, could not see who it was but irritably called over his shoulder, "No needles, no pills, nothing. You're wasting your time."

"I don't think so."

Luke rolled over with a cry of surprised delight. "Sara! Thank God. Where have you been? I've been worried . . ."

"Believe me, I've tried to get in here. Just give me a minute to wash off." She crossed to the sink, turned the cold water on full blast, and started splashing it on her legs, wincing with pain all the while.

"What are you doing?"

She told him about the bucket of disinfectant. "Believe me, you have no idea what I've been through to get in here." She recanted her vigil outside his room for weeks, only to be banned from the hospital once he woke up.

Patting her legs dry with a towel, she went to give him a hug and a kiss, hurting all the while. Her skin was a fiery red and needed burn ointment. She had to get home and tend to that, plus there was no time to waste, anyway, because Security might still be looking for her.

"I'm sorry you're hurt, and I can't understand why you wouldn't be allowed to see me. I've asked for you, and . . ."

"Alma doesn't want me to tell you about Emma Jean," Sara said in an angry rush. "Oh, Luke, are you really going to be okay? You *sound* okay . . ."

He pushed her away. "What about Emma Jean?"

"She killed Rudy, and . . ."

His hands snaked out to painfully grasp her shoulders. She gave a little cry, but Luke held tight. "What the hell are you talking about?"

She twisted. "You're hurting me . . ."

He let her go. "Tell me, please . . ."

"She killed Rudy the night you were shot. She stabbed him. Her trial starts Monday, and she's been charged with murder."

"I don't believe it."

"It's true."

"Then it had to have been in self-defense. Emma Jean couldn't kill anybody in cold blood."

"She told me all about it, how he brought the knife into the bedroom and threatened her with it. She grabbed it and was going to kill herself because she couldn't take anymore, but then he threatened to kill you, and she went crazy."

"But if she claims self-defense . . ."

"The jury won't believe her," Sara said miserably, then explained about Burch, how he'd had himself appointed her attorney and planned to have her plead guilty. "Not only is he sacrificing her but also he's made her think you were going to die. If I hadn't managed to sneak in to see her, she'd still believe it."

"But now she's going to fight back, right?"

"I hope so. But I'm afraid there's more. Everybody thinks she shot you."

"That's ridiculous." Had the whole world gone crazy while he was out of it? "How'd that lie get started?"

"It was Alma. She was suspicious of you two, and when you didn't come home, she went to Emma Jean's house thinking you were there, that maybe you'd fallen asleep in Emma Jean's bed. She knew Rudy was working night shift, or so she thought. But actually he had come home early, apparently unexpected.

"Anyway," she rushed on, fearing any second someone would find her there, "Matt tried to head her off, but they got there at the same time. Rudy was dead, and Emma Jean was holding the knife and covered in blood."

"But what does that have to do with Alma thinking Emma Jean shot me?"

"Somehow she got the idea you'd met her at the cemetery and told her you weren't going to get a divorce and marry her, so she went crazy, shot you, then went home and killed Rudy."

Luke felt like he'd been hit in the gut with a bowling ball. "That's the stupidest thing I ever heard of. And how come Alma was suspicious of me and Emma Jean, anyway? Had there been talk? And what about Matt? Had he heard something, too?"

Sara's smile was sad and wry. "Weren't you the one who told me nothing goes on in Hampton that everyone doesn't eventually find out about? No doubt there had been rumors, but there's no need in worrying about that now. What's done is done. What we've got to do is get Emma Jean out of this mess. We can find out who shot you later."

The muscles in Luke's jaw went tight. "I know who did it, and I'll take care of it."

Sara had no doubt he would and didn't waste time asking, knowing he wouldn't tell her. "We have to get you out of here so you can testify about Rudy beating her in the past . . . how he made her lose her baby."

"Hell, Sara, I can't even walk." He threw his head back on the pillow in frustration, then looked at her with troubled eyes. "What about Matt? Have you talked to him? I'm pissed over him not telling me all this."

"Alma made him promise not to, and he doesn't want to get involved. Neither does Kirby. Believe me, I've tried everything." She told him about talking to Mel Parker and how he'd refused to listen and chastised her for the accusations about Burch.

"So without you, she doesn't stand a prayer," Sara finished miserably. "I just wish I was strong enough to carry you."

Again, his jaw clenched. "Well, you aren't, but I know somebody who is, and I want you to call him and repeat what you've told me. He knows about Emma Jean because I'd arranged for her to live with him and his wife if she left Rudy. Tell him to call our buddy in Mobile. He'll know what to do. Then tell Emma Jean not to worry."

Sara was not as confident as Luke. "Are you sure you can depend on him?"

Luke wished there was time to tell her just how much. Instead, with a firm nod, he said, "We were in Special Forces together in Nam."

He gestured to the blue and white striped hospital gown he was wearing. "Tell him I'll need some clothes, too."

"I'll take care of right now. Just tell me his name."

"Hey! Here she is."

An orderly in green scrubs rushed in after opening the door and seeing Sara. Another was right behind him.

Luke reached for the bar and tried to pull himself. "Get your damn hands off her. Leave her alone."

"Sorry, but she's not allowed in the hospital," one of the orderlies said as he and his partner grabbed Sara and began pulling her out of the room.

Luke let go of the bar, snatched up his water pitcher from the table next to the bed and threw it. "I said leave her alone, damn you."

"Luke, the name," Sara cried, struggling with all her might against the two men dragging her. "I need his name."

"Woody," he shouted. "Woody McElrath. He lives in West Birmingham, and his number is . . ."

The door closed.

"We should have you arrested," the head security guard told Sara with a scathing glare after she was taken to his office. "It'd serve you right to stay in jail a day or two, but you say you've got kids."

"Yes," she said hotly. "And I wasn't doing anything wrong, just trying to see an old friend. And he wanted to see me, too."

"I'm going to let you go." He nodded to the orderlies to release her. "But if I catch you pulling a stunt like this again, I will have you arrested for trespassing because you've been told to stay off hospital grounds."

"Maybe I'll sue your damn hospital," she said, reaching down to rub at her still-burning legs, "for having such a lazy janitor."

She rushed out of the office, leaving the three men to exchange bewildered looks.

Sara stopped at the first pay phone she came to. There was no phone directory, but she dialed information and found one listing for Woody McElrath. He answered on the second ring, sounding annoyed to be awakened. But all she had to say was, "It's about Luke Ballard. He needs your help," and he was all ears.

He listened in silence, then brusquely said, "I'll take care of it," and hung up.

Somehow, Sara felt she could believe him and told herself not to worry anymore. It was out of her hands.

Friday passed with agonizing slowness. She had to wait until dark to sneak to see Emma Jean again. Finally, supper was over, the kitchen cleaned up, and Tim left for his weekly poker game. Sara put the children to bed, waited till they were asleep, then left. She didn't like leaving them alone but didn't plan to be gone long, anyway. When she got to the basement entrance of the courthouse, it was locked. She jiggled the handle, then peered through the glass and knocked. She was about to give up when she saw someone coming down the hall toward her and recognized Mel Parker.

"What are you doing here so late?" he asked, surprised. "If you need to see somebody in the sheriff's office I'll get them for you. We've had to start locking the doors at night. There have been some threats against Emma Jean."

"Isn't that against the law?" she asked irately. "Shouldn't you make some arrests instead of merely locking doors?"

"We have no proof who they are," he said, likewise annoyed. "Now do you want me to get someone for you or not? I'm late enough as it is."

"No. I'm here to see Emma Jean."

"Well, you can't. She doesn't want any visitors."

"Yes, she does. Burch is lying when he says she doesn't."

Mel shifted his briefcase from one hand to the other, his expression one of impatience and disgust. "I'm not going to go into that again. You can see her in court Monday morning."

He stepped out of the courthouse, pointedly closing the door behind him. Sara heard it lock. "Damn you, Mel. You're as big a skunk as Burch Cleghorn."

"Hey, now, that's no way to talk about me."

Burch Cleghorn walked up, smiling and looking at peace with himself and everyone else. He glanced at them in turn, then focused on Sara. "What is your problem?"

It was all she could do to keep from screaming. "You know darn well I want to see Emma Jean, and you won't let me."

He gave Mel a helpless shrug. Mel nodded as though he understood. Then Burch said, "Sara, I'd love for you to see Emma Jean. I've encouraged her to have visitors, but she refuses, and I have to honor that. I can't let you go up there when it will only upset her."

Dismissing her, he focused on Mel. "I hope things go smoothly. I'm real sorry about the Veazey family being so stirred up, but maybe, once this is over, the healing can begin."

"Well, I appreciate your not wanting to drag it out, Burch," Mel said with a tip of his hat. "See you Monday morning."

"Oh, you might see me on the golf course tomorrow," Burch gaily called after him. "I'm playing with Buddy and Hardy."

"Sure thing. Maybe for a drink after."

Sara stood her ground, ready to fight her way in when Burch opened the door. "I'm going in, and you'd better not try to stop me."

She expected him to respond with his usual angry threats. He surprised by remaining quite calm. "Now, Sara. I know you're angry with me, but I can't help what Dewey asked me to do. He just wanted to make sure you didn't hurt his family, and it's a shame he didn't have time to execute the paper saying so. I hadn't planned to show it to them, but if you don't stop saying bad things about me, you leave me no choice."

For a few seconds, she could only stare at him, wondering what he was talking about, if she had even heard him right.

He continued, "As I told you before, he came to me only a month before he died and wanted it made clear you would have no claim on his estate, even though the two of you had an illicit, and what some folks might consider *incestuous*, relationship for many years."

"You are mad," Sara whispered in horror, thinking that this was his plan to see everyone knew about her and Dewey . . . by making up the most dastardly lie possible.

His smile made her flesh crawl as he dared to embellish, "You do remember we talked about this in my office when you inquired about his will. You said you expected him to leave you something."

"I've never been to your office, and you know it. You're making every bit of this up, and you won't get away with it, just like you won't get away with making Emma Jean plead guilty when it was self-defense."

He was holding his briefcase but tucked it under his arm so he could spread his hands in a feigned gesture of concession. "She can plead anything she wants. I do whatever she tells me to. I don't know where you got the ridiculous idea that I was out to see she gets the death sentence. I have only her best interests at heart.

"And, yes," he added, eyes glittering, "Mel Parker told me how you went to him with your slanderous lies. I could sue you for that. But perhaps when all this is over, you'll come to your senses and apologize. I'm sure we can work something out and become good friends." He winked.

"Now if you'll excuse me, I have to visit my client," he finished. He hadn't seen Emma Jean in a few weeks and needed to tell her the trial was about to start, not that it would make any difference. She was like a vegetable with no more personality than a carrot.

He reached for the door. Sara was right behind him.

"Sara, if you insist on making a scene, you leave me no choice but to show Dewey's poor widow that paper."

"There is no paper," she said, not realizing how much she truly hated him till that moment.

"Why, of course, there is," he smiled. "All typed up and ready to be signed. But when she reads it, she won't care about that. She'll believe every word of it.

"Now run along," he added, eyes hooding with malice, "or I'll do it, so help me."

Sara had no choice but to concede. Burch had won the battle, but not the war. Luke would see to that.

At least she prayed that's how it would be.

When Emma Jean saw Burch, she rushed to wrap her fingers around the bars and cry, "I'm going to plead not guilty. I killed Rudy in self-defense."

"Did you now?" Very calmly, he pulled up a bench in the walkway between the cells and sat down. "What makes you think the jury will believe you?"

"Because it's the truth, and because it's time I took up for myself." Her eyes were cold with accusation. "Sara Speight came to see me and made me realize that."

Burch frowned. "When was that?"

"It doesn't matter. What does matter is that I know you lied and said I didn't want any visitors, just like you lied about Luke. He's not going to die. He's out of his coma. He's going to live, and he's going to help me."

"Is he now?" *Carrot*, indeed, he thought, annoyed. *She was spunky as an unbroken colt.*

"Yes, because he can back me up about Rudy's beatings. He's seen the bruises. He can also testify Rudy beat me so bad I had a miscarriage because he took me to the hospital. I'll tell the jury what happened that night, how Rudy came home and threatened to kill me. He's the one who got the butcher knife and brought it into the bedroom. Then he raped me, and I just couldn't take it any more.

"Luke is going to say it wasn't me that shot him, too," she added with a lift of her chin. "Sara told me how folks have been saying I did."

Burch crossed his legs, folded his hands on his knees and sighed. "Oh, Emma Jean, Sara did a cruel thing by getting you all stirred up like this because if you change your plea you'll likely die in the electric chair."

Emma Jean's knuckles turned white as she gripped the bars tighter. "How can that be? If I say I'm guilty I don't stand a prayer."

"Yes, you do, because all you'll be doing is admitting you killed Rudy and you're throwing yourself on the mercy of the court. The jury will then be lenient and give you a prison sentence. You'll be out on parole in a few years. If you plead not guilty, that means a long, drawn-out trial. I'll have to ask the court to have you evaluated by a psychiatrist in hopes that he'd testify you were genuinely in fear for your life when you committed murder. On the other hand, if he doesn't think so, and there's a chance he might not, then the court will show no mercy, and you'll go to the electric chair."

She was swept with terror. "But I have to try. And Luke will help me. I know he will."

"How can he help you when they're saying he has brain damage?" Burch had not heard that, but what difference did it make? Any means to justify the end, by damn.

"No, that can't be . . ."

"But it can. After all, a bullet went in his brain. He probably won't ever be completely normal. He might not remember everything—*everyone*—in his life, including you."

Slowly, her hands slipped down the bars as her knees began to buckle. Sinking to the floor, she rolled into a fetal position and began to weep.

Burch knelt beside the bars, and, making his voice sound husky with compassion, said, "I'm your friend, Emma Jean. You must believe that. Why else would I have offered my services for free to defend you? Everybody else in town hates you for what you did, but I care about you. I want to take care of you, and I will, if you'll trust me and do as I say: plead guilty and throw yourself on the mercy of the court."

He stretched to trail his fingers down her arm. "Emma Jean, will you let me help you? There's no one else. Sara might care, but she can't really do anything for you. She can't be a witness because she wasn't there. Luke won't be able to do anything because he's an idiot. I hear he babbles and drools and can't control his bowels or his bladder and has to wear a diaper, and . . ."

"Stop it! Stop it! Stop it!" She screamed and covered her ears with her hands. "Don't talk about him like that. Don't say things like that. If Luke won't be like he was before, then I don't care what happens to me. I don't care, do you hear me? So do what you will. I don't care . . ."

Her cries became hysterical as she seemed to melt into the floor in her hopelessness.

Burch stood, feeling quite satisfied with himself. "Well, *I* care about you, Emma Jean. Now get hold of yourself and try to get a good night's sleep. You're in good hands."

Whistling under his breath, head high, and feeling better than he had in too long to remember, he merrily went his way.

CHAPTER 31

The courtroom was packed; the atmosphere was tense. Some of Rudy Veazey's kin had camped out on the lawn the night before so they could rush inside the second the doors were unlocked. Then they stretched out on the hard wooden benches to save seats for the rest of their clan, which left little room for anyone else. Just about everyone in the hills surrounding Hampton was related to the Veazeys in some way, and they had banded together wanting revenge for the death of one of their own.

Sara was able to find a seat only by pushing and shoving her way in, but she wound up in the back row. At least she was next to the aisle, where she could watch for Luke. She also intended to run down to the front of the courtroom when Emma Jean entered to give her his message. She had tried to call Woody McElrath the day before, but his wife sounded funny when she said he was out of town. Sara began to fret that maybe he hadn't found a way to help and didn't want to admit it and wouldn't come to the phone.

Alma walked in, saw Sara, and leaned to hiss furiously in her ear, "I heard about you sneaking in the hospital Friday night, you little hussy. Do it again, and I swear I'll have you arrested."

Sara swept her with a gaze of abject contempt. "We both know why you tried to keep me out, Alma, but it won't work. He loves Emma Jean, and he'll be here to help her. Just wait and see."

Alma's hands shook, itching to slap her. "If we were anywhere else I'd claw your eyes out. And you're crazy if you think he'll be here. He can't walk, you fool."

She proceeded down the aisle. Emma Jean craned her neck to watch as Alma sat down with the Veazey family directly behind the railing next to the prosecutor's table and Mel Parker.

The woman sitting next to Sara opened a bag and took out a banana and began to peel it. She saw Sara watching and politely offered, "Want one? I got pig's feet and pickled eggs, too. When they break for lunch, I don't intend to give up my seat."

"No, thanks," Sara mumbled. She'd never seen her before and figured her to be distant Veazey kin.

"Wonder if the murderin' hussy will stand trial for shooting the sheriff, too."

"She didn't shoot him," Sara was quick to convey.

The woman looked her up and down. "How come you know so much? Everybody says she did."

"Everybody is wrong." Sara turned away, and the woman gave a haughty sniff but didn't say anything else.

Suddenly a stirring rippled through the room as the door behind the Judge's bench opened and Matt walked in with Emma Jean. She was wearing orange button-up coveralls, jail-issue. Her hair had been combed but obviously needed shampooing.

Bertha Veazey leaped to her feet. "Murdering bitch. You killed my boy."

Wilbur Veazey joined in. "You better hope they fry your ass before I get my hands on you."

Matt warned, "I've told you the judge isn't going to put up with that."

They sat back down, grumbling.

Emma Jean kept her head down as Matt led her to the chair behind the table where Burch Cleghorn was already seated. Matt unfastened the handcuffs, then took his place behind her. Sara's heart sank. Where was the spirit she had witnessed in Emma Jean when she had seen her before? What had Burch said to make her so cowed?

Rudy's Aunt Pinella was sitting directly in front of Sara and said to no one in particular, "That Burch Cleghorn is a fine man. He knows she's guilty, and he ain't gonna waste taxpayers' money by trying to prove she ain't. When this is all over, I'm going to make him one of my pecan pies."

Sara could not resist blurting, "And I hope he chokes on every bite."

The woman next to Sara poked her in the side with a banana. "You better stick this in your mouth or you're gonna start a riot."

Sara was not about to be quiet. She started down the aisle, intent on telling Emma Jean not to worry, that Luke would be there. But she had not gone far when Kirby grabbed her arm. "Don't make me have to run out of here, Sara," he said apologetically. "Now get in your seat and stay there, please."

"I need to speak to Emma Jean."

"Well, you can't. Now hush. The jury is coming in."

Sara watched as they filed in, tight-lipped and somber. She hoped they would keep an open mind but felt a jury should have been brought in from another part of the state or the trial moved elsewhere. There'd just been too much talk, and too many opinions formed about Emma Jean's guilt. But, of course, Burch hadn't asked to do that.

Next, Matt went to stand in front of the bench and face the room to announce, "All rise."

Sara stood along with everyone else but was not listening to the court preamble Matt was reciting. She was watching for Luke.

Judge Barrett wore a long black robe over a white shirt and tie. Stern eyes peered over the round glasses perched on the end of his nose. What hair he had left was a silver halo around his bald spot. In his personal life, he was a loving husband, father, and grandfather. But when he was in his courtroom, he was known to be harsh and put up with no nonsense from spectators or counsel.

He banged his gavel. "Be seated." He began to read from the docket before him. "The State of Alabama versus Emma Jean Veazey. Superior Court file number SC 1245. Will the defendant rise."

A soft murmur went through the crowd as Emma Jean slowly, shakily, got to her feet.

"You have been charged with the murder of Rudolph Morris Veazey on October 31st, 1969. How do you plead?"

Sara held her breath, glancing towards the door again, then at Emma Jean. She could not hear what she said. Neither could anyone else. Judge Barrett asked her to speak up.

"Guilty," came her feeble croak.

Sara's horrified cry of "Dear God, no," went unheard amidst the relieved chorus ringing all around.

Burch stood, making sure he was loud enough for everyone

to hear. "Your honor, my client wishes to place herself at the mercy of this court. She declines to testify nor offer any evidence on her behalf. Further, she respectfully requests that the sentencing hearing commence at once."

Burch sat down. Emma Jean already had, placing her head on the table, face to the wall. Sara again looked to the door, sick to the pit of her soul. Burch had manipulated Emma Jean into capitulation, and God help her if Luke didn't show.

"How say the state?" Judge Barrett asked of Mel Parker.

Mel stood. "The state requests that the jury hear the evidence against the defendant and then convene to recommend sentence."

"Proceed."

Mel gathered up some papers and went to stand at the railing next to the jury and began to read. "The state charges that on the night of October 31st, 1969, the defendant did willfully, and with malice aforethought, cause the death of her husband, Rudolph Morris Veazey, by stabbing him seven times with a butcher knife."

Mel went back to his desk and picked up a knife with a white tag hanging from the handle. Holding it up for everyone to see, he then placed it on a table near the court reporter. "Please record this as state's evidence: the murder weapon."

He returned to the jury. "In addition to stabbing her husband, Emma Jean Veazey bit off a portion of the victim's penis."

A roar went through the crowd, and Rudy's parents again leaped up to shake their fists and scream out at Emma Jean.

Judge Barrett viciously pounded his gavel. "Another outburst, and I will clear the courtroom."

Like a giant hand sweeping, everyone fell silent.

Mel cleared his throat and continued. "The state maintains that this brutal slaying was premeditated, and, under Alabama law, the death sentence is warranted and justified."

He pointed a finger and swept the jury with a challenging gaze, "And I charge you to recommend that sentence, that you show no more mercy to this cold-blooded murderess than she showed to her husband the night she so ruthlessly killed him."

Sara craned to see Emma Jean. She had not moved, head still resting on her folded arms, face to the wall. Mel returned to his desk and sat down. The Veazeys leaned over the railing to pat his shoulder for what they felt was a job well done. Alma was grinning all around. Burch was leaning back in his chair, staring off into space, trying, Sara knew, to look concerned.

Judge Barrett told the jury they could recommend death or life in prison, with or without parole. Then he sent them out to begin deliberations and declared a recess until they finished. Matt put the handcuffs back on Emma Jean and led her out. Most people stayed in their seats, not about to give them up, confident it would not take the jury long to agree on a sentence of death.

Sara knew it was all over. Luke's friends hadn't been able to find a way to get him there, and Emma Jean was doomed. She took one last look around, and that was when she saw Betsy Borden standing in a corner. Those around her had squeezed against each other to put as much room as possible between them and her because she smelled like fish, and other things, like garbage and chicken droppings from sleeping in roost houses.

Betsy locked eyes with her, then quickly looked away. Was she feeling guilty, Sara wondered, knowing she might be able to save Emma Jean but refusing to do so?

Sara cut her gaze to Burch, despising him more with every breath she drew. As though feeling her wrath, he turned around to flash a triumphant smile. Childishly, crudely, she gave him the finger.

The minutes ticked by. Sara's stomach began to cramp. It was time for her period. All the stress was probably going to make her start early. She clenched and unclenched her fists, stared up at the ceiling, then at the floor, taking long, deep breaths to try and make her heart slow down, all the while wondering what had happened to Luke. Did he give up? No. He'd never do that. The people he was counting on had let him down. That's all it could be. She wished with all her might she hadn't left it to them and insisted on being a part of whatever plans were made to see they were carried out. By not doing so, she felt like she'd failed him, too.

It seemed like hours but only twenty minutes had passed before Matt came to announce the jury had reached a decision. People scrambled to spread the word to those who'd ventured out, and suddenly everyone was rushing back to their seats.

There was some pushing and shoving over seats having been taken, and Matt had to yell above the din and threaten to throw them out. Finally order was restored, and he went to notify the judge as the jury began filing in.

Sara noted how smug they looked and had no doubt they had unanimously agreed Emma Jean should die. She tried to console herself with the hope that perhaps Luke could do something later. She didn't know about the law, but she'd seen movies where people convicted of murder were later freed because it was proved they were innocent. Still, he hadn't actually seen Rudy beat her. And he wasn't there that night. His testimony might not help at all.

Excitement was like electricity popping through the crowd as Judge Barrett returned, and Matt again declared, "All rise," then repeated his speech about court being in session.

Everyone sat back down. Matt led Emma Jean in. She stared at her feet the whole time, and once she was in her chair squeezed her eyes shut.

Judge Barrett asked the jury for their decision, and Sara felt like every nerve in her body was raw and screaming as Marvin Donhenner got up and said he'd been elected foreman, and, yes, they'd made up their minds.

"We think she should get the death sentence."

Cheers and applause broke out, and Judge Barrett started banging his gavel for quiet but no one paid any attention.

Bertha Veazey leaped up and threw her arms over her head as she prayed out loud giving thanks. Wilbur was rocking back and forth in his seat and snapping his fingers in time to a joyful rhythm only he could hear. Alma was bouncing around, shaking hands and hugging everyone close to her. Emma Jean showed no emotion, continuing to sit with eyes closed.

Burch, Sara noted, was putting on a good show of pretending to be disappointed, shaking his head as he patted Emma Jean's shoulder like he was trying to console her. Finally, after Judge Barrett's desk creaked beneath the gavel's pounding like it was about to break, things quieted down.

"The defendant will rise," he said, looking like he couldn't wait to get it over with and have everyone get the hell out. Emma Jean did not move. Burch rose and gently pulled her with him. Sara thought she was going to collapse, but he kept his arm around her. She did not open her eyes.

"Emma Jean Veazey," Judge Barrett intoned, "you have pleaded guilty to murder in the first degree, and a jury of your peers has recommended that you be sentenced to death for your crime. It is therefore the decision of this court to concur with that recommendation. You are hereby sentenced to die by electrocution on the 31st day of December . . .

"And may God have mercy on your soul," he quietly concluded.

"Happy New Year, bitch," Bertha sang out.

The Veazey clan broke into raucous laughter, and Judge Barrett banged the gavel over and over. "Oh, to hell with it," he finally yelled over the din. "Court adjourned."

Suddenly a voice louder than any other heard that day rang out. "Not yet it isn't! Not by a long shot."

Everyone turned to stare at Luke, who was sitting in a wheelchair. There were three men with him, all wearing white shirts, ties, and suits . . . and all tight-lipped and grim-faced.

He was in the aisle right beside Sara, and, with a squeal, she lunged to throw her arms around his neck. "Thank God. I didn't think you'd be here."

Hugging her briefly, he gently pushed her back. "I'd have crawled if I had to."

He was dressed like the men with him, only his clothes were way too big. The clothes belonged to Woody McElrath who was larger. Still, he was neat and clean-shaven, though his face was gaunt and mirrored the strain of the moment as well as the past weeks of illness.

Alma, red-faced and furious, pushed past those in her way to get to the aisle. Luke, seeing her, pointed a finger in warning. "Sit down and shut up. You and I will talk later."

She looked at the men with him. "How dare you bring him here? He has no business being out of the hospital."

"Leave him be," Bertha Veazey said, on her feet like everyone else. "He came to see justice done. The hussy shot him, remember?"

Luke gripped the arms of his chair and tried to stand but couldn't make it. "That's a damn lie. And besides that, when she killed Rudy she did it in self-defense."

Emma Jean, having snapped out of her daze, had slowly risen to her feet to cry in wonder, "Luke . . . oh, Luke . . . praise God . . ."

She started toward him, but Matt, looking like he wished he didn't have to, held her back.

"Let her go, Matt," Luke shouted.

Matt shook his head. "You know I can't . . ."

"Luke, have you lost your mind?" Alma shrieked.

Wilbur Veazey bellowed, "She killed my boy in cold blood, and she's gonna die for it. She's already been sentenced, and there ain't a thing you can do about it."

Luke looked to Sara for explanation.

"It's all over," she hated to tell him. "She pleaded guilty, and the jury asked for the death sentence."

"No. Hell, no," he roared, trying once more to rise, his fury propelling him, but Woody put a firm hand on his shoulder.

"Let Jim handle it. They aren't going to listen to you."

Judge Barrett, so mad the veins in his neck were standing out and throbbing, slammed the gavel down, and, surprisingly, this time, it worked. Everyone got quiet. Pointing the gavel at Luke, he asked, "Now what's the meaning of this, Sheriff? And you'd better have a good explanation."

One of the men standing behind Luke walked down the aisle to stand before the judge and introduce himself. "My name is Jim Burkhalter. I'm an attorney in Mobile." He motioned for the other man who had followed him to step forward, "This gentleman is Stewart Delaney. He is the President of the Alabama Bar Association."

"I know who he is," Judge Barrett said with a curt nod to Stewart. "We went to law school together. Suppose you tell me what this is about, Stewart."

Burch, cheeks beet red, stood to protest, "This case is closed. Court's been adjourned. This is out of order."

Judge Barrett glared. "And since when do you tell me how to run my courtroom, Burch? Sit down, shut up, and let the man speak. He's come all the way from Montgomery, so it must be serious."

Burch whined, dread creeping, "At least wait till everyone leaves."

"They can go whenever they want to." He gave another nod to Stewart. "Continue."

Not a soul in the room budged. They wouldn't have left for the world, sensing something exciting was taking place.

Before Stewart could begin, Luke, having been rolled to the front by Woody, interjected, "Wait a minute, Judge. I want to ask Emma Jean one question."

Judge Barrett sighed. "Oh, go ahead, but be quick about it. I want to get this over with . . . whatever it is."

Luke turned to her, his heart wrenching. "Did you plead not guilty today because that's what you wanted?"

She shot a hating look at Burch. "No. He told me to do it. He said I'd get the death penalty for sure if I didn't. I told him I only killed Rudy 'cause I couldn't take him beating me anymore, but he said the jury would never believe me."

Luke started to say something else, but Stewart leaped in to ask Emma Jean for clarification. "Are you saying, Mrs. Veazey, that you informed your attorney you wished to plead not guilty, and he advised you against it?"

"Yes, and when I told him Luke could testify how Rudy beat me lots of times before, he said no, he couldn't, because his brain was damaged, and he was like an idiot. I just gave up then and let him do what he wanted, 'cause if Luke was like that I didn't care what happened to me, anyhow."

Covering her face with her hands, she began to cry brokenly. Now she had really let the cat out of the bag and only hoped Luke wasn't mad because everybody would know they'd been lovers. But he must not have cared, she reasoned, or he wouldn't have come. She stopped crying and rubbed at her nose with the back of her hand and lifted her chin to let everybody know she wasn't ashamed of anything, anymore . . . not with Luke there.

Mel Parker, holding a pencil, snapped it in two as he wheeled his chair about to face Burch. "Is what she says true? Did you deny your client the right to plead not guilty and tell her those lies?"

"She is guilty," Burch mumbled. His hand went to his chest. His head pitched slightly forward, face twisted as though in pain but no one paid any attention.

Stewart Delaney placed his briefcase on Mel Parker's desk, opened it, and took out a folder and handed it to the judge. "We had this drawn up and signed by Judge Harper in Montgomery yesterday. It's a writ removing Burch Cleghorn as counsel for the defense, replacing him with Stewart Delaney. You should also know that charges are being brought against Mr. Cleghorn by the Alabama Bar for malpractice."

Burch, head still bowed, did not move, made no sound.

Judge Barrett read the writ, then said, "Well, based on this, I'm tempted to declare a mistrial, even though court has been adjourned. I'm just not sure what to do about this." He scratched his head thoughtfully. "I should also point out that, unless the sheriff actually witnessed Rudy Veazey beating his wife, his testimony will be useless."

He started to rise. "Gentlemen, I think we'd better discuss this in my chambers."

Suddenly, from the back of the room, came an indignant cry. "Wait just a dad-burned minute, judge."

Once more, heads turned and necks craned to see what was happening.

"I saw him beat her, and I can testify, by cracky," Betsy Borden announced proudly as she marched up the aisle. "I won't gonna say nothin', but I can't sit back and let you all fry her for somethin' she couldn't help."

Like everyone else in Buford County, Judge Barrett knew Betsy. Spinning completely around in his chair, he threw up his hands and cried, "This has turned into a circus."

Betsy walked right up to the witness box beside his high bench, sat down, crossed her legs, looked out on the sea of startled faces and corrected, "Naw, it ain't no circus, Judge. It's bullshit, that's what it is. Emma Jean killed her old man in self-defense. I know 'cause I was there that night, sleepin' in her roost house, and I seen and heard the whole thing."

Wilbur Veazey stood to shake his fist in protest. "She's crazy. Everybody knows that. And you're crazy to let her babble on."

"And you're crazy," Judge Barrett said, scowling, "if you think I'm going to put up with your outburst. Now either sit down and shut up or get out of my courtroom."

Wilbur sat, but if looks could kill, Betsy would have dropped dead then and there.

"Go on, Betsy," the judge prodded. "Let's hear what you got to say. You probably won't shut up till we do."

Jim Burkhalter asked, "What about the Writ, your honor?"

"Yes," Stewart Delaney chimed in, pointing at Burch. "I came all the way to make sure that man is removed as counsel for the defense."

"Oh, don't worry about that," Judge Barrett said with an airy wave. "It's done. I just want to hear what Betsy's got to say." He looked to Mel Parker. "What about the prosecution? Are you willing to listen?"

Mel looked doubtful but murmured consent.

Unnoticed, Alma had made her way to Luke's side and knelt by the wheelchair to whisper, "I'll never forgive you for this, Luke. You're humiliating me and our marriage in front of the whole town."

"We never had a marriage, and you know it. Now get away from me."

She retreated, stunned. Then, noticing how people were looking at her and snickering, she ran from the courtroom. Outside, she leaned against one of the tall columns at the top of the marble stairs, bosom heaving as she tried to swallow the anger rising from the pit of her stomach. It was over. Luke would find a way to save Emma Jean, and then he would want a divorce so he could marry her. But Alma would take revenge in the worst way possible. She'd tell him Tammy wasn't his, and she'd laugh at him for being fool enough to think she was all these years. That would fix him good, and . . . No, she could never do that. Not only would it break Tammy's heart, but she'd be ruined forever more. She had to go on living in this town, had to be able to hold her head up. After all, people would feel sorry for her over her husband running off with another woman. So Alma would just keep her mouth shut. Besides, she could make him pay child support.

She thought about the new maintenance engineer that had hired on at the plant. He was from Montgomery, not half bad-looking, and he'd just gotten his divorce. She didn't think it was her imagination he'd been giving her the eye. She drew a deep breath and let it out slowly, and, with it, came the rage. To hell with Luke. She'd never given a damn about him, anyway.

Judge Barrett urged, "Go on, Betsy. Tell us what you saw the night Rudy Veazey died."

She wriggled happily in the chair, enjoying being the center

324   Patricia Hagan

of attention. "Well, I heard him beat her lots of times. I seen him, too. One night she ran out of the house, tryin' to get away from him, but he caught her and dragged her back in by the hair of her head with her hollerin' bloody murder the whole time.

"And another night," she continued, raking the courtroom, eyes shining, making sure everyone was listening, "he whipped her with his belt right out in the yard. Yanked her panties down and beat her good."

Luke gripped the arms of the wheelchair and squeezed. Jim patted him on the back. Woody murmured for him to hang on, it was almost over.

"But what about the night he was killed?" the judge reminded. "What did you see?"

"Well, I got to the roost house later than usual. Some smart alecks played a trick on me." She cast an angry glare all around in case the culprits were in the room. "But Sheriff Ballard, he was nice to me, made me see it won't no ghost. I tried to go back to bed, but I decided to move on in case them kids came back. I went over to Emma Jean's 'cause I like her roost house. She's got plenty of chickens, and it's warm with them all nestled around me, and she's got a friendly rooster, too, and . . ."

Judge Barrett gave an exaggerated sigh. "Betsy, please."

"Okay, okay. That night I heard Emma Jean scream so loud I got down off the roost and went to peek in the bedroom window. The light was on, and I saw Rudy holdin' a knife right in her face and sayin' he was gonna kill her. Then he stuck his dick in her face, and . . ."

Shocked gasps ripped through the room, and Judge Barrett admonished, "There is no need to be so graphic."

"Well, you let Mel Parker say it," she argued.

"No. He didn't say it like that."

Betsy held up a hand. "Okay. I'm sorry. He didn't say dick. He said penis. So if it makes everybody feel better, I'll say it: penis . . . *peenuhhsss*. Is that better?"

Someone laughed outloud.

Betsy glanced around to smile at whoever it was before continuing, "So he took out his *peenuhhss* and poked it in her mouth, and she bit him and grabbed hold of the knife and stabbed him to keep him from stabbin' her.

"Now I didn't see that part," she emphasized, "'cause I took off runnin' like a scalded dog. But I reckon that's how it happened. She killed him 'cause he made her, and if you want my opinion, I think the low-life deserved it."

Wilbur Veazey screamed, "Don't you talk about my boy that way, you filthy old bag."

Both he and Bertha started out of their row at the same time, but Kirby and Matt, not waiting for Judge Barrett to give the order, moved quickly to forcefully escort them out of the room.

Luke and Emma Jean had not taken their eyes off each other since Betsy had begun to speak. Luke silently mouthed, "I love you," and she did the same to him.

Betsy was sitting back, arms folded across her chest and grinning. Everyone else had lapsed into stunned silence. Finally, Judge Barrett, with a shake of his head, said, "Well, it sounds like self-defense to me."

Mel Parker got to his feet, cleared his throat, and said, "Your honor, based on the testimony of the eyewitness, unorthodox though it may be, along with the allegations of malpractice against the defendant's attorney, the state moves that a mistrial be declared. In addition, the state will drop all charges against the defendant."

"So granted." Judge Barrett sounded relieved. "Now I want this damn courtroom cleared. I've had enough for one day." He banged the gavel.

Luke looked upwards and whispered, "Yes, Lord. Bring that hammer down one last time!"

And he opened his arms to Emma Jean, who was making her way toward him through the crowd, ignoring the jeers and name-calling. She wasn't afraid of anyone or anything and never would be again.

Jim Burkhalter and Stewart Delaney walked with Judge Barrett into his chambers. Burch, deciding he wasn't going to be blessed with having a heart attack to end the misery after all, doggedly followed.

Woody stayed close to Luke in case anybody tried to start something. When Matt and Kirby walked over, he held up a hand for them to stay back. He didn't like the way they looked angry enough to bite a nail in two.

"It's okay," Matt said to put him at ease. "We just need to speak to the Sheriff, and it can't wait."

Luke unwound Emma Jean's arm from around his neck, his expression as angry as theirs. "You've got something you want to say to me?"

"Yes, we do," Matt said. "We know we let you down, and we're sorry, but we were listening to the wrong people."

Kirby added, "That's right, because I was convinced Emma Jean shot you, and that's why you wouldn't tell us who it was after you woke up."

"I explained I'd take care of it," Luke reminded. "And I will."

"Well, that's something else we need to talk about," Matt said. "The fact is, you aren't able to take care of it right now, and me and Kirby were just talking about how once word spreads about you being out of the hospital, whoever did it is going to run, if he hasn't already. So how about telling us so we can go pick him up."

Kirby, looking more serious than Luke had ever seen him, added, "And we aren't taking no for an answer."

Luke surprised them by saying, "All right. But I'm going with you. And I don't think he's run. He doesn't know I saw his face."

CHAPTER 32

Luke was standing in what had once been Emma Jean's kitchen, circling the date on a calendar hanging on the wall—December 17, 1969. It was a day he had been living for and one he would always remember because, at long last, he was leaving Hampton. The best part was he was taking Emma Jean with him. They had spent the last two weeks living in Birmingham with Woody and his family. Luke needed to go to the hospital every day for physical therapy. He also wanted to be around for the arraignment of the person who had shot him—*Rossie Scroggins*.

Many people were surprised, for they had no idea Rossie even had a grudge. The charge was attempted murder. Luke had identified Rossie's as the face he saw that night. Mel Parker took Luke's sworn deposition so he wouldn't have to be at the trial. It was cut and dried, anyway. Rossie would go to prison for a long, long time for trying to kill an officer of the law.

As it turned out, Rossie had left town right after the shooting and ran off to join the Army. He was still in basic training down in Columbus, Georgia, and wasn't hard to track. Ossie, still living at home, broke down under questioning and told the whole story as to why Rossie hated Luke enough to want to kill him.

Ossie described the day Luke took him and Rossie home after they tried to break into Billy Saulston's store, and their pa had chased after them when they ran into the woods. He had caught Rossie and beat him so bad he broke his nose. Then he took his old '56 Chevy away from him, sold it for a hundred dollars, and used the money to stay drunk for two weeks. That hurt Rossie worse than his nose. By the time Ossie came back after staying with a cousin in Coosa County for a while, his pa seemed to have forgotten all about it, so Ossie didn't get his licks. But Rossie hadn't forgotten and started planning then and there to kill Luke.

Ossie was charged as an accessory and didn't mind a bit. He was happy to be locked up after his pa found out.

Luke had had plenty of time to think about that night and was glad it had been the Scroggins boys instead of Junior, Hardy, Burch, or Buddy. He didn't want to think they had the guts. There had been other things to take care of, also, like filing to divorce Alma. It had gone a lot smoother than he expected because, after what happened in court, she wanted to be rid of him fast. Far be it from her, she told anyone who'd listen, to try and hang onto a man who had been running around with a murderer.

Luke wished it could have been different for Tammy's sake. He never meant to cause her embarrassment. He tried to talk to her and explain how it was, how even though he couldn't live with her mother anymore she was still his daughter and he would always love her, would always be there for her if she needed anything. Her response had been to politely tell him to go to hell, and he told her he hoped she'd feel differently when she grew up.

Luke wasn't leaving with much, but then he'd never had very much. A few pairs of trousers and jeans, some shirts, a pair of Sunday shoes and a polyester leisure suit. Alma got the house, car, furniture, and what money was in the bank. His insurance with the county took care of the hospital and doctor bills. When he got a job, he'd pay Woody back the money he had loaned him to buy the second-hand Ford.

He was drawing a circle around the date on the calendar when Emma Jean came out of the bedroom carrying a small cardboard box. "This is all I could find. I don't know what they did with the rest of my clothes. They weren't worth anything, anyway."

He took the box from her and set it on the kitchen table. "Don't worry about it. When we get to California, I'll buy you lots of new clothes. Pretty ones, too."

She saw the circle on the calendar. "What did you do that for?"

"To mark the first day of the rest of our lives." He lifted her up and spun her around till she was dizzy and giggling and begging to be put down.

He kissed her till she was breathless, and when she finally pulled from his arms looked around the room and said, "Luke, I just want to hurry and get out of here. This place gives me the creeps."

He understood. He didn't like being there either. Even though all the blood and mess had been cleaned up, it still gave him a bad feeling. "Well, if Sara will come on, we can leave." They had gone to the house at first light, wanting to get in and out before people were up and stirring on the roads. They had kept in touch with Sara by phone during the past weeks, but she had wanted to meet them to say good-bye in person.

A rooster crowed. Emma Jean went to the back door and opened it. "The chickens are coming out. They belong to Mr. Dootree. Otherwise, the Veazeys would have taken them like they took everything else that wasn't nailed down. I guess he doesn't have room for them over at his place, but I see he left feed."

Luke joined her. "I imagine he'll have this place rented out in no time, and the new tenants will take them over."

Headlights turned in. "There's Sara," Emma Jean said, waving.

They went to meet her, and after warm hugs and kisses, Sara exuded, "You two don't know how happy I am for you. But I hate you're going all the way to California. I'm afraid I'll never see you again."

"Yes, you will," Luke said confidently, "because you're welcome to visit any time, stay as long as you like, and you know it. I think its the place for me and Emma Jean, and I won't have any trouble getting a job in law enforcement.

"I'm going to school to be a hairdresser," Emma Jean added proudly. "But don't you worry about us not keeping in touch. You're the best friend anybody could ask for. If not for you, I'd be on the way to the electric chair."

"Maybe not," Sara disputed. "Eventually Luke would have found out what was going on and done something about it."

"I'd damn well have tried."

Sara said, "Well, I have to admit I was getting real worried you wouldn't get there."

"I was doing some worrying of my own, not knowing if you were able to get in touch with Woody. From what he told me, Jim was the one who worked his butt off all weekend. Woody called him right away, and he got busy getting in touch with the Bar Association and having that writ drawn up. Then they all had to meet Monday morning and come to the hospital to get me."

"Luke said they tried to stop him from leaving the hospital," Emma Jean contributed.

He smiled. "But not for long. Woody can be very convincing."

Sara asked if he'd heard anything about Burch's disbarment hearing.

"I talked to Mel yesterday to say good-bye. The hearing is next week. He took a deposition from Emma Jean and said Burch will definitely be disbarred."

Sara then bounced up and down on the balls of her feet in her excitement to convey the good news that Burch was moving. "I heard it for a fact. Irene is making him move to Mobile and go to work in her dad's shoe store. Quite a comeuppance, wouldn't you say?"

"Oh, yes," Luke said, agreeing more than she realized.

"Things around here are really going to change," Sara said. "And all for the better. I still can't believe Buddy Hampton has hired a negro to be some kind of executive to improve race relations at the mill, plus he says he won't oppose the union coming in."

Again, Luke smiled but tried not to look like he was gloating, which he was. He had phoned Buddy right after the trial and told him he had exactly two weeks to follow orders or a skeleton was going to leap out of his closet and straight into the arms of the Ku Klux Klan. Buddy had sworn it would be done, and the wheels had been put in motion the very next day, stunning everyone even more than what had gone on at Emma Jean's trial.

Rest in peace, Momma, Luke thought. *I kept my promise.*

As though uncannily reading his mind, Sara assured, "I'll look after your mother's grave and see she has flowers at Christmas and Mother's Day."

"That'll be nice of you."

"Well, I always loved her. You know that. Oh, I almost forgot . . ." Sara went to her car and brought back a paper sack. "Sandwiches for the road. Chicken salad and bologna, chocolate chip cookies, and apples."

Emma Jean hugged her again. "I'm really going to miss you. I wish you were going with us."

Sara was blinking back tears. "Who knows? When the kids are grown, I might just follow you out there."

She walked with them to Luke's car, but just as Emma Jean was about to get in, a familiar voice rang out in the morning quiet.

"I knew if I slept here long enough you'd show up sooner or later," Betsy Borden called sleepily as she crawled out of the roost house. "I've been waitin' for you to see how you're doin', and I figured you'd be back to get Emma Jean's clothes. I nosed around inside and saw some of 'em were still there."

Though it was hard to do, Luke did not flinch as Betsy threw her arms around him. Feathers were stuck in her hair and on her overalls, and she smelled of chicken dung, but she had done a great thing for Emma Jean, and he would always be grateful. "Well, I'm glad I got to see you before we left," he said . . . and meant it.

She let him go to exclaim, "Aw, hell. You mean you're leavin' town? You ain't gonna be sheriff no more?"

"I'm leaving that job to Matt. Emma Jean and I want to make a fresh start somewhere else."

Betsy pursed her lips, thought about it, then allowed, "Well, I reckon that makes sense, but I'll miss you, 'cause you was always good to me." Suddenly she whirled on Emma Jean and shook her fist. "You better be good to him, or you'll answer to me, you hear?"

Emma Jean swallowed against the odor and kissed her cheek. "Don't worry, Betsy. I love this man more than my life."

Betsy stretched and yawned. "I best be goin'. Y'all come to see me when you can."

When it was just the three of them again, Sara couldn't hold back her tears any longer. She threw herself on Luke, and he wrapped his arms around her. "This isn't good-bye. We'll meet again."

He loaded the box in the Ford, and soon he and Emma Jean were driving down the winding road that would take them to Birmingham, and, eventually, on to the west coast.

Emma Jean slid across the seat to snuggle close. Passing a sign that read *"LEAVING HAMPTON—HURRY BACK,"* she said, "Luke, I can't help thinkin' now that you're leaving for good that deep down you wish you knew who your real daddy was. I mean, all those years you lived in Hampton, and you might have passed him on the street and not known it."

"I'm sure I did," he said. "But like I've always said, it doesn't matter. I'm here, and now you are, too, and that's all that ever will matter."

He glanced in the rear view mirror, and the smile on his lips came from his very soul.

The moment had arrived at last.

Hampton, Alabama was behind him for all time.

THE END

Other books by Patricia Hagan...

Invitation to the Wedding
Dark Journey Home
Winds of Terror
Love and War
Raging Hearts
Love and Glory
Love and Fury
Love and Honor
Love and Dreams
Love and Splendor
Love and Triumph
Passion's Fury
Souls Aflame
Love's Wine
This Savage Heart
Golden Roses
Midnight Rose
Heaven in a Wildflower
Orchids in Moonlight
A Forever Kind of Love
Starlight
Simply Heaven
The Desire
The Destiny
Bride for Hire
Groom on the Run
My Child, Our Child
My Irish Love
Ryan's Bride
Spicy Loving
Boy Remeets Girl
Texas Lucky
Arizona Gold
Ocean of Dreams
A Touch of Love

NO LONGER THE PROPERTY OF
THE ST. LOUIS COUNTY LIBRARY.